NO MORE BLOOD

A British Murder Mystery

THE WILD FENS MURDER MYSTERIES
BOOK 13

JACK CARTWRIGHT

CHESTNUT PRESS

ALSO BY JACK CARTWRIGHT

The DCI Cook Murder Mysteries

A Winter of Blood

A Secret to Die For

The Wild Fens Murder Mysteries

Secrets In Blood

One For Sorrow

In Cold Blood

Suffer In Silence

Dying To Tell

Never To Return

Lie Beside Me

Dance With Death

In Dead Water

One Deadly Night

Her Dying Mind

Into Death's Arms

No More Blood

Burden of Truth

NO MORE BLOOD

A Wild Fens Murder Mystery

PROLOGUE

For Debbie Jarvis, life was one big game. Kevin knew it, her parents knew it, and she knew it. Everyone knew that if there was a win to be had, then Debbie was onto it. Her edge, she had called it once when they had sat chatting at the waterside. But Kevin knew it only as her narcissistic tendency. It was the one thing about her he simply couldn't bring himself to like.

A fire burned further into the field. There was always a fire at this time of year. Despite the dozens of posters on the school walls, and even a local fire officer giving a talk on the dangers of summer fires, they still had them.

They were cautious enough, and it wasn't as if they had nothing to lose. If the trees surrounding the fields went up, then at least two of their houses would go up with them and the blaze would probably take their parents, too.

"Shall we join them?" Kevin said to her, but Debs shook her head. They were sitting at the edge of the field, closest to the stile, beyond which was the forest, the river, and all those places he had taken for granted over the years but may never enjoy again.

"I'm going to stay here for a while," she replied. "I'm not sure if I can handle Ross right now."

"Don't worry about him," he said. "Come on."

"No, you go."

He climbed to his feet and stared down at her, giving her one last chance to join him.

"I told you, I'm staying," she said.

"Debs, nobody cares what you did with him—"

"I told you not to mention that—"

"I know, but come on. If we don't go over there, they'll only come over here."

"No, Seb won't leave the fire," she said. "And Anne won't leave the wine. She'll be worried about somebody nicking it."

A scream rang out in the field contained by the trees at every edge. Laughter followed and Kevin felt Debs scorn rather than saw it in her eyes.

"She's a slut," she said, referring to the only other female in their group. "Every one of them lads has felt her up at some point."

"I haven't," he said, quite proud of being the odd one out.

"No," she said with a laugh. "But you would if you had the chance, wouldn't you?" She grinned up at him and then took a swig from her wine bottle. "I've seen you looking."

"Look, are you coming or not?" he said, trying to change the topic.

"Only when you admit you fancy her."

"I *don't* fancy her."

"So, I'll stay," she said, taking another swig of wine and resting on an elbow. "It's fine by me."

The sky was pitch dark, dotted with bright stars, and her skin appeared grey against the grass.

"Come on," he said. "This is ridiculous."

"Go," she told him. "You asked me to come tonight and you said he wouldn't be here."

"Well, I didn't know he would be, did I?" he said. "For God's sake, Debs. What can I say to make you come with me?"

She rolled onto her back and stared up at the sky.

"You can tell her to go home."

"Oh, behave. I'm not going to do that."

"So, I'll stay," she said, then her expression altered. She was on to one of her wins. "Okay, how about this for an alternative?" She sat up, folded her legs, and beckoned for him to sit opposite her. So he dropped into a crouch, took a drink from her bottle, and then handed it back.

"Go on," he said, and her smile reached from ear to ear.

"Tell me a secret."

"What?"

"Tell me a secret," she said. "Something that nobody else knows."

"I don't have a secret."

"Yes, you do."

"What?"

"Tell me."

He thought for a moment but couldn't think of a single thing that he knew that nobody else did.

"I don't have a secret. I tell Seb everything, and if I don't tell him, I tell you."

"There must be something," she replied. "Something personal."

"What?"

"Something personal. What do you think about when you... you know?"

"What's wrong with you?" he said, and she laughed loudly. "I don't do that."

"Oh really?"

"Really."

She gave another laugh, dismissing his weak denial.

"You're on your own then," she said. "I do it all the time."

The confession could have floored him, and he closed his eyes to get the image from his mind.

"Are you picturing it?"

"Debs, come on," he said.

"Do you think about me?"

"What? No! Of course I don't—"

"I bet you do," she said and then cackled when, even in the dim light, she could see his blushes. She sighed, as if relenting, and then rolled onto an elbow again. "Okay then. Last chance. If you really want me to come with you, then tell me about the box under your bed."

The last few syllables came at him like six individual slaps to his face. He hesitated, realising that he should have at least made a noise to hide his guilt, instead of simply staring at her with his mouth hanging open.

"See?" she said. "You do have a secret."

"You're mental," he said, clambering to his feet.

"And you're sick," she replied. "But I'm not complaining."

He stormed off towards the fire, not looking back.

"Tell me about the box, Kev," she called out, in that tormenting sing-song tone she was so good at. She cackled again and it danced around the trees. "I know your dirty secret. I know your dirty—"

She stopped her tormenting when he was a good fifty metres away, and he looked back into the darkness to where she was sitting. He was somewhere between her and the others – not just physically, but metaphorically.

Seb laughed at something. He was always laughing. He was always so positive. One of them was playing music on their phone, but none of them were dancing. He could make Ross out, sitting on the far side of the fire, while the others were back in the shadows, away from the blazing heat of the fire.

They weren't missing him one bit.

He turned on his heels and began marching back towards her, seething more and more with every step he took.

"Debs?" he said, trying to eliminate all traces of his usual friendly tone. "You about?"

But she didn't reply. She didn't step from the shadows and her cackle didn't dance around the trees. He ran to the stile and peered into the forest.

Then he saw it. It was unmistakable. A Vans shoe, her trademark footwear. He bent to pick it up. It was still warm from her body heat.

"Debs?" he said quietly and an ill sense of dread washed through him like a chilled breeze. "I can explain."

CHAPTER ONE

Bells marked the occasion, singing from the tower of St Peter's in Dunston to spread the word as far as the wind would carry their tintinnabulations.

The party was small, a few dozen at the most, each dressed in their fineries—ladies in hats they would never wear again, men in suits they had worn to a score or more weddings and funerals. The day was fine, not too hot and certainly not too cold, and the sky was a sea of serene azure carved into segments by aircraft ferrying holidaymakers to warmer climes. Birds waited in the trees, perhaps for the church doors to open, for a glimpse of the bride and groom, and spring flowers flavoured the otherwise green scene.

The congregation filed out in pairs, forming an avenue for the happy couple to parade through as confetti rained down on them. They stopped once, and the bride smiled up at her groom before gently kissing his lips.

"Look at them," Freya said from her living room window. "I wonder if they know what they're getting themselves into."

"A life of wedded bliss?" Ben replied, looking up from yesterday's newspaper. "Did you know, the residents of Scampton have been protesting about their RAF base being used to house asylum seekers for over a year now? A *year*? Some of them have been camped out on the verge. Can you imagine that? An entire year of shouting and nobody hearing you?"

"I can," Freya said. "It's a bit like working with Gillespie, having to tell him the same thing over and over again, and like the Home Office, he nods his head and does what he wants anyway."

"I thought we'd moved past the whole Gillespie thing. I thought separating him and Cruz had brought out the best in them both."

"He's still a loose cannon," Freya replied. "He's still dangerous."

"But he gets results. You have to give him that."

"I do," she said. "Which is more than can be said for the Home Office."

A loud cheer rose from the wedding party, and Freya shook her head.

Ben, however, made a point of not engaging with her on the events taking place on the far side of the village green, and his feigned ignorance was more than apparent.

"I know you want to say something," she said.

"No," he replied.

"You're fighting it," she said.

"Nope."

"Do you want to know what I think?"

He turned a page, looked up at her, and shook his head.

"Not right now, Freya."

"I read somewhere that forty-two per cent of marriages end in divorce," she said.

"Wow," he said. "That means that fifty-eight per cent of marriages are successful. That's got to be a good thing, surely?"

She reached for her tea on the little side table and took a sip.

"Your positivity is positively sickening."

He snapped his newspaper shut, tossed it to one side, and pushed himself from the armchair.

"Freya, I've done the honourable thing. I asked you if you wanted to marry me. If you expect me to push you for an answer every five minutes, then I'm sorry, but you'll be sorely disappointed."

"It would be nice to see some passion from you, Ben."

"Oh, you've seen plenty of passion from me," he replied, then took a breath. "Look, I've told you how I feel. I'm not going to spend the next God knows how long convincing you to marry me. You either will or you won't. It's that simple. All I can do is bide my time."

"It's not about *you*, Ben," she replied. "You're forgetting that I've been married once."

"Oh, that's right. You're a veteran. You've been married to one bloke, so being married to anybody else will be exactly the same. We're all cut from the same jib, aren't we, us men?"

"I didn't say that," she replied. "I just mean that I should learn from my experiences. It wasn't easy building a life with man and walking away, you know?"

"I don't suppose it was," he told her.

"And I'm not about to jump into the same pool feet first without testing the water—"

"And making sure you have a means of escape?" he said, and she had to give it to him. He was right.

"I'm being pragmatic, Ben," she said. "For both our sakes. If I'm going to marry anybody, then there's nobody else I would rather marry than you. Honestly, I can see my life with you, something I've never been able to do with anybody. I can see us settling down and building a home. I can see all of that."

"It's just the whole marriage thing then, is it?"

"It's a big deal."

He nodded slowly and stepped over to her.

"So, you're not wondering if I'm the right man?"

"No," she said. "I know you are."

"You just don't know if you want to commit to me?"

"Oh, for God's sake, Ben. I am committed. I have committed. I just don't know if I can go through the whole wedding thing again."

"Which would mean that I don't get a wedding," he said. "I never get to be married. I never get to walk down the aisle with all my friends and family looking on. I never get to slide a ring onto your finger or introduce you as my wife. And all because you've been married before, to someone who didn't treat you well enough, or who didn't understand you, didn't love you like I do. I have to miss out on all of that, do I?"

He reached for her shoulders and pulled her close, but she pulled away and returned to the window.

The newlyweds were posing for photographs while the colourful congregation conversed and slowly dissipated, making their way onwards to the reception, wherever that may be.

"Is all of that so important, to you?" she asked, to which he sighed.

"It is, Freya," he told her. "It's not something I ever wanted. Not until I met you, anyway."

Her eyes remained fixed on the couple, who were clearly in love.

"I'm too old for children, you know, don't you?"

"Have I ever raised the topic?" he asked.

"No. No, you haven't."

"And if I said no? Would you stay with me, or would that be the end of us?" She turned to face him. "Is this is deal or no deal scenario?"

"All I'm asking for is to be the centre of your world for one day. One day, Freya. One day when we don't have to think about work or Steve Standing."

"Steve Standing is trying to destroy my life, Ben," she told him.

"Steve Standing is a convicted murderer, Freya," he replied.

"A convicted murderer with friends in the police force. Friends who are keen to see me in ruins."

"I said that I'd help you, and I will, alright? And like I said before, we need to find a way of proving the fact before we can take action. And if you think you can divert this conversation, Freya."

"I'm not diverting. But we need to be aware of what we're getting into. We're two separate people right now. But if we marry—"

"When we marry," Ben corrected her.

"If we marry," she said again. "Then each of us will inherit the other's problems. It would be wise to release some baggage before we begin that journey, don't you think?"

He sat on the back of the sofa and folded his arms, letting his eyes wander over the three pieces of artwork she had bought from a local artist, whose fluid style was somewhere between abstract and landscape. The summer fields of barley or wheat— she could never tell the difference—and the wide Lincolnshire skies were as blue as can be. Perhaps they reminded him of his farming heritage. Perhaps they simply served as a distraction. He was hard to read sometimes.

"If you say no," he told her, "I won't walk away."

"You won't?"

"How could I? I still feel the same for you," he said. "Even with the whole Steve Standing drama hanging over you."

"That's not the only issue I'm dealing with, you know?"

"Freya, your dressing room looks more like the incident room than a room dedicated to dressing and make-up. You've got more research pinned to the wall than we've had for some murder investigations."

"So?"

"So, it could take years to prove that anybody is out to destroy your career. Years, Freya," he said. "Am I to wait?"

"I didn't ask for your help," she told him.

"I told you I would help. I told you I wanted to help. You can't do this alone, and you can't do this without evidence."

"I'm sensing a *but* coming," she said.

He opened his mouth to speak but the loud vibration coming from her phone cut him off as it danced across the side table.

"Do you want to get that?" he asked.

"Not really."

He stared at her and still the phone performed half-pirouettes with every elongated buzz.

"Could be important."

"*This* is important," she told him.

He pushed himself off the sofa, reached for her phone, and hit the green button to answer the call.

"DCI Bloom's phone," he said, then closed his eyes as the caller spoke. He nodded, although the caller wouldn't have known. "I'll tell her. Yep, we'll be there shortly. Thanks, Denise."

He ended the call and slid it back onto the table.

"Look's like lunch is off," he said.

"Right," she replied. "That was Chapman, was it?" He nodded, but refused to meet her gaze. "But?"

He dragged his shoes closer and slid into them, reaching down to coax them over his heels. She couldn't remember the last time she had seen him tie his laces.

"I don't think I'd ever be happy," he whispered. "There would always be this burning ambition or lost opportunity in the back of my mind. I don't know, maybe I'd resent you for it? I can't honestly say. But I suppose that kind of puts a time limit on us, doesn't it?" He pulled his jacket over his shirt and loaded his pockets with his phone, wallet, and keys. "How long can I really live with being unhappy or unfulfilled?"

"You can't," she replied, and then closed the gap between them, pulling his jacket together, before resting her hand on his chest. "I just need time."

"Take as long as you need," he replied, and he wrapped his arms around her. "I wasn't the one pushing for this conversation, you know?"

"I know," she replied. "It won't spoil anything, will it? The waiting, I mean?"

She felt him shake his head and then plant a kiss on her forehead.

"Unless you take ten years to decide," he replied. "In which case, I might start getting a little fidgety."

"Fidgety?"

"Well, you know," he said, and he pulled her away to look at her. "If it takes that long, then I might start having to consider my options."

"Oh, you have options, do you? I suppose there are women all across the county ready to fall at your feet?"

"Hundreds of them," he replied. "Come on, there's a body out there with our name on."

"I want Gillespie at the crime scene," she replied, as she pulled on her jacket.

"Okay," he said, sounding a little dubious. "It's not often I hear you say those words."

"I know," she told him. "Call him, will you? And tell him to pick up some coffees on the way."

He stopped at the doorway and turned back to her, the amusement gone from his expression.

"I mean it, Freya," he said. "I *will* wait."

"I know you will," she replied, as she sidled past him through the front door. "I'd expect nothing less." She glanced around her little front garden, ignoring his shaking head. "It's a pity. I was hoping to go to the garden centre today." She looked back at him to savour his incredulity. "It needs a bit of colour out here, don't you think?"

CHAPTER TWO

Rural crime scenes were nearly always a travesty, in Ben's opinion. The label wasn't so much in reference to the crimes, which were a travesty for far different reasons, but for the attending circus that, due to police procedure, resulted in more than a dozen vehicles and scores of people in white suits, police uniforms, and plain clothes, all of which seemed to spoil the place. Rarely were scenes of murders ever restored to their former glory, at least not in the eyes of the locals.

A few miles northeast of Sleaford, Haverholme Park was an area of outstanding natural beauty. It hadn't been formally recognized as such, but as Ben saw through the toing and froing and the vehicles parked across the lane near the entrance to the park, he saw the place for what it was.

The River Slea ran through the centre of a dense forest, and unlike many parks, which were little more than a patch of green between ugly buildings, fields and forests surrounded this one. Having grown up only ten miles away, Ben knew of the park but had never had cause to visit until now, and something told him that this wouldn't be the last visit.

The cars and vans belonged to a throng of services, including the uniformed police, CSI, the FME, and wider services such as the two individuals who were standing by, ready to remove the body.

At the far end of the mass of vehicles, a familiar figure stepped into view. His hair was longer and scruffier than the service regulations stipulated, and he was taller than the uniformed officers who guarded the cordon. He raised a hand to his lips, placed two fingers into his mouth, and a shrill whistle carried through the trees before he waved to get their attention.

"He beat us to it," Ben said from the passenger seat of Freya's Range Rover.

She flashed the headlights once to let him know they had seen him before he whistled again.

"And I can't see any coffees in his hands," she replied. "His first failure of the day, and I'm sure it won't be the last."

"Ah, come on. Give him a break," Ben said as he climbed from the car. A uniformed officer raised the cordon as he approached, and Ben waited for Freya to catch up. "I thought he was doing okay since we separated him and Cruz."

"Is doing okay good enough?" she said, nodding thanks to the officer as she passed beneath the police tape. "I was rather hoping for something close to excellence."

"Maybe we should take baby steps," Ben suggested as they neared the lanky Glaswegian. "If anything, it'll keep your disappointment in check." He smiled at her eye roll and then caught Gillespie's eye. "Now then, Jim. What have we got?"

"Ah, it's not pretty, mate," Gillespie replied. "I hope you woke up with a strong stomach."

"Where are we going?" Freya asked, ignoring his comment and looking around them through the trees.

"Up here," he said. "There's a wee house buried in the trees."

"A house?"

"Aye. It's a renovation or something. You know, like a grand design or something? The driveway looks like the Somme so I had the vehicles parked out on the lane."

"Well, we'll need the park closed off and any surrounding lanes," Freya told him. "I don't want any dog walkers parking up and destroying what evidence we might have."

"Oh, I don't think that'll be an issue, boss," Gillespie said.

"Oh, you don't, do you?"

"Not in this instance, boss," he replied.

"What about the digging works? Do we have the names of the contractors?"

"Again, I think we should wait until you've seen what we're dealing with."

"Who owns the house? Are we in contact with them?"

"Aye, we are. It was the lady of the house who called us in," Gillespie said, and he checked his notes. "A Mrs MacMillan. Rachel MacMillan, fifty-five years old."

"And is she home?"

"Uniform are taking care of her, boss," he replied. "We've called her husband. He's on his way."

A rudimentary path had been established from the edge of the driveway to the front door, and they walked single file to avoid the large trenches which presumably had been dug to prepare for the services.

The house in question was unassuming, to say the least. Some years or decades before, someone rendered and painted the walls white. The roof needed a good clean, or better still, an overhaul and the windows were ready for retirement. To the front, a little porch offered respite from the weather for guests, but even that appeared to have given up on life, offering only minimal protection from the elements.

"Crikey," Freya said. "It's a fixer-upper that's for sure."

"You might not think that when you get inside," Gillespie

said, holding the old porch door open for them to enter before him. He waited for Ben to pass and then muttered under his breath. "Place needs bloody torching if you ask me."

"Thankfully, you're not in the property business," Freya said without turning, and Gillespie gave Ben a surprised look as if to say, 'How the bloody hell did she hear that?'

Ben grinned and followed Freya through into what appeared to be the main reception room, which was around fifteen feet square and was most likely the living room at one point. However, there was no furniture inside, and someone had stripped the walls of any decoration, leaving only outdated newspapers used as lining paper. An old fireplace on one wall took pride of place, with an iron grate lined with turquoise tiles that Ben presumed had been in place for as long as the house.

"Through there in the kitchen," Gillespie told them, and he gestured at the door to the rear of the room, where a few figures in white overalls moved slowly, leaving little yellow flags to show areas of interest.

"May we?" Ben said when he poked his head through the kitchen doorway and found the lead forensic investigator brushing the architrave down. "Oh, hello, Katy."

She nodded at him and muttered something that was muffled by her mask.

The area they were looking for was clear, but it was far from ordinary.

Someone had lifted the floorboard from one end of the room and piled it neatly against one wall, and in the void, there was a mass of clear plastic close to eight feet long.

"Good lord," Freya said, and she glared at Gillespie.

"I did mention that you'd need a strong stomach," he said.

"Has the forensic medical examiner been in yet?" she asked.

"Not yet," Gillespie replied. "For him to get a good look at her, we'll need to unroll the plastic sheeting."

"And that might take some time," Katy Southwell added, lifting her mask to be heard.

"How long?" Ben asked.

"A few hours, maybe more," she said. "We'll need to lift any prints from the plastic and swab any areas of interest. Plus, there's a chance that whoever did this left some organic matter behind, hairs, sweat, that sort of thing."

"And has anybody searched for identification?"

"Nobody has touched her, boss," Gillespie said. "Mrs MacMillan said she was pulling the floor up as part of the restoration when she found her. As soon as she realised what it was, she called us."

Freya nodded and then crouched beside the plastic-wrapped cadaver.

"How do we know it's a female?"

"Well, it's an educated guess, really. One foot is exposed, and given the size, it's either a child or a female," Southwell replied and then nodded to the far end of the plastic roll. "I might be wrong, and if I am, I'll be the first to hold my hands up."

"So she was barefoot? Do we have some kind of estimated timeline?" Ben asked, to which Southwell sucked in a deep breath like a car mechanic looking down at an old engine.

"Anywhere between a year and ten," she replied, not committing to an exact answer.

"Great," Freya said. "I suggest we get out of here. We'll only slow things down."

"Sounds good to me," Gillespie said. "A nice coffee wouldn't go amiss."

"Indeed," Freya said. "And if I'm honest, I was hoping to have had one by now."

"Aye, well–" he began.

"I'm sure there's a cafe nearby," she said and stood from where she was crouched, nodding to Southwell that the crime scene was back in her hands. "Oh, and you'd better make it a full round. While you're gone, we'll be calling in the rest of the team."

"A full round?"

"A full round, Gillespie," she told him, as she edged past them both. "You should have got them in when Ben told you to. You could have saved yourself a few quid."

CHAPTER THREE

"This isn't going to be easy," Freya said, savouring the cool breeze on her nape. "What did she say, somewhere between one and ten years?"

"Are any of them easy?" Ben replied.

"I suppose all we can do is trust the process," she muttered. "And that process begins with the individual who made the discovery."

"Mrs MacMillan," Ben said, then checked his notepad. "Kerry, Gillespie said her name was. She's at the end of the drive in one of the cars." He pointed to where a hundred feet away, police vehicles lined the lane that led to the park.

"Come on then. Let's see what she has to say," Freya said, and she made her way back across the top of the trenches. "Eerily quiet here, don't you think?"

"Peaceful, you mean?" he replied, to which she turned to look him in the eye.

"No, I mean eerily quiet. Peaceful suggests some kind of positive connotation. This place is surrounded by forest. It's bloody terrifying if you ask me. I wouldn't want to be out here on my own at night, I can tell you. I'd feel like someone was always watching me."

"I'd love it," Ben said, as they made their way towards the lane. "I think it's because the farm is so exposed. There's no escape from it sometimes. The wind tears across the fens and it's relentless sometimes, especially in winter. I think I'd like being hemmed in, having some kind of protection from the wind. You know, so you can take the bins out or nip to the car without being blown over?"

"But you do have a view," she countered. "Which is more than I can say for this place."

"Yeah, we have a view, but I'm just saying that it's nice to have a change, isn't it? It's human nature. We always want what someone else has got. We don't appreciate what we have, or at least we grow tired of it."

"Do you often grow tired of the things you have, Ben?" she asked, as they reached the lane and made their way over to a police transporter, where a uniformed officer was standing quietly beside a middle-aged lady sitting in one of the rear seats.

"I've lived there my entire life, haven't I?" Ben said quietly.

"Was that through loyalty to your father?" she asked. "Or were you simply indoctrinated into farm life?"

Ben shook his head.

"You can be a cold-hearted cow sometimes, Freya."

The sliding door was open, and as they approached, Freya put Ben's comment to the back of her mind and appraised the woman. She wore leather work boots, heavy dungarees over a light t-shirt, and a flannel shirt over the top and had used a clip to hold her mousy hair in a topknot. If she was wearing makeup, then it was minimal.

"Only sometimes?" she said quietly to Ben, then smiled politely at the officer, who took her leave. "Mrs MacMillan?" Freya said, and the woman looked up at them both. Both Freya and Ben presented their warrant cards, which seemed to answer an unspoken question. "I wondered if we might have a quick word."

"I've told them everything," she said. "The big fellow. Scottish chap."

"I know. He did give us a brief run down, but sometimes in these situations, little details can be overlooked. Our emotions can run high."

"Do I look emotional?" MacMillan replied.

"No, you don't," Freya said. "But I was hoping to hear your account first-hand. I understand you're doing the place up. It's a lovely spot."

"It is," the woman said, then cleared her throat. "My dream house, if you can believe that. Well, it will be when we're done." She peered past Ben and Freya and waved. Ben turned to find a middle-aged woman at the cordon being held back by a uniformed officer. "It's Kerry," MacMillan explained.

"A friend?"

"A good friend," she said, and Ben signalled for the officer to let the friend through. She was one of those women who, rather like Freya, carried their youthful good looks into maturity. She wore tight jeans, expensive-looking ankle boots, and a quilted Barbour jacket.

"Oh, my love," Kerry said. "I got your message, you poor thing."

They hugged and Kerry refused to let her friend go. She stood close, holding her hand.

"I'm okay," she said. "Just a shock, that's all."

"I'm not surprised," Kerry said, and she turned to Ben and Freya. "Do you know who it is?"

"We're still minutes into the investigation," Freya said. "I'm sure we'll get there."

"Is it a major renovation?" Ben asked, hoping to get his line of questioning back on track, and Mrs MacMillan looked between the two of them briefly, perhaps deciding on who was the boss.

"You could say that," she said. "We're keeping the original house but extending on all sides. It'll be twice the footprint by the time we're done. It's a three-bed now but we're adding two more. The kitchen will be twice as large. We'll have a boot room, a large utility room, a laundry room, pantry, and another reception room." She spoke with pride and gazed along the driveway as if she could envisage how it would all look. "Five years I've been waiting to do this. Five years. Three weeks in and what do we find? A bloody dead body. Most people find damp or a rotten roof. But no, not us. We found a dead body. I've had to put the ground-work back. That'll cost us, you know? They'll have to reschedule and God knows when they can fit us in. Could be months."

"I'm sure you couldn't have foreseen this," Ben said.

"No, I couldn't have, could I?" she replied, with a touch of scorn in her voice.

"You used the word *us*," Freya said. "Are you referring to your husband?"

She nodded. "He's on his way back from work now."

"And what does he do?"

"He does a bit of this and that. Construction mostly," she said. "Extensions and whatnot. That's why it's taken us this long to get started on our house. Spends all his time on other houses. By the time he gets in from work, he hasn't the energy to do our place. I mean, look at it," she said, presenting the house with her palm. "Five years I've lived like that. We had a lovely place before this. Not big but nice, you know?"

"So you bought the house five years ago, did you?" Ben asked, and Mrs MacMillan nodded.

"Nick sold the idea to me," she began. "That's my other half. He knew I always wanted a large kitchen and a laundry room and all that. Told me this place had real potential. And it does. I love being surrounded by trees and we've got a decent-sized garden all around the house. Honestly, I couldn't have asked for more. But he couldn't get another firm in to do it, could he? Had to do it himself. Which meant that I've lived in squalor for the past five years. And that smell?"

"What smell?"

"That thing," she said, nodding at the house. "We thought it was damp. I mean, we always knew we were going to rip the house to pieces, but Christ almighty, when we first moved in, the smell was unbearable."

Kerry pulled her in for a hug, rubbing her shoulder as friends do when words fail them.

"But the smell subsided, did it?"

"Either that or we got used to it," she replied. "But I daren't invite anyone round."

"I can see how that might grate," Freya said.

"It did," she replied. "So when it started to warm up a bit, I told him. Said we're doing it this year. I want my house the way I want by Christmas. We can have the kids round and really make it something."

"And he agreed, did he?"

"Not at first, no," she replied. "Had to give him an ultimatum. Either I get my house or he can bugger off and I'll get someone in to do it."

"Builder's pride," Freya said.

"Something like that. I mean, don't get me wrong. He's good at what he does. Bloody good, actually. Hasn't advertised for decades. No need. People see what he does and they want him to do their house. First thing he did was tear up the driveway to get the services in. He was planning on having some time off after the job he's on to get the bulk of the work done here. You know, get the footings in, the walls up, and the roof on. Said once it's water-tight the rest is easy and he can get mates in to do the electrics and plumbing and whatnot. Anyways, we put our furniture in storage, moved into a B&B nearby, and got started. I've been doing what I can, you know, forcing the project on. That's when this happened."

"It was this morning, was it?" Ben asked, to which she nodded.

"He went to work, and I got here early. The whole downstairs floor needed ripping and replacing, so I figured I'd make a start. I wasn't an hour into it, and making good progress, I was, when I saw the plastic stuffed between the joists. Thought nothing of it at first. Figured whoever put the floor down way back when had just stuffed it in there. So I carried on, didn't I? Must have been an hour later when I had to move the plastic that I put my crowbar in. That's when I saw it. A bloody human foot sticking out of the plastic. Gave me a right start, it did."

"I'll bet it did," Freya said, as a loud diesel engine roared along the lane and came to a stop at the cordon. A large man in a check shirt and jeans climbed out, and the officer guarding the crime scene approached him.

"That's him," Mrs MacMillan said. "That's my Nick."

"Let him through," Ben called out, waving to the officer, who then held the cordon up for Nick MacMillan to pass beneath.

He ran to the van, and seeing his wife, embraced her.

"You all right, love?" he asked, and both Freya and Ben took a step back to give them some room. "Oh Christ, you poor love," he said, clasping her in his powerful arms. "I told you to wait for me, didn't I?"

"I just wanted to get on," his wife sobbed with her face buried into his shoulder. "I'm tired of it all, Nick. I just want it done."

"I know, I know," he replied and looked back at Freya.

"Give us a minute, will you?" he said, to which Freya nodded and led Ben away, just as the officer raised the cordon once more, to allow Gillespie to pass with a cardboard tray of coffees.

"Well done, Gillespie," she told the big Scotsman, as he set the tray down on the bonnet of a liveried police car. "Did you have to go far?"

"No, just into Ruskington," he said. "Found a nice wee cafe. Cheap too."

"That's good to know," Freya said, taking her coffee from the tray. She sniffed at it and then took a sip to test the temperature. "I don't feel so bad about sending you back now."

"Eh?" he said, his hand poised to take his own cup. "You want me to go back?"

"Yes, I think Mr and Mrs MacMillan need something to calm their nerves. It's the least we can do, really," she said, peering back at them briefly before turning to address Gillespie. "And while you're at it. You could probably get them some breakfast. Some bacon sandwiches or something. I'd hate to be thought of as being inhospitable or, dare I say it," she said with a glance at Ben, "cold-hearted."

CHAPTER FOUR

Nick MacMillan's skin was leathery and tanned from a life of working outside. Cement had chipped and stained his fingernails, his forearms were as broad as one of Ben's calves, and tattoos covered every inch of his impressive arms.

"Sensitive lass, our Rachel," he said, and he gestured over his shoulder at the van where Freya was talking to his wife. "Take her weeks to get over this, it will. Did she see much?"

Ben shook his head, leading him away from Rachel MacMillan to where they could speak freely. He saw Anna Nillson and Jenny Anderson speaking to the officer at the cordon and nodded a brief greeting to them.

"Thankfully, there isn't much to see right now, and whatever your wife saw is severely decayed." Whoever did this wrapped the body in plastic sheeting, and we can't unwrap her until forensics have been over it."

"So it's a her then, is it?"

Ben winced at his mistake.

"It's an assumption," he said. "No details have been confirmed."

"I see," MacMillan replied, seeing through Ben's backtracking.

"So you won't know how long she's been there, either then."

"Like I said," Ben told him. "Details are pretty thin right now. But give us a few hours and we'll be up to speed. You can't rush things, not at this stage anyway. We have to be certain of what we're dealing with, which leads me to my next point. Exactly how long have you owned the place?"

MacMillan puffed his cheeks out, then sucked air in through his teeth.

"Five years," he said, wrinkling his nose. "Give or take."

"And is this the first work you've done to the house?"

"I'd like to think that if I laid a new floor, it wouldn't need to be ripped up in my lifetime, Sergeant."

"Thanks," Ben said. "And it's Detective Inspector if you don't mind."

"Right," he replied, as if he enjoyed Ben correcting his rank, which in a world without formalities, such as MacMillan's, must have seemed quite archaic. He took a moment to pull his phone from his pocket. It was an old Nokia, and he held it a distance to read the screen, using his fat fingers to fumble through a message. He finished and pocketed his phone again.

"Sorry, just a customer wants to know how long I'll be."

"So, to your knowledge," Ben said, hoping to regain some momentum. "The floor hasn't been up since you've owned it?"

"S'right," MacMillan said. "S'pose you'll want the previous owner's details, will you?"

"Why should we want that?"

"Well, I haven't had the floor up, so it must have happened before then. You said there was some decay. It's an old one, right? Been there a while, like?"

Over his shoulder, Ben saw a figure in white overalls step from the house, remove her mask and goggles, and then release her hair from the bun she had worn, as if the act was part of some release mechanism for the tension she had developed during her morning's work. She caught Ben looking and gave him a thumbs-up from afar.

"We'll need to take a formal statement," Ben told MacMillan, then caught Nillson's attention. "Sergeant Nillson here will take the details of the B&B you're staying at, and if there's anything else you need, she'll make the arrangements for you. We'll be in touch in the next day or so for a formal statement."

"That's it then, is it?" he replied. "I'm supposed to be on my way and just leave you lot here in my house, am I?"

"Your house is now a crime scene, Mr MacMillan," Ben told him as Nillson approached, and he turned to her. "See that Mr MacMillan and his wife are taken care of please, Anna."

"Will do," she replied, smiling pleasantly at Nick MacMillan.

"Freya, they're ready for us," Ben called out, to which she nodded and began closing down her chat with Mrs MacMillan. Finding himself with a moment to reflect on the morning, Ben stepped into a patch of sunlight that had found its way through the tree canopy. He closed his eyes and listened, trying his best to block out the sounds of muffled conversation, the rumble of an engine, and the comings and goings of the circus performers. There were birds aplenty and their combined melodies were fragrant with spring.

Her perfume announced her arrival. By now, he thought he might have grown immune to it, but each time he smelled her fragrance, it was as if for the first time.

"You look like you're about to drop into the downward dog," she said, and he opened his eyes to see her.

"The what?"

She grinned.

"Never mind," she said. "Shall we go and see what all the fuss is about?"

"Now there's an offer I can't refuse," he said, hoping the level of sarcasm he was aiming for was clear.

The house was one of a few properties on the edges of the

park, each one barely visible from the next. At the furthest reaches were the remains of the old Haverholme Priory, now a derelict skeleton of what must have once been a glorious sight to behold. And that prominence had carried through to each of the surrounding houses. High brick walls denoted boundaries with elegant gates and the River Slea that carved its way through the area gave life to the banks, adding a calmness to the space.

The MacMillan house, however, had been built at a different time, and though it had not inherited that same sense of pride as its neighbouring properties, there was a charm to it that, with a little imagination, could have been quite wonderful with some wildflowers, climbing roses, and perhaps a bed of spring bulbs. Cracked, rendered walls surrounded old, timber-framed windows, few of which still retained glass. The house was, in Ben's imagination, the very epitome of what they were heading to view – the ruined remains of imagined beauty.

At the front door, Katy Southwell and Doctor Saint met them, both waiting in sombre silence like a pair of pathologists presenting a body to a grieving mother.

Ben nodded to Doctor Saint.

"Peter," he said, extending his hand. "Thanks for coming."

Saint smiled briefly, shook his hand, and then led the way into the kitchen. The room was desolate. Someone had removed the cupboards and furniture, and stripped the wallpaper, leaving behind only sheets of yellowed newspaper as a substitute for lining paper. It had been a common practice decades ago, and Ben fancied that when the day came to decorate his own house properly, he would be able to date the last refurb via the newspaper on the walls.

"As you can imagine, this one isn't really for me," Saint said, stopping in a spot that shielded them from the view, where he turned to face them all. "In fact, there's nothing I can tell you that might give you a head start."

"Cause of death?" Ben asked, to which Saint simply gave an apologetic smile and stepped to one side.

"Good Lord," Freya said from behind Ben, and the foursome shared a moment of silence as each of them contemplated the remains.

"I can tell you from the shape of the pelvis that it is a female, and judging by the wear on the teeth, I would say late teens or early twenties. But it isn't my area of expertise, so that's an educated finger in rather turbulent air. Please don't quote me on it."

"We won't," Freya said reassuringly, and she stepped past Ben for a closer look. Since their initial visit to the house, someone had lifted the plastic from within the floor and opened it up to reveal nothing more than bones and partially rotted clothing loosely arranged in the shape of a human being. Freya inspected the remains. "She had a broken leg."

"At some stage, but that was some years before her death," Saint replied. "It's healed nicely, and the calcium build-up around the break would have taken years to develop."

"Well, are we talking natural causes, here?" she asked, leaning over the bones to examine the skull. "I can't see any signs of violence."

"We've taken samples from the residue on the plastic," Southwell said. "If the sheeting had been sealed, it might have slowed down the decay," Southwell said. "But as it stands, I would say that someone hastily wrapped the body, leaving enough gaps for insects to get in and do what they do best," Southwell said.

"What residue?" Ben asked, to which Southwell hesitated to consider her response.

"When the heart stops, the body begins to decompose. Gravity has an effect on the fluids and sooner or later they find their way out."

Ben dropped to a crouch beside Freya and gestured at the stains on the plastic.

"So this isn't blood?"

"I don't believe so. It's hard to say for definite, of course, and we will do some tests. But from what I can see, nothing here suggests that this girl bled."

Freya glanced across at Ben and then gave her considered response. "So we can rule out blunt force trauma and we're as sure as we can be that she didn't bleed out."

"I'd also suggest that strangulation isn't an option, either," Saint said, and using the end of his pen, he identified the intact hyoid bone at the neck. "These usually break under the force of strangulation."

"She could have bled out elsewhere," Ben suggested. "The body could have been wrapped afterwards and dumped in the floor."

"In which case, she could have been poisoned, or shot, or she could have died from natural causes," Freya said. "In which case, why wrap the body in haste?" She shook her head. "No, this was done in a hurry. Somebody panicked. It's not a neat job. Whoever did this didn't have the luxury of time on their side."

"I doubt even the pathologist could give you an exact cause," Saint said.

"Which won't help us build a case, even if we do find a suspect," Ben added.

"But we have to try," Freya said as she stood. "This poor girl died. Her parents must have been through hell. Even if we never know how she died, we'll damn well do our best to give her justice."

"Where's her other shoe?" Ben asked, and the team peered down to the girl's feet, where the remains of an old, skateboard-style shoe hung loosely from one of the feet. The other foot was bare. He leaned into the hole from which the body had been pulled but saw nothing. "She lost a shoe," he said. "Could give us an idea of her last few minutes."

"Could do," Freya said. "The other one looks to be fairly intact."

"They tend to last a good ten years or more," Southwell said. "Shoes are thicker than the clothing we wear on our bodies. The soles especially can last for decades."

Ben ran his eye across the piles of bones as Freya spoke. Something caught his eye, a dull glint that was alien to its surroundings.

"Katy, can you help me?" he said. "I need tweezers or something."

"What is it?" Freya said as Southwell dropped beside him.

"There," he said, pointing into the gap where the skull lay on the plastic. "What is that?"

Carefully, Southwell eased a pair of needle-nosed tweezers into the space, her gloved hands as steady as rocks. And then she held it up into the light.

"What is it?" Freya asked. "An earring?"

"Close, Chief Inspector Bloom," Southwell said. "This is a nose stud." She dropped it into a small, plastic bag. "Whoever she is, she had a pierced nose."

"Well, that gives us something to go on," Ben said. "We don't know how she died, but we do know she had a pierced nose." He turned to Freya. "We'll need to check the mispers."

"I agree," she replied. "And I know just the man for the job. Gather the team, will you? We'll reconvene at the station."

"Aren't you coming?" Ben asked.

"In a minute," she said, then turned back to the remains on the sheet. "Actually, why don't you go back with Gillespie? I just want a moment alone with her before she's taken away."

CHAPTER FIVE

Weekends were often quiet at the station. Shift work meant that CID on the floor above were always present, but for major crimes covering a broad rural area, shifts would only dilute the resources and add expense.

"I'll see you in a sec, Benny boy," Gillespie said when they reached the first floor. "I just need a jimmy."

He strode off towards the washrooms and Ben shook his head at the big man undoing his belt while he walked.

Inside the incident room, Ben flicked the lights on and they whirred into life, a sound that he only ever noticed when he was alone in the room, when memories of times gone by prevailed. Memories of David Foster, the man who almost dragged Ben through his career, tearing him from uniform into a plain-clothed detective constable, and then to detective sergeant, before cancer had taken hold and left Ben in a cloud of uncertainty. A cloud that had only thickened when Freya had joined the team, leaving him doubtful of his future.

There had been others, too. DI Standing, the man who most would have agreed was more suited to policing in the seventies than the modern day, a sentiment which was strengthened by his recent conviction for murder.

"Ah, that's better," Gillespie announced as he pushed into the room, rubbing his hands on the back of his trousers. He took his seat, dumped his bag onto his desk, and then crossed his legs before staring up at Ben. "You all right there, Ben? You look like you've seen a ghost."

"I'm fine," Ben told him. "Just remembering, that's all."

"Remembering, aye? What is it you're remembering?"

Ben shook his head.

"David," he said. "Steve Standing. Just old times, that's all."

"What about Arthur?"

"Arthur," Ben said, recalling the old man who led the team from the confines of his office for so long.

"Who's Arthur?" A voice said from the doorway, and Ben turned to find Anderson and Nillson entering the room.

"Detective Superintendent Harper," Ben said.

"Arthur Harper? That's an unfortunate name."

"He wasn't actually called Arthur," Ben told her. "It was a nickname, earned by only ever doing half a job and then delegating it to somebody else to finish. Hence, half-a-job Harper became Arthur. The name stuck."

"What about him, anyway?" Nillson said. "Why are we talking about him?"

"Oh, Ben was just reminiscing," Gillespie said. "Thinking about old times, weren't you, Ben?"

"Not old times," Ben corrected him. "Just times. This room has seen a lot. Quite a few people have come and gone."

"Aye, they have, and with any luck, none of them will come back," Gillespie said, to which everyone stared at him, surprised. "What? Arthur's dead, David's dead, and Standing's locked up for murder. And anyone not included in that list who has been and gone was a supporter of Standing, which makes them as welcome as a fart in a balloon."

"Such a way with words," Nillson muttered.

"We should get ready," Ben said, taking control of the room. "Freya will be here soon, so if you need the washroom or a drink, then do so before she gets back."

"I'm afraid you're too late for that," Freya said, as she barged through the doors, followed closely by DCs Cruz, Gold, and Chapman. "This shouldn't take long, so if you do need a comfort break, please hold it." She checked her watch. "It's Saturday at two p.m. and we won't have much to go on until tomorrow at the earliest, so I suggest we make a plan, start with the basics, and by the time the lab has any results and the pathologist has done what she can, we won't be at a standing start."

"Mispers?" Ben said.

"Precisely," Freya replied, taking her usual spot of perching on the edge of her desk. She dragged the whiteboard closer and snatched up a marker from the little tray. The rest of the team took their seats as Freya drew a horizontal line across the board, writing *2024* to the right and *2014* to the left. In the centre of the line, she added a cross and then wrote *2019* above it. She glanced behind her to make sure all were paying attention and then began. "According to the FME and CSI, the body is anywhere between one and ten years old. The decay is significant enough that we are sure it is not a recent death."

"Christ," Cruz said. "What was it, a bag of bones?"

"That's exactly what it was," Freya said, turning to give him a hard stare. "And she deserves the same respect as if she died yesterday. We follow the same rules, but, and I cannot stress this enough, this is not going to be easy."

"Sorry, boss," Cruz said.

"That's all right. Just remember, whilst we are dealing with a bag of bones, that bag of bones was once a human being. She had a personality, parents maybe? She would have had friends or enemies. She came from somewhere and it's our job to find out who she was."

"What do we know so far?" Nillson asked.

"Not much," Ben said. "Female, early twenties or late teens. Nose piercing."

"She had her nose pierced?" Cruz said. "I thought you said it was...well, bones, boss?"

"We found the stud beside her skull," Ben said. "Southwell is analysing it for DNA, along with the residue from the sheeting."

"Residue?"

"You don't want to know," Ben said, then nodded an apology to Freya.

"Thank you. We do have a few lines of enquiry we can make a start with," she said. "First of all, within that nine-year period, the MacMillans purchased the property. Who from?"

"I can take that," Chapman said, making a note on her pad.

"Nillson, Anderson, I want you to look into the MacMillans. Do they have a history? Are there any records of them?"

"Will do, boss," Nillson replied, and she shared a pleased expression with Anderson.

"Gillespie," Freya said, adding a little emphasis to her tone, which did little to ease his anxiety. "Mispers."

"Ah, you're kidding me," he said. "Missing persons?"

"I want a list," Freya said. "Every individual reported missing in a five-mile radius during the last ten years."

He let his head fall back and gave a heavy sigh, leaving Freya to focus on Gold and Cruz.

"You two, police reports. Anything you can get in the area. B and Es, TDAs, disturbing the peace, whatever you can find. We're looking for a link between your list and Gillespie's list."

"That's a long shot," Ben said.

"But it is a shot," she said. "Like I said, this one is not going to be easy. Whoever did this has had up to ten years to develop a story. We're playing catch up, so we need to look down every avenue we come across."

"Agreed," he told her, as the doors opened once more and Detective Superintendent Granger poked his head inside.

"Bloom, Savage," he said. "A word in my office, if you will."

"Be right there," Freya told him, and he slipped from the room, leaving her to finish her briefing. "The last thing I want to impress upon you is this. We have no way of positively identifying how she died. No recent broken bones, no sign of strangulation, and the plastic sheeting she was wrapped in appears to be free of blood. Which means what, Cruz?"

"Eh?"

"What does the lack of blood mean?"

He gave it some thought before responding, rocking his head from side to side.

"Natural causes, boss?"

"Or?"

"Poison?" he said. "Overdose, asphyxiation, there must be dozens of ways to die without leaving a blood trail."

"Unless she bled out somewhere else?" Gold said. "Isn't it possible that the killer wrapped her up an hour or more afterwards?"

"It's possible," Freya said. "And it's the point I was hoping to impress on you all. You see, waiting for the blood to stop suggests that whoever put her there had time on their side. But if that was the case, they would have wrapped her neatly, rolled her up, and sealed the ends rather than simply stuffing her into the sheet like garbage and hammering the floorboards down."

"That's subjective," Cruz said and the comment raised Freya's eyebrows. "I mean, you're probably right, boss, but we can't take that for granted, can we? I mean, we should be keeping an open mind, shouldn't we?"

She held his stare and for a moment Ben thought she might drag him outside for a verbal spanking. But she smiled at the young constable.

"How right you are, Cruz," she said. "And we will keep open

minds. In fact, that can be your job. To look at every option available to us. Keep us on track."

"Eh?"

"That way if we miss something I'll have somebody to blame," she said, and then winked at Gold, who sat closest to him. "Good thinking, Cruz. I knew I could count on you."

"But I didn't—"

"Right then, everyone should have enough to be getting on with," she said, eyeing Ben. "Are you ready for our little chat with Granger?"

CHAPTER SIX

"Close the door," Granger said from behind his desk and then made a show of stacking the few files into a pile, pocketing his pen, and sitting back in his chair. Ben did as he asked and then stood beside Freya until the superintendent proffered them seats with a sweep of a giant hand. "We need to have a serious chat."

Ben glanced across at Freya, who, perhaps purposefully, avoided eye contact with him. Instead, she dragged a seat to the desk and perched on the edge. Ben followed suit and watched as Granger waited for them to settle.

"First of all, I'd like to congratulate you both," he began. "I appreciate that might seem a little late, given that you proposed several weeks ago, Ben, but I hope you can appreciate my reasons when I explain."

"Thank you, guv," Ben replied. "And don't worry, we hadn't noticed–"

"In fact," Freya cut in, "I believe your congratulations are somewhat premature. That's why we haven't told everyone yet. Only one or two trusted individuals."

"Oh?" Granger said.

"I haven't said yes yet," she replied, somehow maintaining a stoic expression.

"I see," Granger said, and did his best to re-establish the status quo. "Well, even so, perhaps you might permit me to make my position clear?"

"Of course," she said and seemed to delight in the fact that she had off-balanced his authority.

"The force has a definitive position on relationships," he began. "It feels, and perhaps rightly so, that married couples should not work in the same team."

"Do they provide a reason for this?" Freya asked.

"I would have thought the reasons were clear," Granger told her. "Should one of you be injured in the line of duty, then the other's ability to give his best would be compromised. Conversely, should the two of you have a disagreement concerning a private matter and this was to seep into your work lives, then it could have an effect on the team as a whole. It could affect an investigation, it could affect your judgement, and when we're dealing with serious crimes such as murder, the results could be devastating."

"That wouldn't happen, guv," Ben said.

"We don't know that," Freya replied, which came as a surprise. "We might not mean for it to happen, but it's plausible." She turned to Granger, who appeared impressed at not having to argue his point. "So, what do we do? What's the solution here?"

"The solution?" He sucked in a long breath. "Is there a solution?"

"We could break up," she said.

"What?" Ben replied.

"I'm sure that's not the answer," Granger cut in, holding his hands up before World War Three commenced. He sighed, collected his pen from his desk, and then leaned back in his chair. "My inclination is to let it go," he said.

"You mean let us marry?" Ben asked.

"I can't stop you from marrying," he said.

"But you can split us up," Freya suggested, to which Granger nodded.

"I can. I can also suggest provisions that would greatly reduce the risk of either one of you letting the relationship get in the way of an investigation."

"Such as?" Freya asked.

"I can make you desk-bound, Freya," he replied.

"Excuse me?"

"Desk-bound," he repeated. "I mean, you're the only chief inspector we've had that I can remember who still works out in the field. Having you at your desk all day wouldn't exactly raise any eyebrows. I stayed at my desk, as did Harper and Standing. There's no reason for you to be out there."

"I need to be out there, guv. I need to be on the ground. It's what I'm good at."

"You're a chief inspector, Freya. You have a solid detective inspector in Ben here. Nillson and Gillespie are both extremely competent sergeants, and beneath them, you have Cruz, Chapman, Gold, and Anderson. That's a good team, you have to admit."

"We are a good team, guv," she said. "We're good because we work well together. I know what works, how they operate, and how to get the best from them. It's taken me over a year to learn them. You can't expect me to give that up just so that we can tick a box that the force has imposed, blindly I might add. There's no context. It's just another blanket rule that somebody has created to protect the force from being prosecuted or to save face. Where's the loyalty in that? Where's the personal touch?"

"I'll transfer," Ben said.

"What? No, Ben–"

"Nillson or Gillespie can take my place. Both are up to the job," he said, ignoring Freya's objection.

"That's a bold move, Ben," Granger said.

"I want to marry her, guv," he said. "You know, I've given the best years of my life so far to the force. But I do have a life outside of it and I will have a life when I'm retired. I want that life to be with Freya, and if that means that I move on, then so be it."

"This is ridiculous," Freya said. "Do you see what this policy does, guv?"

"I suggest we take a little while to consider our options," Granger said, again holding his hands up to calm the room. "The fact of the matter is that you cannot both be out in the field. The force simply won't allow it, and I'm close enough to retirement that I can smell the lazy mornings." He raised an index finger at them both. "And love you both as I do, I won't be risking my pension on this."

"I understand that, guv," Ben said. "I wouldn't want you to stick your neck out for us."

"Good," he replied. "Then, we'll reconvene when this investigation is over. Whichever way you look at it, this investigation will be the last time you're both out in the field. Either you accept your position as chief inspector, Freya, or one of you transfers. Now, go away and think on it."

"Guv," Ben said, as he rose from his seat.

"There is one more thing," Granger said when they both stood at the open door. "While you're contemplating the options, you'll do well to consider the team out there. I've spoken to them all individually, and every one of them is behind you." He nodded as if to reaffirm his point. "Make the right decision, eh? You both know what that is."

"Speaking of making decisions, guv," Freya said. "The Haverholme investigation could prove to be quite a challenge. I'll send you my report later on, but in short, we could be dealing with a ten-year-old murder here."

"So you're on the back foot, are you?"

"The body was found beneath the floorboards of an old house," Freya said. "Female, wrapped in plastic sheeting. The team is pulling together a list of mispers and crime numbers as we speak."

"What do you need from me?" Granger asked.

"I need bodies. Live ones. In uniform," she added.

"What for? Is Sergeant Priest withholding resources, because if he is, I can assure you–"

"He's not withholding resources, guv," she said. "In fact, I rather think that he's overindulged me to the detriment of other investigations. He's thin on the ground down there."

"So you want me to bring in uniformed support from Lincoln?" Granger said, to which she nodded.

"To what purpose?" he asked. "If, as you say, the murder is ten years old–"

"Could be ten years old," she corrected him. "But I want to conduct a thorough search."

"Haven't you done that?"

"I want to check the rest of the floors, guv," she said. "The walls too."

"Crikey."

"I also want to bring in GPR," she said.

"Ground penetrating radar? You want to dig the garden up?"

"Cadaver dogs too. I want the works," she said.

"On what grounds?"

"On the grounds that a body has been concealed under the floorboards, guv, and aside from knowing that it is a young female who had her nose pierced, we have very little to go on. History tells us that victims found either buried or concealed in wall or floor cavities are rarely on their own."

"Are you going to give me a history lesson now?"

"John Christie," she said. "Eight victims. Peter Tobin. Three victims that we know of. And then there's the Wests, of course. Fred and Rose. Should I go on?"

Granger shook his head but was lost in thought.

"We can't ignore the MO, guv," she said. "We can't not investigate due to resources. If I'm wrong, and I hope I am, then we'll find nothing. I can take that. But if we're right—"

"Then your last investigation as SIO will be a good one," Granger said.

"I'm not doing this for glory," she replied. "I have an entire career behind me. If you think I want to go out with a bang or to be remembered for doing something great, then you're wrong. You can call up any one of the families of the victims I've worked with and ask them if they remember me. That's all the glory I need."

Granger sat back in his chair and glanced at Ben, who knew better than to add his two pennies worth in at this stage.

"Leave it with me," Granger said. "No promises, but I'll see what I can do."

"Thank you," she said, straightening her blouse.

"And Freya?" Granger said, always keen to have the last word. "If this happens and you get your GPR, and your dogs, and everything else that comes with it…"

"Yes, guv?"

"Then you'll be under the spotlight," he said, wagging his index finger at her. "Every mistake you make will be front page news."

"I know," she said. "We'd better make the right decisions then, hadn't we?"

CHAPTER SEVEN

The hum of activity in the incident room was inspiring. Nillson and Anderson were huddled around a laptop, as were Gold and Cruz. Chapman worked alone as was her preference, while Gillespie sat by himself, grumbling audibly like an old diesel engine on a cold morning and stabbing his keyboard with two rigid index fingers.

"Guv?" Chapman said when she saw them enter the room, and she gestured at the printer which whirred into life. "That's for you."

Freya collected the piece of paper the printer spewed into its tray and read through it.

"It's a list of names and dates," she said.

"Mispers," Chapman replied.

"I asked Gillespie to look at the mispers," Freya said, and she glared at Gillespie who refused to look up.

"He had a few difficulties," Chapman explained, to which Nillson laughed out loud.

"Even more than usual," she said.

"Ah, shut it, Anna," Gillespie told her. "It's not my fault the printer's racist, is it?"

"Racist?" Freya said. "The printer is racist, is it?"

"Aye, it is," he said. "Works well enough for Chapman and Nillson. Even Cruz managed to scan something once he'd found a stool to stand on."

"Oy!"

"But will it print for me?" he said. "No, it won't. I've got the same model laptop as the others, the same software, and I hit the same buttons. But will it print? Will it bugger."

"Because you're Scottish?" Freya said for clarity.

"Aye."

"You do realise how ridiculous that sounds, don't you?" Freya asked. "Gold, you're Scottish. Are you able to print?"

"I think so," she said. "I printed off my family liaison report last week and it worked just fine. But then again, I am only part Scottish. We moved down here when I was young."

"Right," Freya said. "Well, I'll need to report this, of course. The force is very strong on discrimination, you know? If it turns out that our printer is indeed racist, then I'm afraid it'll be withdrawn from service and we'll have to write everything out freehand. Either that or we'll have to go upstairs to CID to print."

"Aye, well," Gillespie grumbled.

"Or is it perhaps that you simply couldn't be bothered to walk across the room to the printer, Gillespie? So you sent your report to Chapman in the hope that she would do it for you?" Freya stepped over to his laptop and she held the lid open before he could close it. "May I?" she asked, and reluctantly, he relented.

She read through the file he had open and then clicked on the little printer icon. A few clicks later, the printer whirred to life.

"Oh," she said aloud. "Would you look at that?" Gillespie's face reddened, and he feigned ignorance. "Must be because I'm English," she said and then carried the sheet of paper to the whiteboard. "Seventeen names," she said. "Seventeen missing persons reported to the police in the past decade."

"Aye, it's a lot, eh?"

"Too many," she said. "Reduce the search area."

"Did that," he replied. "Narrows it down to the top five on the report."

"Five? Now that's more like it," she said, studying the names. "Two of them are male, which narrows it down further to the three females."

"Only two of which fit the age range," Gillespie said. "Holly Carson and Deborah Jarvis."

"I've taken the liberty of finding the reports, guv," Chapman said and then turned her laptop for Freya to see. "The girl on the left has a nose piercing."

"Had a nose piercing," Nillson said.

"We don't know it's her," Freya replied. "Not yet, anyway. Anna, have you both been through this list?"

"We have," she replied, referring to her notes. "Looks like Holly Carson was the daughter of a couple in Ruskington, with no previous convictions or cautions. Deborah Jarvis, however, has a history of minor offences."

"Such as?" Ben said.

"Breaking and entering," Nillson said.

"Theft? Handling stolen goods? They normally accompany a B and E charge."

"Not as far as I can see," Nillson replied. "The father, a Reginald Jarvis, also has previous. There are reports of domestic abuse which were dropped, disturbing the peace, plus two accounts of GBH and several accounts of drunk and disorderly."

"Sounds like a charming fellow," Freya said.

"No wonder she ran away," Cruz added.

"Sorry, Cruz?"

"I just meant that if the dad was like that, no wonder she ran away."

"Aye, for once I agree with the wee squirt," Gillespie said.

"Who are we to cast aspersions?" Freya asked.

"I'm not casting anything, boss," he said. "But if you recall, I did see my fair share of abusive households when I was growing up. I tell you, I ran away more times than I can remember."

"But you always returned to whatever children's home was supposed to be looking after you," Freya said. "As far as I know, there is no James Gillespie fitting your description on the mispers list?"

"I might have gone back but only when social services found me," he said. "If I'd had my way, I'd have slept on the streets. I'm telling you, if that wee lass was being abused by her da, she'd have been long gone."

"Gillespie, so far, we have the name of a girl who could possibly be our victim and the criminal records of her father. It is far too early to be making assumptions."

"Aye, I agree," he said. "But mark my words, if that is our lass, then the father will have something to do with it. I've got a nose for this sort of thing."

"I'd rather keep your nose out of it, Gillespie," Freya said. "I prefer to rely on hard evidence and not the gut instincts of a man who is too bone idle to walk to the printer."

"Ah, come on. That was just a wee joke."

Freya strode over to the whiteboard and snatched up her pen.

"When was Deborah Jarvis reported missing?" she asked nobody in particular.

"2019," Anderson replied. "May fourth. According to the report she had been missing for two days but the parents had assumed she was just out with friends."

"For two days?"

"She would have been nineteen, boss," Anderson said. "My brother used to be gone for days when he was that age. Used to come home stinking with absolutely no idea where he'd been."

"You grew up in London, Anderson," Freya told her. "And your brother was, I am assuming, a young man." She tapped the whiteboard with the pen. "Deborah Jarvis was a young girl in a rural location. I think it's an entirely different kettle of fish."

"I think we need to have a word with the parents," Ben said.

"Agreed," she told him, then stared at the timeline. "2019, that's five years ago. Which puts us directly in the year the house was sold."

"Coincidence?" Ben asked.

"You know how I feel about coincidences," she replied. "Chapman, see if you can find out the exact date the sale of the house was made. Either we need another word with Mr and Mrs MacMillan or we need a word with the previous owners."

"Will do," came the reply.

"Gillespie, speak to Superintendent Granger. I've requested some support from Lincoln, which he said he would ask for."

"Aye, boss," he said, sounding bored.

"I want you to line up the cadaver dogs, too."

"Cadaver dogs?"

"Do you remember that investigation we did in Woodhall Spa? The one where the wife had been missing for a year or so?"

"I do," he replied. "The husband was a builder or something, wasn't he?"

"That's it. We had a GPR team involved to see what was under the patio," she told him. "Find out who that team was and have them come to the house in Haverholme, will you?"

"Eh?"

"I'm sorry, was I not clear?"

"You want to rip the garden up?" he said.

"Not just the garden," she said. "I want to start with the house. The floor and the walls are all coming down. Once we're done there, I want the garden examined."

"Jesus, that could take days."

"Well, it's a good job you have nothing else to do, isn't it?" she told him. "Because you're the one who will be leading the search."

"Me?"

"You are capable, are you not?"

"Aye, well, yeah, I'm capable," he replied. "I'm just a wee bit shocked, that's all. I was expecting to be sent on the world's most pointless door-to-door mission to see if anybody remembers anything about a young lass from five years ago."

"Even I'm not that cruel," she replied. "This is a chance for you. Don't let me down. Coordinate the resources from Lincoln and our own uniformed officers. Make sure they have PPE, make sure you brief them, and above all else, make sure nothing gets out to the press. If they get wind of this, we'll find ourselves on the front page of the nationals, and if we don't find anything, then we'll have egg on our faces."

"Aye, boss," he said, suddenly enthused. "Do you think I could...you know?" He nodded sideways across the room.

"Are you okay, Gillespie? Do I need to call the on-duty medic?"

"No..." he said. "Can I take Gabby?"

"You want to take DC Cruz with you? You'll have a dozen officers from Lincoln, a dozen from here, a dog-handling team, a GPR team, and most likely your girlfriend in CSI—"

"Aye, well, Katy's not my girlfriend just yet, like."

"And you want Cruz, as well."

"Ah, come on. We work well together."

"Cruz?" Freya said. "How would you feel about working with Sergeant Gillespie again?"

Cruz shrugged.

"Suppose so, boss."

"Well, let me put it a different way," she said. "Who would you prefer to work with, Gold here in the office, or Gillespie out in the field?"

"Gold here in the office," he said.

"Ah, Gabby, come on," Gillespie said. "How can you say that?"

"She doesn't send me for coffee, she doesn't berate me, she

doesn't make me feel stupid or small, and she doesn't take the mick out of my hair," Cruz said. "Should I go on?"

"But we work so well together," Gillespie said. "I can't manage four different teams at once. I need help. I need someone to help me coordinate."

"Coordinate? Not fetch coffees and cakes? You want me to do actual police work?"

"Aye, course, I do, ya dummy."

"That settles it," Freya said. "Cruz, help me out here and work with Gillespie, will you? Just for a day or two until the bulk of the search is over."

Cruz lowered his head and stared at his hands.

"Okay, boss," he said quietly.

"You're my eyes and ears on the ground," Freya told him. "If you see or hear anything untoward, then I want to know."

"That's unlikely," Gillespie muttered aloud.

"Cruz?" Freya said, to which he nodded.

"Yes, boss," he said. "I'll keep you informed."

"Good, in the meantime, Gold, I want you on standby. If we get a positive ID on Deborah Jarvis, then the parents might need some support, in which case I'd like you to step in as Family Liaison."

"Boss," she replied.

"Nillson, Anderson, can you work with Chapman? I want to know everything about the MacMillans and the house sale. We'll call you from the road."

"Got it," Nillson replied.

"Good. Ben?"

"Boss?" he said, mimicking Nillson.

"Get your coat," she said. "And print the mispers report on Deborah Jarvis. You can read it to me while I drive."

"Jesus, married life, eh?" Gillespie said, and he pressed down on the top of his head with his thumb.

"And when you've spoken to Superintendent Granger, Gillespie, perhaps you can pull together a door-to-door strategy?"

"Eh?"

"I've been thinking. It might be a good idea to speak to her neighbours, and I think you're the man for the job," she said, then glanced across at Ben as Gillespie hit his forehead on the desk. "Ben, I'll see you in the car. Don't be long."

CHAPTER EIGHT

"So?" Ben said when they were in the car and heading towards Anwick, a village less than a mile from Haverholme Park.

"You'll have to be a little less vague if you want some kind of response," Freya replied, and Ben sighed.

"Granger," he said. "What do you think?"

She shrugged, which she rarely did.

"He's right, isn't he?" she replied. "And even if he's not right, he's the boss. So for all intents and purposes, he's right whatever he says."

"Can you see yourself sitting in your office all day?" he asked. "You barely even go in there."

"I barely go in there, Ben, because my team are all in the incident room. Doesn't make for great leadership, does it? And as for sitting in there all day, I would rather eat my own shoe, or one of Gillespie's, for that matter."

"Not keen then?"

"How do you feel about transferring?"

"Honestly?" he said. "The very idea of it fills me with absolute dread. But I'd do it if I had to."

"But you would resent having to," she suggested.

"Of course," he replied. "This is where I belong."

"So essentially, what you're saying is that you don't want to transfer. You wouldn't be happy."

"I wouldn't be happy at work, but I'd love to come home to your cooking every night."

"Right, so one of us has to be unhappy for us both to be happy at home," she said, to which he said nothing, instead choosing to stare out of the window as they passed through Ruskington. "Unless we don't marry."

"Freya–"

"Just hear me out, will you?" she said and then waited for him to be silent. "Unless we don't marry, in which case we both get to be happy at work but a little discontented at home."

"Would you be discontent?" he asked. "Really?"

"You know what, I think I would," she replied.

"Honestly?"

"Don't sound so surprised," she said.

"Well, you didn't seem so keen this morning."

"I am keen, Ben. My heart is keen. Everything inside me is keen, except for my brain."

"Oh, that's right. Your pragmatic brain."

"We've been through this," she said. "But the more I think about it, the more it makes sense. We don't have to marry to be happy. It's not like we can have kids, is it?"

"Really?"

She took her eyes off the road to stare at him for far longer than he deemed safe, given the nature of the country lane.

"Ben, I'm no spring chicken, you know?"

"Right, so?"

She looked utterly incredulous.

"You are aware of how a woman's body works, aren't you?"

"I'm learning," he replied with a childish grin that she ignored.

"You're aware of the risks of somebody my age giving birth?"

"Well, I know it's not usual."

"Not usual? Ben, the risks are huge. It could affect the baby. It could affect me–"

"How?"

"Well, for a start, I could die during childbirth."

"What?"

"Ben, children are off the table. Is that a show stopper?"

"No, I suppose not," he said, to which she shook her head in disbelief. "I just always fancied having a kid of my own."

"They're children, Ben, not goats."

He pointed to a side road and she slowed to make the turn.

"I can live with that," he said.

"Are you sure, Ben? It's kind of a big deal. I mean, you're young enough to find somebody to have children with. But I'm afraid that somebody isn't going to be me."

"I want you, Freya, that's all. I want to marry you and I want to live with you. I want to wake up in the morning and smell your cooked breakfast, and I want to come home at night to your delicious cooking."

"Are you deliberately trying to annoy me?" she said, and he laughed at how easy she was to wind up sometimes.

"Freya, I know we won't have children," he told her. "Do I look like father material?"

"Honestly, yes," she said. "I think you'd make a great dad."

"Right," he said then gave it some thought. "Really?"

"Yes," she said. "You'd be excellent."

"I don't know the first thing about babies."

"Nobody does," she told him. "You learn it as you go along. That's the fun part. So I'm told, anyway. And anyway, what makes you so sure that I'm the right person for you?"

"I don't know," he replied. "Gut feeling, I suppose."

"A gut feeling? Nice. So now I'm just a hunch, am I?"

"Just here," he said, pointing to a terraced house with a red front door. The grass needed cutting, the gutters needed cleaning, and the curtains in the windows looked like they were hanging on by threads. He waited for Freya to stop and put the car into park before resting his hand on her knee. "I don't want them. Babies, I mean. I don't want them. I want you, and if I can't have you, then I'll end my days like my old man, sitting on my kitchen chair staring out of the window."

"Don't say that—"

"I don't want anyone else," he said. "I want you. I want to be married to you, and if that means that one or both of us has to endure a little hardship...well, I don't know about you, but I think it'll be worth it."

He climbed out of the car and waited on the footpath. The house had been neglected, and in Ben's experience, that often meant sour occupants who were unwilling to enter into reasonable discussion. It wasn't always the case, but more often than not, the people in houses such as the one before him were difficult to talk to. The challenge was to overcome the barriers they put up. Once their defences were down, they were often receptive.

Nearly a full minute had passed before Freya eventually climbed from the car and joined him.

"Ready?" she said, then cleared her throat before starting towards the door. But he grabbed her arm and she turned to glare at him then stared at his hand. "What do you think you're doing?"

"You've been crying," he said.

"Don't be ridiculous."

"You have. You've been crying," he said.

"Oh, leave off, will you?" she said, snatching her arm away. "If this is going to work, Ben, then you need to learn when to switch us off. We're at work. You heard what Granger said, didn't you? Do you really want to give him an excuse to split us up?"

He stared at her, observing the tiny mascara smudge in the corner of her eye, which on any other woman might have just been nothing, but for Freya, who was meticulous about her appearance, it was nothing short of telling. She had shed a tear or two whilst in the car. The question was, Ben thought, what was the tear over?

"Right," he said, pushing past her and striding up to the front door, where he gave three hard raps and then stared her in the eye. "I'm going to make this work, Freya."

The door was opened by a man in an old Guns and Roses t-shirt and dirty jeans. His hair had receded from the crown of his skull, leaving a horseshoe of greasy, red hair that extended into lengthy sideburns.

"What?" he said, and that first word to leave his mouth was enough for Ben to mark him out as a man with a barrier to overcome.

Ben held up his warrant card and Freya followed suit.

"We're with the Lincolnshire Police," Ben said. "We're looking for a Mr and Mrs Jarvis."

His expression altered from utterly inhospitable to one of confusion and aggression.

"What is it now?" he said. "I've done nothing wrong."

"You are Reginald Jarvis, are you?" Freya asked, to which he simply sneered.

"No, I'm the Queen."

"We're here to discuss your daughter," she told him. "Deborah Jarvis."

At the mention of his daughter's name, a woman came to his side. She had the look of a woman with the weight of the world on her shoulders. The skin around her bloodshot eyes sagged, her hair was thin, lank, and grey, and she looked as if a strong wind might snap her in half.

"Debs?" she said. "You've found my Debs? Is she okay? Where is she?"

"I think it's best if we come inside," Ben said.

"Hold on, hold on," Reginald said, holding his hands up, palms out. "Nobody's coming inside without a warrant."

"Reg, will you listen to them? They've got news of our Debs.

They haven't come here for anything else," she said, then eyed them both.

"She's right," Freya said. "We've come for a brief chat about your daughter. We're following up on a missing persons report made by yourself, Mrs Jarvis. Five years ago, is that right?"

"It is," she said, and somehow she managed to nudge her husband from the doorway. "Please, come in. I'll make some tea."

"You must be Mariam?" Freya said before her husband could interject.

"I am," the woman said, and she held the door to prevent her husband from stopping them from entering. "You'll have to excuse the mess." She gestured at the living room door. "Go through, will you?"

"Please," Freya said. "No tea for us. We've just had coffee."

Mariam Jarvis led the way and then gestured for them to take a seat on a sofa, one side of which appeared flattened through heavy use, presumably because it was the best spot in the room from which to view the TV. Ben took the sagging seat, allowing Freya to remain dignified at the other end of the sofa, while Deborah Jarvis' parents each claimed an armchair. Mariam sat forward, her hands fumbling with a tissue, while Reginald eased himself back, crossed his legs, and stared at them both as if they had just insulted his sainted mother.

"I'm afraid conversations like this are never easy," Freya began. "But earlier this morning, the remains of a young girl were discovered in a house in Haverholme."

"Remains?" Mariam said, and her already loose skin seemed to sag even more. "Oh no. No, no. It can't be. She's alive. I know she is."

"Well, that's what we're aiming to find out," Freya said. "If I can just explain the process we have to follow under these circumstances. With no identification to go on, and very little chance of a visual identification—"

"Oh God," Mariam said, then held her face in her hands and began rocking back and forth.

"We have to rely on DNA evidence," Freya continued. "Now, one of the reasons we believe that it could be Deborah is the proximity of the discovery to the location the missing persons report suggested she was last seen."

"It were Haverholme," Reginald said, his tone gruff and his words so lazy that they seemed to blend into one. "That's what he said. That's where they were."

"We don't know that," Mariam told him.

"He were the last to see her," he replied.

"I'm sorry, who are we talking about here?" Freya asked, to which Ben, who had read the report, responded.

"I think it's Kevin Stone," he said, and Reginald nodded. "He was the last person to see her according to the report. He claims that a few of them were sitting in a field in Haverholme Park on the evening in question. Deborah didn't want to join in, so she sat on the far side of the field. When Kevin went back to try and coax her into joining them, she was gone. According to his statement, he ran into the trees to find her, but all he found was her shoe." He flicked through the papers and found what he was looking for. "A Vans plimsole."

"That's right," Mariam said. "But you have to understand. She was going through a difficult time. She said she was leaving. Said she could get work in London. She wanted to get away."

"Why would she want to get away?" Freya asked, to which Mariam closed up somewhat, then shook her head dismissively.

"There's nothing round here for her, is there? No jobs, she doesn't drive, no chance of meeting a nice boy."

"I see," Freya said. "I have to be frank with you, Mariam. There was a shoe missing from the remains we discovered. I saw it with my own eyes, and I'm sorry to say, it was a Vans shoe."

"No," Mariam said, at which time any ordinary husband might have consoled her and shared her grief. But Reginald Jarvis remained perfectly still. The bitterness had gone from his eyes and he stared sadly at the threadbare carpet. "No, not my baby girl. It can't be."

"We also discovered what we believe to be a nose stud," Freya said. "Am I right in thinking that Deborah had her nose pierced?"

"No, it can't be," she said. "Lots of girls have their noses pierced, and how many have those Vans shoes she always wore? Every kid in the county must have a pair."

"I'm sorry," Ben told her. "I know this must be hard to hear, but what we really need is some way of obtaining Deborah's DNA. I appreciate we're talking about five years ago, but do you still have anything of hers? A toothbrush or a hairbrush, maybe?"

"Everything we had of hers is gone," Reginald said. "We waited a year or more then cleared it out."

"*You* cleared it out," Mariam said, her tone as bitter as could be. "It was you who wanted her stuff gone."

She wiped at her eyes and then blew her nose before looking up at them both.

"I've got some bits," she said.

"What?" her husband replied. "I told you to get rid of it all."

"Well, I didn't," she said. "She's my bloody daughter, Reg. I wanted some bits of hers."

"Are we able to see them?" Ben asked.

"There's a box full," she said. "I'll fetch it for you."

"Perhaps I can help," Ben said, shoving himself out of the sagging seat. He followed her out to the kitchen and into a makeshift conservatory, which was used for storing boxes and old pieces of furniture more than as a sunroom.

It took her a few moments to clear the path, and then, from beneath an old chair, she dragged a cardboard box, roughly twelve inches square.

"This is it," she said. "That's all we have left of hers."

She dropped it onto the kitchen worktop and rested her hand on its lid as if savouring the connection.

"Do you mind if we take it?" Ben said. "It'll be returned, no matter the outcome."

She nodded slightly and stared at the box. Her eyes were lost to some memory of her daughter, or regret perhaps.

"If it is her..." she said, forcing herself not to break down. "If it is her, I want to see her."

"Mrs Jarvis—"

"I know," she said, cutting him off. "I know she won't look the same, but still..." She peered longingly into Ben's eyes. "I want to say goodbye. Properly, like. I want to."

CHAPTER NINE

"So this is it, is it?" Freya said when they were standing in the field where Kevin Stone had claimed to have seen Deborah last. To the edge of the field was the forest, with the River Slea marking the boundary where the field stopped and the forest began. To their left, an old, stone bridge gave means to vehicles and pedestrians to cross the river, and somewhere close by, water thundered over a weir.

"The house is five hundred yards away," Ben said. "Give or take."

"Less if she cut through the forest," Freya added, then looked up at him. "Or was dragged." She walked over to the edge of the field, where the river ran from right to left and a wire fence prevented the thick undergrowth from encroaching onto the open land. A wooden stile gave access to people, and a small sign denoted the route as a public footpath.

"She would have had to climb this," Freya said. "Where was her shoe found?"

"According to Stone's statement, a few metres into the forest," he replied, as he gazed into the trees. "Well, she could only have turned left or right, unless she crossed the river somehow."

"Left towards the road and the house," Freya said. "Or right towards...where does right take us?"

"To the weir, I think," Ben replied. "And I think there are a couple more houses beyond the trees."

"How many houses are here?" she asked.

"At a guess? Half a dozen," Ben said. "Including the farm and the old priory."

"Priory? As in monks?"

"They're not there anymore," he said. "The building is a ruin." He nodded at the trees. "It's in the field on the other side of the forest."

"Do you think it's relevant?"

He screwed his face up and shook his head.

"No. It's closed to the public."

"Oh right, so our murderer would have been worried about trespassing, is that what you're saying?"

"No, but I can't see any reason why they would go there."

"An abandoned building?" Freya said. "If you found yourself in need of somewhere quiet where you won't be disturbed..." She left the sentence unfinished for him to fill in the blanks.

"Let's leave that idea open, shall we?" he suggested. "I'd like to walk the route to the house. We know, or at least we're led to believe, that she climbed this stile, lost her shoe somewhere near here, and then ended up at the MacMillan house. Why would she leave her shoe behind?"

"She was struggling," Freya said, and she pictured the scene, narrating her thoughts as they came to her. "The report said she didn't want to join in with the others. She was sitting somewhere close to here while they were somewhere over there," she said, pointing out into the field. "Why didn't she want to join them?"

"Maybe she'd argued with one of them?" Ben suggested.

"In which case, why be here at all?" Freya said. "Why would you bother?"

"Maybe she had nothing else to do?"

"Or," Freya said, "maybe the place where she should have been wasn't safe for her."

Ben was silent for a moment and there was a joy in the bird-song emanating from the trees.

"Her house?" he said.

"Exactly. I think we need to know more about Reginald Jarvis. Where was he the night his daughter went missing?"

"Christ, Freya, it's a bit early to be pointing the finger."

"Is it?" she said. "Is five years too early? That poor girl has been lying beneath the floorboards for five years, Ben. It's high time she had some justice, don't you think? Her father has a history of abuse and violence. I don't think it's unreasonable to understand his movements during the time in question."

"That's not what I meant and you know it," he told her. "The original missing persons report was just that, a missing persons report. The officer who took the statement would have no cause to interview the parents. You heard what her parents said. She was fed up with living here. I know you and I both cherish the quiet country life but it's not for everyone. Half the people I grew up with have left to go and live in a city or another country. There's nothing here for someone with itchy feet. Deborah had a history of breaking and entering. She was a wild child, a free spirit."

"Oh, she's free all right," Freya said. "Listen, if she climbed this stile and then found herself in a struggle with somebody, then that would suggest that whoever it was was waiting there for her."

"It could have been an opportunist," Ben said.

"What time did Kevin Stone say this happened?" she asked, and Ben referred to the report.

"Sometime around midnight," he said.

"Midnight," she repeated. "Maybe somebody was just out walking their dog in the dead of night? Maybe it was Nick MacMillan going for a moonlight stroll through the forest?"

"Don't be flippant," he said.

"Well, come on. Think about it. She was out here, sitting close to but not with her friends. Why?"

Ben said nothing. Instead, he climbed the stile then held out his hand to help Freya over. Stinging nettles reached across the track which they edged past as well as ducking beneath low-hanging trees.

"They would have heard her," Freya said. "The path runs adjacent to the field. Even if it was too dark for them to see, they would have heard her struggling."

"Unless she was silenced somehow," Ben replied, and he stopped. "What you said about her sitting in the field but not wanting to sit with her friends. Why do that and then go into the forest? If she wanted to get away, why wouldn't she walk across the field to the road?"

They both contemplated the idea in silence, but it was Freya who voiced her opinion.

"Maybe somebody called her over?"

"Right," Ben said. "I mean, if she had had enough and was going to head home, then she would have walked across the field to the road. There had to be a reason for her to climb the stile and go into the forest."

"Okay," Freya said. "Okay, so she climbed the stile for whatever reason. She was grabbed or even hit. Silenced somehow. And then she was dragged or carried along the path to the road beside the bridge, which she would have had to cross to get to the house."

"What if she wasn't grabbed, or hit, or silenced?" Ben said. "What if she didn't lose her shoe in a struggle, but wanted people to think she had?"

"Are you suggesting she staged the whole thing?"

"I'm just throwing ideas out there, Freya," he said. "The girl was troubled. Maybe she was looking for attention."

"I think we need to talk to this Kevin Stone character," she replied and pointed to the file in Ben's hand. "Because that statement is lacking in detail, and if we're going to get to the bottom of this, we need that detail."

"Want to go and see him?" Ben asked, to which Freya checked her watch.

"No, it's late. He can wait until tomorrow," she replied. "Call the team, will you? Arrange a briefing for the morning. With any luck, the pathologist will have some answers for us by then."

"No guarantees there," he said. "No doubt Pip will find something to berate me for."

"True," she agreed. "But we do need some hard facts, Ben. We can't go on theories and gut feelings and expect a positive outcome, can we?"

CHAPTER TEN

The house was cool, and although Ben enjoyed little more than coming home to his own house and slipping into some comfy jogging bottoms, Freya's little cottage was becoming quite comfortable. While Freya paid a visit to the washroom, he dropped into the armchair and let his head fall back with a sigh. Compared to a month before, the weather was a positive contrast. The days were longer and the sky bluer; the early perennials bloomed and filled the hedgerows and raised spirits, the weight of winter lifting from the world.

Through the window, he watched as a young mother minded her daughter as she paddled in the beck. The ducks, which were permanent residents of the village, were out in numbers, one family boasting a flock of more than a dozen, which fascinated the young girl in the shallow watercourse.

Sometimes, the nature of his job proved so disruptive to any kind of routine that the days seemed to merge into one, and it was only the volume of dog walkers and villagers that passed by the window that reminded him it was a Saturday evening. His own home was a similar size but set deep into his father's farmland, where the only people who passed by his window were his brothers, his father, and the postman. So seeing the world go about its business was a rare joy, a notion he hadn't even considered before.

"Busy?" Freya said as she was coming down the stairs.

"Just having five minutes," he replied, as he kicked off his shoes.

"What time's dinner?"

He raised his head and watched her go about her business.

"Sorry?"

"I asked what time dinner is," she replied.

"I suppose that all depends on what you're cooking and how long it takes."

She closed the dishwasher and folded the dishcloth.

"I won't be cooking anything tonight," she said. "I have a few things I'd like to get on with."

"Such as?" Ben asked, then eyed the box from the Jarvis house on her dining table. "I see. Well, how about I do us a nice chicken tikka masala, pilau rice, and maybe one of those lentil Dahl things you like?"

"That sounds ambitious for a man who can barely cook beans on toast."

"Oh, I've been practising," he told her, as he shoved himself from the armchair and strode into the kitchen to stand behind her. He placed his hands on her hips and rested his chin on her shoulder.

"Do you only do Indian?" she asked, and he felt her smile against his cheek.

"You'd be amazed at my new skills," he replied. "I could do you a nice aromatic duck, sweet and sour chicken, and a stir-fry?"

"I'm not in the mood for Chinese," she said. "I'm feeling Italian. I have a nice Chianti I'd like to open."

"Pizza?"

"No, Ben. Real Italian. A tagliatelle or a nice carbonara or something. Do you think you could manage that?"

"Easy," he said. "In fact, I can do that with one hand."

"Oh?" she said, and she turned in his arms. "What will you do with your other hand?"

She reached up to kiss him then pulled away.

"Hold the takeaway menu," he said. "One hand to hold the phone, the other to hold the menu."

"You are a man of many talents," she said.

"Well, you know I do try."

"Indeed," she replied as she pulled out of his arms. "Why don't you order? I want to take a shower before we get started."

"Get started?" he said. "Get started on what, exactly? Should I shower too?"

"Get your mind out of the gutter, farm boy," she said. "You and I will be elbow-deep in the belongings of a dead teenager."

"Not quite what I had in mind," he replied, as he flicked through the plethora of takeaway menus that had been posted through Freya's door since moving in. He found the one he was looking for and tried to remember the dishes she had mentioned. But she was lingering in the doorway. He felt her stare and glanced up at her.

"I do love you, you know?" she said, which, to his memory, was the first time she had said so. "Whatever happens, I do love you. And I know I don't always show it. I don't always know how. But I do."

———

"What the hell is this?" Freya said when she had torn the lid off of an aluminium container. "Spaghetti?"

"That's what you asked for, wasn't it?"

"Spaghetti? I asked for tagliatelle, Ben. If I had wanted spaghetti, I'd have boiled the bloody kettle and made some."

"I thought you said–"

"It doesn't even have sauce. It's just plain spaghetti."

"Well, stick some ketchup on it or something."

"Ketchup?" she said, feeling her chest tighten. "Ketchup on spaghetti?"

"Well, what then? Mayo?"

"Ben, I could write what you know about cooking or food of any description on the side of a rotten carrot. How on earth have you survived this long without starving to death?" She opened another container and peered inside. "Calamari?"

"Don't tell me that's wrong as well," Ben said.

"It's squid, Ben. It's a starter."

"So start with it, then."

"I asked for carbonara."

"It's the same thing, isn't it?"

"Carbonara has pancetta, Ben. It has eggs, olive oil, and herbs. All the things that make it delicious. This is just spaghetti.

"Well, I didn't know—"

"So, we have a plate of dry spaghetti and one and a half pieces of calamari each," she said, then took a sip of her wine.

"You don't like squid, then?" he said, and she felt something lift inside her chest. The tension eased, and she saw the innocence in his eyes. So much so that a smile broke free.

"Oh, Ben," she said. "Luckily for you, I do like calamari. But I'm afraid that three pieces on a bed of soggy lettuce is not going to do much, is it?"

"I can order something else."

"No," she said. "No, we'll make do. Maybe I can knock up a bolognese sauce?"

"Or maybe we can just bin the lot of it and get stuck into the wine?" Ben suggested, which was the most sensible thing he'd said all day. He took a bite of the calamari, pulled a face, and then dropped it back into the container. "It's not even cooked. It's like bloody rubber."

She gave a laugh and shook her head at him.

"Do you know, I would love to take you across Europe. We

could work our way along the French Riviera and then up into Italy. By the time I'm done with you, you'll be able to order from any restaurant."

"I'd also be as big as a house," he said, as he dragged Deborah Jarvis' cardboard box across the table, nudging the takeaway to one side. He pulled open the lid and peered inside. "Ready?"

"Maybe there's a packet of crisps inside," she joked, and she watched as he pulled a toiletry bag from the box and set it down on the table.

He unzipped it and peered inside, while Freya began making an inventory on a clean sheet of paper.

"There's the hairbrush," he said. "And the toothbrush. Should be able to get some DNA from that."

"Presuming the samples have survived this long," Freya added and met his curious stare. "They don't last forever, you know."

Carefully, Ben peered into the bag, calling out what he saw.

"Toothpaste, hairbands," he said, then pulled a tub of something and held it up in the light. "Some kind of cream."

"Moisturiser," she said. "Good stuff, too. That's an expensive brand."

"I think we hand the whole bag over to Katy Southwell at the lab," he said. "If there's DNA to be found, then she'll find it."

"Agreed," Freya replied, making a note of their findings. "What else do we have?"

Ben stood to look inside the box, pulling out the items as he found them.

"Some books," he said, reading the spines.

"Anything of note?"

"Classics," he said, placing the pile on the table. "Brontë and the like."

"How on earth would you know what a classic is?"

"I'm not a complete philistine," he said defensively. "I might not know about Italian food, but I do know a good book when I see it."

"So you've read these, have you?" she asked, fingering the pile. "You've read Emma and Nineteen-Eighty-Four, have you?"

He grinned back at her.

"I've seen the films," he said, as he pulled a notebook from the box. "It's much quicker." He flicked through the notebook and then set it down.

"What's that?"

"Just some doodles," he said. "I thought it might be a diary but it doesn't look like it."

Freya noted the notebook down and then flicked through the pages, stopping periodically to admire some of the drawings. But her intrigue was pulled away from the notebook and onto the next item that Ben placed on the table.

It was an A4-sized padded envelope and the flap was open.

"No address on the front," Ben said as he peered inside and let the contents spill out onto the table. "Photos."

"Of what?" she said, standing to get a better view and Ben looked away.

"Christ," he said. "I didn't need to see that."

Freya dragged the photo in question across the table.

"Saucy," she said. "Are they all like this?"

Ben sifted through the images, his face a picture of absolute disgust.

"Most of them," he said. "Why on earth would her mum keep those?"

"Maybe she didn't look inside the envelope?" Freya replied. "I'm sure if she had found photos of her daughter like this, she would have burned them."

"Is it Deborah, though?" he said, and Freya searched for an image with a clear picture of the woman's face.

"Haven't a clue," she replied. "The camera is too far away to see if she's wearing a nose stud, and she certainly doesn't have a pair of Vans on."

"Who's the man?" he said. "Could be something there."

"Again, no idea. He certainly looks older though. Looks like he has some kind of tattoo on his chest too. What about the other photos?"

"Random stuff," he said. "She might have been getting into photography."

"What makes you say that?"

"Just the photos," he said. "There's one here of a wardrobe, a fireplace, an old, wooden box." He stopped and he held one of them up.

"What is it?"

"A photo of a garden shed."

Freya nodded and considered how she might phrase the entries in the inventory she was making.

"So she was either completely mad or a keen but lacking photographer," he said. "Or there's something in that garden shed."

"I'm going for option one," Ben replied, peering inside the box to see what else he could find. "Oh, that's a shame."

"What is?" she asked, to which he removed a little jewellery box and then tipped the box upside down to indicate it was empty.

"No crisps," he said.

CHAPTER ELEVEN

It wasn't quite eight a.m. when Ben pushed his way into the laboratory where Katy Southwell and her team worked. The receptionist was a young girl with intelligent eyes, whom Ben had come to recognise over the past few years. She buzzed him through into the corridor, and when he reached the door to the lab, he peered through the window.

They were like bees, the lab workers. Each of them was head to toe in white. Some wore goggles and hoods, while others, presumably performing less dangerous tasks or with less risk of contamination, dressed down yet still wore the white overalls. It was one of the less protected individuals who saw Ben at the window and she called across the room, where Katy Southwell looked up and smiled. She removed her goggles and her hood as she walked over to the door, where she buzzed him through.

"And to what do I owe this pleasure?" she asked, leading him politely away from the sensitive equipment and into the more appropriate kitchen, where she flicked on the kettle and then eyed the toilet bag in his hand. "Are you staying the night? Do I need to make a bed up?"

"Very funny," he replied, then placed the bag on the worktop. "I'm surprised to even find you here on a Sunday."

"Well, Jim's working, so I might as well," she replied, and once more she glanced at the bag.

"Deborah Jarvis," he said.

"Ah, a potential name for our Jane Doe?"

"Potential, but we're almost certain," he explained. "Her mother filed a missing person's report five years ago. She wore Vans trainers and had her nose pierced. According to the statement made by one of her friends, the last person to see her, I might add, found one of her shoes in the forest, but there was no sign of her."

"And you need me to give you some kind of positive ID, do you?"

"I'm pretty sure the parents won't recognise her," he said. "We've nothing else to go on. There's a hairbrush and a tooth-brush, so we're hopeful you can find something. Without some kind of confirmation that it's her, we can't really do much."

"I'll give it my best shot," she replied. "Tea? Coffee?"

"Not for me, ta. We've got a briefing in half an hour."

"Right," she said, slowly, as if she had heard him but hadn't quite understood the meaning of what he said.

"It's not a good idea to ask for a toilet break while Freya's giving a briefing."

"Ah," she said, clearly understanding.

"Jim mentioned that she has a certain way about her."

"That's a polite way of putting it," he said, and she hesitated.

"Sorry, I didn't mean that he moans about her. He doesn't, you know? He actually has a lot of good things to say about her."

"Now I know you're fibbing."

"I'm serious. The way he talks about her, you'd think she was sainted or something."

Ben leaned against the worktop and folded his arms.

"Jim? Jim Gillespie?"

"Yes," she said. "You too. In fact, he rarely has a bad word to say about any of you. The only person he seems to put down is himself."

"That sounds about right."

"You were right about him, you know?" she said.

"I was right? Perhaps I could get that in writing."

"When you convinced me to give him a chance?" she said. "You were right about him."

"Yeah, sorry. I feel guilty about pressuring you into that."

"Don't," she told him. "You told me he's a nice man and he is. But he is troubled."

Ben nodded, and he noticed the way her eyes softened when she spoke of Gillespie. At the mention of his name, eyes usually rolled or closed in despair.

"He's been through a hard time," Ben explained.

"I know," she said. "He's told me all about his upbringing. About all the homes he was in and the abuse."

"Crikey, you're actually into him, aren't you?"

"I am," she replied flatly. "And I think he likes me too."

"If he told you about all that, then he must. Those are his darkest secrets."

"He has a gentle side, you know?" she said. "And he knows how to treat a woman."

The statement caught Ben off guard and he stared at her in disbelief.

"Again, Jim Gillespie? The same bloke I work with? He knows how to treat a woman, does he?"

"We had dinner at The Tempest in Coleby," she said, "which for a first date was perfect. Since then, we've been to the tapas bar in Woodhall Spa, The Wig and Mitre in Lincoln, and we've had one or two evenings at my place."

"Have you been to his house yet?" Ben asked.

"I want to," she said. "But he said he's decorating. Doesn't want me to see it until it's done."

"Jesus, Katy, it sounds like you've broken him," Ben said. "In a good way, I mean. Next thing you know, he'll be ironing his clothes."

"I'm working on that," she said and winked at Ben.

"I don't get it. When we were all at Haverholme yesterday, he never said a word to you."

"Of course not," she said. "We're at work."

"Right?"

She shook her head.

"I never mix business with pleasure," she told him. "No, if it's going to work between us, then work is work and play is play. I don't even want to see him at work if I can help it."

"You don't think that could cause problems?" Ben asked.

"Listen, in my experience, working alongside your partner is a no-no." She eyed him and smiled politely. "Every couple is different. But if you want my advice, keep your career out of it and love her when you get home."

He considered her words and suddenly felt a pang of insecurity. He was a grown man taking relationship advice from someone he barely knew, who was at least a decade younger than him.

"I'll bear that in mind," he told her and offered a grateful smile, before glancing at the innocent-looking toiletry bag. "How long?"

"Give me the day. The pathologist has sent over some of the remaining tissue, so I'll have something over to you by tonight," she replied. "If the DNA from the tissue matches whatever is in that bag, then you'll be the first to know. Although, I imagine it means that Jim will have to cancel dinner tonight."

"I don't know if I should apologise or thank you," Ben said.

"Just pay heed to what I said," she told him, ushering him out of the room. "I don't know how you can, but if you want your relationship to work, then find a way to work separately. You'll thank me for it in the long run."

CHAPTER TWELVE

Freya was in full swing by the time Ben pushed through the doors into the room, nodded a greeting, and settled into his seat. Freya paused long enough for him to open his notebook and for the rest of the team to mumble their good mornings.

She stared at him, eyebrows raised in question, hoping he would pick up on the inevitable question.

"Before the end of the day," he said. "Pip has already sent her some of the remaining tissue from the body, so it's just a case of putting the two DNA samples side by side and seeing if they match."

"And if they don't?" she asked.

"Then she'll run them through the database. Although, I wouldn't put your hopes on that ringing any bells. Female, late teens," he said. "Probably the smallest sub-strata on the database."

"Well, then let's hope we get a match with the contents of Deborah Jarvis' toiletry bag," Freya said. "In the meantime, I don't want us to sit on our laurels. Let's do some homework, get our ducks in a row, so when the time comes that we know if it is indeed Deborah Jarvis, then we have some kind of plan to put into action."

"I'll be surprised if another girl is walking around with one shoe and a nose piercing," Nillson said.

"Agreed," Freya told her. "But until we know for certain, we need to stick to the process. Speaking of which, Cruz and Gillespie, are we all set for the search of the house? Could be a long few days for you."

"Aye, no bother, boss," Gillespie said, and he checked his watch. "Actually, the team from Lincoln will be rocking up in about an hour."

"Well, off you go then," she said. "Feedback to Chapman throughout the day."

Both Gillespie and Cruz stood from their seats and began collecting their things. It was only when Gillespie reached the door that Freya called out to him. "And Gillespie?"

"Aye, boss?"

"Please look after Cruz. He isn't your personal gopher," she said. "You'll do well to remember that."

"Aye, boss," he replied. "I'll find one of the Lincoln boys to fetch me coffee then, eh?"

He offered her a wink and a cheeky grin and then left before she could think of anything that might deter him from abusing his rank.

"God help that lad," Nillson said.

"Bloody right," Anderson cut in. "Honestly, if he told me to fetch him coffees, I'd tip it down his trousers."

"Sadly, I think he might enjoy that," Gold said with a smirk.

"As it happens," Ben said, "I've just been speaking to Katy Southwell about him. I think he's turning a corner in his life."

"What?" Nillson said.

"He takes her to nice places," Ben said. "Granted, they're all places I suggested to him, but still, he's trying, and she seems very happy."

"Crikey, can you imagine if those two marry?" Gold said.

"Gillespie in a three-piece suit and a top hat?" Nillson said. "I don't think so."

"Well, he's decorating his house," Ben said.

"Really?" Nillson said. "Now you mention it, I think he was wearing aftershave today. I thought it was just that he had put deodorant on, but it was nicer than that."

"Katy says he'll soon be ironing his clothes," Ben added and Gold laughed out loud. "What?"

"Sorry, I just had a thought," she said. "What if they have kids?"

"Oh my God, can you imagine little Gillespies running around the place? Long-haired, scruffy, little urchins picking their noses and sticking two fingers up at everyone."

"I think Katy will rein them in," Freya said, hoping to draw them back to the task at hand. "Now then, Ben and I paid a visit to Deborah Jarvis' parents yesterday. His mother gave us a box of her belongings, which is where we got the toiletry bag from. But the father, he's one I want to look into. Chapman, you said he has form, but what I'd like to know is dates. According to the misper, Deborah Jarvis went missing on May the eighth five years ago. Where was he during that period? Was he in trouble around that time? If so, what was it for?"

"Got it," Chapman said, making neat notes on her pad.

"Gold, help out where you can for the time being but don't start anything you can't hand over. If Katy Southwell comes back with a positive ID, then Mrs Jarvis will need somebody with her."

"Doesn't she have her husband?" Gold asked. "Sorry, I'm happy to go, but she's not alone, is she?"

"She might as well be," Ben said. "The man has less empathy than a toilet roll. He didn't even hold her hand when we told her what we'd found."

"Heartless bastard," Nillson said.

"Let's not jump to conclusions," Freya said. "We don't know

these people and we don't know the full story. Not yet, anyway. Nillson and Anderson, I want you both on the MacMillans and the house sale. Do we have a date yet?"

"We do," Nillson told her. "I got an email back from the land registry this morning. They exchanged on the twentieth of June, which is around six weeks after Deborah Jarvis was reported missing."

"Kevin Stone's statement said the last time he saw her was on the night of the sixth of May," Ben said. "The misper report was made on the eighth, and then six weeks later, the house changed hands."

"Right, but it takes longer than six weeks to exchange on a house," Freya added. "There are surveys to be done and all the other checks, and solicitors don't exactly rush it, do they?" She snapped the lid back on her marker. "Who were the previous owners?"

Nillson flicked through her notes and then looked up.

"A Liam and Lucy Finch, boss," she replied, then read on further. "Looks like they were in a chain and they ended up buying a place in Ruskington."

"Right," Freya said and turned to Chapman. "Could you do the honours, Chapman? Find out whatever you can for now."

"Will do," she replied, and Freya returned her attention to the whiteboard, removed the pen lid, and then began to write.

"Reginald Jarvis," she began. "The father. He's worth looking into, as is Nick MacMillan and..." She glanced back at Nillson. "What was that name?"

"Liam Finch, boss," she replied, and Freya added the final name.

"Is it worth looking into MacMillan?" Gold asked. "If he didn't get the keys to the house until six weeks after, I mean."

"There's nothing to suggest that the body was placed under the floorboards at any particular time," Freya told her. "So, yes. I want everything we can get on them all, specifically the period between May and June 2019."

"Got it."

"Good. Nillson, I want you to lead the research and create a timeline for me. Use Gold where you can, but be aware she could be pulled as soon as we get a result on the DNA." Freya stared at the whiteboard for a moment longer, then snapped the lid back onto the pen. "That just leaves you and me, Ben."

"Pathology?" he suggested.

"Not yet," she replied. "I think I'd like to speak to Kevin Stone. I want to see if he can give us a little more detail than what's in his statement."

Ben stood, snapped his notebook closed, and stood waiting while Freya reached down and collected the cardboard box from the floor. She placed it on her desk and sighed as she withdrew the envelope of photographs.

"I wanted to wait until Gillespie had gone before I showed you these," she said, speaking directly to Chapman, and she handed her the envelope, hoping her expression conveyed enough to caution her as to the contents.

Chapman took them tentatively and the rest of the team watched on with apparent intrigue as she opened the envelope and fished out a few of the photos.

"Oh, really?" the delicate young woman said after taking a single brief look. Her nose wrinkled in disgust and she turned away but then forced herself to look at more of them.

"What is it?" Nillson asked. "Not the body, surely?"

"No," Chapman said, stuffing the images back into the envelope. "No, it's nothing like that."

"Well, what's in them?" Nillson asked. "Come on, share and share alike."

"They are intimate photographs of a young girl and a...not-so-young man," Freya said, hoping that would be enough to quench any desire to see the photos.

"Ah," Nillson replied. "Gotcha."

"What do you want me to do with them?" Chapman asked, to which Freya took a deep breath.

"Well, I think the girl is Deborah Jarvis, but who is the man?"

"Facial recognition?"

"I'm not sure if they are clear enough, but yes," Freya said, leaning forward to tap the envelope. "This might be something. I want to know who he is, and more importantly, where he was when Deborah Jarvis went missing."

CHAPTER THIRTEEN

The half a dozen or so properties in the Haverholme Park area were all pristine, with well-tended gardens, maintained walls, and cared-for brickwork. But the MacMillan house was the exception. Compared to its neighbours, all of which were more than five hundred yards away, it was nothing more than a sorry-looking building that didn't just need extending and a little TLC; in Gillespie's opinion, the place needed tearing down.

"I'm surprised the neighbours haven't complained," he said to Cruz as they walked along the drive.

"About all the commotion, you mean?" Cruz replied. "I know, but it can't be helped, can it?"

"No, I'm talking about the state of the place. What a hole."

"Well, he was doing something about it, wasn't he? This MacMillan bloke. Apparently, it's going to be a Grand Designs sort of place," Cruz said. "And anyway, it's not like you live in a palace, is it? You've had bolognese on your kitchen wall for as long as I can remember."

"Not anymore," Gillespie said, as he stepped over one of the many trenches. "Jesus, it's like Passchendaele."

"Don't tell me you've finally found a cloth and wiped it off?"

"Gabby, Gabby, Gabby," Gillespie said proudly. "You wouldn't recognise the place. Besides, I couldn't exactly ask you to help me paint the walls with tomato sauce everywhere, could I?"

"No, I suppose not," Cruz replied, then stopped in his tracks. "You what?"

"Sorry?" Gillespie said nonchalantly.

"Me? Help you paint?"

"Well, aye. I mean, I can't do it on my own, can I?"

"Paint?"

"Don't worry, I've got you a ladder."

"Hold on, what makes you think I'd agree to help you paint your house? And why have you got me a ladder before I've even agreed to it?"

"Well, you're not exactly a social butterfly. Not since Hermione left you, anyway. Come on, it'll be fun. You and me. I'll get some beers in, stick some music on. We'll have it done in no time."

"I do have friends, you know?"

"I'll get you dinner too," Gillespie said.

"I can get my own dinner, ta."

Gillespie stopped at the front door and took a deep breath.

"Gabby, I know I'm not always easy to get on with–"

"Very rarely would be more accurate–"

"But I'd really appreciate your help decorating my house," Gillespie said. "It's Kate."

"Has she complained about the smell?"

"No, she hasn't been in there yet."

"Eh? It's been a month. I would have thought you'd have had her in your dungeon by now."

"I don't want to put her off," he explained. "I don't want her to think..." He paused to think of the right words.

"You don't want her to see the real you, you mean?" Cruz said, and then his anger turned to amusement. "Oh, I see. You like her, don't you?"

"Well, aye. She's nice and that—"

"You're in love."

"I'm not in love, ya wee scrote."

"You love her. Just admit it. There's nothing wrong with it," Cruz said, and he laughed aloud as he pushed past Gillespie and into the house where his laughter faded. Half a dozen men in overalls looked up at them both. They were on their knees, using crowbars to prize up the floorboards, while two others were ferrying the discarded wood out into the back garden. "Jesus," Cruz said.

"Alright, lads," Gillespie said. "Anything to report?"

The man who set his crowbar down and climbed to his feet was familiar.

"How's it going, Jim?" he said.

"Not bad, mate," Gillespie said, shaking his hand and turning to Cruz. "Gabby, this is Sergeant Godfrey. One of the Lincoln mob come to do the dirty work."

"Oy," Godfrey said. "Less of that. We're here doing what you lot can't."

"Actually, I think it's a numbers thing," Cruz said, to which both Gillespie and Godfrey turned to face him, and he seemed to shrink under the weight of their stares. "You know? We're a small rural station. We don't have the resources."

An awkward silence followed, which Gillespie broke by clearing his throat.

"Well, why don't you guys crack on," he said. "I don't want to hold you up. I think our lot are in the garden."

"Yeah I did notice," Godfrey said. "They're out there in the fresh air while we're stuck in here. It didn't go unnoticed, you know?"

"Gabby, give them a hand, will you?" Gillespie said and made his way towards the back door.

"Oh right, so you're leaving your mate in here while you go out into the sunshine, are you?" Godfrey called out. "Some things don't change, Jim."

"Aye well," he replied, "I need to find someone qualified to fetch me some coffee, don't I? And I won't find that in here."

———

"He's always been a lazy sod," Godfrey said, shaking his head. He was a stout figure, who appeared to have no identifiable features, the type of man who Cruz would struggle to describe. His dark eyes lent nothing to his appearance. He would have made an ideal model for the images that came as an example when buying a photo frame—the middle-aged father with his equally bland but not unattractive wife.

Cruz smiled back at him, not willing to join in the friendly banter for fear of becoming a target himself. "So, you're here to help, are you?"

"I am," Cruz said.

"Cruz, isn't it?"

"DC Cruz, yeah," Cruz replied. "Where can I start?"

"Well, we've got the entire ground floor to rip out, and when we're done, any partition walls need pulling down, and that's before we've even started upstairs."

"Why not start upstairs?" Cruz said. "Or at least start with the walls? Then we won't have to step over the holes in the floor to get the stuff out."

"Ah, I knew it," Godfrey said. "You're one of the younger lot, aren't you?"

"So?"

"Too much logic, that's your problem."

"Well, isn't that a good thing?"

"The body was found beneath the downstairs floor," he said. "Which means that if there are others, they are most likely beneath some other part of the downstairs floor. Tearing the rest of the house apart is just a process. I doubt we'll find anything, to be honest, but who am I to have an opinion on these things?" He collected a jimmy bar and a hammer from a bag on the old fireplace. "Here, you'll need these. We're working back from the original hole and stacking the wood by the door. Gloves?"

"Sure," Cruz said, and Godfrey threw him a pair of work gloves and then pointed to a box beside the toolbar. "Anything you find gets a red flag. Don't touch it. When we're done, we'll get CSI in to go over our finds. We'll do this room, then move through the house. Take your time. We're on a day rate here," he said and slapped Cruz's shoulder. "There's a couple of days of work here and it beats walking the streets if you pardon the pun."

Cruz nodded. It all seemed straightforward enough.

"Anything else I should know?"

"Mind the nails," Godfrey replied. "Hundred bleeding years old, some of them. You'll get sepsis if you cut yourself. Next thing you know, they'll be cutting your arm off."

The statement came as a surprise to Cruz, and he weighed the crowbar in his hand.

"I should be fine," he told him.

"Good," Godfrey said. "Because if you do end up losing a limb, I'll be doing paperwork for a month, and I won't thank you for it."

He brushed past Cruz and returned to where was working when Cruz and Gillespie had entered. Cruz dropped onto the joint beside him and set to work, watching Godfrey to gain some idea of technique. He slotted the end of the crowbar beneath the outermost floorboard, then hammered it home before levering it up, being careful not to split the wood.

It took a few attempts before Cruz had the gist of it, and he'd only caught his finger with the hammer twice before he was on his third floorboard. Cruz kept a keen eye on Godfrey in case his working too fast became an excuse for ridicule. He tore up the board and swung it around, being careful not to hit one of the other officers, and then added it to the pile by the door. But it was as he returned he caught sight of something in the hole where Godfrey was working.

"Need a flag while I'm up?" Cruz said, and Godfrey looked up at him.

"Eh?"

"You found something," he said, vying for a better look and pointing at the object in the hole, which from where he stood was unrecognisable.

"Oh...no, it's nothing," Godfrey replied. "And slow down, will you? It's not a race, you know?"

"Right," Cruz said, and Godfrey sat back on his haunches.

"Why don't you see about fetching some tea or something? It's thirsty work this."

"Eh?"

"Last in first out," one of the other uniforms added. "Them's the rules."

"Tea?"

"Six of them," Godfrey said. "Just grab a few sachets of sugar and we'll sort ourselves out."

"Right," Cruz said. "Tea it is then."

"Good lad," Godfrey called out as he wrenched another board from the floor. He sat back to wipe his brow. "Well, go on then, or you'll have six more bodies in here. Die of bleeding thirst, we will."

CHAPTER FOURTEEN

The address in Ruskington that Chapman had found for them was easy enough to locate. It was an average end-of-terrace house with an old, white Transit van on the makeshift driveway. It was difficult sometimes for Freya not to look down her nose at such sights. She had to remind herself that not everybody had been given the same start in life as she had and that not everyone was born with the same motivation that had driven Freya onward and upward.

"Ready?" she asked Ben, who hadn't said a word during the entire journey.

"I am," he said after a short pause, and he gave her a fleeting smile before climbing from the car. She found him leaning on the car bonnet waiting for her, and as was once their habit, they spoke with the car between them. "We still don't have a positive ID, you know?"

"I'm well aware of the circumstances," Freya said. "What do you suggest, that we sit in the incident room waiting for something to happen?"

"No, I'm just saying that we should go easy on him. Give him as few details as we can."

"Oh," she replied, making her way toward the front door. "And here's me wondering how to describe the fact that her clothes had rotted from her body and that all that held her bones in situ was the decaying sinew and tendons. Lucky you're here."

She rapped on the front door and then stepped back as Ben came to stand beside her.

"You know what I mean," he said.

"I do," she replied. "But if you think I'm going to fall for that being the reason you've been off all morning then you really don't know me at all." The front door opened before he could respond, and Freya held out her warrant card for the occupant to see. "Good morning, sir," she said. "I'm DCI Bloom and this is DI Savage. We're looking for a Kevin Stone, is that you?"

The man was beyond lean. His shoulders were narrower than Freya's yet he was taller than Ben, who famously claimed to be six-foot-something, never quite specifying an exact number.

"I am," he said, opening the door fully. He wore a pair of jeans that gave him the look of a teenage boy wearing his father's clothes, and his shirt was buttoned up wrongly, as if he'd dressed in haste – or in the dark, perhaps. "What is it? What's wrong?"

"I wondered if we might come inside," Freya said. "We'd like a little chat with you."

"I've done nowt," he said defensively.

"Perhaps we could explain inside, Mr Stone. I can assure you that you're not in any trouble."

He hesitated and both Freya and Ben smiled politely, waiting for him to make a decision. He took a step back and let the door swing open, leaving them to enter the house and close the door behind them. They found him in the kitchen, clearing a space among the dirty crockery and cutlery, where he placed three cups from the cupboard and then flicked the kettle on.

Ben waited in the doorway while Freya moved slowly into the kitchen.

"May I call you Kevin?" she asked, to which he glanced once at Ben and then at her before shrugging.

"S'pose."

"Do you recall, Kevin, about five years ago, you made a statement regarding a friend of yours?"

He leaned on the counter, let his head fall back, and closed his eyes.

"I knew it."

"I'll take that as a yes," Freya said. "Deborah Jarvis. Do you remember her?"

"Do I remember?" he said with a stab of laughter. "Like she was sitting here with us." He reached for a box of tea bags and unceremoniously dumped one in each of the mugs.

"Kevin, yesterday morning, some human remains were discovered near here," Freya said quietly. And he stopped at the cupboard for a moment, perhaps to avoid letting her see his face.

"Haverholme?" he asked, and Freya glanced up at Ben as Stone peered over his shoulder, clearly afraid of the answer.

"I'm afraid so," she said, and he let out a loud gasp and then clung to the cupboard as if he might otherwise fall.

Freya nodded for Ben to step in, and he did, helping Stone to an old, wooden breakfast stool, and then taking over the tea-making.

"I'm sorry, Kevin," Freya said. "This is a very difficult conversation to have but the fact remains that it's one we need to have."

"Is it her?" he asked. "It is definitely her?"

"We should know for sure in the next few hours," Freya told him, and he suddenly looked up at her, his eyes wide.

"You don't need me to...you know?"

"No," she said. "No, you don't need to see her."

"But it might not be her. You said you weren't sure yet."

"The girl we found was missing a shoe," Freya said and watched as memories clouded his eyes. "She also wore a nose stud, Kevin."

"My God," he mumbled amidst a sob.

Ben slid two of the three teas towards them and then waited for Freya to begin.

"What happened that night?" Freya asked. "I'm sorry if this is difficult, but we really need to know."

Stone took a moment and then nodded thanks to Ben for his tea, which he cradled in his hands.

"I told the officer," he said. "I remember being interviewed."

"That's right. We have your statement," Freya said. "I was just wondering if you could tell us a bit more. Maybe something about Deborah that could help us?"

"Help you do what?" he asked, and he looked between them. "What are you saying? Why do you need to know more about her?"

"It'll help with our investigation," Freya said.

"Investigation? What are you saying? Somebody..." He paused and shook his head. "No. No, you can't be serious."

"Kevin–"

"She was killed? Somebody bloody killed her?"

He entered into a state of obvious denial, backing away from them both as if they were out to get him.

"Kevin–" Freya began.

"No," he said. "No, she can't have been. I saw her. She was there. She was just bloody there. She was in the field. I was speaking to her, for God's sake. I was speaking to her and..." His voice trailed off and he stared into space. "I walked away from her," he said. "I tried to get her to join us, but she wouldn't. So I left her. I got about halfway and I could hear her calling out, teasing me, like she always did." He gave off an unconvincing laugh. "The others were by the fire."

"How far?" Ben asked, to which he shrugged.

"Hundred yards or so. Maybe more but not much. There's a spot behind a big tree where we used to sit. You can't see it from the road so nobody could moan about us being there."

"And where was Deborah in relation to the others?" Freya asked.

"She was over by the fence. There's a stile there."

"And that was the last time you saw her, was it?"

"I was hoping she would follow me. You know, get over herself and come with me," he said. "But she didn't. I wanted us all to be together. We were moving house and it wouldn't be so easy for me to meet them at the field anymore. All I wanted was for one more night out there." He scrunched his face in regret and his nostrils flared. "She was annoying me. She was ruining it. It always had to be about her. You know? She couldn't just put her feelings to one side for one moment." His voice quietened as he recalled the moment. "I went back to her. I was going to tell her how selfish she was being. How ridiculous." He shook his head and emitted another stab of unconvincing laughter. "But she wasn't there. She'd gone. I climbed the stile and looked for her, but it was dark. She could only have gone left or right. There's a river, you see? It's in front of the fence and the path follows the fence. I ran a few steps to the right but there was nothing up there. I figured she would have headed back to the road. She could have cut across the fields to get back to Anwick from there."

"But?" Freya said, coaxing him on.

"I found her shoe."

"It was definitely hers, was it?"

"One hundred per cent," he said. "She loved those Vans. She went everywhere in them. She wouldn't have left one behind. Not a chance."

"So what did you do?" Ben asked, and Stone simply shrugged.

"I called the others. We looked for her, but couldn't find her," he said. "I called her parents to let them know and asked them to call me when she got home. But nobody called. Her phone was switched off."

"When you called her parents," Freya said, "who did you speak to?"

"Her dad," he said and winced at the mention of the man.

"And how did he take the news?"

"Sorry?"

"Well, was he angry? Did he sound concerned?"

"Reggie doesn't do concerned," Stone said. "He's...a difficult man. Him and Debs had a strange relationship. She was close to her mum but her dad was always on the edge. Do you know what I mean?"

"I do," Freya said. "And I'm sorry to ask this, but did she ever speak of her dad?"

Stone was silent for a while, and eventually, he shook his head.

"No," he said. "No, she didn't like to talk about him. She didn't really talk about her life away from us. She was quite private like that."

"So she spent a lot of time with you and your friends, did she?"

"I wouldn't say that," he said. "She called herself a lone wolf. I think she liked the idea of it more than anything. I got the impression it made her feel strong. But she wasn't. Strong, I mean. She wasn't. She was troubled, but I could never understand why. She never told me what was going on in that head of hers. There was always a distraction, or a diversion, if you know what I mean? Always a reason to speak about somebody or something else."

Freya sipped at her tea and eyed the young man before her.

"Did Deborah have any hobbies, Kevin? Something she did in her free time, away from everyone else?"

"Hobbies?" he said. "Like what? What could she possibly do around here? That was her problem, see? She was bored. She always moaned about there being nothing to do, and about how one day she would get herself into a city somewhere. She always dreamed of being a tattoo artist. She loved to draw. I suppose you could call that a hobby. I'd often find her out in the fields on her own, just sitting there doodling. And when she wasn't doodling, she was walking somewhere."

"Where?"

"Anywhere, really. She liked to walk."

"On her own?"

"Of course," he said. "It didn't matter about the weather either. She'd be out in the rain, snow, and sun."

"Just walking?" Ben asked.

"I suppose," he said. "If she was going somewhere in particular, then she didn't tell me."

"But nothing else?" Freya asked.

"Like what?"

"Photography?" Freya said, to which Stone appeared confused.

"Photography?" he said, shaking his head. "Not as far as I know. She didn't even take selfies, and as for social media, she hated it, so she certainly didn't take pictures of her dinner and whatnot. She wasn't like other girls. She was different."

"You've given us a lot to think about," Freya said, politely bringing the conversation to an end. "We will, of course, need to corroborate your story."

"Sorry?"

"It's part of the process," Freya explained. "I'll just need the names of your friends who were there that night. I'm sure their stories will match yours."

He looked between them both then his eyes settled on Freya.

"Of course," he mumbled. "I'm sure they will."

Freya made her way to the doorway, gestured for Ben to leave before her, and then turned to face Stone.

"Just one more thing," she said. "You said that Deborah was sitting alone by the fence, which suggests some kind of altercation or argument had taken place." She watched as his eyes darted to the floor. "Is there anything you can tell us about that?"

CHAPTER FIFTEEN

"I need some addresses," Freya said once they were back in the car. They heard the scratching of paper and Chapman's pen clicking open and then a pause. "Ross Elder, Sebastian Grove, and Anne Hargreaves. They will all be around the same age as Kevin Stone and Deborah Jarvis, and I'm led to believe they all still live locally. See what you can find, will you?"

"Will do, guv," Chapman said, and Ben sensed she wanted to say something but was hesitating.

"What is it, Chapman?" he said.

"It's just that we had a call from the pathologist," she said. "The Welsh girl. Doctor Bell."

"Okay. What did she have to say?"

"Well, she was wondering why you hadn't paid her a visit yet. She said she'd been waiting all morning for you. Expected you to arrive early."

"Well, that's typical," Ben said. "We usually push her for answers and get an earful for giving her the hurry up. The one time we give her a bit of breathing space and she's breathing down our necks."

"Should I call her?" Chapman asked.

"Yes," Freya cut in. "If you could tell her we'll be there at lunchtime, I'd be grateful."

"Got it," Chapman replied. "There was one more thing. Katy Southwell asked for Ben to call her. She said she had some news."

"Could be what we've been waiting for," Ben said. "I'll give her a call. Thanks, Chapman."

"What about Nillson?" Freya said. "Am I on loudspeaker?"

"You are and I'm here," Nillson replied, her voice growing louder as she neared Chapman's desk phone.

"Do we have anything yet?" Freya asked. "We're already pushing the limits of what we can do without a positive ID."

"We do, as it happens," Nillson replied. "I can't get much more on Reginald Jarvis. Deborah was reported missing in May, at which time, according to the tax office, he was working for a local agricultural-manufacturing firm. He was arrested for GBH during the previous February, which was his second instance, but the charges were dropped due to lack of evidence. Coincidently, that particular charge is around the same time his daughter was arrested for breaking and entering for the second time. She was arrested on the tenth. He was arrested on the thirteenth. I can't find a link between either of the victims, but it does give us an idea of what the family is like."

"Trouble, you mean?"

"Well, without stereotyping them, boss. It's not hard to draw a conclusion."

"No, you're right," Freya told her. "Anything else?"

"The Finches are clean. He's an accountant. She works in a nursery looking after kids all day. However, there is one interesting link here."

"Oh, really?"

"They adopted a child back in the early two thousands. A young boy."

"Kevin Stone," Freya said, and Ben turned immediately to witness her knowing grin.

"How on earth did you know that?" Nillson asked.

"He mentioned that at the time Deborah Jarvis went missing, his family were moving house," she said. "I wondered if there was a link and I was right."

"But you didn't say anything to him," Ben said. "You didn't press him on it."

"No, it's always good to have a few cards up your sleeve, Ben," she replied. "This could be good. Deborah Jarvis was found beneath the floorboards of the house where the last person to see her alive was living at the time." She stared across the car at him. "I think we've got ourselves a primary suspect, don't you?"

"We can't have a suspect without a positive ID, Freya," he said.

"Well, I suggest you make that phone call," she replied. "It's eleven a.m. now. If we get to pathology by lunchtime, then pay a visit to the house afterwards, we might be in a position to make an arrest by dinnertime."

"That's a bit of a jump," Ben said. "We'll need a bit more to link the death directly to Kevin Stone. A lot more if you're planning on nicking him and having the CPS support us."

"I thought you knew me better than that, Ben," she said. "I didn't say *who* I was going to arrest, did I?"

————

"Do you want the good news or the very good news?"

Katy Southwell's voice came loud and clear over the loudspeaker on Ben's phone. Movement caught his eye, and from the living room window, Kevin Stone watched them curiously.

"That sounds positive," he replied. "Let's start with the good news, shall we? I'll need to build myself up to the *very good* news."

"We've got a match," she said. "There was enough hair with roots on the hairbrush for us to obtain a decent sample, and I can tell you now that it is a direct match with the DNA extracted from the tissue sample that Pip sent across."

"You're a lifesaver, Katy," he told her. "An absolute lifesaver."

"And the very good news?" Freya asked, keen to hear what she had to say.

"The clothing had decomposed, as you saw, but there was enough of it left for us to run some analyses. Specifically, her underwear."

"Oh God," Ben said aloud. "Don't tell me–"

"There's no evidence that she was interfered with sexually. The elastic in her bra had snapped but due to rot. It wasn't torn off, as they so often are."

"And the rest?" Ben asked.

"Also intact. In fact, the elastic was still around her waist and legs. The material had decomposed, but there was enough of the gusset for us to run some checks, and although I cannot confirm that nothing happened, I can confirm that there is no evidence of sexual activity of any description. Now, whilst I appreciate the body could have been there for ten years–"

"Five," Freya said. "May 2019."

"Five then," Southwell said. "It should be enough for you to work with. This isn't a sexual assault gone wrong. I'm almost certain of it."

"Certain enough to testify?" Freya asked, to which Southwell left a lengthy pause.

"Certain enough to give a balanced and experienced opinion in a court of law, yes."

"Good enough for me," Freya said, as she fingered the stitching in the leather steering wheel. "Thank you and well done. That must be some kind of record time to get a result back."

"We're going over the rest of the clothing," Southwell continued, ignoring the compliment. "But I'm not hopeful that we'll find anything."

"What about the plastic sheeting the body was wrapped in?" Ben asked. He stretched his legs into the footwell and pushed back in the seat. The car's air conditioning was running, but still, a layer of sweat developed on his lower back, as it often did during talk of sexual offences carried out by men. He supposed it to be a reaction to shame on behalf of his gender.

"There are some," she replied. "But as you can imagine, they aren't particularly clean. Hypothetically, a fingerprint can last forever given the right conditions, however—"

"Being stuffed beneath the floorboards of an old house with bodily fluids, insects, and God knows what else are not optimal conditions?" Freya added.

"Quite," Southwell replied. "We may obtain some partial prints. I have a technician working on it right now, but if you intend to use the plastic sheeting to develop a case, then you'd be better off finding out where it came from and somehow linking that to the perpetrator."

"And what would such a large amount of plastic sheeting be used for?" Freya asked.

"Decorating," she replied with a shrug. "Building work maybe. It's not particularly thick so it could quite easily have been used as packaging. The entire piece is approximately three metres by two, but only two of the edges are factory cut."

"Meaning it's an off-cut of a larger piece?" Ben said. "That could be useful."

"So, we have a confirmed ID but the killer left no obvious DNA or fingerprints?"

"Either that or time has just been against us, in this instance," Ben said, to which Freya nodded.

"What we don't have is a cause of death," she said with a sigh. "Let's hope our friendly pathologist has some answers for us."

CHAPTER SIXTEEN

"Absolutely not," was the answer that Freya had not been wanting, but the one which Doctor Pippa Bell, the tattooed pathologist, gave, and her thick Welsh accent seemed to add several syllables to the statement. "The hyoid is intact, there are no obvious fractures to the skull or bones, and until we get the results back on what was left of the organs, I'm afraid I have absolutely nothing to go on."

"Damn," Freya muttered to herself.

"I do have a theory, though," Pip said, which inserted some much-needed hope into an investigation which, up until now, had been filled with ups and downs.

Pip wore her usual smock, gloves, and a mask, while Ben and Freya had donned the disposable PPE provided in the small reception area.

Deborah Jarvis lay on her back atop one of half a dozen stainless steel benches. Her bones were partially held in place by decaying sinew and tissue, while those that had become free had been carefully placed in the right area. It was a sorry sight, but somehow easier to view than some of the sights they had witnessed in the mortuary. Perhaps it was the lack of blood.

"Go on," Freya said.

"Well, had the cadaver been fresh, I might have been able to say it with an element of certainty, but given the amount of time the body had gone unfound, I can only give you an experienced opinion."

"Two experienced opinions in one day," Freya replied, to which Pip seemed perplexed but not enough to press her on.

"I examined the contents of the stomach," she began. "Now, the human body's digestive cycle typically takes twenty-four hours. This isn't set in stone, though. It all depends on the types of food."

"Some foods take longer to break down than others?" Ben said.

"Right," Pip replied. "We're also all different. Some of us have faster metabolisms than others, some slower, and of course, the microbiomes in our gut differ too."

"Pip?" Freya said, gently nudging her on.

"The stomach was virtually empty. Aside from some remnants of some type of red meat, there was nothing in there."

Ben pulled a confused expression but was polite enough not to interrupt and to allow Pip to read his face.

"In my opinion," Pip continued, "this girl died from dehydration."

"Dehydration?" Ben repeated.

"There was a significant amount of faeces in the girl's underwear, which isn't uncommon. The body releases its contents through whichever means possible when the heart stops," Pip said. "However, the consistency of the faeces suggests that she passed it naturally, as opposed to post-mortem."

"I'm afraid my imagination is rather letting me down," Freya said. "Either that or it's more accurate than I give it credit for."

"I'm saying that someone wrapped this girl in plastic when she was alive. The killer may have thought she would suffocate, but she didn't. She would have been there for days."

"Christ," Ben said loudly.

"You're aware that the body can typically go without air for three minutes, water for three days, and food for three weeks?"

"I am," Freya replied, staring down at the girl's remains, wondering what her last moments would have been like.

"I can only assume that, given that her digestive cycle had completed and she had no access to water, she died of dehydration."

"Would it have been painful?" Ben asked, his tone sombre.

"Her organs would have given up one by one. Her kidneys and her liver first, then her pancreas and the smaller organs, before those that are critical to life would have failed—her lungs and her heart, for example."

"So in answer to Ben's question..." Freya said.

"Yes," Pip said, and it was in times of sober dignity like this that her voice deepened and slowed, her Welsh accent becoming more pronounced. "It would have been very painful. Very painful indeed."

They shared a moment of silence for the girl, each of them lost in their thoughts. Pip, no doubt, would have been contemplating the process of death under such circumstances. Ben had his eyes closed, perhaps considering the due conversation with the girl's mother. Freya, however, was imagining far darker thoughts. She pictured Deborah Jarvis fighting for her life against a far larger assailant. Two perhaps? The plastic would have restrained her but she would have been kicking and writhing, terrified, until the moment she was dropped into the space between the floor joists, where any movement at all would have been near impossible. The plastic had been transparent. Not clear like a glass window, but transparent enough for her to have seen whoever attacked her, and transparent enough for her to have seen the light being snuffed out slowly as one by one the floorboards were replaced.

Until there was nothing but darkness, quiet, and a fear like none that Freya could even contemplate.

"Thank you, Pip," she said and then cleared her throat. "Are you able to tell us—"

"When?" Pip finished for her. "Not to any level of precision. Doctor Saint suggested anywhere between one and ten years. I'm going to somewhere in the middle of that. Ten years and there would be nothing left of the tissue. Less than five years and I'd expect the clothing to have been more intact, and perhaps even some hair to have survived. The team examining the faeces might be able to determine a more exact date from the bacteria, but don't get your hopes up for anything more precise than what I've given you."

"May 2019 then," Freya said.

"May?"

"She went missing on the sixth and was reported missing on the eighth."

"So she would have died sometime between the sixth and the tenth. She might have lasted until the eleventh, but I doubt it. Not under those conditions."

"Thank you," Freya said, and she looked up at Ben. "Call the team, will you? I want a briefing this afternoon." She nodded goodbye to Pip and then turned on her heels. "And I want a case put together to bring Kevin Stone in for questioning."

"That's a bit premature, don't you think?" he said.

"Not really," she called over her shoulder, as she snapped off her gloves and came to a stop at the doors to the reception. "In fact, I've got a good mind to lock the bastard in a cell and leave him there for a few days. At least until he provides a confession."

"There are rules against that," he said.

"Sadly," she said. "Which means we'll have to do it the hard way, won't we?"

CHAPTER SEVENTEEN

It wasn't unusual for Ben and Freya to hear the team's chit-chat as they emerged from the fire escape stairwell onto the first-floor corridor. The conversation ranged from heated debates between Gillespie and Nillson to more polite interactions between Cruz, Gold, and Anderson, and sometimes even laughter.

Today, though, there was no sound at all. It was as if they had entered a library corridor, and when they peered through the incident room windows, all they saw was Gold, Anderson, Nillson, and Chapman, each of them with their heads down. Anderson and Nillson spoke quietly, referring to something on Nillson's laptop.

There had been a time when the incident room doors used to squeak open and then slam closed, but the DCI before Freya, Steve Standing, had seen to the noise and had the hinges fixed, which was a shame, as Freya used to enjoy the introduction of her arrival.

But today, she pushed open the door and nobody even noticed until Ben dropped his bag onto his desk, causing a few of the team to look up, each of them gauging the progress, not by Freya's actions, but by the expression on Ben's face.

"Let's get Gillespie and Cruz on loudspeaker," Freya said to Ben. "The rest of you, briefing in two minutes, so if you need the washroom, go now."

Nobody moved. In fact, not only did none of them leave, but they all seemed to remain with some kind of defiance in their eyes. Freya eyed them all but said nothing. Instead, she prepared to give the briefing as Ben dialled Gillespie's number on the desk phone.

"Aye, Ben," the loud and gruff Scotsman's voice rang out across the room. "How's life under the thumb, eh?"

Ben's eyes flicked up to Freya, and then to the other women in the room, and he gave a slight cough.

"You're on loudspeaker, Jim," he said, and Freya could have sworn that she could hear Gillespie's teeth scraping against his foot.

"Right," Gillespie said. "Right, good."

"Are you with Cruz?" Ben asked. "Freya wants to hold a briefing."

"Right," Gillespie said again. "Right, a briefing. Aye. Give me a sec, eh?"

Freya yanked the lid from the whiteboard marker and then began updating the board while she waited for Cruz to join them. She'd barely begun to get her thoughts in line when Gillespie's voice came over the line once more.

"Aye, Ben. Ready when you are," he said.

"Cruz, are you there?" Ben asked.

"Erm, yes," he said, and Freya imagined him leaning into Gillespie's phone, slightly tentative about being so close to his superior.

"Give us a rundown of where we are, please, Cruz," she called out.

"Sorry?" Cruz replied, and she sighed. He was a good officer, but his common sense and lack of maturity often let him down.

"How did the search go? Have you found anything?"

"Oh, right," he said. "Well, we've stripped the floor out of the living room. Sergeant Godfrey said we should get a good start on the rest of the downstairs this afternoon."

"So, one room?" Freya said. "Is that it?"

"Well, yeah. He said we weren't to rush it in case we missed something."

"Cruz is running the inside," Gillespie said. "I'm looking after our lot in the garden."

Freya rolled her eyes, knowing full well that Sergeant Godfrey was not in the slightest part concerned that they might miss something and more inclined to enjoy a few days of avoiding paperwork and proper policing. And as for Gillespie looking after their own uniformed officers in the garden...

"I wonder if the circumstances would have been different had it been raining," Freya said.

"Sorry, boss?" Gillespie said.

"Nothing," she said, not wishing to enter into an argument in front of the team. Again. "Cruz, just remember who is leading the search. Don't be pushed around by Godfrey. I know what he's like. He's old-school. He'll try to get the upper hand, and in this instance, despite his rank, you are leading the search at my request. Push on. I want the rest of the downstairs floor removed today and the upstairs done tomorrow. If we're not pulling the walls out by Tuesday, I'll want to know why."

"Right," Cruz said, slightly unsure of himself.

"And, Gillespie, I expect you to support him. Sergeant Godfrey might outrank Cruz, but he doesn't outrank you, and if that means that you swap places and Cruz takes the garden, then so be it."

"Aye, boss," he replied, and again Freya's imagination cast images of the sergeant giving Cruz a filthy look.

"So what have we found, Cruz?" she said, her pen poised at the board.

"Nothing, boss," he said confidently, and she let her pen fall away.

"Nothing?"

"Not a thing," he replied.

"How many of you were searching the one room?" she asked.

"There're four of us, boss. Plus there's two more ferrying the wood outside."

"And you haven't found a single thing?"

"Freya," Ben said, his brow furrowing, "if he says they haven't found anything, then they haven't found anything. They know what they're doing."

"I know," she said, unable to hide her irritation, but recovering her composure quickly. "Thank you, Cruz. Remember what I said. Don't be pushed around. You're running the show. Is that clear?"

"It is," he said, still with a hefty amount of uncertainty in his voice.

"Gillespie?" Freya said, making sure he heard her sigh over the phone line. "What about you? Or have you just been sunning yourself while everyone else does the work? I can imagine you lying in a hammock while your flunkies bring you cold drinks and updates."

"I wish," he said. "Even the bloody garden furniture is rotten. There's not a damn place to sit down."

"Shame," Nillson called out. "You might even burn a few much-needed calories."

"Where are we?" Freya said before the topic of an individual's weight grew into something far more inappropriate.

"Well, the GPR team has been over the place. We've split it into four sections, the front, the back, and the two sides. They did the front first, as most of that has been dug up already for the water mains and other services. After that, they did the back and the two side areas. It'll take an hour or two more for them to go over the findings and get them into some sort of format that you or I can make head or tail of."

The response was far more detailed than Freya had expected and it rather took her by surprise.

"Good," she said, not wanting to sound dumbstruck. "So, what's the plan now? Presumably, you're not sitting around with your cronies waiting for the subcontractor to give you the GPR results?"

"No, boss. No such luck, I'm afraid. We've identified a few areas of interest in the garden, so we're making a start with the digging. The GPR fellow said that the surrounding trees might cause some issues with the results."

"The roots, you mean?"

"Aye, he reckons there'll be some areas that the radar just won't see through, so we've got the digger in."

"How far down are you digging?" Ben asked.

"To the bedrock if we can," Gillespie said. "But the roots are proving to be a challenge."

"You're not cutting them, are you?"

"God no," he replied. "A TPO covers the whole bloody garden and forest. The last thing I need is a bloody tree hugger breathing down my neck."

"What's a TPO?" Gold asked, and she looked around the room for a face that might provide an answer.

"Tree Preservation Order," Ben said. "It stops people cutting down trees that are deemed as significantly important. The problem is that a lot of the local TPOs were created during the eighties and nineties when there was a surge of building work and trees can grow quite high in thirty or forty years."

"Why is that an issue?" she asked.

"Well, the TPOs are put on the trees when they are young and small. Thirty years later, the trees have grown taller, no sunlight gets in, moss grows on the roof and causes damage, birds nest in the roof or the attic, or the tree branches start interfering with the building, and whoever owns the house ends up with mounting maintenance costs," Ben said. "And that's not even mentioning the subsidence issues that the roots can cause."

"Can't they just cut the trees down?"

"Not with a TPO," Ben told her. "No, the owners have to engage with a tree surgeon and request permission from the local authorities. They aren't allowed to prune the tree at all or do anything to cause it to die without risking a significant fine and even prison."

"So? Surely the authorities would just grant permission?"

"Rarely," Gillespie said. "Any work has to go through a tree officer and typically they don't want any trees touched."

"And rightly so," Ben said. "I mean, we can't have people cutting down all the trees so they can build or get rid of moss. But it just seems to be one of those pieces of red tape that has gone too far in the wrong direction. The whole policy needs modernising."

"So, the long and short of it is, Gillespie?" Freya cut in. "Before we get a lecture from Ben on the ethics of modern arborist practises."

The comment hadn't been an insult and Ben laughed to himself.

"The long and short of it is, boss, that as long as we don't disturb the roots and we don't disturb the health of the trees, we can dig around them. But it's slow work. The GPR man thinks we have about three feet of soil before we hit bedrock. The issue we have is that the entire property is surrounded by the damn things."

"Right, so these areas of interest? What do they look like and why are they of interest?"

"Well, digging a hole in this place is bloody hard work," he replied. "There's a few spaces between the trees that might be suitable for digging, so I've got a team on them now."

"That sounds promising," Freya said, again impressed at Gillespie's diligence.

"I wouldn't worry about the trees too much," Ben said. "Dig where you need to. If you hit a root, stop."

"Why's that?" Freya asked.

"Well, if you hit a root, the chances are that nobody has dug there. Certainly not in the last five years, anyway."

"That's a good point," Freya said. "Gillespie, how does that affect the space you're working with?"

"Significantly," he replied. "Let me see what the GPR results look like and I'll get back to you."

"Good, do that," Freya said. "Call us if you need anything."

"Will do."

"Oh, and Gillespie?" Freya said, calling out to ensure she caught him before he ended the call.

"Aye, boss?"

"Two things. First of all, well done. It sounds like you're handling it well. Just make sure Cruz is looked after," she said.

"No bother," he replied.

"Secondly," Freya said before the compliment went to his head. "Ask Sergeant Godfrey to come in and see me before the end of the day, will you?"

"Godfrey? What do you want to see him for?"

"Oh, nothing really," she said, staring directly at Ben. "It's just a little project I've been working on. Nothing for you to concern yourself with." Ben's eyes narrowed as he stared back at her, knowing full well which project she was referring to. "Just see to it that he comes, will you? As soon as reasonably possible."

CHAPTER EIGHTEEN

"Kevin Stone," Freya announced from the front of the room. She tapped the whiteboard with her pen, and even from where he sat, Ben could see a sparkle in her eye. "From what Ben and I have gathered so far, he seems to have been the closest thing to a best friend that Deborah Jarvis had. He was the last person to see her alive, and he lived in the house in which her body was found five years later." She stopped and made a show of meeting them all eye to eye. "He's our primary suspect," she said. "Now, Ben and I have spoken to him, and he was visibly upset at learning that the body could have been Deborah. But there's something he isn't telling us. There has to be. What I want is a full background check done on him. Where does he work? How long has he been there? Does he have children? You know the drill."

"I'll take that," Chapman said, scrawling a neat note in her notepad.

"The father," Freya continued. "Reginald Jarvis."

"Can't get much more than we've already got," Nillson said. "He has previous, but as for his whereabouts in May, we'll have to speak to him."

"That could be an issue," Ben said.

"Well, you and I can go to see him again," Freya said. "We need to deliver the news of the positive ID anyway. If he puts up a fight as to his whereabouts, then we'll bring him in and he can tell us under oath."

"That'll give me something to look forward to," Ben muttered, leaning back in his chair, and hoping that his sarcasm was evident enough.

"Gold, I want you to come with us. Take your car as we'll be leaving you there. Ben and I deliver the bad news and question Reginald Jarvis. Then you can take over as family liaison. We won't be questioning the mother. She's quite fragile, but you might find a way in. You'll have a few days with her, so take it slow. What we want is a picture of events leading up to the disappearance of Deborah Jarvis."

"Understood," Gold said, who then looked across at Nillson and Anderson as if relaying some kind of handover of her existing tasks.

"Nick MacMillan," Freya said, and Ben always admired how she retained control of the room, yet left enough freedom for the team to interact. It was quite a skill to behold. "What do we think of him?"

"Given that he bought the house after Deborah had disappeared, I don't see how we can involve him," Anderson said. She rarely voiced her opinion, but when she did, it usually followed a common-sense path.

"Agreed," Freya said, clearly pleased to have had some input from her. She turned back to the board and tapped the last name.

"Which leaves us with Liam Finch," she said. "Kevin's father. He owned the house during the period we believe Deborah to have been buried there, but other than that, we have nothing on him. He's an accountant."

"*Was* an accountant," Chapman said, looking up from her notes. "Retired two years ago."

"Okay, well if his adopted son proves to be a dead end, we

know where to go next, don't we?" Freya said, moving to the far side of the whiteboard. "Photos. What did we find?"

"I've had them taken to Lincoln, guv," Chapman said. "There's a team there with the facial recognition software that said they could help. It'll take a day or two, I'm afraid. The images were quite blurry."

"That'll be because it's from a video," Ben said. "It's almost impossible to get a decent still from video footage."

"Actually, he disagrees," Chapman told him. "Not with the difficulty of extracting a still image from a video, but the photos themselves. He doesn't think they're stills. He said they're the wrong aspect ratio."

"The wrong what?" Gold said.

"The size of them," Chapman explained. "He said that video ratios are usually sixteen to nine, where sixteen is the long horizontal side and nine is the shorter vertical side."

"And photos have a different aspect thingy, do they?" Gold asked.

"They do," Chapman said. "Video footage is different as it tends to be made for TVs and or laptops. Photos, however, are usually a three-to-two ratio, which is from the days of old, thirty-five-millimetre film."

"But if they were actually photographs, why were they so blurry?" Freya asked.

"And who took them?" Ben said. "Unless, of course, she was into some kinky stuff and enjoyed being photographed."

"No, we thought it was a video camera that she had set up. If we're wrong on that front, then I think we can still assume some kind of voyeuristic theme here."

"Somebody was spying on her?" Gold said, a horrified expression creeping across her face. "Who the bloody hell would do that?"

"Disgruntled lover?" Ben suggested. "Ex-boyfriend, maybe?"

"Kevin Stone?" Freya said, then left the name hanging there.

"Thank you, Chapman. Pester him, will you? This facial recognition man, give him hell. Call him three times per day or more if you have to."

"Won't that just annoy him?" Ben asked.

"Hopefully, yes," she replied. "And usually enough that he will want to get this particular photograph off of his to-do list."

"No wonder you're so popular," Ben told her, and he caught Nillson's eyes widening as she looked away in case Freya's temper revealed itself.

But there was no temper. Freya was in too good a mood for her temper to raise its ugly head.

"Now for the disturbing part," she began. "We can confirm that the body is that of Deborah Jarvis. Katy Southwell has linked the DNA found on her hairbrush to the tissues found on the body. It's also worth mentioning that Doctor Bell's analysis supports our theory so far. Jarvis died five years ago."

"So we're on then," Nillson said. "All systems go."

"We are on," Freya replied. "But we move with respect. Whoever did this was not acting out of emotion. This was not a sudden mistake that he or she tried to cover up."

"What do you mean?" Anderson asked, looking to see if anybody else was following.

"Deborah Jarvis was alive when she was wrapped in the plastic," Ben added. "She didn't suffocate. The plastic wasn't secured. Instead, she died of thirst."

"Thirst?" Gold said. "But that would have taken–"

"Days," Freya said. "Three to four days of excruciating pain as each of her organs shut down. Three to four days in pitch darkness, lying in her own filth, with nothing but fear keeping her alive."

"Why?" Gold said. "Why would somebody do that?"

"That's what I intend to find out," Freya said. "And believe me, when I do find out, I will be making their lives as uncomfortable as the law allows me to."

"Amen," Nillson said, followed by one or two more.

"Amen, indeed," Freya replied quietly, then checked her watch. "It's three-thirty p.m. now. I want to hit Kevin Stone's house at five o'clock. Before that happens, Chapman, find out what you can about him. Talk to the phone network providers to see who he talks to and talk to the home office to see if he's travelled. If he has, where did he go and when? Do we know what he does for a living?"

"He's a delivery driver, guv," Chapman replied. "Self-employed, but he has a contract with a large internet company supplementing its in-house team."

"How long has he been doing that?"

"According to the tax office, he's been self-employed for six years," Chapman replied. "His self-assessments suggest that he doesn't earn a huge amount, but it's a solid career."

"So he was driving for a living when Deborah went missing," Freya said. "Good work, thank you. That's the level of information we need across the board." She sat back on her desk and appraised the remainder of the team. "Nillson, Anderson, I want you to put together a plan to bring Kevin Stone in. We don't need to go in hard, but I want you to have support, so talk to Sergeant Priest downstairs to see if he'll give you a couple of uniformed officers."

"I'll try, boss," Nillson said. "He's a bit thin on the ground right now, though. Gillespie has half his team."

"So he does have another half at his disposal," Freya said, to which Nillson had no answer. "Good. Ask him to come voluntarily at first. If he refuses...well, you'll know what to do."

"No problem, boss," Nillson replied, making no attempt to conceal her glee at a bit of action.

"He's a suspect, but until he incriminates himself, or until we learn of his actual guilt, this is just a box-ticking exercise. If he puts up a fight, tell him he can either come voluntarily or we can arrest him and hold him for twenty-four hours."

"What's that going to do?"

"He's a self-employed delivery driver," Freya said. "He won't want to miss a day's work, and if he's innocent, then he'll be glad to help. Gold, we'll be going to the Jarvis house first thing in the morning. It'll be late by the time we're done with Stone, too late to start the custody clock. Your job over the next few days is to find out what you can from the family, predominantly Deborah's mother. What aren't they telling us? What was Deborah really like?"

"Understood," she replied, as she started loading her bag with her belongings.

"This one isn't going to be solved overnight," Freya announced to the room. "But if we do this right, we'll be able to circle a name on our list. The killer has had five years to prepare, which means that we cannot take the pressure off for a single moment." She turned to read the four names. "At the very least, I want to strike one or two of these names off by the end of the week. So let's get this done. Stone was the last to see her and she was found in the Finch house where he lived. Reginald Jarvis is as bent as they come and he's clearly hiding something. And as for Nick MacMillan, I'm not quite ready to strike a line through his name. Who was Deborah with in those photos? Who took the photos? Why did she keep photographs of random pieces of furniture and a box? Who did they belong to?"

Freya tapped the board with her fingernail.

"Tomorrow will be a big day. Get some rest tonight and be prepared to work late tomorrow. Gold, you may need to find childcare. Nillson, Anderson, I'm going to ask a lot of you while Gillespie and Cruz are otherwise engaged."

She turned to the meek and mild-mannered, young constable who sat quietly.

"Chapman, if we haven't made any progress by this time tomorrow, I want to give a press statement. Line it up, will you? And if you could prepare some wording, I'd be grateful. I don't usually like to involve the public but in the absence of information and evidence, somebody somewhere might just remember something."

"Let's hope Stone has more to tell us then," Ben said. "I can't stand the press. They'll twist the facts into some kind of sordid story."

"Well, in this instance, they'd be right," Freya told him. "If this isn't sordid, then what is?"

CHAPTER NINETEEN

"What's all this about?" Ben asked as they descended the fire escape stairwell.

"What's all what about?"

"Godfrey?" he said. "Why have you asked him to come in?"

"Because he's involved in the house search," she told him. "And I want to make sure all protocols have been followed. I'm not having this investigation fall over through a technicality of which I have no control."

"Freya," he said, and he grabbed her arm. She stared down at his hand and, reluctantly, he released her. "Come on. It's a bit obvious, isn't it?"

"What's obvious?"

"He's on your list. Godfrey is one of the names on your list of officers conspiring against you."

"Is he?" she replied innocently.

"You know full well he is."

"Oh, so what?" she said. "He's an officer who works out of Lincoln, as are the other two names on that list. The odds are that when we request some uniformed support from Lincoln, at least one of them will be part of that support."

Ben studied her eyes and every muscle in her face as he searched for some kind of deceit. But Freya knew him better than most, and all it took was a heavy breath and an expression that said, 'Are we done here?' To put him off the scent.

Or so she thought.

"I'll join you," he told her.

"What? No. You don't have to do that. I'd rather you focus on a strategy to interview Stone when he gets here and Reginald Jarvis. We can't walk in unprepared."

"Oh, I'm prepared," he replied, opening the door to the ground-floor corridor for her. He stood there holding the door. "The sooner we get this done, the sooner we can get on with the investigation."

"All right," she relented and then nodded for him to close the door. "Do you really want to be a part of this?"

"Freya, when I asked you to marry me, what did I tell you?"

"I can't remember exactly," she said. "It's all a bit of a blur. But then again, I was tied to a radiator with no chance of escape, so you can forgive me for not hanging on your every word."

"I told you that you wouldn't have to do this alone," Ben said. "I said I'd be there to help you. No more lies. If you genuinely believe that somebody is out to harm your career, then I want to help you get to the bottom of it."

"Honestly, Ben, is this what married life is going to be like? Are you going to hold my hand every time I face some sort of challenge? I'm quite independent, you know?"

"I am, yes," he said. "And if you honestly think that one or all of those officers on your list are out to destroy your career, and you really want to take action without going through the proper channels, then I'm going to be there with you."

"It could spell trouble. We might have to break a few rules," she told him and then closed the gap between them so that her face was inches from his chest. She peered up into his dark eyes. "I've had my career. They won't fire me but I might be asked to take early retirement. I'm okay with that, but are you, Ben? Are you ready to give it all up? And more importantly, are you ready to give it all up for me? Your career, your pension, your future?"

Her hands hung by her side and he held them loosely then pulled her towards him, just enough to close those few inches.

"It would solve a multitude of problems," he told her. "We could get married. We could start a new life. Buy a little farm, maybe."

"A farm?"

"Yeah, you know, a smallholding? Nothing big, but enough for us to make a living from the land."

"And what would I do?"

"Grow things," he told her. "You could grow grapes and make wine."

"Right, Châteauneuf-du-Lincolnshire? Doesn't really have the same ring as Northern France, does it?"

"I'm just saying that whatever happens, we'll get through it. But whatever we do, we have to do it together. If there are risks to be taken, then we discuss it and we approach it together. I can't help you otherwise, and if you're going to keep me at arm's length while you go off and work on this conspiracy, then you might as well close the door on me altogether. I'm either in with both feet, Freya, or I'm not in at all."

She tried to pull away but he held her there, wearing an expression that she recognised.

"All right," she told him. "All right, but you let me do the talking.

"So you are questioning him about the conspiracy?"

"Kind of," she said, feeling his hands release her. She reached behind her and opened the door. "You're there as a witness and nothing more, okay?"

"Fine by me," he said, clearly preparing himself for whatever might happen in the next thirty minutes or so.

"Good," she replied, then marched along the corridor and into interview room two. Ben followed her and closed the door behind him. "Sergeant Godfrey, thanks for coming in. How did you get on today?"

"Good, thanks," he replied. "Not much to see but we're ticking boxes."

From the outset, he appeared professional with his focused frown, his interlinked fingers, and his neat, short hair.

"Good, good," Freya replied. "I understand from Detective Constable Cruz that you were heading up the uniformed officers conducting the interior search today?"

"That's right," he said, and Freya watched him search Ben's face for some kind of clue. "I'm sorry, but couldn't we do this in the incident room, or something? I feel like a suspect here."

"Oh, really? It's just a room. Are you guilty of a crime, Godfrey?"

He looked uneasily between them.

"I'm not sure what you mean," he said.

It was Ben who broke the tension.

"She's toying with you, Sergeant."

"Right," Godfrey replied, clearly still not convinced.

"I'm sorry about that," Freya replied. "I'm afraid the incident room is pretty hectic this afternoon."

"On a Sunday?"

"It won't take long. I just wanted an update on how we're getting on," she said. "And I wanted to drive home the need for us to follow protocols here. We have recently had confirmation that this is indeed a murder investigation, and being as it's at least five years old, we mustn't cut corners. Whoever was responsible for Deborah Jarvis' death has had five years to develop a story. His or her legal team will pull every trick in the book to have the case thrown out on a technicality, so I need to be certain that procedures are followed."

"They are," he said with a shrug. He was what Freya would have called decidedly average. The type of man that could pass her in the street and leave not a blemish on her memory. He had no defining features, wasn't particularly tall or short, under or overweight, and he had an uncanny ability to maintain a neutral expression. One day, he might do well in CID. If he lasted in the force that long.

"So the floorboards that were removed were handled properly, were they?" she asked.

"We tagged and numbered them and stored them out of the weather."

"Good," she replied. "And any finds were flagged ready for CSI, were they?"

"We've got the flags," he replied. "But sadly, no finds."

He stared at her, unblinking.

"I see," she replied, making a note of the response. "No clothing found beneath the floor, no scraps of plastic sheeting, or dare I say, body parts?"

"Nothing of the sort," he said, to which she nodded and sat back in her chair, deliberating his adamant response.

"This is where I have a problem," she said. "In fact, it's bigger than that. This is where you and I both have a problem."

"Really? What type of problem is that?"

Freya smiled politely at him. It had been easier than she had thought it might be. The difficulty now would be to ensure her own investigation did not in any way affect the Deborah Jarvis investigation.

"You worked with us on an investigation last month, didn't you?" she asked.

"I worked on quite a few investigations—"

"Specifically, the body that was discovered on Viking Way, out near Boothby Graffoe."

"S'right," he said. "I was there. On my hands and knees, if I recall, alongside the rest of us in uniform."

"And if I'm right, it was you who discovered a particular piece of evidence. A wine bottle."

"Several, if I remember rightly," he replied. "Though we don't get told if any of our finds prove to be of significance. We just clean ourselves up, dry off, and then get back to work."

"Well, let me tell you, Sergeant Godfrey, that one piece of evidence you discovered was particularly interesting."

His eyes narrowed and his head cocked to one side.

"That's good," he said, although his voice had lowered in tone.

"Yes, you see, two of the three wine bottles you discovered in the scrub were of no use to us. We assume them to be the result of teenagers enjoying a drink in the trees, where nobody could see them. The same for the cigarette butts and minor drug use," Freya said. "One of the bottles, however, caught my attention. Unfortunately, there were no fingerprints on the glass and no DNA from inside the rim."

"Shame," he said, somehow elongating the single-syllable word with his anticipation.

"Yes, and despite being out there lying discarded in the trees for months, or even years, there wasn't even any dirt on it. Not the build-up that CSI would have expected to see and that they did find on the other two bottles."

"What are getting at, Chief Inspector Bloom? I get the feeling that I'm being interrogated here," he said, adding in a fake laugh for good measure. "We're on the same side, you know?"

"Are we?" she said. "Are we indeed?"

"Look, if you're accusing me of something here—"

"Accusing you?" Freya said and glanced across at Ben. "Have I accused Sergeant Godfrey of anything, Inspector Savage?"

"Not yet," Ben replied. "But I get the feeling you're heading that way, and if that is the case, then perhaps we should involve the IOPC before you make any accusations."

She knew enough of his mannerisms to read the warning in his eyes and acknowledged it with a curt nod.

"The *what*?" Godfrey said. "You can't be serious?"

"The Independent Office for Police Conduct," Freya said, to

which Godfrey shoved his seat back and started towards the door. "I have a report ready," she said and he stopped in his tracks. "All I have to do is hit the send button."

He closed his eyes, much in the way any other guilty suspect might have done in that room.

"What do you want?" he said quietly.

"I want you to empty your pockets," Freya said.

"What? You can't do that–"

"You found something, Sergeant Godfrey. You found something beneath the floorboards, and I will credit you with some level of intelligence, which means that you would not have left a find like that lying around. Nor would you have binned it or left it in your car." She could have smiled. She could have displayed the smug sensation that ran through her veins. But she held fast. "Which leaves only your person," she said. "You see, I believe that the wine bottle you submitted as evidence last month was a plant to somehow disrupt my investigation or cause me to fail. Perhaps, had the defence team picked up on it, then the case might have been thrown out on grounds of inconsistency or reasonable doubt. Thankfully, they didn't."

"Why would I have done that? Why would I want you to fail? I don't even know you, aside from seeing you on a few jobs here and there."

"Well, that's the big question, isn't it? That's what I'm hoping to find out, Sergeant Godfrey. Now I suggest that if you would like to keep your rank and not be shunted into a back office for the remainder of your career, then you should empty your pockets."

"Am I under arrest?"

"Have I cautioned you?" Freya asked, to which he shook his head. "I can do if you would prefer it. But I'm afraid that would limit your options. It would add a sense of formality to the whole affair. I'm sure you don't want that, do you?"

He gave it some thought, and then, with a huff, he folded his arms.

"Do you want to do this the hard way?" Freya asked, her face reddening in anger. "Because I can assure you..." The door opened without a knock and Freya turned at the intrusion, only to find Detective Superintendent Granger in the open doorway. "Guv?"

"I heard that one of our friends from Lincoln was here," he replied and peered at each of them quizzically. "I wondered if there was an update."

"I was just getting to that, guv," she replied with a forced smile. She turned to Godfrey. "Perhaps you'd like to update us all with your finds, Sergeant?"

He hesitated, regained some composure, and then shrugged.

"Nothing yet," he replied, pushing his chair back and sliding it beneath the table. He gave them all a faux-friendly smile while he straightened his jacket. "But if there's anything there worth finding, then we'll find it, and you, Chief Inspector Bloom, will be the first to know."

CHAPTER TWENTY

Interview room one was almost identical to interview room two, save for the variations in wall posters and, of course, the names and insults that had been scratched into the table, although, some of the names belonging to local recidivists could be found in both rooms and on the walls of nearly every one of the cells.

But instead of a uniformed officer sitting behind the table, as was the case in interview room two, the man sitting behind this table wore baggy jeans, dirty trainers, and a t-shirt that was two sizes too large for him.

"Ah, Mr Stone," Ben said and then closed the door behind him. "Thanks for coming in."

The young man peered at him from across the table, his expression a combination of fright and grief.

"DCI Bloom will join us shortly," Ben continued. "I just wanted to ensure that you were comfortable. Have you been offered a drink?"

"I have," the boy said. "I'm fine though."

"And of course, you have been made aware that you are entitled to a duty solicitor? Or to call your own if you have one in place?"

"Yeah, the woman said that," he said, gesturing at the door. "But I don't need one, do I?"

Ben leaned on the seat back, not ready to commit to sitting just yet.

"I'm afraid we can't know that, can we? All we can do is ensure that the correct procedures have been followed."

"What procedures?" Stone said. "I thought I was just here to answer some questions."

"Oh, you are," Ben said. "But these matters have a habit of escalating. Sometimes it's better to start with legal support, rather than to find somebody suitable later down the line."

He began preparing the recording, using the silence to gauge Stone's demeanour.

"Excuse me," he said. "Am I in some kind of trouble?"

"Not yet," Ben told him cryptically. "DCI Bloom will be here in a moment. She'll be able to answer any questions you might have. I'm sure she'll explain everything."

"But I told you everything I know. I don't see what else I could possibly—"

"Good afternoon, Mr Stone," Freya said as she marched into the room. She set her file down on her desk and peered down at him. "We're grateful for you coming in."

Her brisk entrance had taken the wind from his sails and replaced it with the finest Parisian perfume, which even Ben would agree was enough of a sedative to calm most men—and even some women.

But there was a new air about her. It was as if the meeting with Godfrey had released something inside of her. A confidence, maybe? A confidence that he knew, admired, loved even, where before had been an arrogance, a surrogate persona.

"We're set," Ben told her as he hit record and they waited for the long buzzer before commencing.

Freya began by announcing the date, time, and location, and

then she introduced herself and Ben, leaving a space for Kevin Stone to speak his name.

"Kevin Stone," he mumbled.

"Good, thank you. I presume you've been offered legal support, Mr Stone?" Freya said, to which the young man nodded. "For the recording, please."

"I don't understand," he said. "I thought I was coming in to answer some questions. You're recording it."

"Oh, that's just standard procedure," Freya told him. "Should the investigation culminate in a trial, then we prefer to have recordings of the conversations we've had with suspects–"

"Suspects?" he said, and his head flicked from Ben to Freya and back again. "I was just her friend. I was a good friend."

"And witnesses," Freya finished. "However, I would like to confirm the details we spoke of earlier today at your house. Then I have a few more questions for you. All being well, you'll be on your way when we're done."

"So I'm not under arrest?"

"No, Mr Stone, you're not under arrest. Although that can be arranged if you prefer?"

"Well, no," he said.

"Good, good," Freya said in a manner Ben recognised as her brushing over details to drive the conversation towards a destination of her choice. "Now, when we visited you at your home earlier today, you gave us the following facts. I'll just list them, and if you hear me make a mistake, then feel free to jump in, okay?"

Stone, caught in Freya's whirlwind, nodded once, his eyes wide like a rabbit's in headlights.

"On May sixth 2019, you and a few friends, namely Ross Elder, Sebastian Cooper, Anne Hargreaves, and Deborah Jarvis were in a field at Haverholme Park enjoying a few drinks. The sky was dark, which suggests the hour was later than ten or eleven o'clock. Deborah Jarvis was sitting alone close to the stile while the rest of you were gathered around a small bonfire behind a tree out of eyesight of the main road. You made several attempts to coax Deborah to sit with the rest of you, but she was keen on sitting alone. You started to walk back to your friends when she called out to you, so you returned only to find her gone. You climbed the stile to find her in the forest, but she wasn't there. That was when you discovered her right shoe. A Vans skateboard shoe." She looked up from her notes. "How am I doing so far, Mr Stone?"

"Sounds 'bout right," he replied.

"You and your friends searched for her but unsuccessfully, after which time you called her parents and spoke to her father." She paused to clear her throat. "Now, this is where you stated that Mr Jarvis was unemotional."

"That's right," Stone said. "He said that she'd be home when she's ready and that she was probably just looking for attention."

"Very good," Freya said. "But she didn't come home, did she? In fact, it was two days later that her mother finally made the missing persons report."

"Yeah, something like that. A police officer came around to take a statement, but I think her dad had already convinced them that she was prone to running away for a few days. They didn't seem to take it seriously. Not really, if you know what I mean? They didn't seem too bothered whether they found her or not."

"I'm sure they acted in a professional manner," Freya said. "Now, when we spoke earlier, I asked you if Deborah had any hobbies, to which you replied that she liked to be on her own, she was quite private, and that she was often out walking, sometimes in the streets, sometimes in the fields and the forest."

"She liked her own company," Stone replied.

Freya sat back for the first time, a sign she had exhausted their current knowledge and was pursuing a new angle.

"Would you say that you and Deborah were close?" she asked, to which he nodded.

"Yeah. She was one of my best mates. I told her most stuff."

"Such as?"

"You know. Stuff. What I was doing, if I liked somebody."

"If you liked somebody?"

"Yeah. Girls, I mean. If I fancied anyone. She usually had an opinion and was always telling me how to act. She said that I should be more forceful with them. Girls, I mean." He smiled as if recalling a past conversation fondly. "I didn't take her advice often, but it was good to talk to her."

"Because she was a girl?"

"No, not really. She was more like one of the boys anyway. It was just easy, talking to her, I mean. She didn't talk about herself, so I found myself telling her about my own life. She had a way about her. It was like she knew everything about everyone else, but nobody knew about her. Not really."

Freya made a note of the statement and the timestamp on the recording and then clicked the lid back on her pen.

"I'm afraid this is rather personal, Mr Stone, but tell me, did you ever have a relationship with Deborah?"

"A what?"

"A relationship," she said. "Even a fleeting one."

"Did I ever sleep with her?" he said, seeming disgusted by the very idea. "No. No, of course not. She was a mate."

Ben turned away, refraining from stating how fleeting sexual encounters with friends were often the best, and often developed into something far greater, just as his and Freya's had.

"And to your knowledge, did Deborah have any sexual partners? One of your other friends, perhaps?"

"There were rumours," he replied. "Ross reckoned they had spent a night together, but she always denied it."

"Is that it? No long-term boyfriends?"

He shook his head.

"No, like I said, she was quite private. Even if she had a boyfriend, she probably wouldn't have told me." He gave a nervous laugh. "To be honest, if she had a boyfriend, he might not have even known about it."

Both Freya and Ben stared at him until his laughter subsided and he returned his gaze to his fumbling fingers.

Freya reached into her file and extracted some of the photos she had found in Deborah's box. She scanned through the pile, selected two, and then placed them face down on the table.

"I'm going to show you some photos we found amongst Deborah's belongings," she began. "I'd like you to tell me if you recognise anything."

"Okay," he said with a shrug, and Freya flipped over the first image.

"It's a wardrobe," he said, looking more than a little confused.

"Do you recognise it?" Freya asked, to which he simply shook his head.

"No, no, I don't."

"Did any of your friends have wardrobes like this?" she asked, and again he shook his head.

"I don't recognise it, sorry," he said, and Freya flipped the second photo over.

"How about this?" she said, and her manicured fingernail tapped the image of the box. "Do you recognise it, Kevin?"

"No," he said, but could barely tear his eyes from the photo. "It's just a box, isn't it?" He looked up at them both. "Am I supposed to recognise it?"

"Maybe, maybe not," Freya said, sliding the photo towards her, but leaving it in full view. "Tell me about your parents, Kevin."

"Sorry?"

"Your parents," she said. "I mean, you were nineteen. Were you living with them around that time?"

His eyes flicked to the ceiling in thought and then returned to the photo.

"I was, yes."

"And if I recall, you mentioned earlier that you were shortly to be moving house on the night that Deborah went missing. Was that you finally flying the roost? Or were your parents moving house, which indirectly meant that you were too?"

"My parents," he said. "I didn't move out until a year or two ago. Had to save up."

"It's difficult, isn't it?" Freya said. "It's so expensive these days. Tell me about your parents' house."

"Eh?"

"Was it a nice house? Was it run down? Did you enjoy living there?"

"It was okay, I suppose," he said.

"Were you sad to leave?"

"I'm sorry, I don't see what this has to do with anything."

"Well, it actually has quite a lot to do with our investigation," Freya told him. "Considering that you were the last person to see Deborah alive and her body was found in your parents' house."

"You what?" Stone said. "Deborah's body was...no way. No."

"Beneath the living room floorboards," Freya added. "Wrapped in plastic. But I suspect you already knew that, didn't you?" She took a deep breath and then slid the photos back into the file. "So you can understand why we were keen to discuss the matter with you, Kevin. I would advise you to look at the situation from my perspective. You saw her last, she was found in your house, and yet you refuse to provide any answers to the questions I've posed. You claim not to recognise any of the photographs, you claim that Deborah had no sexual partners, despite us knowing otherwise, and above all, you seem intent on diverting our attention to Reginald Jarvis." She made a show of making herself comfortable then crossed her legs suggesting that she was prepared to remain there for as long as it took. "It's time to talk, Kevin."

"It was him," he said. "Reggie. It was him. He was a...bastard to her." He stared up with bloodshot eyes. "She never said nothing, but we all knew. We all knew exactly what he was doing to her."

"And what exactly was he doing?" Freya asked, to which Stone pulled an expression as if they should have already known.

"He...touched her. He spied on her, and..." His chest rose and fell and he squeezed his eyes closed as if ridding his mind of the image. "She was terrified. Bloody terrified of him."

CHAPTER TWENTY-ONE

"He's talking rubbish," Freya said. "Did you see the way his body tensed when he saw the picture of that box? Who does he think he's kidding?" Freya said, as she shoved open her front door, slung her keys onto the little table in the hallway, and kicked her shoes off. "I'd bet good money that he's not telling us something."

"Well, we don't have anything on him apart from circumstance," Ben said. "If we're going to nick him, we'll need something to stick. We need to talk to his friends to see if his alibi stands up."

He closed the front door but said nothing more. Sometimes it was best to let her give off some steam. It was as if she had a pressure valve that sometimes needed to let go in order for her to run efficiently. He set Deborah Jarvis' box down on the dining table, then hung his coat on a chair.

"Anyway," she said, bringing her left foot up so she could rub her heel. "Wine?"

"If you're opening one," he replied and then sauntered into the kitchen to watch her. "I've been thinking."

"Go on," she said, sounding intrigued but dubious as to his selected topic. She pulled two glasses from the cupboard, held them up to the light to inspect them, and set to work opening the bottle.

"We've got twelve uniformed officers at the MacMillan house," he began. "Six locals plus six from Lincoln."

"I see you've been working on your mathematics homework again," she told him.

"And then there's the GPR lads, the cadaver dog handler, and, of course, CSI, not to mention Gillespie and Cruz."

"And all of that adds up to...?" she teased.

"Overkill," he said. "Not by much, I grant you that. But did we need to double up on uniforms?"

"We didn't have to," she replied, sliding a glass his way. "But I am keen to progress this investigation."

"So you were just keen to have Godfrey in place so you could put your little plan into action?" he asked. "You planned this from the start, didn't you? You knew that if you requested a dozen officers from Lincoln, you'd get six. You also knew that by having six officers from Lincoln, at least one of them would be a name on your list, Harris, Sanderson, or Godfrey. You set him up. What did you do? What have you done, Freya?"

"You seem disappointed in me, Ben," she said.

"No," he replied, surprised to hear himself say it. "No, I'm not disappointed. In fact, I find myself in admiration."

"You do?"

"It was a risk, Freya. A huge risk. You could have got us all in a lot of trouble."

"Not us *all*," she said. "That's why I haven't told you. And nor will I." She set her glass down and stepped closer. "It might have been a risk, Ben. But the fact is that I'm not going mad. I was right."

"Right about what?"

"Somebody is trying to destroy my career. Now I know that, I can get on with my life. I can prepare for it. I can take measures to protect myself against whatever else they have planned."

"But you still don't know who's behind it," Ben said. "Godfrey wasn't exactly forthcoming in that respect, was he?"

"No, but he won't be interfering with my career until either the IOPC knock on his door or he finds himself under pressure from whoever persuaded him to get involved in the first place."

"And you still think they are linked to Steve Standing, do you?"

"Ben, Steve Standing is an ex-Detective Chief Inspector currently serving a life sentence at HMP Lincoln, which I need not remind you is a category B prison and was not designed to accommodate lifers. Whatever power he has over these officers will be short-lived. He'll be transferred soon to somewhere like HMP Wakefield, and when that happens, I think we'll find these little interferences will become a thing of the past."

"So why not let sleeping dogs lie?" Ben asked. "Why go to such lengths to catch Godfrey?"

She grinned and then placed her index finger on his lips playfully.

"Oh, Ben," she said. "What I would do to be as trusting as you."

"What's that supposed to mean?"

"It means that if three of them have been coerced into bringing my career to a grinding halt, then there will be more," she told him. "Now I know that I'm not going mad, I can handle that. In fact," she said, "bring it on."

She brushed past him and reached into the box for the envelope of photos, dropping slowly into one of the chairs, still rubbing her foot. She stared at one of the images, which was enough for Ben to know that the conversation had moved on.

"So you're not going to tell me what you've done?" he said. "I can't protect you if I don't know."

"I don't need your protection, Ben," she told him, then eyed the image again. "I wish these bloody facial recognition experts would get a move on. They can't be that busy."

"What do we do if they don't come back with anything

useful?" Ben asked. He leaned against the kitchen counter, enjoying the glass of wine far more than he was expecting to. Perhaps this was another of Freya's influences. Or maybe it simply numbed his infuriation at her.

"I've been wondering about that," she said, almost to herself. She turned the image for him to see, and he was faced with a grainy representation of Deborah Jarvis astride a man many years her senior, both of them as naked as the day they were born. "I can hardly give that to the press, can I?"

"The tech guys might be able to do some careful editing," Ben suggested. "They may be able to enhance it somehow so we can get some detail."

"No, that's about as good as we're going to get on this, I'm afraid," she replied, then looked up at him again. "I did six months on a fairly hectic organised crime investigation. We had surveillance teams out there twenty-four-seven, which meant that we had dedicated media resources doing whatever they could to make the images we received useful. I got to know the limits quite well and, believe me, it is not as the movies would have you believe." She slapped the photo down on the table then, perhaps because of some deep-rooted moral compass, she flipped it over so that it was face down. Or maybe it was because she didn't want to stare at a young girl and a mature man enjoying a moment of freedom. She scanned through the remaining images, laying two of them out as if they were playing poker. "A wardrobe and a box," she said, then uttered to herself. "A wardrobe and a box. A wardrobe and a box..."

"There's nothing else in the photos?" Ben asked. "Nothing to the side or something?"

"No," she said. "No, it's just a Polaroid photo of a pine wardrobe and a Polaroid photo of an old box."

Ben came to stand behind her and rested his hands on her shoulders, giving them a slight squeeze.

"The carpet is different," he said. "And the lighting too. If they belong to the same person then they're in different rooms."

"You're right," Freya said, collecting them from the table. "The light in the image with the box is warm, whereas the light in the wardrobe photo is cool."

"You buy bulbs like that, don't you? Warm or cool. Yellow or white, or whatever? Personally, I just use whatever I find in the house. It's hard enough to get one with the right fitting."

"Oh, I don't know," she replied, tossing the photos back onto the table. She plunged her hand into the box and dragged out the handful of books. But it was only when she flicked through the pages of *Emma*, that her demeanour altered, and Ben felt her body tense beneath his fingers. Three twenty-pound notes had fallen onto her lap, each of them as crisp as the day they had been printed. She upturned the book, letting the pages hang free, and more fell out onto the table.

"Jesus," Ben said, and he reached for one for the notes, only for his hand to be slapped away.

"Don't touch," she said, then pointed into the kitchen, clicking her fingers. "Get me the tongs."

"The what?"

"The kitchen tongs," she said.

"The tweezers, you mean?"

She stared up at him, aghast, and he fetched the utensil he had, until that day, always referred to as the tweezers. She took them from him, failing to conceal the smirk on her face, and then used them to grab each note and drop them back into the book.

"I'd hate to see you plucking your eyebrows with these," she muttered, as she pored over the notes briefly and then straightened. "Consecutive numbers."

"Sorry?"

"Consecutive serial numbers," she said, excitement seeping into her voice. "These came from the same ATM at the same time."

"So what? She could have withdrawn it," Ben said. "How much is it, anyway? Two hundred quid?"

"Three," she said. "Three hundred quid in brand new notes that she clearly didn't want anybody to know about."

"Why keep it secret? Why would she hide money in a book?"

"Have we checked her accounts yet?" Freya asked.

"I believe Chapman has requested the warrant," he told her. "It's a Sunday so I doubt she'll hear back until tomorrow."

She handed him the book.

"Add this to Chapman's list, will you? I want to know who withdrew that amount and when," she said. "And when she's done, she can have the notes sent for fingerprinting."

"Bank notes are pretty hard to pull prints from, Freya."

"Not brand new ones," she said. "Crisp and shiny bank notes straight from the ATM," she said, gleefully. "When we know who withdrew that money, I want to pay them a visit."

She opened the other books in much the same fashion as she had *Emma*, and to their surprise, more notes fell out.

"Oh, bloody hell," Ben said.

"I think she was saving up for something," Freya said, flipping the photo over of Deborah Jarvis and her lover. "And it's quite possible that however she got this money wasn't entirely above board."

"Oh, you don't mean that—"

"Deborah Jarvis wanted to get away from her home. She wanted to move to a city," Freya said. "You heard what Kevin Stone said." She nodded at the table. "There must be two thousand pounds there. I'd say she was close to making her dream come true. Maybe she was close to leaving?"

"But somebody didn't want her to go?" Ben suggested.

"Somebody with a quick temper," Freya said, and she slid the photo forward. "And a hell of a lot to lose."

CHAPTER TWENTY-TWO

The morning's weather accompanied the mood in the way tuna and sharks accompanied the shoals. The sky was featureless and grey, the warmer temperatures that had brought so much spring hope had dropped a few degrees, and the treetops in neighbouring gardens swayed with the strong easterly breeze.

But the Jarvis house was a desolate and lifeless rock in a sea of new, green life. It was as if a sadness cloaked the building, a sensation that Ben felt the moment he stepped onto the driveway for the second time, knowing that the news they were there to deliver would do little to rouse any joy that might be lingering.

Gold slammed her car door and ran the few steps to meet them, her expression conveying an apology for her lateness, which Freya brushed off with a polite shake of her head.

"Do you have everything you need?" Freya asked, to which Gold nodded.

"The first hour or so is the worst," she said. "It takes a while to break down any barriers."

"If you had told us that before we'd left," Freya replied, "I'd have had uniform come with a ram." She eyed the young detective constable, then leaned in to speak quietly. "The husband won't break easily. If I were you, I'd focus on the wife. See if you can get her alone."

"Yeah, I thought as much from what you were saying at the station yesterday," Gold replied, straightening her blouse. "Shall we?"

Ben led the way along the drive, rapped three times on the door, and then stood back.

"This one's on you, boss," he said to Freya who, without altering her expression in the slightest or even turning her head, accepted the weight of the task.

The door opened slowly and Mrs Jarvis peered around the frame. Her hair was still as lank and greasy but she wore a simple dress in place of the scruffy work clothes she had been wearing last time.

"Mrs Jarvis?" Freya said. "Do you remember me?"

"Of course," she said, her eyes glancing over Ben and resting on Gold.

"Might we come inside?" Freya asked, to which Mrs Jarvis appeared slightly hesitant.

"He'll be back soon. Reggie, that is. He's just... He's just popped down to the garage for some milk. He'll be back soon."

"Well, perhaps we can wait for him inside?" Freya said, and Mrs Jarvis leaned out of the doorway to peer along the street.

"You'd better come in," she said and then held the door open for them. They filed into the living room, which, by the time the four of them had claimed a seat, was soon full.

"Is there news?" Mrs Jarvis asked, and she stared at Ben hopefully. "Is that why you're here?"

"We do have some news for you, Mrs Jarvis," Freya said and then waited for her to meet Freya's stare. "In fact, it's probably best if we talk to you alone." She waited a moment for the true meaning behind the statement to sink in, and Mrs Jarvis' expression seemed to just hang.

"It's her, isn't it?" she said. "The girl you found. It's her. I know it is."

"I'm so sorry–" Freya began, but Mrs Jarvis' throat seemed to burst with emotion and she fought to breathe.

"Oh God. Oh God, no. I knew it. I bloody well knew it–"

"Mrs Jarvis," Gold said, and she slipped from the armchair where Mr Jarvis had been sitting during their last visit and dropped into the seat beside the distraught mother. She put her hand on the woman's shoulder and gave a light squeeze, before searching the room for tissues. Ben knew exactly what she was looking for and left the room to search the kitchen.

He heard the hum of their voices and Mrs Jarvis' stabbing sobs, and he saw the box of two-ply tissues on the kitchen table. He turned briskly to head back but came face to face with Mr Jarvis coming through the front door. Jarvis saw Ben and slowly closed the door, not letting his eyes wander for a second.

He caught the voices from inside the living room and his eyes narrowed. Slowly, he made his way past the living room door and came to a stop in the kitchen, where he turned his attention to putting the milk in the fridge. It was as he closed the door that he grumbled his first words.

"Her then, is it?"

Ben said nothing for a while, taking a few moments to fully appreciate the man's arctic demeanour.

"We had confirmation yesterday," he said, to which Jarvis simply flicked his head up by way of affirming that he had both heard and understood. "At times like this–"

"So what now?" Jarvis asked, cutting him off, and Ben was surprised to see a hint of sadness in his downcast eyes. "What do we do now?"

"What do you feel like doing?" Ben asked, matching his subtle aggression with that of his own. He took a few steps towards the man, stopping a few feet away. "Do you want to talk about it?"

"Not really."

"Is there something we ought to know?"

Jarvis stared at him, an accusing expression forming.

"How dare you?" he said, and if he expected Ben to apologise or back down, then he was rightly disappointed. "How dare you suggest that I know something."

"I suggested nothing of the sort," Ben said, raising his head to peer down his nose. He stood at least three inches taller than Jarvis but was perhaps only half as broad. "But if there's something you can do to help us with our enquiries—"

"Your enquiries? What enquiries?"

"Your daughter was murdered, Mr Jarvis, and I plan on finding out who was responsible."

"Why?" he said. "Why put us through all of this? She's dead, man, for God's sake. Won't bring her back, will it?"

"Sadly not—"

"So why then? We've been through it all. We knew she was lost. Mariam clung to the hopes that she'd run away, but I knew," he said, stabbing at his chest with a fat index finger. "I knew she were gone. You know, you know? In your heart, you know when your kid's gone." He shook his head sadly. "Don't make us go through it all again."

Ben searched for a flaw in the first display of emotions in the man but found none.

"I'm afraid we must," he said. "We don't get to pick and choose."

"So what then?" Jarvis said. "So you upset Mariam again, do you? Drag all of this up so we can go over and over? Round and round in circles? She's gone. You can find whoever did this and drag him through here if you need to, but it won't bring her back. As much as I'd like to get my hands on him, nothing will bring her back."

"Closure is often a tonic—" Ben began.

"Closure? Closure? Is that what this is? It were five years ago, man. Do you really think that you'll find whoever did this and they'll simply drop to their knees before you?" He shook his head. "You won't find them," he said. "All you're going to do is bring it all back and leave me to pick up the pieces."

"We don't know unless we try," Ben said, and for the first time, Jarvis didn't cut him off. "If those involved cooperate, then we stand a chance."

"Oh, right. Is that what you want me to do, is it? Cooperate? You want me to tell you how she was a little darling who woke me with a coffee every morning and picked flowers for her ma?" He shook his head again. "She was a cow. There, I said it. I'm not glad she's gone, but I can't lie. We never saw eye to eye, me and her. I'd rather she were here, but she's not and that's that."

'If that's the truth, then I'll bear it in mind," Ben told him.

"It is the truth," Jarvis said. "Mariam no doubt will have something nicer to say, but that's the truth. She were a nasty piece of work, but she were our little girl, and we loved her."

"Thank you," Ben said, refraining from revealing his truest thoughts through his expression.

"Is that all? Is that all you want from me?" Jarvis said. "It better be, because I've lived through this once and I'm all out of ideas on what to do next, save for picking up my wife when you're done and dusting her off."

Ben contemplated his next move, fighting the urge to tell him exactly what he thought. Instead, he closed the distance between them in three slow steps and then shoved the tissue box into Jarvis' chest.

"What you can do, Mr Jarvis," he said, meeting his glare and daring him to push back, "is go and be a husband to your long-suffering wife, and at least pretend to mourn the death of your daughter. Even if you're not."

CHAPTER TWENTY-THREE

Ben let his head fall back onto the headrest and let out a long sigh, which Freya knew to be his way of getting her to ask what was wrong, even if he would never admit it.

"I don't envy Jackie," he said. "Think she'll be alright in there with him?"

"Gold is a fine detective," Freya told him. "She can handle herself. Besides, if you'd seen the way he was with his wife when he came in..."

"How was he?"

"Different," she said. "He showed a softer side. Can you believe he actually held her hand?"

"Oh?" he replied, as she pulled the car onto the road, holding her phone with one hand, from which she read the address Chapman had sent her, which she was entering into her sat nav.

"Shall I do that?" Ben said.

"Nope," she replied, finishing off. She watched as the map oriented itself and displayed a route less than half a mile long. She smiled at him as she dumped her phone into the centre console. "All done."

He shook his head at her blatant disregard for road safety but knew better than to say anything. Instead, he removed his own phone from his pocket and scanned through his emails.

"Anything to report?" Freya asked as she navigated her way through Anwick's side streets and out onto the main road.

"I was hoping Chapman would have come back with the news on the serial numbers of those bank notes," he replied.

"It's ten to nine in the morning," she told him.

"I know," he replied with another sigh. "I'm getting a little uneasy about the lack of information. You know what'll happen, don't you? We're going around talking to everyone involved, basically alerting them to our investigation before we've got a single scrap of evidence."

"We've got the plastic sheeting," she said.

"Right, yeah."

"And we've got the photos. If facial recognition comes back, that'll give us a lead."

"Not exactly damning though, is it?" he replied, as Freya followed the sat nav's directions and pulled off the road. The little lane led beside an old church and then opened out into a large car park.

"It's a garden centre," he said. "What are we doing here? Oh God, don't tell me you're going to get some annuals for that little garden of yours."

"Some what?"

"Some annuals," he said again. "Annual plants? Flowers? I told you, what you need in there are some shrubs. Low maintenance, no fuss, and if you do it right, you'll have something to look at all year round."

"I haven't a clue what you're talking about, Ben," she said.

"Your garden," he said. "Just look at the gardens around your house. The ones that belong to the older folk. You don't see annuals going in their gardens, do you? No, they like shrubs for exactly the reason I just said. No maintenance."

"Right," she replied. "I'm looking for something altogether

different. I wonder if you could use your horticultural knowledge to help me?"

"Shrubs. That's all you have time for, Freya," he said.

They climbed from the car and strode towards the entrance confidently.

Ben checked his watch. "We can't be too long, though. I think we should make the most of being in the area and see who else we can talk to."

"Oh, I agree," Freya replied. "I just need a few moments. It's a shame to pass up on an opportunity like this. I hear this is one of the better garden centres in the area."

"I suppose it is," he replied, and he stopped to hold a plant leaf between his fingers the way a smoker holds a cigarette. "The plants seem healthy enough. They're well looked after."

"Well, that's reassuring," she told him.

"Something like this might work for you," he said, and Freya grinned at how condescending he sounded. "It's hardy enough. A few of those dotted around would give you some interest."

"Oh, really?" she said, scanning the rows of plants for an employee. She spied a young man in a green collared t-shirt and waved at him. "And what is it, exactly?"

"It's a hebe," he said. "Variegated, too." He glanced up at her. "Not a bad price."

"Variegated, eh?" she said, feigning interest. "What does that mean?"

"It's the leaves," he went on, rummaging through the selection. "See how they're different shades or colours? This one's green and white. Quite pretty."

"How can I help?" the young man said as he turned into their row.

"Oh, it's okay," Ben told him. "We're just getting some ideas for her garden. She's not much of a gardener."

Freya read his name badge and smiled at him.

"Well, actually, there is something you could help us with," she began, before removing her warrant card from her pocket and letting it hang open for him to read. "I'm Detective Chief Inspector Bloom and this is Detective Inspector Savage."

His expression turned to concern, which he made to attempt to conceal.

Ben, however, read the name badge and then let his head hang in defeat before straightening from where he was crouched and sighing for the third time in less than fifteen minutes.

"Am I in some kind of trouble?" the employee asked innocently.

"You are Ross Elder, are you not?" Freya said, to which he nodded.

"Yeah. Yeah, I am."

Freya appraised the young man. He was what her father would have called a lanky bean, but at least he was well-groomed and his clothing clean.

"I wonder if there's somewhere quiet we could talk," she said.

"What about?"

"A friend of yours," she replied. "Deborah Jarvis."

His lips parted slightly, and he took a deep breath as he nodded his understanding.

"There's a cafe inside. It's quiet at this time. Usually picks up around ten-ish."

"And your manager? Do we need to tell them?"

"No," he said. "No, it'll be okay. Long as I'm not too long."

"Lead the way," she said and fell into step with Ben a few paces behind him.

"That was a crummy joke," he mumbled. "You could have told me. What does he think of me now?"

"Oh, I wouldn't worry about that," she told him. "In fact, I was rather impressed. I thought you were just a farmer's boy who knew how to grow carrots and potatoes and drive a tractor. I had no idea you were such a green fingers."

"There's a lot you don't know about me, Freya," he said, as

they entered the cafe, where Elder led them over to a table in the far corner.

"Really? I thought I'd cracked you a long time ago. What exactly don't I know?"

"Here alright?" Elder asked, gesturing at the little four-seater.

"Perfect," she replied, taking her seat. "Now, I won't beat about the bush, Ross... Can I call you Ross?"

"S'pose," he said with a shrug.

"I'd like to talk about the night that Deborah went missing," she began. "Now, we've been through the missing persons report and we've read the statements made by you and your friends, but we just need a little more information."

"Information?" he said. "It was five years ago. You're not telling me that you're only just looking into this, are you? I mean, she could be anywhere by now."

"She's not anywhere," Freya said. "In fact, I know exactly where she is."

The statement was designed to place Ross Elder into one of two categories. Either he would screw up his face in confusion and ask where she is or he would read between the lines and draw his own conclusion, thus marking him out as a man of intelligence.

His eyes widened and he let his mouth hang open again. He was the latter.

"Oh God, no. You're not saying that she's back?"

"Sorry?" Freya said. "Back?"

"Yeah. What's she done now? Whatever it is, I can assure you I have nothing to do with her. She was never my mate in the first place, and if you think she's been in contact with me since she's been back–"

"She's dead, Ross," Ben said, stopping the young man from entering into a defensive rant.

Elder stared at Ben, and then at Freya for confirmation, and she nodded enough to support Ben's statement.

"Oh, Jesus. Really? You sure it's her? I mean, she hasn't been around here for..."

"Five years," Freya said. "Since May the sixth 2019, to be precise."

"Right," he said and tried again to read between the lines. "You're not saying... I mean, did she...?"

"If you're trying to ask when she died, Ross, then you should know that we believe she died around the time she was reported missing."

"Oh for God's sake," he said and sat back in his seat, dumbfounded. "We all thought she'd run away to London. That's what she always wanted to do. She was always going on about how we would all rot here and she would go live the high life in the city." Clearly unable to process the information, he looked at them again. "You're sure it's her?"

"Ross, I wonder if you could tell me about that night," Freya said, moving on from the cycle of confirmation. "In particular, who was the last person to see her or speak to her?"

"I said in my statement, didn't I?" he said. "The copper asked me. I went through it all with him."

"I just want to be clear," she said. "Deborah was nineteen at the time and it's not uncommon for girls of that age to take themselves off, which means that a missing persons enquiry might not have been as thorough as it could have been. It's a sad fact, but I'm afraid it's a reflection on the limited resources available at the time." She placed her hands on the table and then waved off the girl who was approaching with her notepad at the ready. She waited for the girl to be out of earshot, then reconnected with Elder. "However, this is no longer a missing persons enquiry, is it? It's a murder enquiry."

"Bloody hell," he said, leaning on the table and burying his face in his hands.

"So you can understand if we go to lengths to ensure the statements you all gave are accurate," she said. "Who was the last person to see or speak to her, Ross? It's not a difficult question."

"I know," he told her, regaining his senses. "I know, it's just..."

"Go on," she said coaxing him on.

"It was Kevin," he replied. "Kevin Stone."

"A friend of yours?"

"Used to be," he said softly. "Not so much these days."

"Had a falling out, did we?" Ben said. "Or did you just grow apart?"

"No, nothing like that," Elder said, lost in thought. He took another deep breath and then stared at them both in turn. "He's not right. Kevin, I mean. He's not right in the head."

CHAPTER TWENTY-FOUR

"So Kevin Stone's story holds up," Ben said when they climbed back into Freya's car. "He was talking to Debbie. He started back toward Ross and his mates and then turned back to her. A few minutes later, she was gone. Stone called them over to help look for her, but all they could find was her shoe."

"Which she could have just lost," Freya said. "It was dark. She might have looked for it."

"The fact remains that Ross and his mates were on one side of the field by the fire while Stone and Deborah Jarvis were on the other. Who's to say that he didn't do something before he even started back towards them? They wouldn't have seen anything, would they? It was pitch black, by all accounts."

"True," she said. "I suppose he could have knocked her unconscious and dumped her in the trees somewhere."

"The whole getting them to help look for her could have been a charade. A way to take the heat off himself."

"Then when they had all left, he could have gone back and dragged her to the house," Freya said, nodding. "Good theory. We'll need to develop it."

"And how do you plan on doing that?"

"By talking to the others," she replied as she put the car into drive. "Beginning with Anne Hargreaves."

"I think they'd be nice, you know?" he told her, and he waited for her to look his way. "The hebes."

"The heebie-jeebies?" she said, offering a playful smile.

"*Hebes*," he said. "Honestly, there's absolutely no point in you putting in a load of plants that need pruning and tending. You don't have the time, Freya. I know what you're like. You'd spend a load of money on plants you know nothing about and then you won't have the time to look after them, and you'll be disappointed when they all die."

"Unless I had somebody to look after them for me," she suggested, as she nosed out onto the main road.

"Somebody?" he said.

"Yes, somebody who knows about these things. You know? Somebody with the knowledge and a good touch with that type of thing."

"Oh, I see," Ben said. "No. I'm not taking on your garden. I barely have time to do my own."

"Yes, but this is the thing," she said. "If we do get married, one of us might end up with more time than we do right now."

"You want me to step down?" he said, laughing out loud. "You are kidding?"

"It's just an idea," she replied. "You could be a househusband. Imagine that? You could spend your days tending the gardens, cleaning the house, and cooking dinner. I can see it now. You look good in a little apron, if I remember rightly."

"Cook dinner? Me? You moan when I order takeaway," he said. "You don't expect me to try to actually cook something, do you?"

"Now you mention it," she said. "Perhaps that's not the solution." She slowed and peered out of the window at the buildings, then seeing a gap in the oncoming traffic, she pulled the car into the car park belonging to a small office building, where she brought the car to a stop. The building seemed out of place in such a small town, but she supposed it to be a sign of the times, and that at one time, even the old pub across the road or the petrol station they had passed would have seemed new and out of place. "We'll just have to come up with a plan B, won't we?"

———

The offices were not exactly at the standard suitable for Alan Sugar, but they were well presented and finished with care, which was far more important to local businesses than a few hundred thousand pounds of glazing and shiny escalators.

The board in the foyer directed them to the second floor, where a friendly receptionist greeted Ben and Freya.

"We're looking for Anne Hargreaves," Freya said, to which the girl, a brunette who somehow still managed to type the name into a computer with fingernails that were nearly as long as her fingers. Her roots were a natural red, like Freya's, but she'd dyed the ends of her hair blonde, suggesting that either she hadn't got around to re-dyeing it, or she was starting some kind of weird fashion and it hadn't had the intended effect.

"Do you have an appointment?" the girl asked, which Freya had been expecting, and in response pulled her best apologetic face.

"It's a last-minute thing, I'm afraid," she said. "It won't take long. But while we were in the area, it just made sense to come and see her."

The girl smiled back dutifully, then collected the phone handset in one of her claws, tapping in an extension with the side of her finger so as not to damage a nail.

"Can I take a name?" she asked, while the call was being connected.

"Oh, Freya Bloom," Freya said, keen not to introduce her warrant card unless it was absolutely necessary.

"Freya Bloom to see you," the girl said into the handset, then tapped on her keyboard while she listened to the other person speaking. "No, I don't know. They said they were passing and needed to see you. Yeah, one sec." The girl put the phone to her chest to block the microphone. "Can I ask what it's concerning, please?"

"It's a personal matter," Freya said. "It's regarding a friend of hers." The girl seemed to be torn between being polite and receiving an earful from Anne Hargreaves until Freya reluctantly and discreetly let her warrant card fall open. "It's quite important," she said, and the girl's expression shifted entirely.

"I think you should come, Miss Hargreaves," she said, then listened for a moment. "It's the police."

The girl had barely replaced the handset and tied her hair back when a pair of double doors opened to reveal a young, buxom woman in a trouser suit at least one size too small.

She looked quizzically at Freya and Ben, her head cocked to one side.

"I'm Anne Hargreaves," she said, and Freya noted the depth of her voice was like that of a far more mature woman. She filled her lungs and the buttons of her tunic threatened to pop off and fly across the room.

"Is there somewhere quiet we can speak?" Freya asked as they made their way over to her. She displayed her warrant card and Hargreaves inspected it closely before nodding slightly.

"My office," she said, then called to the receptionist. "Liz, can you mark me down as engaged, please?"

"Course, Anne," she said. "If anyone asks, I'll tell them you're dealing with a personal matter."

"Appreciate it," Hargreaves said, then with a curt glance at Freya and Ben, she led them down a corridor and into an office with no windows but decent furniture.

Hargreaves took her seat behind the desk and gestured for them to sit in the guest chairs, much as Granger had not so long ago. Behind the desk, on three hardwood shelves, were a selection of books on management accounting, a dying potted plant, and three degree certificates each bearing the name *Anne Hargreaves*.

"So," she said. "How can I help? Liz said it was concerning a friend of mine. Not Seb, is it?"

"Seb?"

"Sebastian," she said, then doubted her initial guess but waited to be told as if she'd recognised that she may have said too much.

In contrast to her approach with Ross Elder, Freya felt that to get the most from Anne Hargreaves, she should tackle the introduction more directly.

"I'm sorry to say that we're investigating the murder of one of your friends," Freya said, watching the young woman's face for any sign of deceit or panic. "A Deborah Jarvis. Do you remember her?"

"Debs?" she said. "Deb Jarvis? Dead? Are you sure?"

"Oh, we're quite certain," Freya told her. "I do try not to deliver bad news unless I'm positive that it's true."

"Sorry, of course. It's just a shock, that's all," Hargreaves said, and she sat back in her chair. "Blimey."

"Anything to add?" Freya said, noting the girl was shocked to learn of the news more than she was upset. "I understand that you were friends and that when her mother filed a missing persons report, you provided a statement to the investigating officer."

"I did," Hargreaves said, and she unscrewed the lid of a posh water bottle and took a long mouthful before replacing the lid. "We all did, I think. The policeman came round to our houses."

"Well, unfortunately, at the time, the officer was investigating a *missing* nineteen-year-old and by all accounts it was presumed that she had gone off somewhere."

"To London," Hargreaves said. "That's what we thought anyway. She was always going on about how she was going to make something of herself."

"Yes, that's a sentiment I keep hearing," Freya said. "But what I'd really like to know is what happened that night. You see, from what we can gather, you, Ross Elder, and Sebastian were in the field beside a fire. You were enjoying a bottle of wine or two, is that right?"

"It is," she said, nodding. "It was for something. Ross kept making a big deal about it." She clicked her fingers twice and pointed at Freya. "Kevin was moving house. It was kind of a good-bye, but not really if you know what I mean?"

"And while you were there by the fire, Kevin Stone was with Deborah on the far side of the field, close to the stile that leads into the woods. How am I doing?"

"That sounds right," Hargreaves said. "He was much closer to her than we were. She wasn't really a friend, certainly not a friend of mine anyway."

"But Kevin Stone was a friend of yours, was he?"

"No, not really. He was more Ross' mate. I never really clicked with him."

"So did you and Deborah have a falling out of some kind?"

"Eh? A falling out? No, not really. She was just... She was a bit of a loner, that's all. Kevin had a thing for her. That's what we reckoned, anyway."

"Oh, did they ever get together?"

"Debs and Kevin?" she said with a laugh. "He should be so lucky. No, Kevin isn't exactly blessed when it comes to women. Unless he's changed, of course. But back then, he was more of a lurker. He liked this other girl at school once but all he ever did was stare at her. He was a bit weird like that, but then he had a bit of a rough upbringing, didn't he? He was never really very confident." She took a breath and her chest heaved. "Where was she then? Are you saying she's been dead all this time?"

"We can't really go into details," Ben told her. "But what we're keen to understand is the timing of it all. How long was Kevin Stone alone with Deborah before he started making his way back to you all by the fire, when, as we understand it, he then went back for Deborah? How long are we talking about here?"

Hargreaves shook her head carelessly as if they had just asked if she had plans for the evening.

"I don't know. Ten minutes or something. Not long," she said. "Wait, hold on. You don't think..." She hesitated and then made up her mind. "You think Kevin Stone did it?"

"We're just reestablishing the facts, Anne," Freya said. "Nothing more at this stage, thank you."

"And you want to rule him out of your investigation," she said, her eyebrows raised as if she knew she was right, and she nodded knowingly. "Well, if you're going to point the finger at one of us, then Kevin is the most likely."

"Why would you say that?" Ben asked. "That's a little unfair, isn't it?"

The door opened behind them and Hargreaves looked up as a man in a woollen suit and knitted tie leaned inside. "Busy, Anne?"

"Sorry," she said, then looked nervously at them both. "We're just finishing up."

"Well, see that you are," the man replied. "We need those accounts by lunchtime."

The door banged closed and Hargreaves shifted uneasily in her seat.

"You've given us a lot to think about," Freya told her, always preferring to leave before being asked. "We might need to speak to you again."

Hargreaves took the hint, and from a little oblong pit on her desk, she withdrew a card.

"Out of hours, please," she said and nodded sideways at the corridor outside. "I'm going for a promotion. He won't take kindly to you lot being here again."

"I understand," Freya said. She rose and waited for Ben to answer the door. "Out of interest, what's the promotion for?"

"Junior partner," Hargreaves replied then softened. "Look, I don't know what else I can tell you. But if I were you, I'd be looking at her old man."

"Reginald Jarvis?" Ben said.

"*Anne?*" the man who Hargreaves clearly revered shouted from outside. His footsteps grew louder along the corridor and he reappeared in the doorway, glaring at both Freya and Ben before turning to Hargreaves. "Meeting over," he grumbled. Then he continued along the corridor, where he called back over his shoulder, "You can deal with your own affairs in your own time."

CHAPTER TWENTY-FIVE

"I've got to say, Gabby," Gillespie said. "Of all the jobs we've had, this one is up with the best of them."

They were standing in the lea of the house, while the uniformed officers from their station filled in the few holes they had dug in prominent places between trees.

"I can't argue with that," Cruz replied. "I was going to say it beats knocking on doors, but didn't the boss ask you to do that?"

"Aye, she did."

"But you haven't done it yet. Jim, she's going to go nuts at you. Why do you always push her? Honestly, she wouldn't give you a hard time if you just did what she asked. I'm telling you, since she split you and me up, I haven't been pulled up once. I just do what she asks me to."

"Alright alright," Gillespie said. "She asked me to draw up a strategy, though God knows why. There's only half a dozen properties and one of them is a business."

"And have you drawn up a strategy?"

"Aye, I have," he replied, tapping his head. "It's all in here. I just haven't put it on paper yet."

"For God's sake. It's not like you've been busy digging, is it? I haven't even seen you hold a spade, let alone dig a hole."

"Bloody hell, Gabby. Who made you the boss?" he said.

"So what's the strategy then, eh? What is this grand design you've come up with?"

"Well, as it happens, it's a good job you asked."

"Oh?"

"Because you're a major player in my plan."

Cruz stared at him, shaking his head in disbelief.

"Oh no. No, it's not happening."

"Come on, Gabby. You can take my car if you want."

"I don't know what part of that statement is the worst," Cruz said. "First of all, your car is both a death trap and a health hazard, and secondly, no. My instructions are to keep an eye on the search of the house and to report back to the boss if I see anything notable or untoward." Cruz grinned up at him, conveying a certain smugness that Gillespie was beginning to dislike. "And that includes you pulling rank to have me do your dirty work. She won't like it if you try to send me off to do your work, you know?"

"And you'd grass me up, would you?"

"I wouldn't hesitate," Cruz replied.

Gillespie coughed to clear his throat and to stifle the abuse that clung to the tip of his tongue.

"Right. No bother. I'll do it. I wonder if there's a broom around here somewhere. I can stick it up–"

"Sergeant Gillespie," a voice said from the far end of the house, and he turned to find Ebeneezer Bennett strolling towards him with a laptop in his hands. Gillespie had nicknamed him Radar Man to avoid having to conceal his grin when the old Dickens character in his bedclothes came to mind at every mention of his name. It was an image strengthened by the man's nasal tone. "Thought you might like to see the results from the back part of the garden."

Bennett was one of life's small men. His hands were small, his feet were small, and Gillespie had known women with broader shoulders. Yet his head seemed to have been designed for a larger body, giving him a top-heavy appearance. One trip and he would be on the floor.

"Aye, right," Gillespie replied. Then he offered a scornful look at Cruz and muttered beneath his breath, "Excuse me, Gabby. I've real police work to attend to."

He approached Radar Man and directed him to the white, cast-iron bistro set on the patio. They took a chair each and Gillespie, keen to see the results, stared blankly at the grey screen with a series of lines running from left to right. It looked like an overhead view of some wild and remote place in America—Utah, maybe.

He stared up at Radar Man. "Well?"

"Well, what?" he replied, suddenly seeming quite confused.

"Are you going to show me the results or are we just going to look at your screensaver?"

"These are the results, Sergeant."

"Eh?"

"This is the image," he said, as if it should have been abundantly clear.

"It looks like someone's taken a rubbing of the frosted bathroom window," Gillespie said.

"Oh, I see it," Cruz said, who had sidled up and now leaned between them. He reached forward and identified one of the wavy lines with a feminine index finger. "This looks like an anomaly. What's this?"

"Eh?" Gillespie said. "An anomaly? It's a bloody line with a hump in it."

"He's right," Radar Man told him. "Of course, we won't know what it is until we dig, but—"

"Hold on, hold on. How exactly is that of interest? All I see is a bumpy line."

"The lines are the layers of soil," Cruz told him, and he glanced at Radar Man for confirmation and received an appreciative nod in response. "When you get a bump like this, it means that particular layer of soil has been disturbed or dug out and refilled."

"Right," Gillespie said. "Of course, I mean, anybody can see that. But what I'm getting at is why you think it's significant?"

"Because somebody dug," Cruz said, speaking to him as if he was a five-year-old.

"Well, how big is the hole they dug then? I mean is it a few inches or a few feet?"

"Hard to say exactly," Radar Man said. "But it's at least a metre. Maybe two."

"Two metres?"

"Give or take," he replied.

"Of course, we'll have to navigate the roots," Cruz said, speaking as if he was the world expert on interpreting the hieroglyphics Radar Man had presented. "But I think we can manage it."

"Tree roots?" Gillespie said and again he studied the image. It was as if they were reading text in a foreign language that used an entirely different alphabet. "What roots?"

"These," Cruz said, and again he tapped the laptop screen. "These thick lines here are roots. See how they push through the layers of soil? We'll need to dig manually. A machine might cut through them."

"Oh, aye," Gillespie told him. "Well, where exactly is this anomaly?" He presented the garden with a sweep of his arm and Cruz stared at him with a wry smile forming on his face.

"Can't you tell?"

"Eh? What do you mean, can't I tell? How do you know so much about GPR?"

Cruz quietened and then stood straight.

"Time Team," he said quietly.

"Time Team? As in, a bunch of bearded nerds digging holes in the countryside? You watch that, do you?"

"They're not bearded nerds. They're intelligent people. Experts, Jim. And anyway, it's interesting. Haven't you ever seen it? You can stream all the episodes, I think. Worth a watch."

"Gabby, you're single, you have no life, and you watch bearded men dig holes in the ground. I, on the other hand, am not single, actually have a life, and I do *not* watch bearded men dig holes in the countryside. Can you see where we differ?"

"But you can't read a simple GPR result?"

"Of course I can't bloody read it. It's a picture of some wavy bloody lines, Gabby. I'm a copper, not a bloody dinosaur expert."

Cruz shook his head in dismay and glanced at Radar Man, who tried to diffuse the tension.

"Well, see this here," he said and pointed to a dark area near the top of the screen. "This is the patio."

"Oh aye," Gillespie said, feigning an understanding and making it quite clear that he was more than happy for Radar Man to provide some kind of narrative.

"Which places the anomaly somewhere near those trees over there." He pointed to the tree line some twenty metres away. "I can mark out an exact spot for the diggers."

"Aye, that would be grand. Nice one, Radar...that is, thank you, Mr Bennett," he said. "What about the rest of the gardens?"

"My team is still interpreting the results, but there's not much to see so far. It's a large area, so we'll need a day or so."

"Right," Gillespie said and he slapped his thighs. "That's a shame."

"What's a shame?" Cruz asked.

"The anomaly," Gillespie said. "It's under the roots, Gab."

"Not necessarily. It could be between the roots. This is a cross-section of the garden. Whatever that lump is could have been buried between the roots. It's a metre down and up to two metres long, Jim. We've got to look into it."

"Hold on, hold on. Ben said anything below the roots could be ignored."

"But we don't know that it is below the roots. If we dig and we hit roots, then fair enough, we'll stop. But we've got to give it a go."

"And what about the trees? I'm not having the local tree officer knocking on my door. It's a twenty-grand fine, you know?"

"And a lengthy prison sentence," Radar Man added.

"Exactly," Gillespie said. "I'm not going to prison just because you, Gabby, have nothing better to do than watch some old codger get himself all worked up over finding a piece of bloody flint from God knows how long ago in a water-logged hole."

"You're such a philistine," Cruz muttered. "We need to dig it. If we hit roots, then we'll stop, and we'll let the boss make the decision."

Gillespie studied their expressions, finding sincerity in both.

"He's right," Radar man added. "It's worth a look. It's a size-able anomaly, alright."

"Alright," Gillespie said. "Alright, I give in. I've got doors to knock on." He stabbed a finger into Cruz's chest. "You can have the team dig the hole, and if it all goes wrong, *you* can explain to the boss why the tree officer is breathing down her neck." He turned and walked away, then called back to Cruz over his shoulder. "And maybe you and Radar Man can pay the twenty bloody grand fine."

CHAPTER TWENTY-SIX

"She didn't seem to be bothered about the news," Ben said when they emerged from the office building and sauntered over to Freya's car. "She was more bothered about getting an earful from her boss."

"I quite agree," Freya said. "But it was interesting what she said about the whole dynamics of the group. She and Sebastian Groves were friends with Ross Elder, who in turn was friends with Kevin Stone, who in turn was friends with Deborah. It's nothing like my friendship group when I was that age."

"I can't quite imagine you in a friendship group," Ben said. "I always imagine you as being a bit of a loner."

"Like Deborah Jarvis, you mean?" she said. "I had friends. Not many, but those I did have were good friends."

"And what happened to them? Did you keep in touch?"

"Life happened, Ben," she replied. "As it always does. Anyway, I want to see the people who owned the house before the MacMillans."

"The Finches," Ben said, and he scrolled through his emails on his phone for the address Chapman had sent. "House is in Ruskington. That's only a few minutes from here. What's your angle here?"

"My angle, Ben, is to understand if they had any connections with Deborah Jarvis and to understand where they were when she went missing." He felt her stare at him across the car bonnet. "It's okay, I'm not going in guns blazing. I just want to have a chat, that's all. I want to get a feel for everyone while we can."

Ben continued to read the email while they spoke, but then stopped and stared at her.

"Get a feel for him, you say?"

"Our jobs are as much about perception at this stage as fact, Ben. Come on, you should know that."

"Liam Finch," he said, and she shrugged. "He's an accountant." She paused and looked back at the office building.

"Not here?" she said, to which Ben nodded.

"Saves us a trip, doesn't it?"

She said nothing at first and Ben recognised when she was lost in thought.

"How long has Anne Hargreaves worked here?" she asked.

"Seven years," Ben said. "I think that's what she said."

"So she would have been working here when Deborah Jarvis went missing."

"Probably, yeah."

She grinned back at him.

"So there's our link," she said, and she hit the button on the fob to lock the car. "Let's go and talk to him, shall we? The pieces are falling into place, Ben. They are falling into place."

"Hang on, it's a bit of a stretch to connect Liam Finch to Deborah Jarvis through Anne Hargreaves. You literally said two minutes ago how strange the friendship group was."

"There's only one way to find out," she said. "A connection is a connection, remember? No matter how fragile the circumstance."

————

Liz, the girl with the outgrown roots and bad taste in fingernails, did a double take when Freya and Ben re-entered the reception on the second floor.

"Hello again," Freya said as they approached her. "I wonder if we could speak to a Liam Finch?"

"Mr Finch?" she said, her voice rising in pitch. "I'm guessing you don't have an appointment."

"We were in the area," Freya said, smiling at her and hoping she caught the joke, which she clearly didn't."

"I'll have to see if he's free," she said. "I know he's very busy and doesn't like visitors unless—"

The double doors swinging open cut her short and the angry man who had interrupted their meeting with Anne leaned into the reception.

"Liz, I need you to keep an eye on calendars. That's the second time this week Anne has had—"

It was his turn to do a double take, and he glared at both Freya and Ben.

"You again?" he said. "If you're here to see Miss Hargreaves, then can I please ask that—"

Freya let her warrant card fall open, which stopped him from finishing his rant.

"I'm Detective Chief Inspector Bloom and this is my colleague Detective Inspector Savage," she said.

"Well, what do you want with Ms Hargreaves? What's she done? I'll need to know if she's in some kind of trouble."

"They're here to see you, Mr Finch," Liz said. "I was about to call through."

"Me?"

"You're Liam Finch?" Freya said.

"That's right," he replied. "What do you want with me?"

"A little chat," Freya said. "Somewhere quiet, preferably."

He checked his watch and seemed flustered at the idea of an unscheduled meeting.

"I can do four p.m."

"How about now?" she said.

"I'm sorry, but may I ask what this is concerning? I'm sure you have good intentions, but you can't just march into my office and disrupt people's days. I'm trying to run a business here."

"I could tell you what it concerns, Mr Finch," Freya said, and her eyes darted to Liz and then back to him. "But it might be best if we go somewhere private."

He was sharp enough to understand that, whatever the topic, it was weighty enough to warrant discretion.

"Very well," he said with a sigh. "I'll see you in my office. Liz, send some coffees through, will you? And cancel my eleven-thirty. Tell them...oh, I don't know. Tell them something has cropped up." He glanced once at Freya and then back at Liz. "Something unpleasant that demands my attention."

————

Liam Finch's office was on the opposite side and at the far end of the corridor to Anne Hargreaves' office. The view across the town was pleasant, but not alluring enough that Ben found himself gazing out over the rooftops.

They took their respective seats while Finch closed the door. Then he sat on his side of the desk, before closing some files, shifting them to one side, and switching his computer monitor off, presumably for client confidentiality.

His desk was relatively tidy, large, and moderately expensive. It was dark wood with a touch of red, which Ben presumed was mahogany, but he could have been wrong. Two framed photos sat at the far end. The first was of Liam Finch and a woman who Ben recognised from somewhere but couldn't quite place. The second was a black-and-white image of a baby wrapped in a knitted blanket.

"Now then," he said, exhaling loud and heavy enough that Ben smelled the coffee on his breath. "What's all this about?"

Freya crossed her legs and laid her hands on her lap, forcing Finch to be silent for a moment, which was just one of the little power plays that Ben had come to learn and be mindful of.

"You were the owner of a property in Haverholme Park, were you not? A property named Priory View. Is that right?"

"That's right. A few years back, mind."

"Five, to be precise," Freya told him. "You exchanged in June 2019."

"Right," he replied with a slight shrug. "Well, if you say so. Is there a problem? I can assure you my affairs are up to date—"

"It's not a tax enquiry, Mr Finch," Ben said. "I'm sure, given your position here, that your affairs are in all in order."

"No, I'm afraid the reason for our visit is rather more serious than that," Freya said. "Do you, or did you, know a girl named Deborah Jarvis?"

"Deborah Jarvis?" he said, then cocked his head. "The missing girl, you mean?"

"That's her," she replied and prepared to deliver the line that, should he know anything at all about the murder, provide the most telling of reactions. "She was reported as missing five years ago, right about the time that you sold Priory View, in fact."

"That's right. I remember now. I doubt there's anyone in these parts that doesn't remember."

"Her remains were discovered beneath your old house, Mr Finch," Freya said, and not a single muscle in his face tensed, moved, or twitched. In fact, he might as well have been frozen in time, at least for a few seconds.

"Her remains?" he said. "Beneath my old house?"

"Hopefully now you can appreciate my discretion," Freya said, and he nodded as he sat back.

"Yes. Yes, I can, and thank you."

"How well did you know her, Mr Finch?"

"Me? I didn't. Not really—"

"But you knew of her?"

"Of course. This isn't exactly a metropolis, is it? People tend to know one another." He fingered his lips in thought then narrowed his eyes. "Is that why you were talking to Miss Hargreaves?"

"We are in the process of making preliminary enquiries," Freya said. "We're talking to everyone who knew her."

"So you've spoken to him then, have you?"

"Spoken to who?" she replied, and he pursed his lips while he considered his phrasing.

"Kevin," he said. "You've spoken to my boy, have you? I remember it now. You lot came round and questioned him. She was his friend. She was good to him. Better than those others were anyway."

"We have spoken to him," Freya said. "But like I said, at the moment, all we can do is follow a preset procedure. We speak to those who knew her, re-establish that the stories all add up, and of course, we need to eliminate certain individuals from our enquiries."

"Eliminate?" he said, and his eyes danced from Ben's to Freya's and back again. "So, I'm part of your enquiry, am I? Is that what this is? I'm a suspect, am I?"

"You owned the house, Mr Finch. It isn't exactly a leap to make."

"I was selling it," he told them. "I didn't have anything to do with it. Why on earth would I?"

"I'm sure if we can just understand your movements, Mr Finch, that all this can be cleared up and we can let you go about your day."

"We're looking at May the sixth," Freya said. "I'd like to know where you were from that date to the eighth."

"Why the eighth?"

"Because that was when the missing persons report was

made," Freya said. "She was missing for a full two days before it was reported."

There was a knock at the door, and it was opened by Liz carrying a tray of coffees.

"*Not now, damn it*," he yelled at her, and she jumped back, spilling the coffee onto the tray.

The door closed and he closed his eyes to regain his composure. Then suddenly they opened.

"Hang on," he said, and he switched his computer monitor back on before clicking a few times on the mouse and then scrolling through the information on his screen. Eventually, he turned it for them to see. "There," he said. "That's where I was."

"Page and Bookers?" Ben read. "Estate Agents?"

"We exchanged on Priory View in June but we moved out in May." He studied the email trail a little more closely. "May the seventh, to be precise."

"You moved out before you exchanged?"

"We were in the fortunate position of buying our new house for cash, so we did. The sale of Priory View came a month or so later if I recall." He sat back, seeming pleased with his find. "Does that tick your box, Miss Bloom?"

"But you would have still had access to Priory View, surely?" Ben said.

"Oh, for God's sake," he said. "I was moving house. What do you think I did, just popped out between unloading the vans so I could bloody well murder a girl I barely knew?"

"But you did still have a key," Ben said, which only seemed to tease at the man's temper even further.

"Yes, I did," he said. "But I didn't go back. In fact, I don't think I've ever been back there." The three of them sat in silence for a few moments until he spoke again, softer in tone. "May I ask how she died?"

"No," Freya replied quietly and thoughtfully.

"What about...what I mean is, where was she found?"

Freya glanced across at Ben and gave him the nod.

"Thank you for your time, Mr Finch," she said as they stood. "If we have any further questions—"

"Then feel free to stop by," he said, then gave a weak, apologetic smile. "If I'm free, I'll see you."

"Perhaps you'll be having a better day," Freya said, which Ben knew to be her way of accepting his subtle apology. "I do hope so, Mr Finch."

CHAPTER TWENTY-SEVEN

A cloud hung over the Jarvis house, but since becoming the team's family liaison officer, Jackie had grown used to it and felt confident she could navigate the turmoil.

"What was your name again?" Mr Jarvis asked. He was sitting on the sofa beside his wife. But where she was leaning forward with her face buried in her hands, he had leaned back into a rather slobbish position and stared vacantly at the ceiling. Only his eyes moved, and he watched her while he waited for her reply.

"I'm Detective Constable Gold," she began. "I'm your family liaison officer."

"And what does one of them do, then?"

"Well, first of all, I'm here to answer any questions you might have regarding the investigation," she explained. "And I'm here to support you. I can help you while you grieve. I'm happy to muck in. The important thing is that you do have that chance to adjust without feeling overburdened by everyday life."

"I see," he grumbled. "So, how long will you be here?"

"Reggie, leave the poor girl alone, will you?" Mariam said, pulling her hands from her face. "She's just told us that she's here to help. The least you can do is be civil." She looked at Jackie apologetically. "I'm sorry. He wasn't blessed with a heart, you see."

"Not blessed with a heart, no?" he said, and he pulled himself out from the sunken sofa seat and marched across the room to the door. "If I had no heart, Mariam, I would have been gone a long time ago."

"Five years ago, you mean?" Mrs Jarvis stared at the floor, but her expression was clearly bitter.

"That was low, even by your standards."

"Just go, Reg," she replied. "Just go, will you? You're no use to me, so you might as well just bloody leave."

He loitered by the door for a few seconds, as if contemplating a retaliation or an apology, but then made up his mind. A few seconds later, Jackie heard the rattle of keys and then the front door slammed.

It was as if the sun had burned through that claustrophobic cloud but had yet to rid the house of the chill that endured.

"I'm sorry about that," Mrs Jarvis said. "He does have a heart. I was wrong to say different. It's just that..."

"You don't need to explain anything to me," Jackie told her. "Honestly, in this game, you learn to turn a blind eye. I'm here to support those who want it."

"Well, I'm grateful to you. You should know that," Mrs Jarvis said. "These last five years, you see, they've not been kind to us. Well, to me, really. I'm not sure Reggie even thinks about her anymore. If anything, his life is probably easier without her. Is that wrong to say?"

"Not at all," Jackie replied. "Relationships are tricky things to manage, aren't they? Who am I to say what's wrong or right? I'm not here to judge, Mrs Jarvis."

Mrs Jarvis softened again and dabbed at her eye with her tissue.

"This is what you do, is it?" she said. "You sit with the families, do you?"

"When there's cause to," Jackie explained. "For the most part, I'm a detective. I work with DCI Bloom. You know, the woman who was here earlier?"

"Right. Well, if you'll be here for a bit, then you might as well make yourself useful."

Jackie smiled at her.

"Tea?"

"Stick a sugar in it, will you? I'll need something to get through the rest of the day."

"You just sit there, Mrs Jarvis," she said. "Then maybe we can talk."

"About my Deborah, you mean?"

Jackie stopped at the door.

"We don't have to, of course. But I find it helps, you know? To get things off your chest. To talk about the good times."

"That would be nice," Mrs Jarvis replied. "And please, call me Mariam. Mrs Jarvis sounds so..."

"Formal?" Jackie suggested, to which she laughed but shook her head.

"Well, yes, but that wasn't what I was going to say," she said. "No, I was just going to say that it reminds me of Reggie." She looked up at Jackie from where she was sitting. "And right now, all I want to think about is my little girl."

———

When they left the office building this time, Ben and Freya had at least managed to climb into the car and Freya had even started the engine before being distracted. But before she could pull away, the phone rang and a familiar number displayed on the dashboard's screen.

She leaned forward to hit the button to answer the call, then sat back.

"Chapman, how is everything going?" she said.

"Slowly," Chapman replied. "I'm sorry to bother you, but Anna and Jenny said that you should have been back by now and that maybe we should have an update."

"Quite right," Freya told her. "We have quite a few moving parts and it wouldn't do any harm to go over them as a team. I'm on loudspeaker, I presume?"

"You are, guv, yes."

"Good. Well, I hope you're all ready for this because we've gathered a lot of information, and apart from a few snippets, absolutely none of it makes sense. So far, we've been to see Deborah's parents, Ross Elder, Anne Hargreaves, and Liam Finch."

"You've done all that this morning?" Anderson asked.

"Yes, I wouldn't ordinarily choose to hit so many of them all at once, but given that we're waiting on facial recognition and the serial numbers from the bank notes, it made sense to get a feel for who they are and to establish some connections. Besides, we're five years behind whoever's responsible for her death. We have some catching up to do."

"And what are your thoughts?" Nillson called out. "Are we still looking at the dad?"

"In my head, he's the one with the character to do such a thing," Freya said. "However, with the little evidence we do have, we would be remiss to ignore the doors that are opening before us."

"What doors are they?"

"Such as the fact that Kevin Stone was the last person to see Deborah Jarvis alive, and she was found in the house that his parents owned. Not only that, but there's a key detail that I believe we have missed up until this point. You've all read the misper on Deborah Jarvis, so you all know that Kevin Stone and Deborah were on one side of the field, while the other three were on the other. All four of their statements claim that he left her there and was heading back to the group when he returned to try to get her to go with him. That's when he realised she wasn't there. That's when he climbed the stile and ran into the woods. A few minutes later, he called for the others to help him, and all he could find was her shoe. The original investigation was weak, and given her parents' statements, it's not hard to understand why. But what happened before Kevin Stone was walking towards the group? And before he turned back? There's a significant window of opportunity there for Kevin to have assaulted Deborah, perhaps knocked her out, and then hidden her body in the woods. It's not unreasonable to assume that when he called the others to join him, it would have been quite feasible for him to ensure they didn't search where he had hidden her."

"How did he get her to the house?" Nillson asked.

"His father showed us evidence that the exchange on the new house took place on the seventh of May. The day after Deborah was last seen. How easy would it have been for Kevin to have hidden her body somewhere? They still had access to Priory View right the way up until June. The fact remains that Kevin Stone should be a primary suspect."

"Are we bringing him in?" Anderson asked.

"No," Freya said. "Not yet. We simply don't have enough. There are too many unanswered questions, and to add some complexity to the mix, there are other avenues for us to explore. All I'm saying is that Kevin Stone's name should not be struck off our list."

"But didn't he try to put it on Deborah's dad?" Chapman said. "You interviewed him, didn't you?"

"We did," Freya said. "And there is something about that young man that just doesn't sit right. And as for the father, well, if there's something to be learned about him, then Gold will be the one to find out. She'll be based from the Jarvis house for a day or so. Let's see what she finds out, shall we?"

Ben tapped her on the leg and nodded through the windscreen. She gave him a confused look and searched the street for whatever it was he had seen.

And then she saw it.

"Well, well, well, Reginald Jarvis must have had enough of grieving for one day," she said. "He's just walked past our car and gone into the local pub."

"Sign of guilt?" Anderson suggested.

"Maybe. Maybe not," Freya said. "Can one of you message Gold and let her know?"

"Is that wise, boss?" Nillson asked. "Do we really want to get involved in a marriage?"

"Personally, I think it's very wise," Freya said. "Nothing annoys a wife more than a drunken husband."

"I'll do it," Anderson said.

"And in case you're wondering, there is more," Freya said, hoping not to lose their attention for too long.

"More?"

"Ross Elder," she began. "Seems like a decent young man. No record, clean cut, and hardworking. But he did say something which has been playing on my mind."

"Go on," Nillson said.

"It was something that Anne Hargreaves concurred with," she said. "Deborah was Kevin's friend. Nobody else really knew her too well. But Kevin was Ross' friend."

"So nobody really liked him?"

"They all thought him a bit weird," Freya explained. "And while that is the very definition of subjective, for some reason, I cannot shake it. There's something there."

"Anything else?" Nillson asked.

"Oh, yes," Freya said. "There's plenty more. Anne Hargreaves and Deborah didn't get along, and she didn't seem too surprised when we told her."

"So you think she's a potential suspect?"

"No, not yet, anyway. But she is hoping to become a junior partner in a local accountancy firm."

"So?" Anderson said, and she imagined her seeking some kind of explanation from Nillson. "How does that fit in?"

"Who else works at an accountancy firm?" Freya asked.

"Oh Jesus," Nillson said. "Liam Finch? Kevin's adopted dad."

"Bingo," Freya said in mock excitement. "So, although the links are tenuous at best, they are there and they are worth exploring. She's worked there for seven years, which meant that she would have known Liam Finch at the time Deborah Jarvis went missing."

"But you said they weren't friends," Nillson said.

"Like I said, it's not the strongest link, but it's a link nonetheless. Can one of you see if you can put some meat on that rather anaemic bone, please?"

"I'll pick that up," Chapman said.

"No, you've got too much on," Freya told her. "Nillson, can you handle it? Just map them all out and see where they overlap. Finch might be a successful accountant but he's not the nicest of men. See where it takes you."

"Will do," she replied, and the sound of her notepad pages came over the call.

"Now, is that enough information for you all to be getting on with?" Freya asked.

"Bloody hell, boss," Nillson replied, and Freya sensed there was some miming going on between them in the pause.

"What is it?" Freya asked.

"The facial recognition," Chapman said. 'It's a non-starter. Whoever it is, is not on the database."

"Damn it," Freya said. "What about the money?"

"Nothing yet," Chapman said. "I've been on at them already this morning. I'll try again in a while."

"Please do," Freya said. "We haven't crossed a single name off our list and we're no further on than we were two days ago. At this rate, I'll have to give that press statement, and honestly, it's something I really don't want to do."

"Erm, guv," Chapman said, "I've got Cruz on the other line. He said he's been trying to get hold of you."

"They might as well join us. Can you patch him onto this call?" Freya asked. "And when we're done, perhaps one of you would be kind enough to update him and Gillespie? I'm not sure if I can stomach going through all of that again."

"Will do," Chapman said.

The line silenced for a moment and then Cruz came on.

"Hello?" he said as if he had answered the phone to a stranger.

"Cruz, how are you doing over there?" Freya said. "Keeping things in order, I hope?"

"Hello?" he said again, and then they heard him wildly tap a few buttons on his phone.

"Cruz?" Freya said, and she was just about to give up on him when he spoke again.

"Boss, are you there?"

"Cruz? What on earth is happening? Where's Gillespie?"

"Jim?" he said. "Oh, he's gone somewhere."

"He's gone somewhere?"

"Door knocking," he replied. "Although I don't think he was very happy about it."

"So what are you doing?" Ben asked, taking over from Freya before she said something she might regret.

"I'm in the garden with Radar Man."

"Radar Man?" Nillson said. "Who the bloody hell is Radar Man?"

"I presume you're referring to the GPR team, Cruz," Freya said. "Have they found anything, other than tree roots and dirt?"

"That's just it, boss," he said, and she heard his breathing quicken. "We've got another one."

CHAPTER TWENTY-EIGHT

"What a bloody awful mess this is," Freya mused aloud, and Ben knew better than to tease the musings into a full-on rant by answering. "Everything points to Kevin Stone, yet his alibi holds up and we have no way of accurately determining what he did before he got his friends involved. The victim's father is as crooked as a baby's arm picking its nose. And as for Liam Finch... well, I won't tell you what I think of him. Not publicly anyway."

"That good, eh?" Ben said.

They were standing at the end of the long driveway with the house before them. The GPR team had set up camp in a van on the road, where they worked on laptops in an awning that seemed to be hemmed in on all sides by CSI vans. One vehicle that was missing was Gillespie's old Volvo.

They walked the driveway, much as they had done twice already, dodging the trenches and ditches, and finding a solid path through the groundworks. But instead of walking to the front, they headed to the side of the building, from where they could hear Cruz's voice.

The garden was a mass of activity. Centring the large hole in a space in the trees, around which Katy Southwell and her team were crouched, uniformed officers sifted through the undergrowth where the garden met the forest, two of the GPR team were re-scanning certain areas, and Cruz, who stood on the threshold of the rear door, was giving instructions to them all, directing the Lincoln officers to relocate the floorboards, which had already been moved from inside, and keeping the rest of the officers busy in the garden.

"How's it going, Cruz?" Ben said, hoping to inject a bit of life into his voice. "Looks like you've got everything under control here."

"I'm doing my best, Ben," he replied, then peered around them both. "No, not there. We need to keep the boards in order and in the dry so that CSI can go over them."

The officer he was instructing rolled his eyes and carted three boards off on his shoulder.

"And don't damage them," Cruz told him, before returning his attention to Ben and Freya once more. "Sorry. That Lincoln lot needs constant attention, I tell you."

"Well, it looks like you're the man for the job," Freya said. "I'm impressed."

"Thanks, boss. To be honest, I could do with another pair of hands, so I'm glad you're here."

"Is Gillespie still knocking on doors?"

"He's been two hours now," Cruz said. "I wouldn't mind, but it's only five or six houses."

"Is there a pub between them?" Freya asked.

"There's nothing," Cruz said, missing the joke. "It's just a forest and river with a handful of nice houses dotted about."

"Have you told him about the new arrival?" Ben asked, and he nodded at the CSI team working in the hole.

"Jim? No, I was going to give him a call, but to be honest, it's been easier without him."

Ben smiled at Freya, hoping to stop her from adding any

weight to the statement, and then he put his hand on Cruz's shoulder. "Come on. Let's see what we've got."

He felt Cruz's muscles relax under his touch and led him over to the hole.

"You know, he didn't even want to dig the hole," Cruz said when Freya was out of earshot.

"What?"

"Yeah," he said, keeping his voice low. "He said because the anomaly was under the roots that we needn't bother digging. He said that was what you said."

"Do you mean the anomaly in the GPR results?"

"Yeah."

"Well, that wasn't quite what I said, but it's a good thing you pushed for it," Ben told him. "I think Freya's genuinely impressed, mate. You did well. You should be proud. Not many with your experience could have handled a dozen officers plus two third-party teams."

"Cheers, Ben," Cruz said as they reached the hole.

"Now then," he said, catching Southwell's attention. "What do we have here?"

"Afternoon," she replied, standing up from where she was crouched and pulling her hood from her head to relieve the tension in her neck.

Freya, who had been watching the Lincoln team, ambled over to them and smiled a greeting. She peered into the hole and sucked in a deep breath.

"It's not exactly fresh, is it?" she said, to which Southwell shook her head.

"And don't ask me for a date. Not yet anyway. We're still exposing the bones."

"Rough estimate?" Freya pushed. "It's been in there longer than Deborah Jarvis, that's for sure. There's nothing left but bones."

"That could be down to the environment," Southwell

explained. "There's a few more bugs and critters out here than in the house beneath the floor."

"Fair enough," Ben said. "So, despite the body being far more decayed than Deborah Jarvis', whoever this is could have died at the same time."

"It's possible," Southwell said. "Although, there's also the chance that whoever this is could have been in the ground for a decade or more."

"Do we have anything to go on at all?" Freya asked.

"As it happens, we do," Southwell said. "The MO is different. Broken femur, broken pelvis, which by the way is looking like a female's, a few broken fingers, collar bone, and some slight damage to the skull."

"Blimey," Ben said. "She wasn't a skydiver, was she? Sounds like someone whose parachute didn't open. I doubt anybody even needed to dig a hole."

"Don't be flippant, Ben, please," Freya said. "This was a person, after all. They had a family."

It was one of those comments that used to wear Ben down, but these days, he simply smiled them off.

"So no chance of DNA then?" he said to Southwell.

"It won't be easy, and even if we do manage to find a sample to use, it won't be quick," she replied. "What are your concerns?"

"Identifying her," Ben said. "What else? I mean, if she didn't fall from the sky, then she had to come from somewhere, and as Freya said, she had a family somewhere."

"Well, in times like this, we can resort to more primitive methods," Southwell said. "Her molars are intact and are well looked after. She ate well and took care of herself, and judging by the wear, I'd say she was around the same age as the other one."

"Deborah Jarvis," Freya said.

"Right," Southwell replied. "And there are one or two features that might help."

"Features?" Ben asked.

"No two mouths are the same, Ben," she said. "I'd say she had a wisdom tooth extracted, which has resulted in a slight variation to the rear of her lower jaw."

"A variation?"

"Some of her teeth are out of line," Freya said.

"That's right," Southwell continued. "They're in great condition, and wouldn't have caused her any pain, but they're just out of line."

"And that would show up in an x-ray," Freya added, to which Southwell smiled knowingly. "Sadly, dentists do not share patient records the way the police do, which means that we'll need a name, and then we'll need to understand who their dentist was, and then we'll need to hope they still have the records."

"Ten years for patient data," Southwell said. "If you can put a name to her, then there's a good chance that whoever extracted that wisdom tooth would still have their records."

"Hang on," Ben said, and he grabbed his phone from his pocket. He dialled Chapman's number and then set the call to loudspeaker for the others to hear.

"Hi, Ben," Chapman said, in her pleasant sing-song voice.

"Denise, I need a favour."

"Another one?"

"The mispers," he said. "There were five names on the list and three of them were male. Do you remember?" Freya's eyes widened and she gave him a proud-looking smile just as he had given to Cruz. "There was one other name. I need it."

They heard her flicking through her notes and then the handset bagged against the desk.

"Holly Carson," she said.

"Holly Carson," Ben said. "Chapman, I love you."

"Oh," she replied, clearly unsure of how to respond.

"Chapman, it's me," Freya said. "Don't worry, I'm not going to declare my undying love for you, but I would be grateful if you could dig out whatever you can on her. And if it's at all possible to do so without alerting her parents, could you contact the local dentists to see if they have her records? Katy Southwell seems to think our victim had a wisdom tooth extraction."

"Lower left," Southwell said, leaning in to be heard.

"Lower left," Chapman repeated, and Ben imagined her scribbling her notes down. "Right, leave it with me."

The call ended and Ben pocketed his phone.

"It's a long shot," Freya said.

"It might be a long shot, but it's the only one we've got," he replied. "And if it's not Holly Carson, then we'll take whatever Katy can give us and ask the dentists to go through their entire patient database if needs be."

Freya's eyes narrowed as she smiled and her crow's feet seemed especially deep in the afternoon light. "You're quite tenacious," she told him.

"And I'm quite busy," Southwell said, pulling her hood back onto her head. "So, if you'll excuse me."

"Thank you, Katy," Ben told her. "And I'm sorry."

"For what?" she asked.

"Well, if you were hoping to see Jim anytime this week, I'm afraid you might have to reset your expectations."

"To be honest, I was expecting to see him here," she replied and then winked at Ben. "But that's okay. You know how I feel about mixing work and pleasure."

CHAPTER TWENTY-NINE

"I'm sorry about my husband," Mariam said. "He's...he's a difficult man sometimes."

Jackie reread the message from Anderson and pocketed her phone.

"At least you're still together," she said. "You know, I've been in this job a while now and you'd be surprised at how long some people take to break. Some never do. They just carry their burdens with them. Others welcome the grief. We're all different. We all handle trauma in our own way."

Jackie paused to consider the question she needed to ask. She considered framing it innocently and letting Mariam read between the lines. But something told her she should just come out with it. Rip the plaster off, as they say.

"Mariam, is Reggie a drinker?" she asked, and Mariam squeezed her eyes closed. "My colleagues have just seen him go into the pub up the road. I thought you should know."

"He is a drinker," she said sadly. For a moment, Jackie thought she might add to the sentence, but she left it there.

"Was it Deborah that led him to it?" Jackie asked. "Something like that can trigger—"

"No," she said, cutting her off. "No, he's always drank." She let her hands drop to her lap with a slap and sighed. "Look at us," she said, looking around the room. "We're one step away from living in squalor. The bills need paying, the car needs work, and where's he? In the pub, squandering it, while I'm here trying to hold it all together. You must think I'm mad for staying. Anyone else would have upped and left a long time ago."

"I'm not here to judge," Jackie said.

"But I couldn't," she continued. "Do you see? I couldn't. What if she came home? What if Debs came home and I was gone? Then what? How would she find me?" She shook her head. "No, I had to stay. I stay for her."

It was a fact that no longer held true, yet to voice it would have been unprofessional. Had Jackie been a friend of Mariam's, who was there simply to console her, then she might have said the words.

You don't have to stay anymore. Not if you don't want to.

But that wasn't her place. Besides, the look on Mariam's face suggested she had drawn the same conclusion.

"I told you, I'm not here to judge," Jackie told her. "This is a difficult time for you."

"It is. It really is," she said. "It's odd. Reggie said that we should just let it lie. That we've done our grieving and we should just move on. That we shouldn't let you lot drag everything up again. But I'm not quite sure if I *have* grieved. You know? I always thought she was out there somewhere. I genuinely believed that she'd just upped and left and gone to Lincoln, or London even."

"It's understandable," Jackie said. "And if it's any help at all, I totally agree. I would have been the same, I think."

"Do you have children?"

"I do. A boy."

"How old?"

"He's ten now."

Mariam turned away, perhaps remembering what it was like to

have a ten-year-old. Perhaps wondering if Jackie was prepared for the turmoil that was to come when Charlie reached his teenage years and then adulthood. That time when a parent thinks they've made it. They've guided, steered, and raised their child all the way so that they're armed with the information and experience they need to survive. Only to have those thoughts quashed. Not in an instant, but in a five-year-long state of limbo where the parent is left wondering where they are, what they're doing, and at the back of their mind, if they're still alive.

"We can put you in touch with some support groups, Mariam. They can really help, and they're free."

"Sit with other parents, you mean? Other failures?"

"You're not a failure. Don't think like that."

Mariam let her face drop into her hands and her body stilled until she gave a loud sob.

"I should have stopped it. I should have known," she mumbled through her tears and then looked up at Jackie. "I'm her mum, for God's sake. I was her mum."

"Should have stopped what?"

"I should have helped her," she said, ignoring Jackie's question. "You know? When she used to shut herself in her bedroom, I should have been more forceful. I should have probed and prodded and...I don't know. Got through to her somehow. Like a real mother would have."

"You can't blame yourself, Mariam."

"She was hurting," she said. "I should have seen the signs, but I was too busy. Too busy trying to make ends meet. Too busy working all the hours under the sun. You know, I used to see her walking around town on her own, head down, lost in her own world. And people I'd meet, friends, they'd tell me how they'd seen her walking in the fields on her own while they were walking their dog."

"She must have had friends," Jackie said. "What about Kevin Stone?"

Mariam hissed through her teeth dismissively.

"Kevin Stone," she said. "He was just a plaything. A lad she used to distract her from her own world. That's what she did, see? She'd bury herself in other people's lives but she'd never speak about her own. I should have known it when they brought her home in a police car. I should have known it would end in tears. But you don't, do you? You tell yourself it's a phase. That growing up is difficult and that she'd come out of it one day. Maybe even find a job. It kept happening."

"The breaking and entering episodes?" Jackie probed, and Mariam gave an ashamed nod.

"I know why she was doing it. She needed the money. I had none to give her, not enough for her to do what she wanted to do anyway. Maybe if I had, then this wouldn't have happened. Maybe if I'd understood how badly she wanted to get away, I could have helped her make a start. You know, got her a flat or helped her find a little job or something. I could have taken her shopping on my days off, as real mums do, you know? Made sure she had the basics, milk, bread, and whatnot. Maybe I could have even helped her with her housework, and over time, she might have come out of her shell and joined the real world."

"Nobody is blaming you, Mariam," Jackie said. "Okay? Nobody. None of this is your fault."

"I thought she was saving to get away. In fact, I knew she was. I know she was stealing it now, but she had a purpose. She needed a deposit on a place. She needed enough to get by until she found a job. A few thousand, at least. But every time she'd get some cash together, he'd find it."

"Reggie, you mean?" Jackie said, and she nodded. "He took her money?"

"The money she stole, yeah," she grumbled. "Beer money, no doubt. I never saw a penny of it, that's for sure. But it didn't stop her. She'd come home with more, find more ingenious places to hide it. But he'd always find it." She smiled suddenly. Not a beaming grin that lit up her face but a sad smile. A proud smile. "When she went, I looked through her room. Couldn't find a penny. That's why I figured she'd finally done it. She'd finally got enough to make a go of it."

"But she didn't say goodbye," Jackie said. "Wasn't that odd?"

"No, not really. She hated it here. She hated him," she said. "I always thought she'd be back one day when she didn't need us anymore. When she could stand up to him. Maybe we could have stood up to him together. I just thought she'd be back for her clothes and whatever else she needed. Then one day became two, and I don't know, I just had this feeling. I was positive she was okay, but what if she wasn't?"

"That's when you filed a missing person's report?" Jackie said, and she nodded.

"Maybe if I'd taken the time to understand her, she might have told me what was going on. I would have known how much she had saved and even helped her hide it from him. But I didn't. I failed her."

"Mariam—"

"I failed her," she insisted. "I should have known she had nothing and that she was missing, but instead I just told the policeman what I thought."

"And you thought she had run away to make a start somewhere else," Jackie said, and the conversation faded into memories and regret. "Listen, why don't you go upstairs and get showered? I'll have a tidy-up down here for you. How does that sound? You'll feel better after a nice shower."

Mariam was still for a moment, lost in her thoughts. She gazed at the carpet, unblinking, and then stared up at Jackie.

"You're nice, you are," she said. "I can see why you do this."

"I just want to help," Jackie said, and she began collecting the mugs from the coffee table, hoping to spur the grieving mother into action. "And when you come down, you can tell me what she was like when she was ten."

"The same age as your boy?"

"Maybe you can give me some pointers," Jackie said as she left the room. "Because believe me, I am not ready for whatever is coming my way."

"That's just it," Mariam said, and she smiled genuinely for the first time. "Nothing can prepare you for what's coming."

CHAPTER THIRTY

Freya flitting around the incident room, preparing her briefings, always reminded Ben of his school days, when the room would hush at the teacher's arrival and hissed conversations and silent gestures would pass between him and his friends. The only real difference in the adult world was that people replaced the hissed conversations and silent gestures with expressions, usually centred around wide eyes or shrugs.

"If you thought this investigation was growing heads faster than we can chop them off, then you should prepare yourselves," Freya said, as she wrote on her whiteboard with her back to the team. She snapped the lid back on the pen and then turned. "In fact, it's rather becoming a modern-day hydra."

Those wide eyes and confused expressions returned on more than one of the faces in the room.

"It's Greek mythology," Freya explained, slightly disappointed in the team's general knowledge. "The multi-headed beast?"

"Cruz would have known that," Chapman said. "He's the one for useless facts."

"With all due respect, Denise," Nillson said, "Cruz spends his life watching documentaries and attending quiz nights. Some of us have lives."

"True," Freya replied. "But in his defence, what we witnessed at the MacMillan house this afternoon was actually quite remarkable. I'd go as far as to say that he has become quite competent, and I'd appreciate it if we could all treat him with a little more respect. The last thing I want is for his newfound confidence to be destroyed because, believe me, he could give us all a run for your money."

"So splitting him and Gillespie has worked, has it?" Nillson asked. "How does Gillespie feel about that?"

"Frankly, I don't care how Gillespie feels. What I'm concerned with is ensuring that each and every one of you performs to the highest possible standard. And do you know what? It's taken a year but I finally feel like we're there. If Granger walked in here now and told me I had to lose a member of the team for budgeting reasons, I would have an extremely difficult time making that decision." She let the sentiment rest for a moment and then gave a friendly smile. "But don't, for heaven's sake, tell Gillespie that."

And just like a few of the better teachers from Ben's schooldays had managed, Freya raised a few warm laughs.

"Now then," she said. "Let's see if we can cut some of these heads off, shall we? Has anyone heard from Gold?"

"Nothing yet," Chapman said.

"Give her a quick call," Freya said. "See if she's in a position to talk. If not, can one of you send her the minutes of the briefing?"

Chapman assumed her usual role and quietly dialled Gold's number, leaving Freya to continue.

"Primary suspect," she said, tapping a name on the board. "Kevin Stone. I still want more on him before we can bring him into custody. He was the last person to see her, he had access to the property, and from what we can gather from Anne Hargreaves, he had a thing for Deborah. Now, that doesn't tie the noose around his neck, but it does bathe him in a new light. He had the means and opportunity, but until we know more about their relationship, we can't begin to understand his motive. Did he make an advance and she turned him down? Did he force himself on her?"

"Southwell did state there was no evidence of a sexual assault," Ben said.

"The act of rape, Ben, is not the only definition of a sexual assault. Just because we cannot prove that they had intercourse, consensual or otherwise, does not mean that he did not satisfy his urges by some other means."

"How do you prove that five years after the fact?" Anderson asked, with more than a hint of flippancy in her tone.

"You tell me, Anderson," she said. "What does all the research on sex offenders tell us?"

"Hold on, we can't label him as a sex offender on the back of a theory," Ben said.

"For the purposes of developing a theory, I will label him Father Bloody Christmas if it brings us one step closer to the truth."

Ben stayed silent, and although he was clearly unhappy with the decision, he knew when to step back from an argument.

"They're typically recidivists, boss," Nillson said, and Freya clicked her fingers and pointed at her.

"Repeat offenders," Freya announced and then circled his name again before turning back to face the team.

"He's done it before?" Anderson asked.

"Or since," she replied, and she pointed to Anderson. "There's one for you. Every unsolved sexual assault within a mile radius of Stone's house. No, expand that. Within a mile of Stone's house and a mile of the MacMillan house. We know they moved house in May 2019. See if there's a trend. You're looking for anything from stranger rape and date rape right the way down to flashing. Just as history tells us that serial killers progress in their careers through an escalation of severity, so too do sexual predators. They start small and their habits develop. They grow more confident, they develop trademarks, but most of all, they grow hungry for it. It's like a drug habit that needs feeding, and every time, they need more."

Anderson nodded, taking on board every word Freya spoke.

"I've got her," Chapman said, and Freya gave the nod to put Gold onto loudspeaker.

"Gold, how's it going?" she asked.

"Oh, it's as I expected," Gold replied. "She's taken the news badly, I'm afraid."

"And have you learned much?" Freya asked, not wanting to delve into the emotional side of the account and focus more on the objective details. "Where is she anyway? Are you alone?"

"I sent her upstairs to have a shower," Gold said, her voice quiet and reserved presumably so that she wasn't overheard. "What we thought about the misper was right. She thought Deborah had run away, so when she filed the report, the details were overlooked. It turns out that she knew about Deborah's B and E charges. She knew that Deborah was saving up so she could leave the house and move to a city somewhere, but every time she built up a sum of money, Reggie Jarvis found it and spent it in the pub. Then when she finally disappeared, Mariam searched her room but couldn't find any money, so she assumed that she'd finally got away." Gold paused and the saliva clicked in her mouth. "She waited for five years, hoping that one day she'd come back."

The room was quiet, each of them imagining just how painful that must have been.

"Well," Freya said, "that gives us a little insight into Deborah's state of mind. Thank you, Gold. But to bring you up to speed, Cruz has made a discovery at the MacMillan house."

"What?" Gold said. "Not another body?"

"This one was in the garden," Freya said. "Multiple broken bones, so the MO is different, and due to being buried in the soil, there isn't really a great deal left from which Katy Southwell can extract DNA, which leaves us with very little in the way of a means to date the remains and also to identify them. Now, Ben has a theory that the remains could belong to Holly Carson–"

"The girl on the mispers list," Nillson said.

"Right. I, however, am doubtful that it would be that easy. In fact, given the number of heads on our mythical beast, I'm inclined to believe that our jobs just became significantly harder."

"Christ," Gold said. "Have we spoken to the parents yet?"

"No, and we're not going to," Freya told her. "At least not until we know for certain. I'm not putting another family through what Mrs Jarvis is going through until we can be sure."

"How are we going to do that?" Gold asked.

"Dental records," Freya said. "And before you pass judgement, it served us well before the days of DNA. In fact, dental records were one of the deciding factors that put Ted Bundy behind bars. They are as unique as DNA and fingerprints."

"Hold on," Gold said, and they heard her fumbling with her phone, and then walking through the house. "Mariam, are you okay?" The team waited for Gold to deal with her charge. "Sorry, guv," Gold said. "I just want to make sure she's okay. I think I heard something."

Freya caught the team's attention.

"Let's get our heads into this," Freya said. "Facial recognition was a dead end, but we still have the bank notes and that plastic sheeting, and we still need something on Kevin Stone."

"Guv, I've got something here," Chapman said. "I've been looking into Holly Carson's social media accounts."

"Right?" Freya said.

"Most of them have been closed down, but her LinkedIn account is still active. It says here that her current position is a Junior Accountant."

"Don't tell me–"

"At Liam Finch's firm," Chapman said. "The last time she logged on was 2017."

Freya stared at Ben across the room, knowing that he had similar feelings about the man. But the news remained the focus of their attention for only a few short seconds.

"Oh God," Gold said. Her voice was no longer whispered and discreet, and they heard a commotion across the phone line as she ran across loose floorboards. "Mariam? Mariam?"

"Gold, talk to me," Freya said, noting the concerned expressions on every face in the room. "Do you need assistance?"

Gold was breathless and her movements hard to interpret.

"I need an ambulance, guv," she replied eventually. "She's bloody overdosed."

CHAPTER THIRTY-ONE

"We seem to have grown yet another head," Freya said when Gold had ended the call to deal with her own emergency. But the remark did little to raise a smile. "Ben, find Reginald Jarvis, will you? I think we both know where he'll be."

Ben considered the instruction thoughtfully and then stood to leave the room. He stopped at the doorway.

"And if he wants to go to the hospital?" Ben asked. "I doubt he'll be in a state to drive."

"And I doubt that visiting his wife in hospital will even occur to him," Freya said. "I'll leave you to handle it how you see fit. But stay with him. Don't let him out of your sight."

Ben nodded and left the room, letting the doors close behind him.

"Am I still looking into sexual offences, boss?" Anderson asked. "Given that there's a strong possibility that the second body is Holly Carson, considering that she worked for Liam Finch, I mean."

"Yes," Freya said. "I'm not ready to let go of Kevin Stone yet. Nillson, I want you on Liam Finch. Chapman, round up the evidence, will you? Chase the dental records and the banknotes. If the remains do belong to Holly Carson, then we have a strong link to Liam Finch. If they do not, then we'll need to link whoever it is to one of the names on our board."

"I've made some initial enquiries, guv," Chapman said. "I've requested warrants for Holly Carson's bank statements and phone records. I'm hoping the judge gets it back to us today, given the momentum of this investigation. Sorry if that was a bit presumptuous, but he came back to me with warrants for Liam Finch's and Kevin Stone's, so I thought I'd get in there while he was responding."

"Not presumptuous at all," Freya told her. "So, when can we expect Liam Finch's bank records?"

"An hour or so," she replied. "I've had to take the long route via customer services."

"Oh, well, rather you than me," Freya said.

"Boss, Anderson and I were thinking," Nillson said, and she pushed herself up from her chair and then walked across the room to the whiteboard. "Do you mind?"

"Be my guest," Freya said. "Are we cutting off a head? I do hope so."

"Not cutting it off, exactly," Nillson replied. "But I like to think that we're sharpening the blade."

Freya grinned at the analogy and nodded for her to carry on. Handing Nillson the marker, she uncapped it and then circled a date on the timeline.

"We know that Deborah was last seen on the sixth of May," she began. "Now, Anderson and I spoke to the estate agents and we can confirm that the move happened on the seventh. He even put us in touch with the removal firm."

"He has a good memory," Freya said.

"Local firm," Nillson said. "And the house is quite distinctive. He remembered it well."

"Go on," Freya said.

"Well, we spoke to the removal firm to double check and as it happens the manager was one of the team who did the move. It was before he was promoted, so he was still on the tools, as it were. Now, he remembers the entire family being involved. The husband, the wife, and the boy—"

"Kevin Stone."

"Right. He also remembers them being involved at the other end. Shifting boxes and unpacking. You know, the usual routine?"

"I know it a little too well," Freya said.

"Well, that leaves us a window," Nillson said. "If she went missing on the sixth and the house was presumably full of people going back and forth on the seventh, then when was Deborah moved to the house? I mean, we're talking about Kevin Stone or Liam Finch being our primary suspects now, but they couldn't have ripped up the floor on the night of the sixth, could they? They would have woken the whole house up."

"Funnily enough, Ben and I had a similar discussion," Freya said, nodding her agreement.

"Which also begs the question, where was Deborah for the duration? I know Haverholme Park quite well and I know the footpath that runs along the fence line. Even if Kevin Stone was responsible and he hid her body in the trees while his mates helped him look for her, there's no way that nobody would have discovered her during the seventh. The place is dog-walker heaven. I just don't think it's feasible."

"Are you leading up to a theory?" Freya asked.

"Kind of," she replied. "You see, if it was Kevin Stone, then he wouldn't have had a great deal of time. He couldn't have carted her off and then gone back. There simply wasn't time. He had what, ten minutes? No chance. But he could have stashed her in the trees, prevented the others from finding her during the search, and then gone back for her when they had all gone home."

"But if it was Liam Finch, then he would have had time to cart her off," Freya surmised.

"Right," Nillson said. "I think we need to find out exactly

what he was doing on that night, and given that it was the night before the house move, then I think it should be quite prominent in his wife's memory."

Freya nodded.

"Good work," she said. "I have to say that I quite agree."

"There is one other thing," Nillson said. "Regardless of whether it was Kevin Stone or Liam Finch, whoever was responsible had to have somewhere to keep her at least until the eighth when the house was empty."

"Somewhere?" Freya said, leaving the question open. "Do you have somewhere in mind?"

Nillson grinned.

"We do," she said. "We have the perfect place."

———

The pub was like any other at that time of the day. A single barman worked the bar, the tables and chairs were mostly empty, and the only people drinking were those that were either there for lunch or were there for the long haul.

Reggie Jarvis was there for the long haul, as depicted by having positioned himself on a bar stool from where he could find somebody to talk to, benefit from a speedy service, and watch the football highlights on the wall-mounted TV.

Not being much of a drinker, Ben found the practice an absurd waste of time, but he did have a friend called Snowy who adopted a similar strategy in his local, and he rarely had a bad word to say about anything. So, he surmised, there must be some kind of peace to be found from sitting at a bar all day long.

He dropped onto the bar stool beside Jarvis and caught the barman's attention.

"Just a water for me, thanks," he said. "No ice."

The request was enough to stir Jarvis' memory, and he stiffened at the sound of Ben's voice.

"Wondered if you'd turn up here," he grumbled, without turning to face Ben. A team in red and white was playing a team in light blue, but as for who was winning, who the teams were, and the significance of the game, Ben had no idea.

"I thought it was time we had a little talk," Ben said. "A serious talk."

"Then you thought wrong," Jarvis said, and finally he tore his eyes from the TV and turned in his seat to face forward, still refusing to look Ben's way. "I've said all I have to say on the matter."

"Well, I doubt it would come as a surprise to you to learn that in these circumstances, you don't get to decide when the conversation ends."

The barman placed a glass down before him and then positioned the half-empty water bottle beside it. Ben slid a five-pound note across the bar and nodded his thanks. The barman returned a moment later with two pound coins in change, and then sloped off to the far end of the bar, leaving Ben to consider his three-pound bottle of water in silence.

"We knew, you know? I told you, we all knew she'd gone."

"That's not what your wife has to say," Ben told him. "According to her, she was under the impression that Deborah would return one day. That's what she was holding out for."

"Well, she's a fool," Jarvis said. "She's been living in denial. Maybe now she'll come back to the real world. Maybe now I'll get my wife back," he said, and then finally turned to look Ben in the eye. "I know what you think," he said, then checked to make sure he wasn't being overheard. "You think I did it."

"Nobody has said that, have they?"

"They didn't need to," Jarvis said, and he took a large mouthful of his pint, wiping his mouth with his sleeve. "I know how these things work. Daughter goes missing. Dad's got form. It doesn't take a rocket scientist to put two and two together to get three, does it?"

Ben sipped at his water. It was no different at all to that which he drew from his kitchen tap.

"So help me get to four," he said. "I'll show my workings and you can tell me where I went wrong."

Jarvis grinned at how Ben had expanded on his little cliche and then cleared his throat.

"Go on then," he said. "Tell me how you came to three."

Somebody in one of the teams scored and Jarvis was momentarily distracted, but the pull wasn't enough to keep his attention for long.

"You have previous charges against you for domestic abuse—"

"Which were dropped," Jarvis said.

"Which were dropped," Ben agreed. "Which means that we couldn't use that as evidence in a court of law, but it does give us cause to believe that you are potentially capable."

"Eh?"

"We don't need a charge to develop a theory, Reg, and we'd be remiss if we ignored the fact that your own wife has reported you on multiple occasions and subsequently dropped the charges."

"Loyalty was never her strong point," he said, sipping at his beer as if he was untouchable.

"And if you are capable of violence against your own wife, then it does raise questions about what else you're capable of," Ben said.

"Ah," Jarvis replied. "Hence, three."

"Deborah stayed away from home as often as she could, didn't she?"

"No doubt sleeping with whoever would put her up for the night," Jarvis replied, and his eyes rolled around to meet Ben's incredulous stare. "You'd be amazed at what that girl would have done for money."

"Oh yes. I've heard about her methods of raising money so that one day she could get away. Breaking and entering, for example. But it's not her methods that bother me, Reg. It's her reasons for wanting to get away in the first place."

"Back to me then, yeah?" Jarvis said. "All roads lead to me, do they?"

"Not all roads," Ben said. "But even you must be able to see why we'd want to take a drive down them to see where they go. Talk to me properly, Reg. Honestly, why did Deborah want to get away from you so badly? What were you doing to her that could have possibly driven a child from her home?"

"It's not what you think before you say it." He shook his head. "I never touched her. Not like that, anyway. I'm not an animal, you know?"

"Well, I'm sure the forensics team will be able to tell us," Ben said, taking a large mouthful of his drink to give Jarvis enough time to react.

"You what?"

Ben swallowed hard and used a napkin to dry his lips.

"Oh, you'd be surprised at what they can do these days."

Jarvis turned his head away and Ben waited patiently. It was time to say nothing. It was an old sales technique that translated to police work. A salesman would, after his pitch, deliver the price, and then remain silent. The theory was that whoever spoke next lost. If the customer spoke, then he would no doubt buy, but if the salesman spoke, then the customer would walk away.

Jarvis spoke.

"She were a difficult one, our Debs," he said. "From the outset, she made life hard. Takes after her grandma on her mother's side, she did. Always had to have the last word, always poking her nose in. Your forensics people can do what they like," he said. "They'll find nowt on me. I'm not like that. I'm many things, but I'm not one of them."

"But you did beat her," Ben said, and again Jarvis fell into silence. "I'm going to ask you a simple question and then I'm going to leave you alone."

"Alright," Jarvis grumbled.

"Where were you the night she went missing?" Ben asked, and Jarvis shook his head.

"In here most likely," he replied. "That were a dark period."

"Darker than now?" Ben asked.

"Darker," he replied. "Much darker. Money was tight. I was out of work. Wife hated me, daughter hated me. What do you think I was going to do, sit at home where I weren't wanted?"

"So, presumably nobody can vouch for you?" Ben said. "Given that it was five years ago, which I'm afraid confirms it."

"Confirms what?"

"That two and two add up to three," Ben said, as he rose from his seat.

"You can ask her if you like. She'll tell you. No doubt she'll have some story about how I came home steaming drunk."

"Oh, I doubt she'll have much to say on the matter," Ben said, and he leaned in to whisper into the dreadful man's ear. "She attempted suicide about an hour ago."

"You what?" he said, loud enough to gain the attention of the punters.

Ben made his way over to the door, where he turned to give him two last pieces of advice.

"She's in Lincoln County Hospital, Reg," he said. "But don't drive, eh? I'd hate for a drunk driving charge to get in the way of nicking you for what you really are."

"And what's that?" he said, but Ben ignored the question and let the doors close behind him. He had just climbed into his car when the doors burst open and Jarvis ran out into the car park, coming to a stop at the car bonnet.

"Well? What am I?" he said. "Aren't you going to take me to see her? Is that it, is it? You came all this way to wind me up and tell me what she's done?" He ran around to the passenger door and Ben quickly hit the button to lock the doors. Jarvis rattled the handle a few times and then banged on the glass. "You taking me, or what?"

Ben's phone announced a new message had arrived and he glanced down to read it.

"Well?" Jarvis said. "You gonna take me to see her, or what?"

"Oh, I don't think so," Ben said, sliding the gear selector into drive. "In fact, in my opinion, if she pulls through this, she'll be better off without you."

CHAPTER THIRTY-TWO

The little stone bridge that crossed the River Slea was adjacent to the field in which Kevin Stone and his friends had spent the evening five years earlier. But Ben wasn't interested in the field, or the fence, or the stile, or the trees. He crossed the bridge and pulled the car into a small car park on the right-hand side, where he found Freya's Range Rover waiting. He parked beside her and climbed out, knowing full well that she would take her sweet time. It was another of her power plays to make people wait for her. But Ben didn't mind. In fact, after his run-in with Reginald Jarvis, a short wait in the fresh air was a welcome tonic.

"You summoned me," he said.

"I wouldn't have put it like that," she replied. "But thanks for coming. How did it go?"

He puffed his cheeks and considered how he might respond.

"Are we using the lots of heads metaphor?"

"If you wish."

"Well, I did try to chop one off," he said. "But I think I just made it angry."

He grinned at her and she shook her head.

"Did you tell him?"

"Eventually, yes," he said, as she opened the rear door of her car and began changing her footwear. "Wellies?"

"These shoes were nearly two hundred pounds, Ben," she told him.

"Mine were about forty quid," he replied, and he looked down at the scuffed Oxfords he'd been wearing for as long as he could remember.

"That much?" she said, in mock surprise. She closed the boot lid, locked the car, and then led him across the car park. "What did he have to say?"

"Only that he swears blind he wasn't abusing her. Not sexually, anyway," Ben said. "But then he would say that, wouldn't he?"

"Physical abuse?"

"Almost certainly," he replied. "We'll never prove it, of course, but he doesn't know that."

"And on the night his daughter went missing? Where was he then?"

"In the pub, apparently."

"Another claim we'll never prove."

"Hence the lack of head in my hands," Ben said. "I got what I needed from him before I told him about his wife."

"No wonder he was angry," Freya replied. "You need to be more careful in future. Either that or you need to sharpen your sword."

"Something tells me that even if we cut this particular head off, another would grow back in its place," Ben told her, as they came to a stop at the three-bar fence, behind which was a ploughed field, and beyond that the ruined remains of Haver-holme Priory.

Ben glanced down at her boots and then back at the ruins.

"No, don't tell me—"

But Freya had already started to climb. She held out her hand and Ben found himself helping her despite his protests. She dropped down into the mud and made a show of waiting for him to follow.

"Freya, this is private property," he said. "There are bloody signs everywhere."

"Oh, damn," she said, and he immediately recognised her sarcastic tone. "I forgot, whoever went to the lengths of murdering Deborah Jarvis wouldn't have dared to climb a little fence and do a little trespassing."

He shook his head at her.

"We could call the owner," he said. "I'm sure they would let us in."

But Freya turned on her heels and began walking towards the old building.

"The killer didn't call the owner, did he?" she called back, leaving Ben no option but to climb the fence and traipse after her. "How far do you think it is? Two hundred yards?"

"Something like that," he said, looking back at the car park to gauge the distance. "It's close enough to carry someone on your shoulder, that's for sure."

"Or drag them," Freya said.

The ruins were relatively small but the undulating ground suggested it had at one time been far larger. At one end of the building, a hexagonal tower stood taller than the rest, with a parapet wall sitting on top. The rest of the building was a simple skeleton of what it used to be. Now all that remained were empty windows beneath roofless walls, mostly built from what looked like local stone, apart from one wall to the rear.

"This wasn't the original building. You know that, don't you?" he told her.

"Was it here five years ago?" she asked, as they came to stand in its shadow. "That's all I care about."

"It's a designated ancient monument. We can't go inside before you try."

"I wonder if our killer knew that," Freya said, and she winked at him before stepping up closer to peer in through the windows.

"I mean it, Freya. The bloody thing could fall down at any minute."

"Stop whining," she told him. "I'm not going inside. I just want to have a look."

They found exactly what Ben thought they would find – leaves blown in by the winds across the field all piled into corners, along with pieces of rubbish, and, of course, the inevitable graffiti. Not lots, but no doubt some of the local kids had taken refuge in there at some point and had, for some reason, decided to scratch their name in history so that everyone knew they had broken the law.

Freya walked with her hands behind her back, as if she was walking through a crime scene and making efforts not to touch any surfaces. Ben kept his hands in his pockets, keeping a keen eye out for the owner, and praying that, should they come out to shoo them off, Freya wouldn't antagonise them further.

"Have you given much thought to Granger's proposition?" she asked.

"His what?"

"To transferring," she said.

"Yes, as it happens," he said. "And if I have to, I will."

She glanced back at him, caught his eye, and then looked ahead.

"You would do that, would you?"

"To be with you, yes," he said. "And you?"

"Would I chain myself to a desk to be with you?" she asked. "I wouldn't be keen on it."

"I didn't say I'd be keen to transfer," he told her.

"You know my office doesn't even have a window?"

"Nor does Granger's."

"And you're aware that I would be insufferably irritable?"

"Oh, that would make a nice change," he said with a laugh. "The point is, Freya, that you either would or you wouldn't."

"No," she said, coming to a stop. "The point is that we must make a decision. Either we marry and one of us becomes unhappy or we don't marry."

"And one of us becomes unhappy," he said.

"And one of us has to reset their expectations," she corrected him.

As if by divine intervention, or sheer belligerence, Ben's phone began to vibrate and Gillespie's name showed up on the screen.

"Jim," he said, answering the call. "What's up?"

"You with the boss, Ben?"

"I am," Ben replied.

"Am I on loudspeaker?"

"No," he replied, and he gestured for Freya to hold on a second. She took the hint and sauntered off to peer through another empty window frame.

"I've just got back from knocking on the doors, mate."

"I know, I heard," Ben told him, checking his watch. "Four hours, Jim. That's nearly an hour a house."

"I know. I ran into a spot of bother."

"Car trouble? I told you those brakes need sorting, didn't I?"

"It's not the car, Ben. It's one of the owners of the house."

"Okay," Ben said, and he walked away from the ruins to ensure Freya couldn't hear his responses. "What about them? Are they worth investigating?"

"Definitely not," Gillespie snapped. "That's the bloody last thing I need."

"Jim, if you need my help, mate, you're going to have to start explaining."

"I knew her, didn't I?"

"Sorry?"

"I've met her before," Gillespie said. "You know?"

"You've *met her* met her? As in, you're well acquainted with her?"

"Very well acquainted," he replied. "And when she worked out who I was, she tried to reacquaint herself with me."

"Oh God, Jim. Don't tell me that you–"

"No, of course I didn't. I've got bloody Katy a few hundred yards away."

"Well, I'm sure there are other reasons for not getting involved with a woman down the road from a crime scene."

"I'm not bloody daft, Ben. But she wouldn't let me go. Bloody threw herself at me."

"Well, why did you go inside? Why didn't you just walk away and send Gabby?"

"I didn't realise who she was until I was inside and she was putting the bleeding kettle on. By that point, I was stuck."

"So, how did you leave it?"

"I left it by walking out of the door and her yelling abuse at me, threatening to make a complaint about me. She chased me down the drive with her bloody blouse hanging open, Ben. You should have bloody seen it. It was like a scene from Benny Bloody Hill."

"Oh, for God's sake."

"I know. What do I do? I knew I should have sent Gabby to do the door-knocking. I bloody knew it."

"Just stay calm," Ben told him.

"But what if Katy finds out? She'll hit the roof, Ben."

"I think Katy is the least of your worries right now," he said, eying Freya. "Just leave it with me. I'll have a word with the front desk. If anything comes in, I'll see if it can come my way."

"The boss can't find out, Ben. She doesn't need a reason to give me a grilling. I'll be a bloody coffee boy for the next ten years if she finds out."

"Just...just leave it with me, alright? Go and see Cruz. He could do with some help."

"Aye, I'm here now. They've excavated the remains and are working on the lift."

"Right, and if I were you, I would do everything you possibly can to keep Freya on your side. If any of this comes back to bite you in the backside, you want to be on the front foot, all right?"

"Aye, gotcha," Gillespie said. "Nice one, Ben. I knew I could count on you."

"Just help Cruz. And for God's sake, do something right. He's done a great job in your absence, so you've got some work to do."

"Aye right."

"One more thing," Ben said. "You were gone for four hours."

"Aye, I know."

"And you didn't–"

"I promise, I didn't," he said. "I didn't know what to do, so I legged it."

"You did what?"

"Well, I didn't want to go back to the house straight away in case she followed. So I legged it. Hid in a lay-by up the road."

"You're your own worst enemy, James Gillespie," Ben said.

"Aye, I know I am. But what was I to do? What if she'd followed me? Listen, I'm going to crack on and just pray she doesn't come marching up the driveway, and if she does, then I hope to God she's got some bloody clothes on. I'll catch you in a bit."

"I'll talk to you later," Ben said, and he ended the call.

"Trouble in paradise?" Freya said when Ben approached her from behind. She was peering into the old building, being careful not to touch any of the stonework.

"Oh, I think he really likes Katy Southwell," Ben said. "I think this is his first relationship."

Freya nodded slightly as if she didn't quite believe his explanation. But to expand on his lie would have only served to heighten her sense of deception.

"Is Katy still at the house then, is she?"

"He says they're just lifting the remains out," Ben explained.

"They'll be transported back in boxes and we can get the GPR team back in. Why's that?"

"Oh, no reason," she said, quietly, and then nodded at something through the window. Ben followed her gaze, and let out a gasp. "Except that I want her to look at that before she leaves."

CHAPTER THIRTY-THREE

"She's gone, Ben. She didn't make it." Gold's voice was weak and cracked with emotion.

Ben heard the words, considered the consequences, and then translated them into feelings.

"You okay?" he asked.

"Yeah, I will be," she replied. "I was just getting to know her. I really felt for her, you know? She was a good mum. She was hurting and I should have seen it."

"Hey now," he said. "You can't blame yourself. You weren't to know, and it's not in your remit to keep people alive. Your job is to provide support to those who need it and to report back on anything you find. Nothing more."

"But she *did* need support," she said. "She needed someone to support her. Her bloody husband isn't going to do it."

"Oh God," Ben said and again he checked his watch. "He's drunk, and he's on his way, hopefully in a taxi and not driving himself. Listen, find a uniformed officer and commandeer them. I don't want you alone. The man's a menace to himself and those around him, and judging by the way I left him, who knows what he's capable of?"

"There are officers here," she said. "I'll tag along with them."

"Good, and if he does show up, call me, all right?"

"I will," she said and then lingered.

"You sure you're okay, mate?" he asked.

"Yeah," she said, which was a lie, and Ben knew it. "Yeah, I'll be fine. I just need some time, that's all."

"I'll talk to Freya," he said. "It's getting late, so go straight home when you're done. Don't go back to the station. I doubt we'll be going back today. It looks like we'll be here for a while longer, anyway."

"Why, what's happened? Don't tell me they've found another one?"

Ben gave a little laugh and realised that she just needed to hear a friendly voice. So he crouched down beside the ruins while Freya spoke to the owner of the land. Southwell and one of her colleagues worked inside with the added complexity of wearing hard hats and boots over their coveralls and hoods.

"No, but Freya had an idea about searching the priory. The theory is that whoever murdered Deborah needed a place to keep her until the family had moved out of the house, and this is the only viable option."

"Right?" she said, and Ben realised his explanation hadn't been complete. He was too concerned with the dramas that had unfolded in a single day.

"We discovered some plastic that seems to be a match for the material used to wrap up Deborah."

"After all this time? Wouldn't it have blown away?"

"Not necessarily, and it's not like anybody comes in here. And even if they did, it's just a scrap of plastic sheeting you'd see on the side of the road or in a ditch or something."

"It could be something, though," she said.

"It could be," Ben said. "In fact, I'd bet it is. There's no other reason for it being here. And sadly, it means that instead of cutting a head off the beast, it grows another one."

"Sorry?" she said. "What on earth are you talking about?"

"Nothing," Ben said, realising that she hadn't been part of that particular and bizarre conversation. "It's probably just added a layer of complexity, that's all."

"Well, I'd better leave you to it," Gold said softly.

"Go straight home when you're done," he told her. "And if he turns up, call me, all right?"

"I will," she said. "Thanks, Ben."

"Just take care of yourself," he said. "It's just a job at the end of the day. You can't take it home."

She said nothing to that, yet he knew she would be smiling politely. Even when he ended the call and pocketed his phone, he found himself wondering if she would be okay.

Immediately, he pulled his phone from his pocket again and navigated to his recent calls.

"Jim," he said when Gillespie answered. "I've had an idea that would get you out of there and still do a good deed."

"Oh, aye," Gillespie said.

"Mrs Jarvis has died," he said, knowing full well that without any context the statement could have come as a total surprise.

"Eh?"

"Long story, but I need you to get to the hospital to get Gold. She's not coping very well. To be honest, I'm quite worried about her. That should get you away from the house in case the mad woman turns up and it should also put you on the front foot."

Gillespie hesitated and sounded quite breathless.

"You want me to go to the hospital?"

"Gold needs help," he said. "To make matters worse, Mr Jarvis is drunk, unhappy, and on his way down there. Look, this is just what you need, it's what Jackie needs, and to be honest, I could do with it just being taken care of, mate."

"The thing is," Gillespie said. "You told me to make a difference, so I did."

"What are you talking about?"

"I found something," he said. "One of the anomalies that Radar Man found was too small and shallow to remain, so while everyone else was busy, I figured I'd get digging."

"You're digging a hole?"

"I've dug it, Ben," he said. "And I've bloody found something. I need Katy to get back here and help me. Do you know where she is? Some of her team are still here, but–"

"Found what? What is it you found, Jim?"

"Do you remember those photos the boss was going on about? You know, the wardrobe and that? They were in with the mucky images of Deborah Jarvis," he said.

"How could I forget?" Ben said.

"Well, I've found it, Ben," he said. "I've found the bloody box."

"You what? Are you sure?"

"And that's not all," Gillespie said, sounding more and more excited by the second. "You should see what's bloody well inside it!"

CHAPTER THIRTY-FOUR

In comparison to Freya's little cottage, Ben's house was relatively dark and cool. There were no little nicknacks and very few framed photos, but somehow, over the years, it had come to take on Ben's persona. If he were a house, then the walls would be thick and strong and devoid of clutter.

"You're doing that thing again," he said, and Freya shook her thoughts away and found him in the living room doorway staring at her. "Everything okay?"

"Everything is just fine, thank you," she replied. "Now, what are we eating? I'm famished."

Ben crouched to open the coffee table drawer and then pulled out a stack of takeaways menus, which he slapped onto the tabletop.

"Take your pick," he said. "You can order. I'll go and freshen up."

"Have you heard of a little something called chivalry?" she said, collecting the menus from the table. She flicked through them and was faced with the choice of pizza, kebab, Chinese, or Indian.

"Nothing else?"

"Not that delivers," he said.

"And what's in the fridge? Could we make something?"

"If you can make a dinner out of butter, ketchup, and out-of-date milk, then be my guest," he told her, with a sweep of his arm as if to accentuate the invitation.

"Pasta?"

"I might have a Pot Noodle?" he said, and she groaned at the thought of eating it.

She stared at the four options again and then with a heavy heart selected the pizza menu.

"No pineapple," she said, slapping the menu into his chest. "And no chicken. God knows how many times they've reheated it."

"So, I'll order then, shall I?" he said, by which time Freya had dropped into an armchair, kicked off her shoes, and was scrolling through her emails. Fully aware of what he had said, she continued to read her emails until he had huffed and puffed as much as he was going to and ventured off into the kitchen, hopefully, to find a decent bottle of wine.

"If you bring me any of that rubbish with the little ship on the label, you'll be wearing it before the end of the night," she called out and then noticed an email come through from Gillespie. She opened it and saw that there were attachments, so she dug into her bag, dragged her laptop out, and opened the email there. "Ben?" she called, but heard him on the phone to the pizza shop, so she scrolled through the photos. "Oh my God."

"Forty-five minutes," he said when he burst into the room and plonked a bottle of Pinot Grigio onto the coffee table, along with two glasses and a bottle opener. She gave the bottle a cursory glance and then held the laptop up for him to see.

"Have you seen this?"

"Gillespie?" he asked without looking.

"You knew about it?"

"Of course I did. I was the one who told him to send them through."

"You knew about this and you didn't say anything to me?"

"You were too busy insulting the owner of the property," he said. "And then we came home in separate cars."

"Have you ever heard of a telephone?"

"Of course I have. I've been on it all bloody afternoon dealing with Gold, Nillson, and Gillespie, not to mention lining up Pip to work with Katy Southwell, which believe me was no easy feat."

"The box, Ben? He's found the box?"

"Yes, I know. Did well, didn't he?" Ben said. "Apparently, Radar Man said they should ignore it as the anomaly was too small to be human remains." He avoided eye contact, choosing instead to focus on opening the wine. "Good job he did, eh?"

"There's something you're not telling me. What is it?"

"Sorry?"

"Ben, I know your poker face—"

"What? For God's sake, Freya, the poor bloke has done a good job. Can't we just be grateful for it? Maybe even send him a well-done email to keep his spirits up?"

Freya studied him. He poured the wine, as he usually did, but instead of leaving his glass on the table for half an hour and then downing the lot in one gulp, he took a few polite sips.

"Ben?"

"What? Just be glad for him," he told her and then took the laptop from her. "Doesn't look like a shop-bought box. Home-made maybe?"

"Ben?"

"Ah, here we go, the contents. Apparently, there were nine pairs of women's underwear inside." He glanced back at her. "Not to mention the jewellery."

"Ben?"

"Katy Southwell is pretty certain she can get something from the underwear if there's anything to be had. The box preserved them fairly well, considering."

"Ben?"

"That might help us understand who they belonged to. Now, if any of them belong to Deborah Jarvis or our mystery body, then I think we'll have enough for the CPS to give us the go-ahead."

"Ben?"

"What, Freya?" he said. "Just what is it?"

"You're hiding something."

"Aren't I allowed to hide anything?" he said. "Must I recite every conversation I have to you?"

"If it pertains to the investigation, then yes," she said.

"Well it doesn't," he told her. "Believe it or not, not every conversation I have with Jackie, Jim, Gabby, or anybody else for that matter, is about the investigation. Believe it or not, they're my friends. I care about them, and when one of them is in trouble, I want to help them."

"So he's in trouble, is he?"

"Who?"

"Gillespie," she said. "What trouble is he in? Nothing to do with Katy Southwell, I hope. She's bloody good at what she does. It would be a shame to lose her because of a relationship with Gillespie—"

"Freya, you're missing the point," he said. "Look, the bloke tries his hardest to make a difference. He really does. Yes, sure, he sometimes cuts corners and sometimes he takes his rank too seriously, but for the most part, he's a bloody good detective, and more to the point, he's a mate, all right? I suggested that when he got back from door-knocking, he should work his socks off so that you can see how hard he works."

"I know he works hard," Freya said. "I don't need you to tell me that—"

"But does *he* know that? Do you ever show him your appreciation?"

"And now we're venturing into the realms of a lecture on leadership, are we? Well, I can assure you that—"

"It's not a lecture," Ben said, sounding weary. "But look, today I've had to deal with Gold who was close to tears over Mrs Jarvis, Cruz, who was clearly running on pure adrenalin, a drunk and potentially dangerous Reggie Jarvis, Gillespie who is terrified of losing his job—"

"He's what?"

"He'll never admit it but he's terrified," Ben said. "And there's you. Hell-bent on either not marrying me or having me transfer. Heaven forbid that you should even contemplate sitting in an office, which, I might add, every other DCI in the station before you, has done perfectly well and been content."

"Ah," Freya said. "There it is."

"There's what?"

"The real reason for all this...emotion," she said.

"Emotion? Freya, just listen to yourself, will you? What do I have to do to convince you that I love you and want to be with you? What is it going to take, Freya?" he said. "Because honestly, I am running out of ideas here, all right? I can handle all your little foibles—"

"What foibles?"

"I can handle the way you seem to piss everyone you meet off. In fact, I find it quite funny now that I know that it's all a charade. Now I know the real you. But what I can't handle is this pig-headed notion that you think you can cruise through life with your head held high, while the rest of us bend over backwards, not to make you happy, Freya, oh no. We do it to stop you from going off into a rant or a rampage, or worse still, going silent. That's when we know there's danger ahead. When you say nothing. I don't know how you do it, but somehow, it's worse. It's like you have no concept of how hard people try to make you happy, and if you do, then it can only be sheer bloody arrogance that causes you not to acknowledge it."

"Are you finished?"

"No," he said. "Because, if all of that wasn't bad enough, this whole thing about you being the victim of a few Lincoln officers is an absolute joke. I've played along with it so far, I've tried to empathise, but honestly, just think about it. You say that they're purposefully targeting you, that they're trying to destroy your career somehow. One of them had you down for leaving the scene of an accident, another made a complaint about your professionalism, and the other apparently tried to set you up with some false evidence in the hope that your investigation would fall apart. But think about it. Just *think* about it, Freya. It's not a conspiracy. This isn't The bloody Bill. This is real life and they're actual officers, and all you've done is piss them off, just like you piss everyone else off with your arrogance. There's no big vendetta against you. You just make enemies, that's all. I've gone along with it as far as I can. I've tried to accommodate your wild accusations. And for God's sake, I've even said I'd risk my career to help you. But the sooner you realise how you make people feel, the better, Freya. The sooner you realise that you are not the victim here, the sooner you can move on. Try being nice to people. Stop being such a..."

"Such a what, Ben?" she said. "What is it I should stop being?"

"A narcissist." He took a few steps towards the door, then turned back. "You know, being with you is like dating a bloody crate of beers. I like them a lot. In fact, I love them and can't wait to get home to have one or two. But I know that if I'm not careful, I'm going to have too much of a good thing, and I'm going to regret it the next day. Or maybe even for the next week."

"So I'm crate of beer, am I? Not a nice bottle of wine, but a crate of beer? Christ, Ben, even your analogies are lacking."

She spoke with mock boredom as if she had grown tired of hearing him bleat on and on.

"Freya, you're infuriating," he said as if it took every ounce of his remaining strength to say so. He shook his head sadly and let his arms flop to his sides. "Are you even listening to me?"

"I'm trying, but I must confess, I'm finding it all quite tedious."

"Will you even consider taking a desk job? Will you even think about what Granger said? For us?"

"I'm not one for sitting in an office, Ben," she replied. "I'm far more effective in the field, as you well know."

"So either I apply for a transfer," he replied, then hesitated, as if verbalising the alternative was to cement the fact in history. "Or we don't marry."

She sipped her wine, pausing for thought.

"I believe those are our options, Ben," she told him, and as if he was a puppet and his puppet master had relaxed his strings, he deflated.

"I can't do this."

"You can't do what, Ben?"

"This," he said, his aggression dissipated. "I'm done. I'm truly done."

She said nothing, which was often the best course of action to take when somebody's emotions had bubbled over. She picked up her laptop and examined the photos, clicking through them one by one. She had to admit that Gillespie had done a fine job of photographing the box before Southwell and her team took it away. There were at least a dozen images of the exterior, plus a couple of dozen of the interior and the contents. There were photographs of every garment against a plain, white sheet of paper with specific attention to the labels, which Freya noted stated sizes ranging from a size six to a size ten. A six to an eight might have belonged to the same person, but a six to a ten almost certainly showed multiple owners.

"Did you see the sizes on these labels?" she asked and looked up to find that Ben was no longer standing there. "Ben?" she said, but the only reply she heard was the slamming of his front door.

She heard his engine start and his tyres crunching across the drive, and then she heard his car fade into the distance. She sat still for a moment, his words sloshing back and forth in her mind like the wine in her glass, which she had to admit, was excellent; better than usual for Ben's house. But unlike the wine, his words left a bitter aftertaste that she could not cleanse. She set her glass down and collected her phone before dialling a number from her recently dialled list.

The call rang for a few seconds, and then a few seconds more, and she was about to end the call when he answered with a voice that sounded like he'd smoked a packet of cigarettes.

"Boss?" he said.

"Gillespie, it's me," she said. "Listen, I need some help with something. I know it's late, but I'd like you to arrange a briefing with everyone first thing in the morning. Everyone except Gold. Let's leave her for tomorrow. She's had a rough day. But get everyone else in, will you? Shall we say eight a.m.?"

"Aye, I can do that," he said. "No bother."

"Good, thank you," she replied. Then, before he hung up, she added, "Oh, and by the way, good job finding that box. That was good work, and genuinely, I think it could make all the difference to the investigation. So thank you for that. Thank you very much."

CHAPTER THIRTY-FIVE

It was more than a little strange for Ben to wake up in Freya's bed alone. Her scent still lingered, but that was the case in almost every room she occupied for any length of time. He had come to know the perfume she had bought from a little boutique store in a Parisian backstreet like he knew his own.

But what he wasn't used to was her not being there. He half expected to hear her making coffee downstairs, but he knew she wouldn't be.

It was with a strong sense of sadness that he packed his bag, not only with his clothes from the previous day but with the few items he kept at her house.

The last thing he packed, he did so with trepidation – a framed photo of his parents way back when his mother had been alive and his dad had his own teeth. They were young and free-spirited, and the photo, which was on his side of the bed, despite him not officially having moved into her house, was an identical copy of the one on his own bedside table at home. She had bought it for him to make him feel at home. It was just one of those little things that she did. One of those things that other people didn't see. They just saw an arrogant but brilliant woman with an exceptional mind who rubbed nearly everyone she met up the wrong way. But he knew her. He knew things about her that nobody would ever believe. Like the way she liked to be held at night, or the way she would run him a bath and rub his feet, or the way she would go out of her way to cook him his favourite meal, even if it meant travelling to five different shops to get the ingredients.

And he knew that if he took that frame and placed it in his bag, it would be over.

He zipped the bag up, gave the upstairs a quick sweep through to make sure he had left nothing behind, and then made his way down the stairs.

He considered writing her a note but thought better of it. He'd said enough. Now it was her turn to speak. Besides, who needed a note when she could recall a conversation from months ago, verbatim?

Yet he knew she wouldn't sink to that level. And even if she did, would he listen? Would he actually bother to listen to her anymore?

He nearly laughed to himself when he emerged from her house, locked the front door, and posted his key through the letterbox, only to turn and find the church looming there on the far side of the village green.

It had been a pleasant dream, but not all dreams came true.

He started his car and gave her little cottage one last look before he pulled away. Only a few hundred metres from her house, he re-tuned the radio from the classic station she had selected to the local station, where people spoke with local accents, spoke of local places, and gave local weather updates.

Dunston faded in his rearview mirror, and by the time he had crossed the bridge into Metheringham, he was preparing himself for the day. Not to do battle with her over their personal lives, but to find a way of working with her. He had to find a way of somehow putting the whole marriage thing behind him, and (he laughed to himself again) doing what Katy Southwell had suggested.

He envied Gillespie, probably for the first time in his life. He envied the fact that after a life like that of a teenager and a life of sleeping with women from all walks of life, he had finally chosen to settle down with somebody who had the potential to be with him for the foreseeable future.

And then he considered his relationship with Freya, which had been a battle since day one. Since the very first time he had met her, when Granger had put the two of them together, there had been friction.

He glanced down at his radio when it went silent then jumped when his phone rang through the car's Bluetooth system. He fumbled for the green button, not to speak to the caller but to just stop the bloody racket.

"Ben Savage," he said.

"Ben?" the voice said, female, alluring, and level-headed. "You're not going to believe this."

———

By the time Freya had finished, the house was not only tidy but clean. The bathroom didn't exactly sparkle but then it probably never had done, even when first installed, which must have been some time in the eighties, judging by the frankly shocking shade of blue somebody had chosen.

The kitchen was now also cleaner than she had ever seen it. The wooden floors throughout the house shone, and the smell was divine. She had found the sandalwood diffuser that she had bought for him and that he had stuffed into a cupboard to forget about, and she had placed it by the front door, which she had left ajar to carry the smell through.

The next time Ben walked through that front door, she was sure that he would wonder if he'd got the right house. And of course, he would know for sure when he discovered the note she had left him on the kitchen worktop.

She knew him so well that she could almost picture the scene. He would step through the door, frown in confusion at the smell, and then tentatively make his way into the living room as he always did. There, he would dump his bag on a dining room chair, kick his shoes off, and then go through to the kitchen to make a drink, all the while staring at the hues, tones, and grains in the wooden furniture that she had polished.

It would be like stepping into a brand-new home.

She had loaded his fridge with essentials. There was no food and buying it for him was nigh on pointless. But wine, good wine, was essential. He could open his fridge and take his pick of the bottles that he had commented on during the past year or so since she had known him. They were his favourites, and even if he didn't know it, she did, and she knew they would make him smile when the day came to open them.

Because he could do that now. He knew which wines paired well with certain foods, and although he might feign indifference, he understood how it worked.

After loading the car with her bags, taking several trips to do so, she locked the front door and stared out at his family's farm. For more than a century, the Savage family had worked that land, and the very idea of such a heritage was almost inconceivable to Freya. Sure, her family had been wealthy and houses belonged to a chain of inheritance, but not a single Bloom had built the houses. Not a single member of the Bloom family had worked the land, save for cutting some flowers from the walled garden to freshen up a bedroom for a guest they had invited to stay.

There were three Savage houses in total, all laid out in a small arc. Ben's was the first, and then was his father's house, and finally the house that his two brothers lived in. They were far enough apart to afford them all privacy, but close enough that, should one of them call for help, it would arrive in an instant.

She fumbled with her keys, working her thumbnail into the small steel ring, and then sliding the key out. She pushed the letterbox open with one hand and held the key with the other, but clung to it for a few seconds, not quite ready to let go. This tiny act could be the deciding factor. When he saw that chunk of faded brass on his doormat, he would know exactly how she felt.

And then she dropped it, uncertain if she had made the right choice but content to have made a choice at all. Now all she had to do was deal with the consequences.

She stayed there for a second or two, picturing the dull brass key on the doormat inside, and then picturing him at his desk in the incident room.

She would remain professional, of course. She had to. They were three days into a battle with a hydra. She would need every pair of hands and every mind she could get her hands on.

Now was not the time for personal feelings to get in the way.

When he arrived home that night, he would know how she felt.

All she had to do was be civil to him, which wasn't hard. He deserved so much more than she could give. He had been so patient with her. More patient than anybody she could remember.

He deserved better.

And better he should have.

CHAPTER THIRTY-SIX

The room was buzzing with activity. Gillespie and Cruz were standing at the wall placing photos from the investigation into some semblance of order. Nillson and Anderson were in deep discussion as they pored over what looked like either bank statements or phone statements, and Chapman was standing beside the printer creating five neat piles of paperwork, which she would dutifully bind to create up-to-date investigation files for each of them.

Freya, however, was at the whiteboard with her back to the doors, and when Ben entered the room, although nobody had uttered a word, she grew still. With her hand poised to write, she turned her head slightly, as a prowling leopard might sense an antelope foraging among the trees. If she had a tail, he was sure it would be swishing from side to side.

He set his bag down quietly, opened his laptop, and hit the power button. It was something he did every time he entered the incident room, but rarely did the old machine actually let him get on and do some work. His emails worked just fine, but any other application seemed to cause some kind of severe malfunction and it would just freeze.

"Good, we're all here," Freya said quietly.

It was a technique he had noticed her use fairly often. She spoke quietly, and the team hushed so as to hear her. Eventually, she lulled their attention from their tasks, like she had wafted some kind of potion throughout the room. He had expected her to avoid eye contact, but she didn't. And if she looked his way, then he had expected her to sneer at him.

But she didn't.

She seemed pleasant somehow like something had shifted inside her. Like his words last night had struck chords, and she was making amends somehow, or perhaps she was just being calm, as was so often the case before one of her tempestuous storms.

Or perhaps she knew he had packed his belongings, taken the photo, and returned her key, and this was how it was to be. A silent resolution. Perhaps she had decided that the best course of action was for them to remain as they were. Part of a team. And that their relationship was merely a hindrance, in which case, why bother with an argument? Why bother with emotions? Working together had been the foundation of their relationship. Perhaps she was seeking to restore the status quo, and perhaps that was for the best.

He nodded once at her and then settled into his seat.

"Liam Finch," she said, eventually pulling her gaze from him and turning it onto Nillson. "What do we have, please?"

"Bank statements and phone records," Nillson said excitedly. "And Jenny and I have managed to make some pretty solid links."

"Go on," Freya said, settling onto the edge of her desk where she often perched.

"Well, to begin with, Chapman managed to get the details of those bank notes that you found among Deborah Jarvis' belongings," she said. "At least two hundred quid of them came from Liam Finch's account."

"Sorry?" Freya said. "The money we found hidden in Deborah Jarvis' books was from Liam Finch's bank account?"

"At least two hundred quid of it, yes," Nillson said. "Which gives us a direct link between him and Deborah Jarvis."

"Well, that's a good start," Freya said. "Well done. What else?"

"Ah, this is where it gets really interesting," Nillson continued. "In his phone records, we found text messages from him to Deborah's number. Obviously, the statement doesn't tell me what was said, and we don't have her phone, but we know they were in contact."

"He told us he knew of her," Ben said. "He said he didn't actually know her."

"He was lying," Freya said. "This is good. This is really good."

"So, Anderson and I went back a couple of years," Nillson added. "All the way back to when Holly Carson made her last posts on LinkedIn."

"And?"

"He knew her."

"Of course he knew her," Freya said. "She worked for him."

"He was texting her."

"Again, it could have been a work thing."

"At midnight?" Nillson said, and Freya's head cocked to one side with intrigue. "Or how about at three a.m.?" She flicked to the next page in her stack of papers. "Or how about two-thirty in the morning?"

"Right," Freya said. "This shines a new light on our beast, doesn't it?"

"Wait," Nillson said. "There's more."

"More?"

"Plenty more," Nillson said, grinning from ear to ear. "Chapman, do you want to tell her?"

"Tell me what?" Freya asked.

"It's the misper, guv," Chapman said. "Holly Carson's mother said that Holly had arranged to go out for drinks with somebody after work and that she'd be late home. She never came home."

"So?" Freya said, slowly, so as not to sound negative.

"Liam Finch's credit card shows he was out at a local bar at six p.m. that night," Chapman said. "He bought three rounds, each costing six pounds and seventy-four pence."

"Six pounds?"

"Two glasses of wine?" Nillson suggested, still grinning, and Freya slowly nodded her agreement.

"So Liam Finch becomes a primary suspect," she said, and she turned to the board to make a note.

"Wait," Nillson said.

"There's more?"

"Sadly," she said. "We might have grown another head."

Freya placed the cap back on her pen and, with a glance at Ben, waited for the bad news.

"In Holly Carson's phone records, we also found calls and messages to and from two more phones that are significant to the investigation."

"Who?"

"Anne Hargreaves and Sebastian Groves," Nillson said.

"Anne Hargreaves?" Freya said, shaking her head. "What's the link there? She's been at the accountancy firm for–"

"Seven years," Anderson cut in. "She joined the firm a month after Holly Carson went missing."

"Hang on," Ben said. "I don't want to be the one to drag all of this down, but we're talking about Holly Carson as if it's a done deal. We don't even know if it was her yet."

"Actually, we do," Chapman said, and in a rare display of excitement, she beamed at everyone in the room. "I've got the dental records. The wisdom tooth, the molars that were knocked out of line, they match, and not only that, the practitioner is willing to testify to that effect. He's certain."

"Brilliant news," Freya said, and she shoved herself off of the desk and scrawled the name *Holly Carson* on the board beside *Deborah Jarvis*. "Bloody brilliant." She turned to face them all, closed her eyes, and held her hand up for them to be silent for a moment so that she could gather thoughts. "So we've got Liam Finch withdrawing money to give to Deborah Jarvis. We've potentially got him taking Holly Carson out for drinks on the night she went missing. And we've got text messages between him and both victims, is that right?"

"Plus the text messages with Anne Hargreaves," Nillson said.

"I've also got some news," Ben said. "I spoke to Katy Southwell early this morning." The room fell into an instant silence. "She's found traces of semen in some of the underwear found in Jim's box."

"Hey, careful how you phrase that," Gillespie said.

"Oh, so you don't want the credit then?" Freya asked.

"Aye, I'll take the credit, no bother. But...you know?"

"Has she got a positive ID?" Freya asked.

"No, but I'm sure Liam Finch would be willing to provide a sample," he replied. "And if he isn't willing, then I'll want a damn good reason why not."

"The question is," Nillson asked, turning her attention to Freya, "is all of that enough to nick him?"

CHAPTER THIRTY-SEVEN

The answer to Nillson's question had been a resounding yes.

"You all know what to do," Freya said. "But let's not take our eye off the beast's other heads, namely Kevin Stone and Reginald Jarvis. Chapman, while we're gone, please take a deeper look into Anne Hargreaves and Sebastian Groves. Groves is the only one we haven't spoken to yet but I'm more than happy to if need be. As for Anne Hargreaves, she's callous and calculated. I'd be keen to learn some more about her."

"Will do," she replied.

"Once we have Finch in custody," Freya continued, finding Ben amidst the team. "You and I will pay a visit to Holly Carson's parents. Chapman, if you could send us the address, please?"

"Already on it, guv," she said.

"Good, thank you. Gillespie, Cruz, who do you have at the house? Who's in charge in your absence?"

"We've got Godfrey running the Lincoln team, guv. But I think they should be pretty much done by lunchtime."

"Anything to report?"

"Not a thing," he said. "If anything, all we've done is save Nick

MacMillan a few quid by tearing the house apart before he renovates."

"Well, that's no significant loss."

"What about the local lads in the garden?"

"Sergeant Yates," he said. "Good bloke."

"Okay, well, leave the Lincoln mob there but ask Yates to send two of his officers to Finch's firm. Ask them to be there for eight forty-five," she said. "But they should wait for us. They're just there for support and to transport him back here."

"Aye, no bother. I'll do it now."

"Is it worth giving some thought to the different MOs, boss?" Cruz called out, which caught Freya's attention enough for her to stop and listen. "I just mean that someone wrapped Deborah Jarvis in plastic and left her to die a slow and painful death, but Holly Carson looks as if..."

"She fell from the sky?" Ben suggested.

"She might as well have done," Cruz replied. "She's got a broken collarbone, broken pelvis, legs, fingers, and God knows what else. Doesn't it strike you as odd?"

"It does indeed," Freya told him. "It strikes me as very odd indeed, and I'm pleased you mentioned it. In fact, why don't you take a trip to pathology? See what Pip has to say about the injuries. I want to know what type of weapon was used to do such damage and if the poor girl was alive when it happened. Gillespie, go with him, will you? And while you're at the hospital, you could inquire about the whereabouts of Mariam Jarvis. We'll need a death certificate for the investigation, but most of all, I want to see if her husband bothered to visit her."

"If he did, then I didn't see him," Gillespie said.

"Check with the nurses, will you? I'm sure he would have caused a memorable scene."

Cruz seemed a little disheartened at having to be accompanied by Gillespie, but he pushed through with a forced smile as he packed his things away.

His demeanour was clear enough for even Gillespie to pick up on. He appeared genuinely saddened at Cruz's reaction.

"You can drive if you like," he said to Cruz.

"Oh right, then you can berate me for driving too slow."

"Ah, I won't say a thing," Gillespie replied. "In fact, if the boss is okay with it, we could stop for a coffee."

"Fine by me," Freya told him, sensing that Cruz was slowly coming around.

"My shout," Gillespie added.

"All right," Cruz said after a few moments of deliberation. "But I want a pastry as well."

"Done," Gillespie said.

It warmed Freya to see Gillespie adapt his usual brash and abrupt nature to accommodate Cruz. There was a genuine friendship in there somewhere and it pained her to think it wasn't too dissimilar to her relationship with Ben.

"Right, are we all clear on what we have to do?" Freya said to the room.

"Aye, crystal," Gillespie said.

"Good, last thing. Chapman, I wonder if you could arrange for some flowers for DC Gold, please? If it all goes well with Finch, then maybe Ben and I can drop them round to her this afternoon."

"That's a nice idea," Chapman replied.

"Thank you," Freya said then collected her jacket from her chair. "Right then, Ben, are you ready for this?"

"I suppose that all depends on what it is I need to be ready for," he replied, pushing himself from the chair and closing his laptop.

"To put an end to all of this," she told him. "To slay our nine-headed monster."

CHAPTER THIRTY-EIGHT

They drove in silence for a while. It was one of those journeys where Ben expected an attack at any moment and, as a result, found himself tense and uncomfortable. He likened it to finding a place to cross a river. He knew that at some point he would have to commit and that he would no doubt get his feet wet. Nevertheless, there might just be a more suitable place further along.

But when she finally spoke, his feet did not touch the water.

"I'd like to do this as smoothly as possible," she said. "Preferably without alerting his colleagues, especially Anne Hargreaves and the receptionist."

"Liz?"

"That's her. The last thing we need is for her to spread a rumour through the office. If Hargreaves has something to do with all of this, it'll be better for us if she is ill-prepared."

"Do you think she'll run?"

"No, not particularly," Freya replied. "But she is smart. She's going for a junior partner position in a fairly decent accountancy firm in her mid-twenties. There are only two reasons that I can see for that to happen. Either she's outrageously smart, and by that, I mean next-level smart, or she's sleeping with the boss."

Ben glanced at her to see if the last part of that comment had been a joke. But Freya wasn't smiling and her crow's feet were smooth. In fact, her entire face seemed smooth, more so than usual, which was saying something for somebody who took such great pride in her appearance.

"I didn't get the impression they were very close," he said, eventually. "In fact, I would have said there was some underlying bitterness between them. Something we weren't privy to."

"That must make for an awkward working day," she mused, then causally peered through her window as they passed a field of rape that seemed golden in the morning sun.

"I agree," he muttered to himself. "In fact, I couldn't agree more."

A single police car was waiting in the car park outside the office building. The two uniformed officers climbed out when they saw Freya's car arrive.

"He's not here yet," Ben said, glancing around at the handful of cars. "According to Chapman, he drives a dark blue BMW." He spied a vacant spot close to the main entrance bearing a reserved sign with the company logo in the top-right-hand corner.

"Oh damn," Freya said, and Ben looked up to find her staring at a little Mazda sports car. The door opened and the buxom brunette climbed from the car, straightening her dress, which even Ben could see was far too small. It was in times like this that Ben was glad to be a man. Had he been born a female, he felt he would find a career in which he could wear baggy clothes. Aside from appearing professional, she looked incredibly uncomfortable. In contrast, Freya somehow always seemed to appear relaxed and effortlessly professional.

"You again?" Hargreaves said as she hit her key fob to lock her car. Her shoulders sagged under the weight of a large satchel, presumably filled with files, and she walked uneasily on her heels. It was another observation of how Freya achieved her appearance with apparent natural ease. Never once had he seen her stumble in her heels. "Am I in trouble?"

"No, but I think perhaps we should have a word," she said, and Hargreaves came to a stop before them.

"About?" She looked at Freya and then at Ben as if she dared them to make an accusation. "Nothing then," she said and brushed past them towards the doors, just as Finch's BMW rolled into the car park and parked in the reserved spot.

He climbed from his car in an instant rage.

"What on earth is this?" he said, leaving his car door open and marching over to where they stood. But instead of berating either Freya or Ben, he turned his wrath on Hargreaves. "Is this you? Have you any idea what having a police car on the forecourt looks like for business?"

"Actually, Mr Finch, it's you we've come to see," Freya said, her voice unnervingly calm and creamy smooth.

"What?"

"Liam Finch, I am arresting you on suspicion of murder," she said. "You do not have to say anything but it may harm your defence if you do not mention when questioned something which you later rely on in court. Anything you do say may be given in evidence. Do you understand?"

"What? No, of course, I don't bloody well understand."

Ben gave the nod to the two uniformed officers, who pulled Finch's arms behind his back and slipped on the handcuffs.

"We'll see you back at the station, Mr Finch."

"This must be some sort of joke," he said as they led him away. "If this is you, Hargreaves, then you can pack your bloody bags. Do you hear me? You're bloody finished."

The officers helped him into the car's back seat with far more grace than Ben might have.

"And then there were three," Freya said, turning back to Hargreaves. "Shall we talk inside?"

"That depends on what you have to say."

"Oh, I just wanted to pick your brains," Freya said. "What can you tell me about Holly Carson?"

Hargreaves stiffened at the mention of the name but possessed enough self-awareness to appear indifferent.

"I know the name," she said.

"A friend, maybe?"

"No," Hargreaves replied. "Not a friend. Wasn't she the girl that..." She hesitated and her eyes widened. "She went missing, didn't she? Is that who you found? You told me it was Debs. Are you saying that Liam had something to do with it? You just arrested him for murder. Are you saying you were wrong about Debs?"

"Oh no," Freya replied. "I'm rarely wrong. Misguided, yes. Misled even. But rarely wrong."

"So, what then? What about her?"

"I just wondered how well you knew her, that's all. Was she a part of your little group?"

"No, she wasn't. She was older than us. And besides, she wasn't exactly like us."

"Oh?"

Hargreaves shook her head as if the entire conversation was a ridiculous waste of time.

"Look, I've got a busy day ahead. No doubt it'll be even busier now."

"So, you never met Holly?"

"At school, yes. But only in passing. She was a bit of a teacher's pet if you know what I mean."

"And you were a rebel, were you?"

"I didn't say that. But no, actually. We were somewhere in between."

"So, it's safe to say that you wouldn't have spoken to Holly outside of the school environment?"

"I think that's very safe to say," Hargreaves said. "Now, if you'll excuse me—"

"Just one more thing, Miss Hargreaves," Freya said. "You see, the reason I'm asking you these questions is because, as you have probably guessed, we are now investigating Holly Carson's death, and as part of our investigation, we are looking into her old records, as you can imagine. Health records and financial records," she said. "Phone records. That sort of thing."

"Okay," Hargreaves said softly.

"And we were wondering why your phone number appeared on her phone records," Freya said.

"There must be some kind of mistake," Hargreaves said. "I don't recall ever—"

"Well, if it's a mistake, then perhaps we should speak to the network provider," Ben added. "Because your friend's phone number is on there, too."

"Ross? He wouldn't have had anything to do with her, just like I wouldn't."

"I wasn't talking about Ross," Ben said. "I was talking about Sebastian Groves."

CHAPTER THIRTY-NINE

The custody suite consisted of a space large enough to accommodate half a dozen unruly drunks plus a handful of officers to keep them in check. A large counter took pride of place, behind which was the door to the cells and the door to the back offices. At the helm, Sergeant Priest worked tirelessly to ensure the smooth running of what they mutually agreed to be the spearhead of the station, where uniformed and plain clothes operations met. The fact was that none of the various teams that worked from the building could operate without the custody suite.

Sergeant Priest, a proud and red-faced Yorkshireman, had managed that space for longer than any other officer he knew of, a fact that he was keen to share as often as possible, and which was made clear by his meticulous planning and scheduling.

"How's our man?" Ben said, as he came in from the car park and leaned on the counter while Freya took a private phone call outside.

"Interview room two," Priest said.

"And have you done as I asked?"

"We have swabbed, fingerprinted, and processed him," Priest replied, never taking his eyes off the computer keyboard that he operated with two fat index fingers. Finally, he looked up at Ben. "Although he's not one of our most friendly guests."

"Do you think he'll leave a bad review?" Ben asked.

"I doubt he'll have the chance. But his solicitor might?"

"Are they here already?"

"Arrived while we were processing him," Priest said. "A Mr Matthew Morrison."

"Never heard of him."

"Well, you can't miss him. He's six-foot-six and built like a garden rake," Priest said. "Looks like you're in for a fun morning."

The door to the car park opened, and the breeze carried Freya's scent with it.

"Are we ready?" she asked, to which Priest simply looked at Ben.

He shoved off the counter and opened the door into the corridor, holding it open for Freya to pass. He gave Priest a friendly wink and then followed.

"This could be a long one," she said as she strode towards the interview rooms. Being a small, rural station, there were only two interview rooms, and she hovered between them, silently asking which one they were in.

"Two," he said. "And don't worry, I've had a wee."

She paused with her hand on the door and smiled sorrowfully up at him before pushing through, leaving Ben alone in the corridor. He took a moment to collect his thoughts and find some dark corner to tuck his emotions. He so wanted to grab her arm and force her into a conversation. He needed some kind of resolution, yet she seemed content simply to leave things where they fell.

"Mr Finch, I hope you're being treated well so far. All settled in, are we?"

"Is that some kind of joke?" he asked.

She looked across to Ben, who finished preparing the recording and then waited for the buzzer to end.

As was usual, Freya began by stating the date, time, and location, and then introduced herself and Ben before waiting for the solicitor and Finch to follow suit.

"Matthew Morrison, legal representative," Morrison said, in a voice that was surprisingly light in tone for a man of his size.

"Liam Finch," Finch said and then stared hard at Freya. "Victim."

"Very good," Freya said, feigning pleasantness. "Right, Mr Finch, can you confirm that you have been read your rights?"

"I have," he said.

"And you understand the reason for your arrest?"

"Not really," he said.

"Well then, perhaps before we begin, I should take the time to educate you. You see, you have been arrested on suspicion of murder, which, in case you aren't aware, is contrary to common law. Do you now understand?"

"I think it's a little early in the proceedings for flippancy, Chief Inspector Bloom," Morrison said, clearly trying to smooth the path ahead.

"The point I was trying to make, Mr Morrison, is that this is a serious crime and I will take as long as it takes to ensure that the proceedings, as you call them, are not inhibited by your client's blatant disregard for police procedure. If, at any time during this interview, your client is unsure of anything at all, then I will endeavour to educate him. What I will not do is tolerate what I can only describe as poor behaviour from a man who should clearly know better. I am, as far as I know, not dealing with a young, scruffy teenager with a chip on his shoulder. I'm dealing with a successful man of business, and quite frankly, if he behaves like the aforementioned teenager, then I will treat him as such. Have I made my position clear?"

Morrison inhaled long and hard and Finch straightened in his seat like a naughty schoolboy.

"Quite," Morrison said. "Thank you for making your position abundantly clear."

"Good, well let's move on then, shall we?" she said. "Mr Finch, what I would like to do is just go over the conversation we had yesterday in your office." She referred to her notes briefly but Ben knew her well enough that she would have memorised anything she would need to recall. "We asked you if you knew of a girl named Deborah Jarvis. Can you just remind me of your response?"

"You're trying to catch me out," he replied. "You want me to say something different to yesterday so you can pull me up on it?"

"Surely if the answer you provided yesterday was the truth, then today's response would be similar, if not the same?"

Finch glanced at his solicitor, who nodded for him to go ahead.

"No," he said finally. "No, I did not know Deborah Jarvis. I told you I knew *of* her, much the same as anyone else in the village."

"Thank you," Freya said, offering him a beaming smile.

"We also went over the details of the sale of your house, one Priory View in Haverholme Park," Freya said. "Which you claim to have moved out of on May seventh 2019, despite exchanging with the new owner some six weeks later."

"That's right," he said. "Our new house came up and it made little sense to wait for the chain, not when we had the capital. We're quite fortunate in that regard."

"Very," Freya said. "Just so you are aware, we have been in touch with the estate agent and the movers, who have both confirmed this. So I see no reason to pursue that matter any further."

"Well, that's something," Finch said.

"What is troubling me, Mr Finch, is that Deborah Jarvis' remains were discovered beneath the floorboards of the living room at Priory View. Now, you moved out of the house on the seventh, but you did still have access to the property until the exchange took place."

"Well, of course I did. I hadn't got my money yet. I was hardly going to hand it over beforehand, was I?"

"Quite," Freya said. "Now, the last time that Deborah Jarvis was seen alive was on the sixth of May, somewhere close to midnight."

"Okay?"

"And you moved out on the seventh, along with your family, which, by the way, is not being disputed."

"Right, so you think I murdered her the night before I moved out? Have you ever moved house? Do you know how stressful it is? Because, believe me, popping out for a quick murder was the last thing on my mind."

"What was on your mind?"

"Sorry?"

"What were you doing the night before you moved out?"

He shrugged and pulled a bemused expression.

"I don't know. It was five years ago. Packing boxes, most likely."

"But you were at home, were you?"

"Of course I was. Lived there damn near twenty years. Have you any idea how much stuff a family can accumulate in that time?"

"So if we were to speak to your wife, she could corroborate that, could she? She'd tell us you were home all night, helping her pack boxes?"

"I don't know," he said. "And I'll thank you for leaving her out of this. Last thing I need is for her to worry. She'll be bloody hysterical."

"I'm not looking for your thanks, Mr Finch. I'm investigating a murder. I thought I made that clear at the beginning of this interview?" He didn't take the news favourably, but he knew he had been beaten and sat back in his seat, flaring his nostrils. "Of course, until we speak to your wife, we won't know for sure, so I suggest we move on. I'd like to talk about your phone records, Mr Finch. Specifically, the messages you sent at the beginning of May 2019."

"What do you want me to do, recite them?"

"No, but I was wondering why Deborah Jarvis' phone number appears in your call history.

"What?"

"Oh, it's quite clear. You made a call to Deborah Jarvis on the second of May."

"I don't know," he said, shaking his head. "I probably dialled the wrong number."

"Oh, I see," Freya said. "It's easily done, isn't it? I do it all the time if I'm honest." She stilled for a moment, unsmiling and predator-like. "What I rarely do, though, is send a text message to the same number shortly afterwards. Were you apologising to the stranger for disturbing them?"

"What?"

"You sent a text message to Deborah Jarvis' phone, Mr Finch. In fact, over the course of two years, you sent her several messages, and made the mistake of misdialling her number frequently."

Morrison caught his attention and shook his head.

"No comment," Finch said.

"I see," Freya replied. "Shall we park that for the time being? We have a lot to get through."

"I wonder if I might be permitted to have a word with my client?" Morrison asked. "In private."

"You can," Freya said. "Let's have a scheduled break in ten minutes, shall we? What would be preferable for me would be to outline the evidence against your client, and then you can discuss it all at once. It'll save us all time, and if your client is innocent as he claims, then he'll be back at his office in a jiffy."

Her mannerisms amused Ben but did little for Finch other than to aggravate him.

The pair on the far side of the table conferred for a moment and then Morrison nodded his agreement.

"Ten minutes," he said.

"Thank you," Freya said with more than a dash of faux charm. "Do you carry cash, Mr Finch?"

"Sorry?"

"Cash? You do remember cash, don't you?"

"Of course."

"And do you carry it? Maybe a little float or something?"

"I'm not sure what you're asking me," he said.

'It's quite simple," Freya continued. "How often do you use a cash machine? Once a week? Twice a week?"

"Less," he said. "I use a card wherever possible."

"I see," Freya replied. "In that case, I wonder if you could tell me how a number of banknotes withdrawn from your account came to be in the possession of Deborah Jarvis?"

"That's absurd," he said.

"I'm afraid not. You're aware that each banknote has a unique serial number?"

"Of course—"

"And you know that those serial numbers can be traced to an individual who withdraws the notes?"

"I suppose," he said, his voice weakening. "But they could have come from anybody."

"They could," she said. "I totally agree. But they didn't, did they? They came from you."

"What? Just because I withdrew them? I could have spent them in the bar or a restaurant and they could have been passed to her."

"All ten of them?" Freya said. "Ten crisp twenty-pound notes? You withdrew two hundred pounds and that same two hundred pounds somehow ended up in Deborah Jarvis' possession. Tell me how that might have happened."

The persistent barrage of evidence slowly wore Finch down. His confidence waned, apparent by his sagging shoulders and despondent expression.

"Shall we pick that up later?" Freya said. "Before we break, though, I would like to discuss one more thing." She sifted through her file and produced three photos, all of which she laid face down on the table.

Finch closed his eyes and his frown deepened.

Slowly, Freya slid a well-manicured fingernail beneath the first image and then flipped it over for both Morrison and Finch to see.

"Perhaps you can tell me about this, Mr Finch?" she said. "For the recording, I am showing Mr Finch evidence number NKDJ003, a photo of a mature male and young female engaged in sexual intercourse."

"I've never seen it before," he said and turned his head to avert his eyes.

"And the individuals?"

"Haven't a clue," he said, glancing briefly at the photo, then staring at Freya.

"Are you sure?" Freya said. "Because we had the image run through facial recognition software. It's a reliable technique with astonishing accuracy."

He shrugged, feigning indifference.

"Mr Finch, I should make you aware that this image proves your connection to Deborah, and any attempt to separate yourself from the contents will only sway a jury into believing you have more to hide. You will, in effect, be demonstrating your ability to lie. And juries tend to notice those things-"

"Okay, it's me," he snapped, and he shoved the photo onto the floor. "Of course it's me. You can see it's me."

Freya leaned forward and spoke quietly.

"I know it's you. If I were in your position, I would give serious consideration to your statement, because believe me, you are not doing yourself any favours by withholding information," she said, and Finch sank further into his seat. "Perhaps we'll break there. Shall we say thirty minutes?"

CHAPTER FORTY

"Ah, that hit the spot," Gillespie said as he dumped the empty coffee cup into a bin in the hospital corridor. "It doesn't matter what coffee they get in the office, it's just not the same as when a pretty girl behind a counter serves you with a smile, eh?"

"Or a boy," Cruz replied.

"Eh?"

"I'm just saying it's not just a job for girls. Men work in coffee shops too."

He guided the big Scotsman into the corridor that led down to the morgue, doing everything he could to stay positive and in control.

"Well, aye. I was just saying that I prefer it when it's a wee lass that serves me."

"I know, and I was saying that sometimes a wee fella will serve you, and it's totally fine."

"Aye," Gillespie replied, then pulled a confused face and dropped the topic. "Anyway, have you heard much from Hermione?"

It was the one name that Cruz couldn't bear to hear. It had

been months since she had left him and he had done his best to move on.

"No," he replied. "No, and I'd prefer to keep it that way."

"Ah, right, I see. Yeah, shocker that, eh? I didn't see it coming, did you?"

"No, Jim. No, I didn't."

He reached up to push the buzzer that would alert the pathologist of their arrival.

Gillespie rocked back and forth on his heels with his hands behind his back.

"A wee birdie told me she'd shacked up with a fella out of Skegness."

"How nice for her," Cruz said, praying that the pathologist would hurry up and open the door. None of what Gillespie had said was news to him, but still, it wasn't a topic he relished discussing.

"Pregnant apparently," Gillespie continued, and as usual, he failed to pick up on any social cues. "Still, I expect she's happy. Could have been you, eh?"

"Yes," Cruz said, and he found himself picturing his ex-girlfriend with a swollen belly. Then the image grew wider to include a faceless, six-foot-something officer with broad shoulders and barrel chest.

"Lucky if you ask me, mate," Gillespie said, still rocking back and forth. "Dodged a bullet, eh?"

Cruz reached forward again and stabbed at the buzzer a few times, only to find the door being ripped open by a disgruntled, tattooed, and very Welsh pathologist.

"Now then," she said, her voice booming along the corridor. "Who are you and what the bloody hell do you think you're doing?"

"Sorry," Cruz said. "I—"

"Hang on, I remember you two. You're Ben's boys."

"Pip," Gillespie said and held out his hand for her to shake.

But she just stared at it in disgust, as if it was roadkill. "Seregant Gillespie."

"Doctor Bell," she replied, then turned to Cruz. "What about you, finger boy?"

"Er, Cruz. Detective Constable Cruz."

"So, where are the other two? Thought they'd be here themselves, I did. Been working on her all morning, I have."

"Chief Inspector Bloom and Inspector Savage are otherwise engaged," Cruz told her, doing his best to make a good impression and hopefully repair any damage he had caused by pushing the buzzer too much.

She studied him and his attire and then did the same to Gillespie.

"You'd better come in," she said, holding the door open for them. "Wipe your feet though, eh?"

Cruz stopped in his tracks and searched for a mat to wipe his shoes on, but found nothing – until he looked up at her.

"A joke, it was," she said, and Gillespie laughed out loud. "Get cloaked up and meet me inside," she told them then pushed through a second door, allowing a cold blast of air to enter the room. The door closed with a swish and Cruz felt his heart rate going like he'd just sprinted for the ice cream man.

"Otherwise engaged?" Gillespie said.

"All right, all right, I was trying to make a good impression."

"Aye, I can see that. But you might be better off not trying to make a good impression with this one. In fact, I plan on saying as little as possible. Scares the bejesus out of me, she does. I've never known anyone like it."

Cruz followed suit and stayed quiet while they pulled on the various articles of PPE.

"What do we look like, eh?" Gillespie said when they were ready to go through. But then he paused and gave Cruz a look that he both recognised and feared. "Tell you what, Gabby, mind how you take this lot off when we're done."

He gestured at the disposable coveralls, mask, and hat.

"Why?"

"Because they're bloody ideal for when you help me paint my house, that's why. Eh?" he said, tugging at the coveralls. "What do you reckon?"

"I think you're clinically insane," Cruz told him and then pushed past him into the morgue, where whatever joviality they had shared in the reception was blown away by the air conditioning.

"Come on," Bell said. "Don't be scared. She won't bite."

Thankful that his mask concealed his expression, Cruz walked over to the stainless steel bench, where he was joined by Gillespie.

"Ready?" Bell asked, to which Cruz nodded, and when he glanced up at Gillespie, he saw only blank eyes that revealed nothing of his thoughts, until Bell pulled the thin, blue sheet back, and those dark, Celtic eyes closed in horror.

Holly Carson had been laid out in almost the same manner as Cruz had seen palaeontologists do with dinosaur bones. It was a flattened version of the human form. Where the ribs should have stood proud, they lay flat, and where the feet should have relaxed at forty-five degree angles, they pointed down to demonstrate their connection to the leg. But, by far the worst of the differences was the skull, which had been placed, minus its lower jaw, staring down at its own remains with dark and hollow eyes.

"Got a name for her, have we?" Bell asked, and Cruz roused himself from his thoughts.

"Eh?"

"A name?"

"Oh, yeah. Holly Carson."

"Right," Bell said, and she seemed to sympathise with his despondency. "So the teeth helped, did they? I scanned them for one of Freya's lot. Chapman."

"Yeah," Cruz said. "Yeah, the dentist matched them this morning."

"You okay, are you?"

"Me? Oh yeah. Fine, ta."

"Looking a little pale, that's all."

"I just...I wasn't quite ready to...you know?"

"Thought-provoking, aren't they?" Bell said, and she ran a gloved finger along the length of what Cruz thought to be a fibula. "More so than when they have skin on, don't you think?"

"Yeah," Cruz said quietly.

"I expect Ben sent you here with some questions, did he?"

"I think his expectations are fairly low," Cruz said. "You know? Given the...given the..."

"Bones?"

"Not the bones, no," he said. "More the lack of anything else."

"You found her, didn't you?" Bell asked. "Katy said so. Sure of it, I am."

"I did," Cruz explained. "But there was all the dirt and...you know? It's not the same, is it?"

"Put you out of your misery, shall I?" she said, to which Cruz smiled and then realised the mask covered his mouth. "Well, sadly, it is not good news. This girl suffered. Badly, in fact. The sheer volume of broken bones would have been excruciating."

"She was alive, then?" Gillespie said, speaking up for the first time.

"Oh, she was alive, all right," she said and then indicated the broken collarbone. "See here?"

"Collarbone?" Cruz said, and she nodded.

"There's no sign of calcium deposits, which means the body hadn't begun to repair itself."

"Surely that could mean she suffered the injuries after she died?" Cruz said, and Bell nodded thoughtfully.

She waved him around to her side of the bench, and he sought some kind of support from Gillespie, who took a step back.

"Come on, I haven't got all day, have I?" Bell said, and Cruz reluctantly took a few steps and then stood before her. "I'm going to come at you," she said and then started towards him. Instinctively, he raised his hands and stepped back. "There," she said. "There, see?"

"See what?"

"What did you do when I came for you?"

"Moved?" he said, doubting his response but not able to come up with another.

"You put your hands up," she said and then went for him again. Instinctively, he reacted the same way. She took his left hand in hers. "Broken fingers," she said, then slid her hand up his arm. "The force transferred along her arm, breaking her radius, and then her collarbone."

He thought about her explanation and could almost see it play out in his mind.

"What about the skull? It's cracked on the back."

"She hit the ground," Bell said. "Hit it hard too."

Cruz studied the remains before them, but Bell clung to his arm and his hand as if preventing him from moving.

"And the..." He nodded at Holly Carson's lower half.

"Broken pelvis and a broken femur," she said. "Well, shattered really. If she had survived, I doubt she would have walked again."

"But, how did—"

"It's a car," Gillespie said, and he stepped forward, risking Doctor Bell's ridicule. He put his hands out before him as if he was reenacting the scene. His hips swayed to the right to portray the front end of a car slamming into her legs, and then he bent over, with his hands out, just as Holly Carson might have fallen forward onto the car bonnet. Then he recoiled in slow motion, but there was no need to fall to the ground. The message was well and truly received. He looked up at them both, his eyes wide and moist. "She was hit by a car."

CHAPTER FORTY-ONE

"That was crafty," Ben said as they pushed into the incident room.

"That was *lucky*," she replied. "I was going to ask him if he recognised Deborah."

"Oh, leave off," he said, and she grabbed onto his arm to drag him back into the corridor.

"Despite what you think, not everything I say or do has an ulterior motive," she told him. "Look, Ben. We've managed to get through the day so far without rowing. I'm making an effort–"

"I can see that."

"I hope you can. Look, I don't want us to be a factor in our working days. I just want to get on with my career and I want to see you get on with yours. Whatever happens between us should have no bearing on what happens here. It can't do. Something will break eventually."

"Or someone," Ben said.

"So, while we're here, I'm DCI Bloom and you're DI Savage."

"Should I use your full title or do you mind if use the abbreviation?"

"Don't be flippant," she said, and he caught the beginnings of a smile.

He pushed the door and held it for her, then waited for her to pass.

"I still think it was crafty," he muttered.

"It got a result, didn't it?" she replied, and then sauntered across the room to her desk, where she dumped her bag down and gathered her thoughts.

"How did it go?" Nillson asked, searching for an answer from either Freya or Ben. "I'm guessing he didn't drop down to his knees and confess?"

"Not quite," Ben told her. "The solicitor requested a break so they can go over their story."

"You see, that's where it's all wrong," Nillson said, slapping her pen down on her desk. "We're hamstrung by bloody human rights."

"Wow, where did that come from?" he asked.

"It's infuriating," she continued. "We've spent three days developing a case against the bloke and the moment his solicitor requests a break, we're forced to give in so they can confer. It doesn't make sense."

"Them's the rules," Freya said. "Them's the rules."

"I think it's wrong."

"I agree," Freya said. "But what are we going to do? Make our own rules up? I'm not sure we'd get very far."

"If I had my way, any rights would be sacrificed the moment the cuffs go on."

"Well, then let's pray that nobody wrongfully arrests you for anything, Nillson," Freya said. "Because believe me, you'll be grateful for those little breaks."

"Yeah, I know. I get it. It's just bloody annoying. They could be down there now, coming up with a pack of lies, and there's nothing we can do about it."

"We could be up here coming up with a pack of lies," Ben said.

"But we couldn't, could we? If we tried that and the case goes to trial, the first thing the defence lawyer would do is bring up our attempts to pin the murder on them. We'd lose all credibility."

"Do you need a coffee break, Nillson?" Freya asked, which seemed to deliver the message.

"Sorry," she said. "I just get bloody annoyed by it all."

"Get used to it. The way this country is going, it's only going to get worse," Ben added. "But you will be pleased to know that it's him in the photos."

"It's what?" Chapman said.

"It's Liam Finch."

"But the facial recognition—"

"Doesn't have him on their database. They have no frame of reference," he told them.

"So how do we know it's him then?"

"He told us," Freya said, cutting in before Ben described the confession in a less than flattering manner. "He's down there now working out if there's a plausible explanation for the bank notes coming from his bank account and hopefully worrying that his wife will give him an alibi for the night of the sixth. Which reminds me, I need somebody to go and see her, preferably before his custody clock strikes twelve."

"We can do that," Anderson said and then looked at Nillson. "Can't we?"

Nillson nodded.

"Good. Make that your job for this afternoon," Freya said. "We'll be going back inside, and with any luck, Ben and I can pay a visit to Mr and Mrs Carson to tell them that not only have we found their daughter but we have her killer in custody. That'll make a nice change."

"What did he have to say about Holly Carson anyway?" Anderson asked.

"We haven't got that far yet. I'm trying to lead him into it gently. Hopefully, he'll make another mistake."

"I wouldn't be surprised if Morrison advises him to go no

comment from here on in," Ben said. "He's already said too much, and the more he says, the harder it will be to defend him."

"Well, if he wants to play the long game, then I'll have to have a little look in my toolkit," Freya said. "I'm sure I can find a way to make his life more difficult than it needs to be."

"I thought you said we couldn't break the rules?" Nillson said.

"Who said anything about breaking the rules?" Freya replied, confident that she could manipulate the processes to work in her favour.

"Guv, I've got Gillespie on the phone," Chapman said, and Freya nodded for her to route the call through the loudspeaker.

"Give me some good news, Gillespie," Freya called out.

"Aye, well, I'm not sure if it's good news or not if I'm honest, boss. But I can give you a cause of death."

"Go on," she replied and found herself closing her eyes to focus on his voice and his voice alone.

"Hit and run."

"A hit and run," he said. "Well, more just a hit, really. The car hit her legs, breaking her femur and pelvis, she put her hands out instinctively, breaking her fingers, arm, and collarbone, and then she hit the deck. And when I say she hit the deck, boss—"

"Okay, we get the message," Freya said.

"Pip seems to think she would have suffered massive internal injuries. If she regained consciousness, her last few minutes or hours would have been unbearable."

"Loud and clear," Freya said. "Thank you very much. I think we'll all be trying to shake that image from our minds for the rest of the day. Okay, I want you both back here, please."

"There's one more thing," he said. "Well, two actually."

"What is it?" she said. "I'm about to go into an interview."

"I spoke to Kate, boss."

"Kate?"

"Aye, I mean Katy Southwell. You know?"

"Ah, I see," she said. "You mean you had a little private chat with your girlfriend?"

"Only to see what she was doing tonight," he replied. "Anyway, she asked me to tell you that the plastic is a match. Not sure what it means, but she said you and Ben would understand."

"The plastic is a match," she repeated and found Ben on the far side of the room at his desk giving a reluctant but complimentary nod. "She's referring to the plastic that Ben and I found in the old priory at Haverholme. It's a match with the plastic that Deborah Jarvis' body was wrapped in."

"So she was hidden in there?" Nillson said. "Whoever killed her dragged her across the field and stashed her in there until the house was empty?"

"Looks that way," Freya said. "Good work, Gillespie. Well done."

"There's another thing," he said. "From Kate, I mean."

"Go on," she said tentatively. Over the past year or so, she had come to know the team well and knew Gillespie enough to understand how his mind worked. He was the type of man who sought the higher ground and shied from trouble. He would always deliver the good news first, to get Freya on his side, and then leave her with the bad news, allowing him to end the call.

"It's the DNA she found on the underwear, boss. She ran it against Liam Finch's and that of Deborah Jarvis," he said, and for a brief and glorious moment she thought she heard a smile in his voice. "Two of the pairs belonged to Deborah Jarvis."

"Yes," she said and stopped herself from fist-pumping the air. "And?"

"Well, we haven't got Holly Carson's DNA, so we won't know if any belonged to her, but the rest of the underwear belonged to at least four other females."

"Four other females?" Nillson said. "Four?"

"Aye, that's what she said."

"And Finch?" Freya asked, knowing that a DNA match on the underwear would secure her the win she so desperately needed.

"Well, in Kate's own words, the distribution of semen was not in line with that of a rape."

"What the bloody hell does that mean?" Nillson asked.

"It means that when the semen was deposited," Freya explained. "The owner was not necessarily wearing the underwear at the time. In fact, the owner didn't even need to be there at the time the...deposit was made."

"Eh?" Anderson said, screwing up her face.

"The DNA was not collected from the gusset," Freya said, trying to explain it as delicately as she could. "In fact, it could have been anywhere on the garment."

And then Anderson fell in.

"Oh, God. Really? You mean, he used...used them to...on his own?"

"Afraid so," Gillespie said. "It's not a pleasant moment to be a man if I'm honest. Always feels like an own goal when men do that sort of thing."

"I second that," Ben added.

"Nobody in this room thinks either of you are capable of that," Freya said, hoping to reassure them both. "Is that all, Gillespie?"

"Well, there is one more thing," he said, and he hesitated for long enough that the pause had become awkward. "It's the DNA, boss. It's not Liam Finch's."

CHAPTER FORTY-TWO

"Bugger!"

Freya's voice echoed in the fire escape stairwell and Ben smiled to himself. He felt the same way about the setback, but the word on his mind contained one less syllable and began with an F.

"Bugger, bugger, bugger," she said and nearly threw herself against the wall. "That was our last card."

"We've got the plastic," Ben said.

"Oh, that doesn't mean anything though, does it? All it proves is that whoever killed Deborah Jarvis stored her there, alive, I might add, until the house was empty. All that would have done for us is connect the dots and allow us to develop the theory."

"He still needs to explain the money."

"And if he does? If he confesses to the money being his, what then? He gave her some money. So what?"

"And the calls?"

"He called her. He sent her text messages, and he called her."

"But he lied."

"Of course he did. Anyone would lie if they were wrongfully

accused of murder. Any defence would say the same," she said and then laughed. "I'd bloody well lie as well."

"We've got photos of him with her."

"So what? He was having an affair with a younger girl. She was nineteen. What are we going to do, ruin his marriage and then let him go?" She let her head fall back against the wall and lowered her voice. "Right, Holly Carson. What do we have on him?"

Ben climbed the few steps until their faces were level.

"Phone calls and text messages," he replied, and her eyes met his. "All right, we can place him in the local bar on the evening she went missing."

"Do you think they have CCTV?" Freya muttered. "And if they do, do you think they still have the files from seven years ago?"

"For God's sake, we had it all lined up," he said.

"And now we don't. The fact is that without it, we can't prove a thing." Aside from sitting beside each other in the interview room, it was perhaps the closest they had been since the previous night. He closed the gap a little, testing the water. "What are you doing, Ben?"

It was enough of a red flag for Ben to doubt what he was about to do, what he wanted to do. Their eyes met, and hers softened, and given the chance, Ben would have gazed into them for the rest of time.

But the doors on the floor above them burst open and Chapman seemed to erupt from the corridor, coming to an abrupt halt when she saw them.

"Oh, sorry," she said.

"What is it, Chapman?" Freya asked, and Ben dropped back a few steps to put some distance between them all.

Chapman held out a stack of papers but seemed reluctant to come closer. So Freya climbed the steps and took them from her.

"Finch's bank statement?" she said. "Is this about the bar bill? Because we've just been through this—"

"It's not the bar, guv," Chapman said. "Look at the dates after Holly Carson went missing."

"After?" She pored over the statement and Ben climbed again to read over her shoulder.

"Oh, Jesus," he said and beamed at Chapman. "Bloody good work, Denise. Bloody brilliant."

———

Finch and his solicitor sat in silence as if performing in the first act of a well-rehearsed play. Freya, accustomed to the ploys of the guilty, took her seat. However, if what Ben had said the previous night bore any truth, then her silence would bear sharper teeth in greater numbers.

The buzzer sounded again, like the bell before a fight, but instead of the fighters charging from their corners, Freya continued her silence until Finch appeared unsettled and sought some kind of statement from his solicitor.

"Are we going to move forward?" Morrison asked, sounding unsure of himself.

"If your client is ready to discuss the evidence against him, then yes," Freya replied, and she waited some more.

Finch cleared his throat, licked his lips, and then took a breath.

Freya watched, unmoving.

"Regarding the serial numbers on the erm...on the bank notes," he began, stammering slightly. "They *were* mine."

"I'm well aware they were yours," Freya said. "What I was keen to understand was how they came to be in Debroah Jarvis' possession."

"I gave them to her," he said, forcing the words from his mouth as if they might run back inside should he falter.

"When was this?" Freya asked. "Do you remember?"

The question was apparently unexpected, and Finch glanced

at Morrison again. But aside from advising him to offer a no-comment response, he was in no position to assist.

"It's a simple question," Freya said, keen to keep the pressure on. "You withdrew the money from the ATM on Ruskington High Street, and you handed the money to Deborah Jarvis. Was this the day before she went missing? The week before? Or was it the year before?"

"I can't remember. Honestly, I can't–"

"Well, perhaps you can tell me where you met her to give the money? Was it in the bar? Did she come to your office? You must remember that, surely? If I handed somebody two hundred pounds, I'd remember, wouldn't you, Detective Inspector?"

"Certainly I would," Ben said.

"I won't ask for your opinion, Mr Morrison. Don't worry. You won't be obliged to lie on the recording."

Morrison's face reddened, and he focused on making his notes.

"I really can't remember," Finch said. "But the notes were mine. Although, we've been through it and I don't see how this proves that I had anything to do with Deborah's death."

"The money is irrelevant, really, Mr Finch. Just as when or where you gave it to her is irrelevant. See, I didn't expect you to know. How could you know? It was five years ago. Even if you had claimed to remember, it would never stand up in court. `Five years is a long time to remember such details."

"So, why–"

"The point is that had this been a solitary event, you might have remembered. But it wasn't, was it? It was a common occurrence."

"Sorry?"

"It wasn't the first or the last time you gave her money, was it? It can't have been or you would have remembered."

Morrison gave a shake of his head and Finch resorted to those two fatal words.

"No comment."

"That's okay. I think we've explored that enough for now," Freya said. "Now, I have a pair of officers on their way to question your wife concerning your movements from the sixth to the eighth of May 2019, so until I hear from them—"

"You what?" Finch cut in. "I told you not to go there. I'm talking, aren't I? Leave my bloody wife out of it."

Freya waited for him to resettle before speaking.

"Moving on," she said, and out of frustration, he flung himself back in his seat. "I'd like to talk to you about somebody else. Another poor girl who was reported missing, and coincidentally or not was recently discovered at your house."

"What?" he said. "What is this, a wind-up?"

"Sadly, we're not paid to play pranks on people, Mr Finch. We're paid to investigate murders, to bring justice to the victims, and to bring closure to the families. Which means we're often short of time, so playing pranks isn't at the top of our agenda."

"Who?" he breathed more than spoke. "Who is it?"

"I was hoping you could tell me—"

"Oh, how can I possibly know?" he said. "How can I? I didn't put Deborah under my floorboard and I certainly didn't put anybody else there. So how can I possibly know? What do you want me to do, make a name up? Should I work my way through the bloody alphabet until I get lucky?"

"Start with H," Freya said, and his face turned ashen grey in the blink of an eye.

"What?" he whispered, but Freya said nothing. "H?" He studied Freya's expression and glanced at Ben briefly for some sort of confirmation. "No. Not..." He laughed like a madman and shook his head, letting that laugh morph into a cry. "No. Not Holly. Please, no."

"When did you last see her, Mr Finch?"

"Oh, God, it is her," he said, letting his head fall back. He covered his face with his hands and his entire body seemed to tense and convulse until, at last, he erupted, screaming at the ceiling above. The whole episode lasted more than a minute, and only when he leaned forward and rested his head on his clasped hands on the table did Freya succumb to the temptation to utter a few well-selected words.

"Were you and Holly well-acquainted?" she asked, and he lunged at her with his hand only falling short due to the table being bolted to the floor. Freya moved back casually, but Finch had reseated himself before Ben could reach him. "That was a silly move," Freya said.

Ben opened the door and summoned a uniformed officer who arrived moments later.

"I want him cuffed," Ben said, then returned to his seat, his anger dissipating.

The officer followed the order and now, cuffed to his seat, Finch entered into a meditative state of deep breathing.

"Could you please get him some water?" Freya asked the officer and then waited for him to leave. "Mr Finch, we have to discuss Holly's death."

"May I ask on what grounds you believe my client to have any involvement in this second murder?" Morrison asked.

"Of course," Freya replied. "Aside from her remains being discovered at his home, Holly Carson was reported missing while Mr Finch was in possession of the home. Two years before Debroah Jarvis was reported missing, in fact. So there can be no doubt that he had access to the property."

"That in itself doesn't prove that he—"

"Secondly," Freya said, "Holly Carson worked for your client. She was a junior partner, in fact. An esteemed position for somebody so young, as you very likely know, Mr Morrison."

"Again, and please let me finish this time, none of this is tangible evidence."

"The day Holly Carson went missing, she told her parents that she would be home late, as she was going out for drinks. She didn't say who with," Freya said. "But needless to say Mr Finch's bank statement shows three payments of just over six pounds at a local bar. This demonstrates that he popped out for a drink with somebody after work, although in fairness, we can't know who."

"Quite, but–" Morrison said.

"But it's not proof," Freya finished before he did. "I understand. But just like with Deborah Jarvis, we have text messages and phone calls."

"She worked with him. Of course there are messages and calls. My colleagues call me all the time."

"At two-thirty in the morning?" Ben asked, and Morrison quietened.

"Now," Freya began. "One of these investigations alone, I agree, would amount to nothing more than coincidence. But two? Your client interacted with two missing girls within days of them being reported missing, both of whom ended up being found dead at his home. Now, Mr Morrison, answer me this. How will a jury interpret those facts? How would you even begin to defend them?"

"One at a time," he said. "I'd defend them one at a time."

"Agreed," she said. "Individually, they amount to nothing, but collectively, they suggest your client is privy to some seriously sinister secrets."

"I'm interested in the box," Morrison said. "You have it listed on the evidence you submitted, but it's not been mentioned. Why is that?"

"What box?" Finch said, and he stared at them all. "What box is this?"

"It was found buried in your garden, Mr Finch, and, Mr Morrison, you cannot expect me to discuss every piece of evidence at once."

"No, but given the contents of the box, I would have assumed it would have been higher up on your agenda."

"What contents?" Finch said. "Can someone tell me what is going on here?"

"The box that we found buried in your garden contained several pairs of female underwear, Mr Finch."

"So I presume these items have been analysed by your forensics team?" Morrison said.

"They have," Freya said, feeling the balance shift in his favour. "And I can confirm that at least two of them belonged to Deborah Jarvis."

"And the others?" Morrison said.

"We're still investigating," Freya told him.

"And can I assume that you or your team have found some kind of evidence that links the box or its contents to my client?"

"We have discovered DNA," Freya said. "DNA from multiple semen samples."

"This is crazy," Finch said. "This is all lies. It has to be lies—"

He stopped when Morrison held his hand up and leaned forward to meet Freya across the table.

"Does the DNA found on those items of clothing match that of my client, Chief Inspector?"

She stared at him and needn't have said a thing had it not been for the recording.

"Not yet," she said.

"Not yet," he repeated. "Thank you. So you have nothing but coincidence and conjecture. Do you seriously intend to keep Mr Finch in custody for the duration, or perhaps you have something else up your sleeve, because if you do, then I would love to hear it?"

"You don't have to hear it," Freya said, and she slid the pile of papers that Chapman had given her on the staircase from the file and pushed it across the table. "You can read it."

Morrison nudged his glasses further up his nose and peered down at the bank statements.

"What am I looking at here?"

If the balance of power had shifted briefly from Freya to

Morrison, it had begun its return but now hung somewhere between them, ready to be snatched by the keenest of the two.

"Shall I tell you how Holly Carson died, Mr Finch?" she said.

"Chief Inspector, I rather think you should—"

"She was walking along a road. A country lane, more than likely. Somewhere quiet. Somewhere dark. She would have seen the headlights and maybe even stepped onto the verge to let the car pass." Freya shook her head. "But the driver had no intention of passing." Finch, red-eyed, raised his head and listened intently. "The front of the car connected with her legs, shattering her femur and snapping her pelvis like the branch of a tree. She put her hands out, just as any of us might. Several fingers broke, and her arm, and her then collarbone." Freya let the image settle, and he watched as a tear meandered across his face. "The force of the impact sent her flying through the air. Nobody can know how far, but suffice to say that when she hit the tarmac it was with sufficient force that the back of her skull fractured. She would have laid there dying. Her organs would have been ruptured causing massive internal bleeding. She died alone, scared, and in terrible, terrible pain."

Just as it had in the incident room, the story had garnered empathy, and each person in the room digested it in their own way.

Morrison, having found the particular line on the bank statement, slid it across to Finch, who read it and exhaled audibly.

"Two thousand seven hundred pounds spent at A2B Auto Repairs, just three days after Holly Carson was reported missing. Do you want to know what the garage said when we called them?"

"That it was my car?" Finch said softly.

"What did you tell them? That you hit a deer or a badger or something?"

Finch shrugged and dismissed the comment. He leaned into his solicitor, whispered something, and then waited. Morrison's eyes flicked from Freya to Ben, and then to the handcuffs. He gave Finch's words some thought and provided his own whispered response, which the suspect listened to intently, before spending a few seconds to prepare himself.

"I had a Ford back then. A Focus," he said, by way of an introduction.

"That's right," Freya said. "So, Mr Finch. I'm going to ask you this once, and please think carefully before you answer. Did you murder either Deborah Jarvis, Holly Carson, or both?"

Finch let his head hang low. He rubbed at his scalp slowly, as if he couldn't quite decide if now was the time to confess.

"To deny the offence is the advice Mr Morrison will give," Freya said. "But there does come a point when all the evidence is stacked against you that a jury will look upon a persistent denial unfavourably. That's my advice, and I'll understand if you choose not to take it, but for what it's worth, I've seen the damage denial can do, and I've seen juries look upon the truth far more favourably. You'll appear human, Mr Finch."

"Human?" he said. "Is that what I am, human?" He slid the bank statements back to them, glanced briefly at Morrison, and then stared down at his handcuffs as if coming to terms with the fact that his incarceration had already begun. "If I say what you want me to say, will you let me tell my wife? Before your colleagues get there, I mean. I want to see her. I want to explain it in my own words."

"Arrangements could be made," Freya said, checking with Ben, who immediately pulled his phone from his pocket, ready to make the call. "However, I'm not in the habit of negotiating with people in your position."

"I rather think you should reevaluate your position," Morrison said. "My client has stated clearly that he is ready to provide his version of events on the condition that, for the benefit of his marriage, he is given the chance to speak to his wife. Now, Chief Inspector Bloom, you can either give him that opportunity or you can take the long road, and I think we all know that the majority of the evidence put before us today still needs a great deal of work." He paused for a moment, perhaps to read Freya's expression. "You know as well I do that could take weeks. Months, even."

"It's a bold move, Mr Finch," she said. "When the prosecution hears this recording, they could easily convince a jury of your guilt."

"I think to convince them of his guilt is a push," Morrison said. "And if we're going to foresee a subsequent trial, then perhaps it's worth considering how the jury would feel about the DNA on those...items of clothing you found, and what a claim of reasonable doubt would do to your case."

The full weight of power shifted to Morrison who closed his file, clicked his pen closed, and then, like any good businessman closing a deal, sat back and waited.

Ben's stare bore into Freya but she couldn't look his way. She found herself lost in Morrison's patient eyes.

She gathered her photos and slid them into her file then closed it.

"Have Mr Finch taken back to his cell please," she said to Ben, without looking at him. "Then make the call."

CHAPTER FORTY-THREE

"Where are you?" Ben said, without even saying hello.

"Just pulling into the road now. Why? What's happened?"

"Change of plan. We need her here."

"What?"

"We need Mrs Finch here. He's ready to talk, but in doing so, his infidelity will become public knowledge. He wants the chance to speak to his wife before she finds out from anyone else."

"Sod that," Nillson said. "He can't make demands."

"That's just it. He can. If we want him to provide a full confession, then we'll need to play the game."

"Oh, come on–"

"What's the alternative, Anna? What have we really got apart from coincidence and conjecture? He gave Deborah Jarvis the money. He's admitted to that. But so what? What man his age doesn't treat his much younger mistress if he has one? He was at a bar on the night Holly Carson went missing, but again, so what? We can't prove he was with her."

"Phone calls?"

"He was having an affair with them both, Anna. Of course

there are phone calls and messages. He probably gave money to Holly Carson, too."

"But surely anyone in their right mind can look at this and see he had something to do with it. It's bloody obvious. And while it might be obvious, we still have one huge hurdle to get over. The DNA on the underwear."

"So?"

"So, it's not his."

"Then we drop it. We don't use it as evidence."

"We can't," Ben said. "His defence would bring it up. In fact, it's the first thing they would do. If it's somebody else's DNA, then there are grounds for reasonable doubt, and reasonable doubt is enough to put the frighteners on any jury. You can't send a man down for twenty or thirty years if there's a shred of doubt that he was innocent. It's not up to him or his defence to prove he is innocent—"

"No, it's down to us to prove he's guilty," Nillson replied, and let out a heavy sigh. Ben heard her slam her hands on her steering wheel. "I bloody hate this."

"Don't get yourself worked up. We'll get there. Look how far we've come, and remember, these deaths are five years old and more. We've had what, three days? Four? We'll get him. And if takes a little longer, then so be it. Right now, it's about crossing the Ts and dotting the Is."

"I know, I know," she said.

"Anderson, can you hear me?" Ben said.

"I'm here," she replied.

"Go knock on the door, will you? I need a word with Anna."

A few seconds of silence followed, and then he heard the car door open and close.

"Sorry, Ben," Nillson said. "I know. I shouldn't let it get to me. I just feel like the rules are stacked against us, you know? It baffles me that in a civilised society where law and order prevail, every minute detail of what we do has to conform to some regulation or other, while the criminal which, let's face it, Finch is, gets to use those same regulations and processes to his advantage. No wonder so many of them go free on technicalities. Honestly, it just winds me up."

"Are you finished?" Ben asked and she huffed.

"I am. Sorry."

"Right, do me a favour, will you? Pull yourself together. Take a few moments to breathe. You're one of the best detectives I know and what you're doing is letting your emotions get the better of you. To be honest, I didn't even know you had emotions, so it's actually quite reassuring to learn that you're human like the rest of us." She gave a quiet laugh but said nothing. "Anderson looks up to you, Anna. Just remember that. It's fine to empathise with Deborah Jarvis and Holly Carson, but instead of pitying them, work for them. Fight for them. Fight for their justice. When technicalities get in the way, then outsmart the technicalities. Beat them, Anna. Because if there's one thing I know about you, it's that when you get knocked down, you get straight back up. Quicker than anyone else I know. It's one of the things I admire about you, and I'm not just saying that. I mean it. I wish I was as strong as you are. So dust yourself down and let's get those girls some justice, alright?"

He wondered if she was still listening but then heard her breathing.

"I wish I had recorded that," she said. "I could have played it on repeat while I slept like one of those stop-smoking CDs."

"It's the truth, Anna," he said. "I admire you. We all do. And you know what? Sometimes I need a bit of a pep talk too. Sometimes I let it all get to me."

"I suppose the boss drags you back to your feet, does she?"

"Not always," he said. "If I'm honest, more often than not it's her who knocks me down in the first place."

She laughed and then let it fade.

"Cheers, Ben," she said. "You're right, of course. I'll try not to let it get to me. Hold on, she's coming back."

The car door opened, and the sound of the street came over the line.

"She's not there," Anderson said. "There's nobody home."

"Brilliant," Nillson's flippancy suggested the beginnings of another rant.

"It's okay, it's okay," Ben said before it escalated. "Find her. Alright? Just find her and bring her here, and remember, this is for those girls, and it's just another part of the fight. So what do you do?"

"Fight back," Nillson said. "We get up, dust ourselves down, and fight back."

CHAPTER FORTY-FOUR

Ben entered the incident room and slid his phone into his pocket before strolling over to an empty desk and perching on the edge. Freya watched him from the corner of her eye. She finished the sentence she was writing and then set her pen down, indicating she was ready to listen.

"The wife's out," he said.

"At work, maybe?"

"She doesn't work," Chapman said. "Not according to HMRC, anyway."

"I thought the days of being a kept woman were over," Freya mused.

"Nillson and Anderson are looking for her in the high street, and I've got an ANPR alert set up just in case her car is picked up on camera."

"Maybe it's not a bad thing," Freya said. "I've managed to get a custody extension, so we've got about thirty-two hours before he goes free. I suggest we use that to close off any remaining loose ends. If the CPS sees reasonable doubt, they'll reject the prosecution, and then we'll be forced to let him go." She held an index finger up to Ben. "And we are not letting him go. Not now when we're so close."

"Agreed," Ben replied. "So what are we looking at here? The DNA, obviously."

Freya turned to the whiteboard.

"If the DNA isn't Finch's, then who else had access to the house?" She stood and examined the list. "Nick MacMillan?"

"The exchange took place six weeks later," Ben said. "Finally, we get to cut a head off."

"Sadly, our beast has many heads," Freya said and moved down the list. "Okay, Sebastian Groves. He was Kevin's friend and we haven't spoken to him yet."

"He would have known the house was empty, and like Anne Hargreaves, he wasn't a fan of Deborah."

"He also knew Holly Carson, remember?" Chapman said. "His number was on her phone bill."

Freya gave it some thought and then returned to the board.

"Have we overlooked him?" Freya asked. "What does he do? And please don't tell me he works for the accountancy firm."

"Actually, he works in the local recycling centre," Chapman said, flicking through her notes. "His employment history is a broad mix of short-lived, unskilled work. Factory worker, security guard, refuse collector. It seems he hasn't quite found his vocation."

"Find out what you can about him. Is he known to us at all?"

"Not directly, guv," she replied. "He attended the same school as the others, went to college with Anne—"

"Went to college?"

"And university," Chapman added.

"Then what the hell is he doing working in a recycling centre?"

"Some people aren't cut out for the jobs they were going for," Ben said. "He might have grand ideas about being an accountant, or a...I don't know, a doctor—"

"Law," Chapman said. "I checked his Facebook page. He studied law at Lincoln Univeristy."

"Right," Ben continued. "Imagine being in education all that time and then getting a placement at a law firm? It's enough to put anyone off."

"I don't buy it," Freya said. "He's going from unskilled job to unskilled job when he must at least have some kind of acumen. Even if he doesn't practise law, you'd think that an individual with those credentials could at least do something like...I don't know, manage a shop. Just do something a little less arduous for a lot more money."

"He doesn't have credentials, guv," Chapman said.

"He what?"

"He doesn't have credentials," Chapman said. "Aside from his a A-levels."

"Then why go to university? Why on earth did he leave University with nothing but bloody A-levels and O-levels?"

"GCSEs," Ben corrected. "It's not the seventies."

"Whatever. The point is that it's unheard of."

"Don't you think you're trying to find something that isn't there?" Ben asked. "Are we talking about Sebastian Groves' education or are we talking about two murders here? What he does for a living is irrelevant. We should be asking what he was doing in 2019 and 2017, and where he was on the nights the girls went missing."

"And if his DNA matches the underwear," Chapman said.

"Right. Why don't we start there? Nillson is in the area. She can go and take a sample. She must have a kit in her car. If he has nothing to hide, then he won't mind helping us, will he? Worst case scenario, we can cut another head off."

"And the best case scenario?"

"Then we're no worse off than when we started," he told her. "It's a process of elimination, isn't it? We work through the list. Sebastian Groves, Ross Elder, Kevin Stone−"

"Kevin Stone," she said. "Liam Finch's adopted son."

"We've spoken to him already. He's still down as a primary suspect."

"But we don't have his DNA. Or do we? He was processed, wasn't he?"

"He was," Chapman said. "But at the time, we didn't have the box of undies, so there was no actual need to fast-track it. It's probably still in the batch waiting to be sent in."

"Well, fast-track it then," Freya said. "He's a primary suspect."

"In Chapman's defence, Freya, he was questioned when all we had was a pile of bones. One pile, I might add."

"Yes, I'm sorry, Chapman. I didn't mean to snap. But this could lead somewhere."

"What about Groves and Elder?" Ben asked.

"What about them?"

"Well, should I divert Nillson and Anderson to help out? It's a better use of their time than driving around looking for Finch's wife."

"I agree. Get Gillespie and Cruz to help out, too," Freya said. "The problem is, Kevin Stone is a multi-drop delivery driver. He could be anywhere."

"I called the firm he works for last time. They use GPS to track all their drivers," Chapman said. "Had a unit from the local station pick him up."

"Can you repeat the process?"

"Probably," she replied.

"Good," Freya said, checking her watch. "It's one p.m. now, so by close of business today, we should have all three samples. Assuming Southwell's team doesn't mind a bit of overtime, we could put a name to the DNA by this evening."

"That's twelve hours or more to bring whoever it is in for questioning," Ben said.

"There is something I don't understand," Chapman said. "Let's say the DNA belongs to one of these boys. All that proves is that they obtained the underwear somehow and...you know?"

"Deposited their DNA?" Freya suggested.

"Right," Chapman replied. "It doesn't prove they murdered Holly or Deborah."

"But it does prove they had access..." Freya stopped mid-sentence.

"What?" Ben said. "It proves they had access to what?"

"To the underwear," Freya said. "Who had access to both victims' underwear?"

"Liam Finch," Ben said.

"And?" She waited for one of them to pick up on where she was leading them, but grew impatient. "Oh, come on, if Deborah Jarvis and Holly Carson were both, at different times, sleeping with Liam Finch, it makes sense that both of them would, at some point, have been to his house."

"Where Kevin Stone could easily have discovered them," Ben said, and Freya clicked her fingers.

"Where Kevin Stone could have found out about the affairs, and if, for example, he had a little underwear fetish going on—"

"He could easily have stolen them," Ben said.

"And," Freya said, growing excited, "what did Ross Elder and Anne Hargreaves say about Kevin Stone?"

"That he was a little odd and not great with the girls."

"Creepy is the word I would have used," Freya said.

"Hold on," Chapman said, flicking through her files. "We had that report on local sexual offences. Here it is." She held up a single sheet of paper to the light and nudged her glasses up her nose. "There's a few indecent exposures, two of which were in Haverholem Park."

"Stone, do you think?" Ben asked Freya, who shrugged, not wanting to commit.

"Then there's a sexual assault claim on the other side of Anwick that is still unsolved."

"We can't pin them all on Stone," Ben said. "That could have been anyone."

"You're right. But I think we can employ a little experience to make a judgement call. Which leads me back to my point. Who, of all the people on this list that might have known about Stone's fetish, might have cause to defend him?"

"Liam Finch," Chapman said. "He's protecting him. He knows his son is a weirdo and he's protecting him. That makes perfect sense. When Holly Carson was killed, Finch was on a twelve-month driving ban and Stone had a provisional licence."

"So Stone was using his dad's car?" Ben asked.

"I can check to see if he was insured at the time, but it's very likely," Chapman said. "What are you going to do if you get a ban, leave your car to rot on the drive or let your family use it?"

"Let's not run away with ourselves," Ben said. "We don't know that Stone was...into that sort of thing. Not yet."

"Ben's right. We haven't time to get this wrong, so let's go over it. Liam Finch is sleeping with Holly Carson, who worked for him. He wouldn't bring her back to his house while his wife was there, but there's every chance Kevin might have stumbled upon them."

"Stealing her underwear is a far cry from mowing her down," Ben said. "How does he make that leap?"

"He doesn't," Freya said. "Not purposefully, anyway. I mean, we could dream up all kinds of reasons for him going after her in his dad's car and knocking her down, but it's far more likely that if he did knock her down, then it was some kind of accident."

"So, he panicked then?" Ben said, and Freya nodded. "He dumped her in his father's boot, took her back to the house and buried her in the garden."

"Why the garden?" Freya asked. "Why not somewhere in the woods or the river?"

"There's far more chance of getting away with it. Dump her anywhere public and there's every chance she'll be found. Let's face it, you saw the spot where she was buried. It's not exactly

Kew Gardens, is it? I doubt anyone has set foot in those trees since he buried her."

"Fair enough. How do we prove it?" Freya asked, which resulted in prolonged silence, save for Chapman's fingers on her keyboard.

"We search the car," she said.

"Sorry?"

"We search the car," Chapman repeated, and she nodded at her laptop. "It's registered to an address in Woodhall Spa."

"It was seven years ago," Ben said.

"Well, our friends in CSI had better polish their goggles then, hadn't they?" Freya replied. "Besides, if Holly Carson's body was in as bad a state as Gillespie would have us believe, then it would take more than a ten-pound car wash to get rid of the stains."

"Not to mention the hair," Chapman added. "There's always hair."

"Right. I think there's a real chance here, Ben."

"So we're going to knock on a stranger's door, impound their car, have Southwell and her team go over it, along with everything else we're throwing at them, analyse the results, and then put a case together for the CPS all before Finch's custody clock expires?"

"Are you up for the challenge, Ben?"

"I am," he said with a new lease of energy. He grabbed his phone from his pocket, dialled a number, and then sat back on his desk. "Jim, it's me. I need you to do something for me."

CHAPTER FORTY-FIVE

Cruz stopped his car beside a skip that was so large that it required a set of steel steps for people to dump their unwanted belongings into it.

"This is the tip then, is it?" Gillespie said.

"I'm not sure they call it that anymore," Cruz replied. "No doubt that phrase offends somebody somewhere. This is the recycling centre."

Before them, a line of cars queued to use the dozens of bays and skips, identical to the one he had parked beside.

"Look at them,' Gillespie said. "That bloke just threw a perfectly good radiator into the skip. There's nothing wrong with it."

"He might have bought a new one."

"A radiator? Who buys a new radiator? It's not like a pair of curtains, is it? You don't just switch them out with your soft furnishings." Cruz held his breath as the onslaught of one of Gillespie's rants took hold. "Do you think they wake up in the morning and say, I know what I'll do, I'll change my cushions, get a new rug, swap out my curtains, and do you know what? I'll get myself a new radiator to go with the colour scheme."

He was still going on when Cruz climbed from the car and searched for somebody who worked there.

"If we wait here long enough, we'll probably see him come up with some doors," Gillespie said, then put on a deep and slow voice. "Thought I'd really push the boat this year. Got meself some new doors, so the handles match my new radiators."

Cruz flagged down a man in a yellow, high-vis vest.

"Excuse me, mate," he said, and immediately the man came over to them, shaking his head.

"Now then," he said, and Cruz was pleased to be in the company of somebody sensible. But he pointed to his little hatchback. "You can't park there."

"Oh, it's okay. We're just here to see someone. I wonder if you could tell us where we could find–"

"That's the electrical appliances skip," the man said.

"Right," Cruz replied. "Like I said, we're just here to–"

"You're in the way. You'll have to move it."

"Sorry, but can I just ask?" Gillespie said, and Cruz sensed this was not going to be easy. "What is it we're in the way of, exactly?"

"The skip," the man replied. "That's for electrical appliances, that is."

"I understand the purpose of the skip, but right now nobody is using it, are they?"

"But there might be," he replied. "Anyone could come along and use it. That's the point."

"But they aren't, are they? And if, heaven forbid, somebody did come along to use it, they could simply park beside us, couldn't they?"

"That's not the point. You can't just park anywhere."

Gillespie gestured at the wide expanse of concrete around them. The lanes for cars to navigate the multitude of recycling bays had been painted on and Cruz understood the man's point. Had somebody parked beside his car, then the next car would have to drive around them, thus crossing the lanes.

"Well, where are we supposed to park?"

"You're not," he said with a surprised laugh. "It's not a bleeding picnic area, you know? You come here, drop your recycling off, and then be on your way."

"What if we were, say, the police?" Gillespie said, and he fished his warrant card from his pocket, which seemed to make no difference to the man's attitude whatsoever.

"Then you'd park in the car park like the rest of us." He turned and pointed to where half a dozen cars were parked beside a portacabin so old it could have been mistaken for a skip. "What do you want, anyway? Nobody said you were coming."

"I didn't realise we had to make an appointment," Gillespie said. "It's the bloody tip."

"Look," Cruz said, "I'm sorry, we got off to a poor start. We just need two minutes with an employee of yours and we'll be on our way. That's all."

"An employee?"

"Sebastian Groves," Cruz told him. "Can you tell us where we can find him?"

"Seb? He's on greens, I think." He nodded sideways to where the majority of the cars were lined up beside rows of bays.

"Greens?" Gillespie said. "What, is he sorting through broccoli and cabbage, or something?"

"He means garden waste," Cruz said, tiring of the entire ordeal. He nodded a thanks to the man and started off towards the bays.

"Whoa, whoa, whoa," the man said and ran the few steps to catch up. "You can't just walk over there."

"Sorry?"

"You can't walk across here like that. It's health and safety, you know?"

"I can't walk across this concrete to get to over there?"

"No way. The boss'll hit the roof if he sees you walking across there without a high-vis vest on."

"So how do I get there?"

"You drive," he said as if the answer was obvious.

"I drive?"

"Unless you want to come with me and I'll fix you up with a vest each."

"Sorry, come with you where?"

"To the office." He nodded again to the portacabin where the employees' cars were parked, and then Gillespie started up again.

"Hold on, mate. So we can't walk across the concrete to where Sebastian Groves is sorting brussel sprouts from carrots and beans, but we *can* walk across the concrete to the office, which is clearly further away."

"Because that's where we keep the vests," the man said. "Besides, you could get hit by a car. Then what? I'm not going to lose my job just because you can't follow the rules, copper or no bleeding copper."

"There's a five-mile-an-hour speed limit," Gillespie said, exasperated. "I've got more chance of being knocked down in the bloody tortoise exhibit at the zoo. This is madness."

"Well, if you'd made an appointment, we could have accommodated you without any of this fuss."

"We're investigating a murder, you half-wit. The whole point of us arriving unannounced is to surprise the fella. Catch him off-guard, you know?"

"A murder? Seb, involved in a murder?"

"He's not involved, we just need to ask him a few questions," Cruz said, flinging his hands up. "I've had enough of this. The pair of you are driving me mad. I'm going to walk across the concrete, I'm going to talk to Sebastian Groves, and then I'm going to leave. If you try to stop me, I'll nick you for obstruction. Do I make myself clear?"

Even Gillespie shut up. Both men stared wide-eyed at him.

"Right," Cruz said, and, turning his back on them, he marched across the concrete only for an old man in a red Honda to slam on his brakes and lean on his horn. He mouthed abuse and tapped his temple with his index finger.

Cruz let the man pass but refused to turn back, knowing full well that Gillespie and the health and safety policeman would be shaking their heads at him.

"Sebastian Groves?" he said when reached what appeared to be the garden waste section. A young man in a yellow high-vis vest leaned against the barrier. He held a folded newspaper in one hand and in the other a biro. He looked up from his paper and appraised Cruz's clothes from his feet to his shirt.

"That's me," he said, dropping the newspaper to his side, revealing a half-completed crossword."Why?"

He glanced about him, perhaps searching for some kind of clue as to who Cruz was, but not even the patrons paid them any attention. They just went about their business taking bags and items from their cars and dumping them into the skips.

Cruz discreetly held up his warrant card and then slipped it into his pocket.

"I wonder if I could ask you a few questions," Cruz said, as a car pulled up beside the bay. A mature lady climbed out, making a show of her frailty.

"What's it about?" Groves asked.

"Is there somehwere we can go? Somewhere private?"

"Not likely," he said, and he folded the newspaper again so that it fit into his back pocket. He strode over to the woman's car. "Need a hand, love?"

"Oh, you are a dear," she replied, glancing up at Cruz as if she expected him to help. "My husband used to do all this, you know?"

"That's okay. I don't mind."

"I lost him a few years back. It's the little things he did, you know? There's not a day goes by I'm not grateful for what he used to do."

Groves may have been intelligent enough to attempt the

Express crossword, but he had failed to see what was abundantly evident to Cruz. The woman was clearly able enough to load her car in the first place.

He heaved a bag of grass clippings from the boot and dumped it into the skip, and all the while, the lady smiled at Cruz, as if she silently judged him for not being as helpful as Groves.

"I don't work here," Cruz told her. "I'd help, but you know? It's a health and safety thing."

She didn't reply, but she waited for Groves to return for the second bag.

"I'd get one of those brown bins, I would. Used to have one when my husband was alive," she said. "But they wanted forty pounds this year. Forty pounds for a plastic bin? Well, I don't know who can afford that, but I certainly can't."

Groves closed the boot for her and then tipped the last bag into the skip. He folded all three bags, and then returned them to her, and by way of thanks, she fished a fifty-pence piece from her purse and slid it into his hand with a wink.

"Get yourself something nice," she said.

Groves pocketed the coin and then turned his attention to Cruz.

"What's this about, mate? I'm busy, and the boss isn't a fan of private conversations."

"But the crossword is okay, is it?"

Groves sighed and then raised his hand to flag a colleague.

"I'm taking my break early," he called out. "Keep an eye on my bays, will you?"

"What am I, a bloody octopus?" the reply came. "You've already had a visitor this morning. Don't let old Grimy catch you or you'll be out on your ear."

They walked past the other bays, where drivers tossed lumps of wood, bags of rubbish, and all manner of perfectly good pieces of furniture into the line of skips.

"This about Debs, is it?" he asked while they walked, and Cruz gave him a questioning look. "Anne told me."

"Your earlier visitor?"

"She was worried. Said you lot had been hounding her. She also told us you nicked her boss."

"We're making enquiries into Deborah Jarvis' death, Sebastian," Cruz told him as they came to a set of three steel steps leading up to the portacabin.

"I don't see how I can help. I barely knew her."

"I'm sure it'll all become clear when we're inside," Cruz said, urging them into the portcabin, which was exactly as he had expected it to be. Their footsteps boomed on the thin floor. Tables and chairs were set out for the workers to drink tea, and health and safety posters covered the walls. To one side of the room was a table with tea-making facilities, and Cruz was quite glad that Groves hadn't offered a drink. The mugs looked like it was only the grime that held them together.

He led them to the corner table beside a window, from where Groves could keep an eye out for his boss.

"As I expect you'll appreciate," Cruz began, "I can't go into too much detail. But there are certain questions you can answer that might help us."

"So I'm in no bother then?"

"You? Oh no. Not yet, anyway. You see, as part of our investigation, we developed a list of people who saw Deborah Jarvis last."

"And I'm on that list, am I?"

"You are," Cruz said, as the door opened and Gillespie came in. Groves eyed him curiously. "My colleague, Sergeant Gillespie. He's just been having the health and safety briefing from one of your diligent colleagues. Anyway, what we'd like to understand is what happened that night. As far as we can gather, Kevin Stone and Deborah were close to a stile in the field, while you, Ross

Elder, and Anne Hargreaves were beside the fire a few hundred feet away."

"That's right," Groves said.

"Didn't you think that a little odd?" Gillespie asked, as usual taking over from Cruz.

"Not really. Kevin wasn't really a good mate. He was Ross' mate, but not ours."

"Yours and Anne's, you mean? What about Deborah?"

"She wasn't anyone's mate, as far as I know. I mean, Kevin liked her, but she was probably just leading him on. She was like that, Debs. He was just her plaything."

"But there was nothing between them? They weren't in a relationship, or anything like that?"

"Kev, in a relationship?" He laughed. "I wouldn't be surprised if he was still a virgin. Not exactly what you would call a ladies' man if you know what I mean?"

"Aye, we all know someone like that," Gillespie said, and his eyes rolled around to Cruz. "We understand that when Kevin realised she was missing, he called you all to help find her."

"That's it, yeah. He'd found her shoe, I think. He was in a right old state."

"But you didn't find her?"

"Of course not, no."

"So, you couldn't find her," Gillespie said. "And then you all went home?"

"No. No, we went back to the fire. I said all this in my statement. I'm sure I did."

"All of you? Including Kevin Stone?"

"Yeah. He called her parents. Her old man told him not to worry and that she was probably just seeking attention."

"But she left her shoe."

"It was dark," he said. "You couldn't see your hands in front of your face."

"But you were calling for her, I presume," Cruz said. "Surely she would have heard you and called back?"

"I suppose," he replied. "Assuming, of course, she wanted to be found."

Cruz took a moment to imagine the scene and felt a certain allegiance to Groves' explanation. There was no reason that Cruz could see to doubt his sincerity.

"What about before that?" he said. "If it was that dark, am I right in thinking that you couldn't see them sitting near the stile?"

"I could barely see Ross and Anne and they were sitting beside me," he laughed.

"And how long were they there? How long was Kevin Stone alone with her before he called for help?"

Groves shook his head and screwed his face up.

"Dunno. Fifteen minutes? Bit more maybe? No longer than half an hour, as we hadn't been there long."

"Half an hour?" Cruz said thoughtfully. "And nobody thought to mention this to the officer who took the missing persons report?"

"Why would we? What is it..." He paused. "Hang on. You don't think that Kevin could have–"

"We're looking into all possibilities," Cruz said.

"But you think it's him don't you?" he said. "Anne said she was found at his old house. It was empty. They were moving out."

"What we're not doing is jumping to conclusions, Sebastian."

"Bloody Kevin?" he said, sitting back in his chair. "Of course it is. After all this time."

"Sebastian, is there anything we should know about Kevin Stone? You seemed to have made that jump with barely any help at all."

"Aye, it won't go any further," Gillespie said. "This conversation is confidential, you know?"

"He's a pervert," Groves said. "Everyone knows what he's like."

"I'm not following," Cruz said. "That's quite an accusation."

Groves leaned forward and lowered his voice.

"He used to break into people's houses and..." he started.

"He's a thief?" Cruz asked.

"Not a thief, exactly. He used to...you know?" Groves' eyes flicked down to his groin. "Watch them while they slept."

From the corner of his eye, Cruz saw Gillespie's mouth hang open. Groves simply nodded to support his statement.

"You'd be willing to put that in a formal statement, would you?" Cruz asked.

"It's no secret," Sebastian told them.

Cruz nodded then reached into his pocket for the DNA kit, comprising of a swab, a sticky label, and a plastic tube, all contained in a small plastic bag.

"There is one more thing, Sebastian," he said. "We'll need to eliminate you from our enquiries."

"You what?"

"We just need a DNA sample," he said, holding up the kit. "It's not a problem, is it?"

CHAPTER FORTY-SIX

"What the bloody hell am I supposed to do without it?" Steve Potts said. He studied the warrant, then marched across his driveway and gesticulated at the low-loader lorry that came to a stop with its air brakes hissing loudly. "How am I going to get to work?"

"We can help you in that regard," Nillson said. "We'll just need to take a copy of your driving licence so we can get you on the insurance. You're okay with an automatic, aren't you?"

"Do I even have a say in this?" he said. "Surely this is illegal?"

"You do have a say, yes," Nillson said, and she stepped over to the red Ford Focus to examine the front end. "We were rather hoping that a man of good standing, such as yourself, would be more than willing to help us in our enquiries."

"Don't butter me up, sweetheart."

"We have reason to believe that the car was involved in a crime," Anderson added.

"A crime? I drive it to work and back. It's my commuter car. What do you think I've done, stopped at the Co-op for some frozen chicken and held the place up while I was there?"

"The crime took place before you bought it, Mr Potts. I can assure you, if we thought otherwise we wouldn't have asked the judge for a warrant to remove your car, we would have asked him for a warrant to remove you, and we would be having this conversation in an interview room. All we're asking for is a little cooperation on your part."

"But I don't see how it can make a difference. I've had it for years."

"Do you see that little white van over there?" Nillson asked, and she pointed to Southwell who had parked behind her.

"Yeah."

"That is Katy Southwell. She's one of the finest forensic investigators in the county. She's going to look at the car, and if she finds something, then I'm afraid it will have to be taken away for further examination, in which case, we'll make the arrangements for you to have a rental."

"So if she doesn't find anything, you won't take it away?"

"If Miss Southwell feels it unnecessary to inconvenience you, then yes, you can keep hold of it. But if she does find something of interest, then we'll have to impound it. I'm being as reasonable as I can, Mr Potts. We're just trying to do our jobs."

"And what is it you're looking for?"

"I'm afraid I can't go into detail," she replied.

"Right, so I'm supposed to hand over my keys and sit here and watch your mate take my car to bits, am I?"

"She's extremely professional," Nillson said. "And you don't have to sit and watch."

"No?"

"No, you could always put the kettle on," she replied with a smile.

The splash of humour could have gone one of two ways. Thankfully, he relented and held the keys out.

"I want it put back exactly the way you found it," he said.

"Thank you," Nillson said gratefully and then winked at him. "No sugar for me. One for Anderson here."

———

It wasn't often that Ben felt uncomfortable in Freya's car. If he had felt uncomfortable in the past, it was usually down to her fractious mood. But today, despite everything that had happened, the mood between them was better than it had been for a long time. With such a complex investigation to work on, their own relationship woes seemed to have been set to one side, and Ben was glad of it.

The reason for his discomfort, however, was due to her driving. Two-and-a-half tons of Range Rover navigating the meandering road from Metheringham to Ruskington at more than seventy miles per hour was enough for any passenger to watch the driver's movements like a hawk.

She slowed to go through Scopwick, and then, before she could regain her speed, the dashboard screen lit up and Gillespie's number displayed on the screen. She touched the button to answer the call and Ben tensed a little as her hand left the wheel.

"Gillespie, give me some good news," she said, checking her mirror, and then chancing a glance in Ben's direction.

"I'm not sure about good news, boss," the big Scotsman began. "But if it's news you're looking for, then I hope you're sitting down."

"Did he volunteer his DNA?"

"Oh, aye. He volunteered his DNA freely," Gillespie replied. "Among other things. Turns out that our man Stone had a wee fetish after all."

"A fetish?" Freya replied. "That's not a crime in itself."

"Depends on the fetish," Ben added.

"Aye, well. Nicking young lass' panties is one thing, but

according to Groves, our man Stone used to break into people's houses and watch them sleep."

"That's a bit weird," Ben muttered.

"A bit?" Freya said. "Bloody creepy, if you ask me."

"Well, there's a bit more to it than that," Gillespie said. "He didn't just watch them. He, erm…"

"It's okay, I get it," Freya said. "So he escalated from stealing panties to that, did he?"

"Not to mention what Anderson found," Ben cut in. "I'll bet if we put all those offences together, we'd see his entire creepy journey."

"What troubles me is what lies at the end of the journey," Freya said. "Alright, nice work, Gillespie. We've got Nillson and Anderson with your girlfriend. They're looking at Finch's car. Meanwhile, Chapman's tracking down Stone and researching Anne Hargreaves. I'm sure she has something to do with all of this."

"Well, she's probably back in her office by now," Gillespie said.

"Back from where?"

"According to Gabby, she paid a wee visit to Sebastian this morning. Not sure why, though."

"You didn't ask what she wanted?"

"Did we need to?"

Freya pulled the car to the side of the road and then stared ahead, lost in thought.

"Boss?" Gillespie said. "You there? Was it something I said?"

"I'm here," Freya replied. "Sorry, I thought I had something. But it's gone."

"You okay, boss?"

"I'm fine," she said, then must have felt Ben's stare because she turned to him as she reached for the door handle. "I'm fine. Come on, let's get this done."

"I'll catch you later then, eh?"

"Yeah, cheers, Jim," Ben said, and he reached for the button to end the call.

"Gillespie?" Freya said.

"Aye?"

She hesitated for a moment as if she was unsure of what to say.

"Good work," she said. "Both of you. Good work."

CHAPTER FORTY-SEVEN

When Mandy Carson opened her front door, Freya saw a woman of similar age to herself wearing tight jeans, a flowing blouse, and a peacock patterned, silk scarf. Her loose ponytail hung over one shoulder, and her bare feet boasted nails painted in a delicate, sapphire blue.

It took approximately four or five seconds for the woman's expression to fade from intrigue at the two strangers at her door to doubt, and then the fear set in.

"Mrs Carson?" Freya said, and she flashed her warrant card with as much discretion as could. The street was undoubtedly middle-class. Large and shiny SUVs occupied the driveways, and the gardens were well tended as if none of her neighbours wanted to let the street down.

"Oh God," she said, clutching for her heart. "Oh, dear God, please."

"Might we come inside?" Freya asked.

Mandy Carson stood transfixed, lost in some other time when her daughter's feet padded around behind her or on the landing above.

The time to be invited in had passed. The lady needed somebody to take charge, so Freya entered with Ben behind her and then waited politely.

"Let's find somewhere to sit, eh?" Ben said, closing the door behind them. His gentle nature belied his size but appeared natural enough that Mrs Carson was happy to be led through the first door they came to, a large living room with a thick pile, cream carpet, stone-coloured sofas, and solid oak furniture. The room was bright and cheerful and reminded Freya of a furniture showroom, save for the family photo above the mantlepiece, which had been taken at a much happier time, with the Carsons laid on a white, fluffy rug.

"Is your husband around?" Freya asked, to which Mandy shook her head.

"He's at work. Do I need to call him? He's down in Cambridge today, I think."

"Perhaps we should speak first," Freya said. "I'm sure you've realised by now why we're here."

Mandy nodded and held a hand to her mouth, fighting the urge to cry.

"You've found her, haven't you?" she said, and her eyes looked fit to burst from their sockets.

"We have," Freya told her, and a cry erupted from somewhere deep inside Mandy Carson. "I'm sorry. It's not good news, I'm afraid."

"I knew it," the grieving mother said, as she tugged a tissue from her pocket. "I knew it. Jamie was always so positive. He said she'd be home one day, but I knew. I knew she wouldn't." She looked up at Freya. "How did she—"

"We can go through the details a little later," Freya said. "The important thing for now is to help you."

"I need to know," she said. "I need to. Did she suffer?"

It was one of those times when Freya wished she could lie, if only to ease the pain. But such untruths rarely did any good.

"The pathologist has examined her," Freya said. "It's likely that she was hit by a car."

"Oh God. Oh God, no."

"She would have died from her injuries."

"Oh, my poor girl. My poor sweet girl," she said. "So, she was left there? She was left there to die? Who would have done that? Do you know who did it? Where was she? In a ditch? Please don't tell me she's been lying in a ditch all this time. Please."

"She hasn't been in a ditch," Freya explained. "Listen, Mrs Carson, there are some things we need to go through that might be difficult to hear. Perhaps it's best if we call your husband, Jamie."

"No, I need to know. It'll take him hours to get home. I can't wait that long. Not now."

"Well, perhaps there's a friend we can call for you?"

"There's nobody," she said, longing to learn more.

Freya looked across at Ben, who accepted the task and then steeled himself.

"Holly was found buried in a property nearby," he started.

"Buried? She was buried?"

"Early indications suggest that she's been there for some time. Most likely since you reported her as missing."

Mandy closed her eyes but did not attempt to stop him or to interrupt.

"We are working on the basis that whoever was responsible for knocking her down then buried her."

"Whoever knocked her down? Do you know who did this? Have you arrested somebody?"

"We're working with a number of individuals who were close to Holly, but as you can imagine, the passing of time creates certain challenges."

"The passing of time? What's that supposed to mean?"

"It means that people's memories aren't as reliable as we'd like them to be."

"What would be helpful," Freya said, "would be for us to know a little more about Holly. What was she like?"

"What was she like? She was the kindest, sweetest, most adorable girl a mother could ask for," Mandy said softly. "There's nothing she wouldn't do for you. Anyone who knew her would tell you the same." She laughed and then clung to a smile. "I wish I could tell you what it was we did, but honestly, I have no idea. She was just one of life's angels." She sat thoughtfully for a moment. "Who is it? Who are you speaking to?"

"I'm afraid we can't–"

"I'm her mother," Mandy said, for the first time revealing another side of her, a bitterness that seven years of hell had nurtured.

"Just some friends, that's all. We're trying to find out what she was doing around the time she disappeared."

"She was working," Mandy said. "She told me that she had arranged to meet a friend for drinks after work. But she didn't come home."

"And do you know who the friend was?"

"Haven't a clue," she said. "I called around to all her friends." She gave another weak laugh. "Must have called everyone she knew to see who she was supposed to meet."

"But she didn't say where she was supposed to meet them?"

"I know, I know. Bad mother, right?"

"That's not what I was–"

"The thing is, Holly was a good girl. She was trustworthy. She was an A-star student, for God's sake. She spent most of her time studying, so on those odd occasions she did want to go out, I had no cause to say no or to question her. You know, like a normal mother would. The fact is, she wasn't like the other kids. I know, I know, there's a hundred mothers out there that all say the same thing, but she wasn't. People looked up to her. They came to her for advice. That's who she was. The kindest soul you could ever meet."

"What type of advice?" Ben said. "Sorry, I'm not doubting you, but I just find that quite fascinating."

"Study stuff, mainly," Mandy replied. "She used to help some of her classmates. You know, for some extra pocket money. I'm sorry to say that we weren't doing so well back then. All she ever wanted was her own house and a family. But before that, she knew she needed a good job. She used to talk about having kids and giving up work, you know? Be a stay-at-home mum or maybe run a business from home. Online tutoring or something. Anyway, before she had kids, she wanted to make something of herself. Have a career, that sort of thing."

"She was junior partner in an accountancy firm," Freya said. "That's quite astonishing for a girl of Holly's age."

"See? I told you she was different, didn't I?"

"It sounds to me like Holly had a bright future ahead of her. She could have chosen any job and had suitors lining up," Freya said. "That's both admirable and astonishing in equal measure."

"It just goes to show, doesn't it? You need to make the most of the ones you love now. The rug can be pulled from beneath your feet at any moment." Mandy smiled sadly. "Then you spend the rest of your life regretting the things you didn't do and the things you never said."

"How true," Freya said.

"Do I need to..." She wiped her eyes and composed herself. "Do I need to come and...you know, see her?"

Freya stood and placed a hand on her shoulder.

"There's no need," she said.

"But if I want to? I mean, Jamie might want to."

"Then I would suggest discussing it with your husband first," Freya said. "I think you should be with somebody, so I'll arrange for a family liaison officer to come and see you."

"Oh, I don't need–"

"Her name is Detective Constable Gold," Freya explained. "She'll help you through the process. She's very experienced in managing these circumstances. She'll also be able to help with some free support groups, and before you turn them down., Mandy, just listen to what she has to say. You might be surprised, okay?"

"So what now? Do I just wait for this Gold woman to arrive?"

"She'll be in touch today," Freya told her.

"And what about...you know, whoever did it? Will you let us know if you find him?"

Freya dropped to a crouch before her.

"Mrs Carson, you've coped so well so far. Believe it or not, you and your husband are our greatest priority. If I can help close this chapter of your life, then I will."

Mandy Carson reached up and gave Freya's hand a gentle squeeze.

"How very reassuring," she muttered. "You know, if you don't find him, if for some reason she's been gone too long, please don't worry."

"I'm not following," Freya replied.

"I just mean that, unless you're sure it's him, then she wouldn't have wanted the wrong man to suffer." She licked her lips and cleared her throat. "That's who she was, you see? We've got her back now and that's more than we had before. It's more than I hoped for."

"I am going to try, Mrs Carson," Freya replied. "For Holly."

CHAPTER FORTY-EIGHT

Freya didn't bother to find a parking space in the car park. She brought the Range Rover to a stop outside the main entrance and was out of the car before Ben could put up an argument. She told him to lock it, knowing it would buy a few extra seconds to climb the stairs before him. On the second floor, she marched straight through the reception, with Ben following close behind.

"Excuse me?" Liz said from behind her desk. "You can't go through–"

"I wouldn't," Freya heard Ben say, and he ran the few steps to catch up with her in the corridor. "I hope you know what you're doing, Freya."

"Of course, I don't," she replied and then felt his hand on her arm. "What on earth?"

"Freya, just stop," he said. "Just take a breath."

"Like Holly Carson, you mean? Like Deborah? Why should I take a breath when they can't? They can't because one had the breath knocked out of her and the other took her last breath under a floor, Ben, bloody terrified out of her mind. So why should I take a breath?"

"You know what I meant," he told her when she tore her

arm free of his grip. "Just think about what you're doing and how you speak to people. We can do this. We just need to be calm."

"Calm?" she scoffed. "I'll show you calm." She turned on her heels, marched down the corridor, and burst into Anne Hargreaves' office. A client or a colleague, Freya neither knew nor cared which, occupied one of the guest seats, and he startled at the commotion.

"What the—"

"Meeting over," Freya announced. "You, out."

"Excuse me?"

She held her warrant card a few inches from his face.

"Unless you want to be included in my little chat with Miss Hargreaves here, then I suggest you make yourself scarce."

He snatched up his papers, pocketed his pen, and then stormed out in a huff.

"That was unnecessary, Inspector," Hargreaves said, and Freya leaned across her desk.

"Don't talk to me about unnecessary, you little minx. Not when you've watched us go back and forth trying to understand Deborah Jarvis' last few moments, seeing your phone number and Sebastian Groves' phone number on both of their phone bills and wondering how on earth the pair of you could be involved when you stated all along that you never liked her, that she wasn't your friend."

"She wasn't my friend. What did you want me to do, lie?"

"I want you to tell the truth, Anne. I want to hear you say it."

"I've told you the truth," she said and tried to gain some moral ground by peering around Freya at Ben. "Is she always like this?"

"Don't you dare ignore me when I'm talking to you. I have got a good mind to drag you down to the station, lock you up for the full twenty-four hours, and then charge you for wasting police time, or obstruction."

"How have I wasted—"

"Holly Carson," Freya said. "You lied. You told us you didn't know her."

"I didn't–"

"Stop lying to me," Freya said.

"Everything all right in here, Anne?" a voice said, and Freya turned to see a man in the corridor. He was at least a foot shorter than Ben with a smooth, bald head, and thick glasses. Freya spun around, grabbed the door, and slammed it closed before completing the circle and leaning on the desk again. She glanced up at the three certificates on the shelf. "It takes somebody quite special to make junior partner at your age, doesn't it?"

"I wouldn't be the first."

"No. No, Holly Carson was the first, wasn't she? Holly was a brilliant mind. Gifted, you might say." Hargreaves refused to meet her eye to eye. "And she wasn't just clever. She was smart. Smart enough that, to save for her education and her own home, she helped others out. Other students with far less chance of success. Other students like you, Anne."

"What are you talking about?"

"I'm talking about Sebastian. The only student to ever drop out of a university course in law and work in a bloody dump. Now, the way I see it, that could have happened for one of two reasons. Either he resisted the idea of a lifetime in an office and chose to eke out a living that provides him an element of freedom."

"Or?"

"Or he didn't drop out of university. He was kicked out. He was cheating, just like you were. Only, he was found out somehow."

"Excuse me?"

"He was thrown off his course, wasn't he?" Freya said. "He was caught cheating. He would have been stripped of his accomplishments. Was Holly writing his papers for him? Is that what happened?"

"I don't know," Hargreaves said. "You'd have to talk to him."

"Oh, we have spoken to him. We spoke to him this morning, shortly after you paid him a visit. Funny how a young man with such a brilliant mind could wind up working in a recycling centre. What did they do, report him? Is that it? Did they throw him off the course? How did *you* get away with it, Anne? How come you managed to complete your course? Do you know what I would find if I contacted the university and the college? I would find an almost perfect score in your A-levels. I expect your first year at university would be flawless, too. But then I'd see a slip in your results, right about the time Sebastian was thrown off the course, when you had to stop all contact with Holly and do the work yourself. Looks like you scraped through though, Anne. Looks like you somehow managed to convince Liam Finch you were right for the job. Who does he report to? Who's the big boss here? I wonder what they would say if they discovered how you cheated your way through your education and pulled the wool over his eyes?"

"You wouldn't," Hargreaves said. "He wouldn't believe you."

"He might not believe me at first," Freya told her. "But after he's spoken to my researcher, he'll be straight on the phone to facilities to have that nameplate removed from your door, and you'll be on your way to Sebastian asking if any jobs are going down at the recycling centre."

Hargreaves huffed, her face reddened, and her already swollen chest heaved.

"So what? It's not a crime."

"Oh, I know," Freya said. "I'll tell you what is a crime, though. Withholding information during a murder investigation. Lying to the police while being questioned. It's called obstruction, Anne. Perhaps if you'd have followed Sebastian into law, you might have known that."

"What do you want?" Hargreaves said. "You come in here, you're rude to my client, you're rude to my colleague, and then you threaten to expose me. What do you want? Or did you come here just to prove a point? Is that it? Is that how you get your kicks, by being a bitch? Or are you jealous? I'll bet you work every hour under the sun dealing with the scum of the earth—"

"If the cap fits," Freya said.

Hargreaves glanced down at Freya's hand.

"You're not married. No surprise there. Who in their right mind would choose to spend the rest of their life with you—"

"I'm not here to discuss me," Freya said.

"I'd guess that you're unhappily single, but somehow I doubt someone like you could live alone. No, you need someone in your life. Someone you can assert yourself over. I'll bet he's a loser. Pretty, but a loser. Somebody weak," Hargreaves continued. "I'll bet he lives in your shadow. He probably has years of pent-up frustration building up like a volcano. One day he'll go pop and you'll be left all alone wondering what on earth happened." She leaned forward and stopped with her face just inches from Freya's. "The sad part is that you probably won't even look at yourself. You'll blame him or somebody else, because it can't be your fault, can it? *You* can't be the reason that nobody wants to spend their life with you."

"You're sailing close to the wind," Freya warned her.

"Am I? Are you going to arrest me? What is it you want from me? Do you want me to tell you about Kevin Stone? Do you want me to tell you how he's a creep? How he used to flash his little willy at women in the park or how he used to watch them while they slept?"

"I'd prefer to understand why you didn't just tell us in the first place," Freya said.

"What, and have you lot keep coming back? No, thanks. It was him, wasn't it? I always knew he wasn't right in the head."

Freya straightened and smoothed her jacket.

"Having us return wasn't the real reason you kept the truth from us, was it, Anne?" she said. "You can deflect the attention onto me as much as you like, but there's no escaping the truth."

"Excuse me?"

"It wasn't the real reason, was it? You see, one benefit of working with the *scum of the earth* as you put it, is that when I meet somebody who fits that bill, somebody like you, for example, I know when you're lying. It's like a sixth sense. I know when you're hiding something. The question is, what are you hiding, or more importantly, *why* are you hiding it? And now I know."

"Oh yeah?" Hargreaves said, and she met Freya's stare with far less confidence than she had a few minutes before.

"It's what you do, isn't it? Is it a power thing? You don't like other women having something over you, so you deflect, you insult, and you resort to behaviour which, quite frankly, is beneath a woman with your capabilities. You did it with me and you do whenever you feel threatened."

"Has this become a therapy session?" Hargreaves said.

"Two words," Freya said, ignoring Hargreaves' attempts at breaking the momentum. She leaned in again, grinning like she hadn't done for days. "Deborah Jarvis."

CHAPTER FORTY-NINE

"We've drawn a blank, boss," Nillson said, her voice filled with frustration. "I can't believe it. I thought that was our chance. I really did."

The news came as a blow when Ben was hoping to calm Freya down. She pulled the car to a stop on the side of the road and leaned on the steering wheel in thought.

"You had Southwell there, didn't you?" Ben said.

"We had Southwell and one of her team there. We had a low-loader ready to take the car away had she found anything, and we'd even convinced the new owner to help us out without having to exert the warrant. The last thing we need was for him to go to the papers with a complaint."

"Agreed," Ben told her. "And nice try. I can't believe Southwell didn't find anything, though. I mean, Holly Carson was seriously hurt. If Stone carted her off in that car, then there would have been something left over. No valet service is that good, surely? Not the ones I've used, anyway."

"Ben's right," Freya replied. "There would have been traces of blood in the fibres. If Southwell couldn't find anything, then there was nothing there. Our theory is wrong."

"So what now?" Nillson asked, and even Ben's enthusiasm had been railroaded.

"We need to rethink the plan," Freya said. "Stay by your phone."

Freya ended the call, thought for a moment, and then dialled Chapman.

"Afternoon, guv," Chapman replied. "Good news. Kevin Stone is sitting in the back of a transporter on his way to the station. They picked him up in Grantham."

"Well, that is good news," Freya told her. "Listen, there's no time to explain. Can you dial everyone in, please? I want us all on a conference call."

"That shouldn't be a problem," Chapman replied. "Is everything alright?"

"Not really. Every time we cut a head off, another one grows in its place."

Chapman had enough awareness about her to know when and when not to press for information.

"Call you back in one minute," Chapman replied and ended the call.

"So Stone is still an unknown," Ben said. "We could always issue the press statement."

"The press statement is a last resort, Ben," she replied curtly. "I've done enough of them to know that inviting the public to come forward with information will see us all working double shifts. We'll be too tired to think straight, and to top it off, we'll be deemed incompetent despite our efforts. No doubt, you, I, or both of us will be on the front of the local papers in some kind of sex scandal, and neither of us will be able to leave our houses without a member of the press shoving a camera in our face."

Ben digested the rant, interpreted her response, and formulated one of his own.

"So you haven't given it much thought then?"

She sighed but was unable to keep her smile at bay. She

reached for Ben's hand and gave it a light squeeze in one of those moments of affection that were becoming increasingly regular.

"I don't want to be on the front page of any newspaper," she said. "Not for the wrong reasons anyway."

She stared up at him, and for a moment, the investigation took a back seat. He opened his mouth to speak but that moment was fleeting.

Freya's phone rang over the speakers, cutting the head off an opportunity to settle things.

"Go on," Freya said when she answered the call. "Are we all here?"

"We are, Chapman replied.

"Good, I'm sorry most of us are doing this from our cars, but I felt we needed some kind of update. This investigation has many moving parts, more so than most."

"Heads with teeth, you mean?" Cruz suggested.

"Precisely," she replied. "Update from Ben and me. Holly Carson was everything that Deborah Jarvis was not, in her parents' eyes anyway. She was an A-star student who worked hard to pay for her own education and was saving for a house. Now, how do you think she earned her money?"

"Not on the tills at Tescos, I'll wager," Cruz said.

'Think about it," Freya said. "Sebastian Groves was kicked off his university course. We don't need to follow this up, but I believe both he and Anne Hargreaves were employing Holly Carson to help them through their exams."

"She was a cheat?"

"Holly Carson wasn't cheating. Hargreaves and Groves were. I don't know how they were doing it, but I would imagine she wrote their dissertations and any other papers and the University's plagiarism software picked up on it. They take that kind of thing very seriously, you know? The point is that we can strike Groves off our list, and Anne Hargreaves too. She may be unpleasant, but she isn't a murderer."

"So going after her was a waste of time?" Cruz said.

"Not entirely," Freya said. "In fact, I think she rather opened my eyes." She glanced across at Ben briefly. "What do we know about Deborah Jarvis?"

"She was a loner, guv," Chapman suggested.

"Right, a loner. How many people have told us that she was seen walking the streets or the fields? We've got the photos."

"I don't get it," Gillespie cut in. "So what?"

"Anybody?" Freya asked, to which she received only silence. "Alright, think of it this way. We have good reason to believe that Kevin Stone is a sexual deviant. His habits have escalated from stealing underwear, flashing, and even breaking into people's homes to fulfil his fantasies."

"Not to mention what he did to that underwear," Gillespie said, hoping to raise a laugh.

"And then there's Anne Hargreaves," Freya continued before somebody took Gillespie's bait. "A cheat with a lot to lose if anybody found out."

"What are you saying, boss?" Gillespie asked.

"Finally, there's Liam Finch. Cheating on his wife. How much did he have to lose? His home, his family, his livelihood? We have the photos. We know he was unfaithful."

"Aye, but Deborah Jarvis was in the photos herself, boss. She's hardly likely to–"

"That is not Deborah Jarvis," Freya said. "We were wrong. We were wrong to think the image was a still from a camcorder. It is in fact a photo from a camera, taken through a window at night, hence the poor quality."

"What makes you so certain it's not Deborah?"

"Because Deborah Jarvis wore Vans trainers, not heels like those on the floor beside the bed. According to her mother, she never wore anything else. And if that isn't enough, she didn't wear smart dresses like the one on the floor beside the heels. Accuse me of stereotyping if you like, but a girl like Deborah Jarvis wouldn't be seen dead in office wear."

"So Deborah Jarvis *took* the photos?" Nillson said, then repeated the statement as she fell in with where Freya was leading them. "Deborah Jarvis took the photos. She took them of Liam Finch and Holly Carson, and, of course, of Kevin Stone's box. She was blackmailing them."

"That's why she died," Freya said. "That's why money from Finch's account was in her belongings. That's why Anne Hargreaves and her didn't get along. It's why she wouldn't join them in their little gathering way back in May 2019. That's who she was."

"But we've no evidence of Kevin Stone paying her anything," Chapman said.

"Not yet, we don't," Freya replied. "I believe that Deborah knew about Kevin's accident. She knew what he'd done to Holly. They weren't friends. He was beholden to her. He had to do what she told him. He had no money to give her and she was the only person who knew what he'd done."

"But how did she know?"

"The same way she knew about Hargreaves' cheating and Liam Finch's affair. The same reason she had multiple charges of breaking and entering against her. Because that's who she was. It's what she did. She discovered people's secrets, and she exploited them. Kevin Stone murdered them both, and as much as I'd love to be the one to charge Liam Finch, all he's doing is saving his boy from prosecution and saving himself from the shame of facing his wife."

"He wanted to tell her about the affair, boss," Anderson said. "He was going to come clean."

"He wasn't going to come clean, and he certainly wasn't going to tell her about the affair," Freya told her. "If anything, he was preparing her for a bumpy ride. He would have told her that he was protecting Kevin and that in doing so he would have to admit to an affair. Whatever he might have told her, it would have been lies."

The team absorbed the revelation in silence, but as usual, it was Nillson who spoke first.

"It's going to be tricky to prove, boss," she said. "I mean, it all makes sense, but we've got nothing on Kevin Stone. Even if the DNA on the underwear comes back positive—"

"We don't have his DNA sample yet," Gillespie said.

"Well, we will do," Freya said. "He's on his way to the station. I want him processed and I want that sample in Southwell's hands immediately."

"I'll take it, boss," Gillespie replied.

"Good. I want the rest of you on hand in the incident room. I want the theory we just spoke of evidenced as best we can. We may not have the means to prove he killed either of them yet, but we can prove that Deborah Jarvis was blackmailing Finch and Hargreaves and we can prove he damaged his father's car in 2017. If Southwell can help us prove that the DNA on the underwear is his, then we've got a chance of proving that he was being black-mailed by Deborah too."

"The photo of the box," Gillespie said.

"Exactly."

"But he could still go no comment. His legal rep would advise it."

"Over the past few days, I've had to tell two distraught mothers that we've found the remains of their missing daughters," Freya said. "He'll talk, believe me." She waited for an argument but none came. They would have all recognised her tone and known not to step into the line of fire. "Ben and I will be back in fifteen minutes. Chapman, what is Stone's ETA?"

"Half an hour or so," she replied.

"Good. Get to work, everyone," Freya said, then caught Ben's raised eyebrow. "And...thanks. Thanks for all your hard work."

She ended the call, leaned back on the headrest, and waited for Ben to say something.

"If Stone takes the no-comment route, we'll be no better off than we are now," he said. "Only we'll have a ticking custody clock to work against. We'll actually be worse off than when we had him in for questioning."

"Oh, I wouldn't say that. When we had him in before, we had everything to play for," she said, calmly and quietly.

"And now?" he asked, studying her composed state. "Oh Christ, Freya. You're going in hard, aren't you? You intend to break him. Freya, that's a huge risk."

"Risk? Risk, Ben? Everything I bloody do has risk. Whatever decision I make now, I lose. Be that the investigation, the freedom my job provides me, my sanity, or even you," she replied, and she stared at him sadly. "Can you let *me* decide which of those is to be my downfall? Allow me that dignity, at least."

CHAPTER FIFTY

The uniformed officers who had stopped Stone had done a fine job of setting the tone for the next twenty-four hours of his life. Limits of acceptable police conduct were often stretched when it came to offences such as those of which Stone was accused. Sergeant Priest, the dutiful custody officer who had processed him, Freya knew to be fair but lacking in bedside manner. So by the time Freya and Ben entered the interview room, Stone had undoubtedly experienced an over-zealous arrest, a joyless and terrifying car journey, a curt handover to the local team, and a brief but efficient processing, leaving him, in no uncertain terms, a snivelling mess.

A duty solicitor attended at Freya's request and sat calmly beside Stone, watching Freya's every move. She was dark-skinned, short-haired, and dressed far more professionally than many duty solicitors Freya had encountered. It was as if her style and charm came naturally and Freya admired that in a woman. She had the bright eyes and flawless skin that Freya envied of African descendants.

"Hello again, Kevin," Freya said, and his red eyes rolled up to meet hers. "You remember me, don't you?"

Stone said nothing, so Freya gave Ben the nod and he hit the button to begin the recording. Most officers would state that the few seconds at the beginning of the recording, during which time a loud buzzer sounded, were for the avoidance of data being lost. But Freya preferred to think that the intrusive blast raised the fear level somewhat. That was if they hadn't already realised things were about to get real.

Freya introduced herself, as did Ben. The duty solicitor introduced herself as Agnes Noor, leaving Stone to finish up.

"Kevin Stone," he said quietly.

"Good, thank you. I'd like to start by thanking you for coming in. I'm sure you can appreciate the complexities of an investigation that dates back to 2017, so if you find the narrative jumps about a little, please be patient with us."

"Understood," Noor said.

"Thank you. So, for the purpose of clarity and the benefit of the recording, Kevin Stone, you are under arrest on suspicion of murder…" Stone exhaled as if somebody had punched him in the gut. Freya waited for a second for him to compose himself before she continued. He buried his face in his hands. "You do not have to say anything, but it may harm your defence if you do not mention when questioned something which you later rely on in court. Do you understand what I said, Kevin? Do you need me to repeat any of that?"

He shook his head, wiped his nose with the back of his hand, and stared at the various names scratched into the table.

"I'd like to talk about Holly Carson," Freya started. "Kevin, do you know Holly Carson?"

"Not really."

"But you knew of her?"

He nodded.

"Yeah, everyone did."

"So if you were to pass her in the street, for example, she would have known who you were?"

"She worked for my dad. Of course she knew me."

"And how would you describe your relationship with her, Kevin?"

"My what? Relationship? I didn't have a relationship with her–"

"But she was in a relationship, wasn't she?"

He shrugged.

"Don't know. She was pretty, so I s'pose so."

Like many who had sat before Freya, Stone found interest in the mundane – a mark on the wall, the timer on the recording, his fumbling fingers.

Freya opened her file, slipped a photo from the plastic envelope, and then slid it across the table.

"For the benefit of the recording, I'm now showing Kevin evidence number NKDJ002, a photo of a wooden box discovered at Priory View." Stone studied the image and then looked away when he realised he was being watched. "Can you tell me what's in the box, Kevin?"

"You can see what's in it."

"I want you to tell me," she said. "What do you see?"

He shrugged.

"Underwear."

"Can you describe what you see?"

"I don't know. It's underwear."

"Is it men's underwear, women's underwear?" she said. "Maybe it's children's underwear–"

"No," he said. "No, it's not children's. It's women's."

"I see," she said, and Ben tapped her arm and then showed her an open email on his phone. She nodded her thanks and then returned her attention to Stone. "Do you know who the underwear belonged to, Kevin?"

"Why would I know?"

"Because you put them there, didn't you?" Freya said, leaving no room to manoeuvre. "You see, I was interested to know how honest you would be with me. We know the box belongs to you, Kevin. We know you put the underwear inside. And we know you buried it in the garden at Priory View."

"Why would I do that?"

"Do what? Keep the underwear in the box or bury it in the garden?"

He hesitated then shook his head and turned away.

"You said Holly Carson was pretty. Did you like her, Kevin?"

"When did I say that?"

"About five minutes ago at the beginning of this interview," Freya said. "Did you like her?"

"She was nice, yeah."

"Did you fantasise about her? About being with her?"

"I think we're pushing the boundaries here," Noor said.

"I'll tell you when we're pushing boundaries, Miss Noor," Freya said, cutting her off and staring her down until she scribbled a note in her notebook. "You see, Kevin, our forensics team discovered traces of your DNA on the underwear."

"If that's evidence, then we need to be made aware of it," Noor said. "You can't just bring up new—"

"The email has just come in," Freya said. "You just saw Inspector Savage show me the email, and don't worry, it'll be submitted in due course. Now, if you don't mind, I'd like your client to tell me how his DNA came to be on the underwear." Stone said nothing. His head hung low and a tear dropped into his lap. "Kevin, I won't ask you to go into detail, so can you answer yes or no to the following question? Do you use women's underwear during masturbation?" Stone remained silent and still. "Have you *ever* used women's underwear during masturbation? It's not a crime, Kevin, but we do need an answer."

Slowly, he nodded but refused to look up at her.

"Did you ever use Holly Carson's underwear for this purpose?" Stone blinked away his tears and then nodded.

"For the recording, please," Ben said, and Kevin nodded again.

"Yes," he said with a string of saliva connecting his jaws.

"Kevin, how did you come to be in the possession of Holly's underwear? Did you go to her house? Maybe you stole it from the washing line?"

"No," he said. "No, she was at ours."

"Was this when she was with your father, Kevin?" she asked, and again, he nodded.

"She used to stay sometimes when Mum was away. Mum used to go to Grandma's. She'd stay over and take her out. And Dad used to..."

"Your dad was unfaithful. Is that what you're saying?" Freya asked.

"He thought I was asleep or out or something. He used to sneak her in."

"And that's when you stole her underwear, is it?"

"He knew I liked her," Stone said. "I couldn't help it. I waited until morning when Dad was downstairs, and she was..." He paused.

"She was what, Kevin?" Stone closed his eyes, ashamed of what he had to say. "Until she was what, Kevin?"

"Asleep," he said, his voice rising to a whine. "I couldn't help it. I didn't know what I was doing. She was just so...so lovely."

"Did you watch her, Kevin? Is that what you did?" He turned away in a huff. "You watched her sleeping and then stole her underwear from her bag. Kevin, do you think it's fair to say that you were obsessed with Holly Carson?"

"No," he whined.

"Kevin, while she slept, did you...find her sexually appealing?"

"Chief Inspector Bloom," Noor started.

"I can assure you my line of questioning is pertinent, Miss Noor. I'll thank you not to interrupt unless you have either grounds or something of value to add, but please do not detract from this interview." Freya left her reeling with an icy glare and then eyed Stone. "Did she catch you, Kevin?" He squeezed his eyes closed, clearly reliving the memory. "Did she wake up and find you standing over her?"

"What?"

"That's what you do, isn't it? You creep about in the night, watching people sleep. You watch women. You watch girls. Children even–"

"No, never children," he said, then hit his forehead with the palm of his hand.

"Who else? Freya asked. "Girls you meet? Girls you see on your rounds as a delivery driver, maybe? Is that where the rest of the underwear comes from? How does it work? You spot them on your rounds and then go back at night? Is that it? Was Holly the first? Is that where this started, with your obsession with Holly Carson? Because you were obsessed, weren't you?"

"No," he cried. "Not obsessed. I was in love with her. I loved her. And she could have loved me. She would have."

"Did you tell her how you felt?" Freya asked, and he looked to Noor before casting his sorrowful gaze on the floor. "When she woke up and found you, did you tell her how you felt? Did she reject you, Kevin? Is that what she did? You told her how you felt and she rejected you? Or did she threaten to scream? Did she threaten to tell the police? Or your dad, even?"

"If she knew me," he whined. "If she had only given me a chance."

"Kevin, what did you do when she rejected you? How did you react?"

"What?"

"Were you upset?"

"Of course–"

"Did you cry? Did you try to convince her?"

"No," he said.

"Maybe you lashed out?"

"No. No, I didn't. She left. Dad said that Mum was due home, so she had to go."

"And that's it, is it? She just left the house, did she? She didn't tell your dad about seeing you? She just left the house and you went back to your room, where presumably, you had hidden the underwear you had stolen?"

He didn't reply. There was no need to press him for an answer. His silence spoke volumes.

"I don't believe you went back to your room, Kevin," she said, and his grief paused long enough to stare at her, confused.

"I did. I went back to my room and..."

"Perhaps. But that was afterwards," Freya suggested.

"Afterwards? After what?"

"After you had taken your father's car and gone after her."

"What?"

"You took your father's car. A red Ford Focus. He couldn't drive it, could he? He was on a twelve-month ban. You were learning to drive. You had your provisional licence, and so you knew how to drive. You just weren't allowed to drive alone. You went after her. You wanted her to love you. Or maybe you wanted to take her home? Maybe you wanted to show her how nice you could be?"

"I didn't–"

"Did you lose control, Kevin? Is that it? Did you fail to stop?" Freya asked. "Or perhaps you were still angry? After all, she hadn't even given you a chance–"

"No!" he yelled. "No, I went to my room and closed the door."

"And where was your dad when this happened? What did he do after she had left?"

"He was outside," Stone replied. "He was in the garden. The builder had turned up and they were going over some bits. I don't know, but I heard them talking."

"The builder? Was there work being done to the house?"

Stone nodded.

"The extension," he said, to which Freya nodded. "He'll remember. I know he will."

"I have no doubt he will," Freya said. "But you see, the problem I have is that Holly Carson left your house after turning you down, after you stole her underwear, and before your mother got home. And somehow, she ended up in your back garden, buried between two large trees."

"Buried?" he said, and there was something in his expression. A sincerity.

Freya watched as the possibilities turned over in his mind.

"Kevin, are you sure your father didn't go after her for some reason?"

"I'm sure of it," he said. "He spoke to the builder. He asked him for a lift to the office."

"This would have been a Saturday," Ben said.

"He often worked on Saturdays," Stone replied. "He sometimes rode his bike, but the weather wasn't great. I don't think he wanted to get soaked."

"So, your father and the builder left together?"

"Yeah. He said he had to get something from the builder's merchants, anyway. I don't know what. I just remember them talking and then I heard the van starting up. After that, Dad was gone."

Freya turned to Ben and wondered if he was thinking the same thing.

"Kevin, do you know the name of the builder?" she said. "Perhaps his van was sign written?"

"Course," he said. "It was Nick."

"Nick? Nick who?"

"Nick MacMillan," he replied. "He did all the work in our house."

CHAPTER FIFTY-ONE

"Nick MacMillan," Ben said, barging into the incident room. "What do we know about him?"

He marched over to the whiteboard, where MacMillan's name had a line struck through it. He rubbed it off with his sleeve, then rewrote the name in capital letters.

"Not much," Chapman replied. "We ruled him out early on."

"Well, rule him in again," Ben said. "He was there the morning Holly Carson left the Finch house."

"The morning she left?" Cruz said. "I thought it was an evening."

"What comes after the evening, Gabby?" Ben asked.

"Morning, I suppose," he said.

"Right. Liam's wife was away at her mother's house, and so Liam had Holly stay at his. He sneaked her in when he thought Stone was asleep. But what he didn't know was that his boy was infatuated with Holly Carson."

"Infatuated? You mean like photos in his wallet?" Gillespie asked.

"Infatuated as in standing over her while she slept–"

"Oh, for God's sake," Cruz said, pulling a face to match his words.

"We all know those people are out there, Cruz," Ben told him.

"I know, but you don't expect to bloody meet them, do you?"

"Well, in an ideal world, we wouldn't have to. But we do and here we are," Ben said. "Stone has admitted to the box and the underwear, but he's come up with a story we need checked out. He's saying that the builders were in working on the extension to the back of the house. According to Stone, Holly left the house shortly after she caught him...looking at her, and his dad went into the garden to speak to the builder."

"And that's when Stone took his dad's car and went after her?" Nillson added. "He wanted to shut her up."

"That's the theory we're working on," Ben said. "But it's not the story Stone is going with. He claims that his dad asked the builder for a lift to the office. Given that he was on a driving ban, this isn't implausible, so we need to get it confirmed."

"What's the builder's name?" Chapman asked. "I'll see if I can find him."

"Here's the interesting part," Ben said. "It's Nick MacMillan."

"Hold on. He owns the house now, doesn't he?" Cruz asked. "Why would..." He paused, and Ben imagined the cogs in his head whirring away. "He bought the house from the Finches."

"He did," Ben said.

"So, either Stone is lying, and he went after Holly in his dad's car, or..."

"Or he's telling the truth," Ben finished for him, "and Nick MacMillan knocked her down."

"On his way into town or on his way back to the house?" Nillson asked, and Ben grinned. He had hoped somebody would raise the question on his mind.

"We need to speak to Nick MacMillan," he said.

"Should I request a warrant for his bank details?" Chapman asked.

"Start the process," he told her. "But we won't get a warrant before Liam Finch's custody clock runs out, and maybe even Kevin Stone's. Whatever we do now, we have to work with what we've got. Freya is making a few calls and cooling off. While she's gone, I want to go through every scenario we have."

"Cooling off?" Gillespie said. "Get a bit heated in there, did it?"

"You have no idea, Jim," he replied and wrote the numbers one to three as a list. "Scenario one, Stone is lying about his dad and he went after Holly in his dad's car. Prove me wrong."

The team exchanged looks, but it was Nillson who spoke.

"We've got the report from the car garage," she said. "So we know his car suffered some sort of damage to the front, which would coincide with hitting somebody."

"Or a deer," Anderson said. "It's common enough for a deer or a badger to be hit."

"What else?" Ben said. "Phone calls, text messages?"

"There's no mention of Stone's number on Holly's statement," Chapman said.

"There's also no evidence that he threw her in the back of the car," Nillson said. "Southwell would have found it."

Ben stared at option one but nothing came to him.

"Option two," he said. "Liam Finch and Nick MacMillan mowed her down in MacMillan's van. They threw her in the back and buried her in the garden."

"Are we talking about an accident here?" Nillson asked. "She would have been walking along the lane. It's possible MacMillan didn't see her."

"What's the alternative?" Ben asked, and Nillson quietened for a moment.

"It wasn't an accident," she said quietly as if still deciding if it was an option.

"Why would he do it on purpose?"

"Because Finch asked him to?"

"Or because Finch told him to," Gillespie said.

"And why would MacMillan listen to Finch? This is serious. It's not jumping a red light, is it? It's murder."

"Then it must be an accident," Nillson said. "Option three. MacMillan took Finch into town, picked something up from the merchants, and on his way home, he knocked her down. Nobody had to know about it. He could have buried her in Finch's back garden easily."

"He would have had tools there," Cruz said. "Maybe even a digger?"

"And then seven years later, when Finch decides to sell–"

"MacMillan buys it. It's the only way to make sure she's never found," Cruz said.

"This is good," Ben said. "This is very good. We're getting close, but we have some work to do." He circled the original name on the board. "Deborah Jarvis."

"You think he killed her as well?"

"The chances of there being two killers in a village of six houses are slim, Cruz," Ben said. "No, what we need to do is link Deborah Jarvis to Nick MacMillan. How do we do that?"

"I'm checking her phone records and I have his number from his website," Chapman said. "But there's nothing here."

"Maybe he's got a second phone?" Gillespie suggested.

"No, I met him," Ben said. "He can barely work the one he has. We need to make the link, guys. Come on. If we can't make the link between MacMillan and Deborah Jarvis, then we have to assume that–"

"It's option two," Freya said. Ben looked up and saw her in the open doorway, a paradox of girlish femininity and power. "We've had Liam Finch in custody for hours. He's had every chance to tell us his house was being worked on, but he hasn't. We've accused him of murder and explained where we found Holly Carson's remains, and yet he still hasn't mentioned that a man with tools to complete the job was at his house. What does that tell you?"

"He didn't want us to know," Nillson replied, as Freya took slow steps into the room.

"He didn't want us to know," Freya repeated. "Because he's hiding something. He knows that if we link him to MacMillan, then we're one step closer. All he's done so far is muddy the waters with his requests to talk to his wife and his endless lies. He's involved." She stopped at her desk and perched on the edge as she so often did. "Ben's right. If we can't link MacMillan to Deborah Jarvis, then Liam Finch has to be involved. The question is, why would Liam choose not to mention MacMillan?"

"Because MacMillan mowed her down accidentally?" Cruz suggested.

"So why wouldn't Finch have told us that?" Freya said. "He knew we were pursuing his boy. Surely he would have rather given up MacMillan than his boy?"

"Here we go," Chapman said, her fingers a blur on her keyboard. Finally, they stopped, and she turned her laptop for them to see, then sat back smiling. Freya leaned forward to read the information on the screen and Ben came to stand beside her.

"Finch does his books," Ben said. "He's his bloody accountant."

"So what?" Cruz said, always the voice of naivety. "What does that matter? Why would that mean that Finch chose not to give him up?"

"Because he has a hold over him," Gillespie said, which came as a surprise to both Ben and Freya. "He's cooking the books."

"He's what?"

"Chapman, did a large sum of money leave Finch's account around the time Holly Carson went missing?"

"Yeah, I think it did," she said, flicking through her paper files. She found what she was looking for and held it up to the light. "Nineteen thousand."

"For the extension," Nillson said.

"It must be," Gillespie continued. "But when we eventually get a warrant for MacMillan's bank records, my guess is that we won't see that nineteen grand go into MacMillan Construction. That'll have gone straight into his private account, or better still, somebody else's account."

"He's cooking the books," Ben said. "Which means that Finch would have a hold over MacMillan."

"And vice versa," Freya said. "MacMillan would lose everything if HMRC were to investigate, but Finch would lose a lot more. They were, for better or for worse, beholden to one another."

"So when Finch killed Deborah Jarvis," Nillson began, "there was only one person he could turn to for help. Somebody he had a hold over and who had a hold over him."

"Nick MacMillan," Ben said, circling the line on the whiteboard. "They were in it together."

CHAPTER FIFTY-TWO

"I could have driven," Freya said from the passenger seat as Ben pushed his old Ford harder than he'd had cause to for some time.

"You need to focus on the plan," he told her.

"I am capable of multitasking."

"What you're not capable of, Freya, is listening. For once, can you just trust me? I know what I'm doing. Focus on the investigation. Is there a link between MacMillan and Deborah Jarvis?"

"We've established there isn't."

"No, we've established that we haven't found one yet," Ben replied as he tore through Scopwick. "Listen, if we put him in cuffs, we're going to need something more than a theory. So far, all we've got is one thread of, let's face it, an elaborate tale."

"Elaborate as it may be, Ben, given the actual evidence that we have, it's the only theory that adds up. Liam Finch and Nick MacMillan killed Holly Carson. Deborah Jarvis knew about it somehow. Whether she saw the incident first-hand or came to know it by some other means, she used that information to get money out of them. But when she asked for more, they refused."

"Where did that come from? We never discussed that."

"Sometimes it's not what is said but what is not said, Ben," she replied. "Had Deborah Jarvis had proof, then she would have used it to her advantage. But she didn't. So she sought some other means. She was using them as a cash cow, but the cow runneth dry. So she followed him or watched him. She saw the affair and used that against him. He paid, of course, but he wouldn't do that forever. How tired must he have grown of the girl who seemed to know the ins and outs of all his affairs? So, he brought it to an end. Perhaps that's why he sold the house? Perhaps it was part of his plan to sever Deborah Jarvis and Holly Carson from his world? Sell the house where Holly was buried, and while he was at it, get rid of Deborah Jarvis?"

"But why put her under the floor?" Ben asked. "Why put one girl in the garden and the other beneath the floorboards?"

"Oh, that's an easy one," she replied. "You see, Nick MacMillan buried Holly Carson. As Cruz rightly said, he had the tools there, and let's face it, a builder wouldn't have any trouble digging a hole, would he?"

"But an accountant might struggle with all those tree roots?"

"I don't wish to stereotype, and if this goes to trial and we end up with a woke jury, then that argument might set us back. But in my defence, who discovered Deborah Jarvis?"

"MacMillan's wife," Ben said.

"Right, which suggests that an ordinary person who isn't used to handling tools can lift the floorboards."

"I see," he said. "As a narrative, that stacks up. But what do we have to prove it?"

"We have the photos of Liam Finch and Holly Carson, we have the bank transfers, we have phone calls and text messages, but, more importantly, we have solid evidence that Deborah Jarvis was capable of blackmail and was willing to employ such tactics for financial gain. She blackmailed Anne Hargreaves and Kevin Stone. That's certainly enough for us to pursue our theory."

They turned off the main road onto the quiet lane that led to Haverholme Park, so Ben put his foot down. Freya, however, may have appeared content in her summary but perused the evidence in her folder as if seeking something to add weight to her argument. Ben crossed the stone bridge, passed the little car park on the right, and then slowed as the lane narrowed.

Freya flicked through the photos from Deborah Jarvis' box. She paused on the photo of the box and held it up for Ben to see.

"She was certainly a brave girl," she said. "Breaking and entering is one thing, but to use evidence of your breaking and entering to blackmail somebody is either brave or incredibly stupid."

"She got away with it," he replied, as he brought the car to a stop in the lane at the end of the MacMillan's driveway.

She held up the last photo in the pile, the only image they had yet to link to anybody.

"Uniformed support is five minutes out," Ben said, reading a message on his phone as he climbed out and stared up at the house. It was different now that the GPR team had left and Southwell's team had completed their work. Even the uniformed teams had pulled out, taking with them the police cordons, and leaving in their wake an innocent house surrounded by trenches and building materials. "Looks like he's started work already."

"What makes you say that?" Freya asked as she came to his side.

Ben pointed up the driveway.

"That pallet of bricks wasn't there before, and those bags of sand, they're new too," Ben said. He cocked his head. "And I think I can hear a cement mixer going."

"He's not wasting any time, is he?"

"He's lost a few days with us lot," Ben told her. "Probably trying to catch up."

"Or move the rest of the bodies," Freya suggested, and they made their way along the driveway side by side until the trenches forced them into a single file. The cement mixer grew louder as they neared the house and Ben signed for Freya to walk around one side while he took the other.

During his earlier visits, he had wondered what grand designs MacMillan had for the place, or if he intended merely to make good and sell it on, tainted with blood and memories that many estate agents would baulk at.

But this visit was different. They were close enough now that the truth would be outed soon enough, even if the evidence was lacking. It wouldn't be the first time they had seen a guilty man walk free on the grounds of insufficient evidence. It was gutting, of course, to watch a guilty man walk free. But there was peace to be had in the knowledge that they were indeed guilty. It meant the chase was over and only those technicalities that infuriated Nillson were to be overcome.

But technicalities were often systemic. To let their consequences drag him down would be to give in.

They met at the rear of the house. Freya walked as if it were Kew Gardens, perusing the house and the surrounding mess. Perhaps she saw the potential? Perhaps she had her own ideas for what she might do to such a place?

The cement mixer rumbled on, a stain on the otherwise peaceful plot. So Ben found the switch, and it came to a stop, its contents sloshing back and forth until they settled.

They both peered at the back door but said nothing. Ben nudged the door open and cautiously peered inside.

"MacMillan?" he said. "Nick MacMillan, it's Detective Inspector Savage. Are you here?" He waited a moment, glancing back at Freya, who had lifted the corner of a tarp to examine the pile of materials Cruz and the Lincoln mob had extracted during the internal search. "I'm coming in, Nick," Ben called, and he took a step inside.

The floor was as he had expected, no more a series of joists than a complete floor. All the furniture had been removed and all that remained were the walls, stripped of wallpaper, with only patches of old and stubborn newspaper remaining. He listened for a while, presuming the upstairs to be similarly inhospitable.

"He's not here," he said, leaning out of the door.

But Freya didn't turn. She had pulled the tarp further off the pile, examining the contents with fervour. But then something occurred to Ben. Something he hadn't noticed before. He left her to her devices and strode around the side of the house.

"The mixer was running," he called out. "The bloody mixer was going but his van isn't here." He ran back to the rear of the house. "What builder leaves a mixer running while he—"

He stopped in his tracks. In the mud beside the mixer, a tool had been dropped carelessly – a club hammer, short, squat, and weighty enough to drive a bolster through bricks and concrete. A tradesman with MacMillan's experience would not leave tools in the mud like that. It was only when Ben stooped to pick it up did he notice the blood on one side of the handle.

He looked up for Freya, but she was nowhere to be seen.

"Freya?" He ran to the other side of the house but she wasn't there, so he ran to the back door and leaned inside. "Freya?" He made his way through the kitchen, across two joists, until he came to the living room, where he stopped and listened. The noise of boots on wood was clear in the silence. Carefully, he made his way up the stairs and found Freya balancing on the joists, using a wall for support. "What is it?"

She didn't reply. She just nodded and he clambered over to her to see what had caught her interest.

"A wardrobe," Ben said.

"I noticed the roll of carpet the team had removed, which led me up here. It's the same wardrobe as the one in the photo," she said, in case he hadn't connected the dots. "It's built-in, so Cruz and his team wouldn't have been able to remove it."

"Well, surely they looked inside," Ben said, and carefully he stepped across the network of timbers and opened the pine doors. "It's empty."

"No," she replied, not in denial but with certainty. She held out a hand so he could help her across and she leaned inside, tapping the sides and the back, and each tap returned a weighty thud until she tapped the floor. She stopped as if the difference in noise had surprised her. Then she tapped again.

"Move," Ben said, and he got down onto his hands and knees beside her. She edged to one side to give him room and he searched for a weakness, which he found in a tiny space where the wardrobe floor met the rear wall. He wedged his car key in the gap and levered the pine plank backwards and upwards until it yielded and came away in his hands. The next few boards came away with ease and they stared into the space beneath the wardrobe. He fished inside his pockets for the pair of latex gloves he carried and then slipped one on, reached inside the space, and lifted out an old, plastic bag.

"Careful," she said when he upturned the bag and emptied the contents onto the loose boards.

The garment that fell out needed very little examining to see the dark brown stains on the soiled denim. But still, Ben raised the old jeans into the air for a better look.

"Women's," Freya said.

"Did you see the hammer?" Ben asked and their gazes met.

"I was wondering when you'd notice it," she replied. It was the closest they had been for some time. Their faces were just inches apart and the memories of their first few days working together came alive in Ben's heart. They stayed that way for what seemed like an eternity, thinking of their relationship and the private times they had shared.

But the moment, as always, was broken by a vibration in Ben's pocket. Reluctantly, he answered the call, enabling the phone's loudspeaker for Freya to hear.

"Ben, it's me," Gillespie said, his thick Glaswegian accent needing no introduction. "We've had a report of a white van speeding through Anwick. The driver hit a few parked cars and then sped off."

"And the number plate?" Ben asked. "For God's sake, tell me they got that number plate."

"It's MacMillan's," Gillespie replied. "We've got a unit following him. Last update was that he was headed towards North Kyme. He's on the run, Ben. If that's not a sign of guilt, I don't know what is."

"It's a sign of guilt, alright," Freya said. "But not MacMillan's. In fact, I think Nick MacMillan is in serious danger."

CHAPTER FIFTY-THREE

He would never admit it, but Ben wished they had taken Freya's car. His old Ford was a good runaround, but for a fast response, her Range Rover was leagues ahead. Still, she proved her competence by casting aside her rank and refusing to mention the Ford's shortfalls. Within moments of their speeding from Haverholme Park, Freya had initiated a call to Gillespie so he could relay any updates.

"Uniforms have the road closed off at North Kyme," Gillespie said, as Ben tore through the usually peaceful Anwick, wincing at the flash of the speed camera. "Unless he turns off beforehand, we've got him penned in."

"Just keep the updates coming," Ben said. "We're two or three minutes behind."

The road from Anwick to North Kyme was mostly arrow-straight. With deep dykes on either side, the narrow strip of tarmac cut between fields, and if it hadn't been for the uneven surface, the risk could have been minimal. He overtook other cars when the need and opportunity arose, and when he deemed it safe to do so.

"Gillespie," Freya said. "We're going to need medical support, and judging by the roads around here, I might suggest having the air ambulance on standby."

"Chapman's on it already," he replied. "Let's hope it doesn't come to that."

"It already has," she told him. "In fact, in addition to a potentially fatal traffic collision, you should prepare them for a severe head injury."

"Is there something you want to tell us, boss?" Gillespie asked.

"Not until I know for sure," she replied, as something caught Ben's attention in the fields to his left. A white dot, unnatural against its green surroundings.

"Just got an update through," Gillespie announced. "The support unit has reached the roadblock—"

"And MacMillan's van has vanished?" Ben said.

"Aye, how did you know?"

"I've found it," Ben said, and he sought the entrance to the field.

"The what?"

"I've found the van," Ben repeated, as he saw the gate and slewed the Ford onto the rough track. "In the fields north of the A153. We've got a white van approximately eight hundred yards from the road. It looks like the driver's door is open."

"He's legged it? Do I need to get the area closed off?"

"Just make the calls, Jim," Ben said, and he leaned forward to end the call. "I hope you're ready for this, Freya."

"Oh, I am now," she replied. "I bloody well am now."

In the rear-view mirror, Ben saw the support unit follow them into the field, so he opened his window, reached out and signalled for them to hang back in case the driver turned on them. Only when he was fifty metres from the parked van did Ben slam on his brakes. They were out of the car and running in moments. He made his way around the van's rear doors, beckoning for Freya to stay back just as he heard the side door slide open.

Then he stepped into view.

"Stop there," he called out, and Kerry Finch startled at the sound of his voice, stumbling backwards, and spilling petrol from a jerry can. Fumes bellowed from the open van and Nick MacMillan's limp, tattooed hand hung from the open door. His skin was wet and liquid dripped from his fingers onto the fertile soil. "It's over, Kerry. Don't do anything stupid. Too many people have died."

In one hand, she held the jerry can, but in the other, she held a lighter. She gazed up at Ben, her eyes lost to some faraway memory.

"You don't know the half of it," she said.

"I do. We do," he said. "We know about Holly and Deborah. We found the clothes you hid beneath your wardrobe. We know it was you who killed Holly. You don't have to do this."

He took a step forward, hoping to lure her away from the van.

"No closer," she snapped. "I'll do it. I'll blow us all to kingdom bloody come if I have to."

"It was an accident," Ben said, trying to reassure her. "That's all it was, wasn't it? An accident?"

"An accident?"

"You didn't mean to hit Holly, did you? You didn't mean to knock her down?"

"I didn't mean to knock her down," she repeated, as if in a trance.

"You were coming home from your mother's. Is that right? You didn't see her walking along the road. It's a narrow lane. It could have happened to anyone, Kerry."

"I didn't see her."

"That's right," Ben said. "You panicked. That's all. What did you do, Kerry?"

"What did I do?" she repeated. "I panicked."

Ben stepped forward, far enough to see the wound across the big man's forehead. "Look at him, Kerry. Look at him. He's hurt. He needs help."

"He knows," she cried out.

"We all know," Ben said. "What are you going to do, kill us all?"

Her eyes softened, as if in apology, and Ben read far more into her vacant expression. He took another step, far enough to see another three jerry cans, each with their lids off, and vapours rising from within. Kerry had doused the entire cargo area in petrol, and Nick MacMillan was lying in a pool of the stuff. He turned to her, and she held the lighter up.

"No, Kerry. No one else needs to die here. No more blood, okay? We can help you through this."

"We all need to die," she told him flatly.

"It was an accident—"

"She's in there," she screamed. "That bitch is inside."

"She's dead, Kerry—"

"Her blood. Her hair. She's in there. There's no escape from her."

Ben considered her choice of words.

"Nick moved her?" he said. "You put her body in the back of the van and he buried her in the garden?"

"Even now," she said. "Even after all this time, she's still here, tormenting me. It's not enough that she had my husband. But even when she's dead, she's still around. I've got to get rid of her. I need her gone. Can't you see?"

"You called Nick, didn't you? You knew he was working on your house. You called him to help you."

She stepped backwards, blinking away her tears.

"He's a friend," she said softly.

"He's a friend, is he?" Ben asked, then gestured at the motionless body in the van's cargo area. She turned her face away in shame. "Tell me about Deborah Jarvis."

"No," she said, and she struck the lighter. The flame was instant, and she held it before her in one hand, slowly raising the jerry can with the other.

"She was blackmailing you, Kerry. She was blackmailing everyone, wasn't she? She knew about the clothes beneath the wardrobe, she knew about Liam and his affairs, she knew about Kevin's fetish. She knew everything about everyone."

The flame still burned, and the fumes from the van watered Ben's eyes. He checked around him for Freya, but there was no sign of her.

"What did you do, Kerry? Did you wait for her to be alone? Is that it? Were you listening to her and Kevin speaking? Did you hear what they said?"

"She was a devious little cow—"

"She was a human being, Kerry. She was trying to get away from an abusive father."

"At my expense?"

"Did she deserve to die?" Ben asked. "Did she really deserve to die?"

Kerry tore her eyes from the flame and the fuel and stared at him coldly.

"If I hadn't done it," she said, "somebody else would have."

"Who? Kevin? Liam?" Ben asked. "Is that it? You'd already killed once. You might as well do it again. Is that it? Is that why it had to be you?"

"My life was over the moment Holly Carson hit the ground," she told him. Slowly, she moved the flame to the jerry can until the vapours caught, and a fierce flame rose into the air. Then, undeterred by the heat, she stared through the haze directly at Ben. "Kevin's has only just begun."

And with that, she hurled the fuel can at Ben.

He raised his arms to deflect it, but it fell at his feet, spilling its contents across the bare earth. The flames were instant, but time seemed to stop. He saw her run as a mirage in the heat haze. He saw the petrol drips from the van finding the burning soil. His eyes roved over MacMillan's still body, his fuel-soaked skin, and the flames that licked at the wood on which he lay.

And he saw Freya step into view, her face contorted with a scream that was lost to the fire, her arms outstretched as she ran to him.

"Freya, no. Stay back," he wanted to yell.

But no words came. It was too late. The rear of the van seemed to suck the air from around them in a rush of hot wind. When it had consumed its fill, the mixture of air and fuel spread its vaporous tentacles and found the fire's potent breath.

There was no time to call out, no time to turn away, and no time to tell her how he felt—those words he had been longing to say.

Instead, that vile and hateful coincidence of time and distance forced him to witness Freya's perfect face one last time as she shoved him hard in the chest.

He stumbled back onto the soil and raised his head in time to see Kerry Finch in the distance, watching the scene play out and Freya standing at the open side door. It was as if she realised her folly and knew that the image of her would leave a scar on his mind for the rest of time. Her eyes found his, and she hesitated, openmouthed. Then, perhaps for all the things she hadn't done or said or all the things she *had* done and said, or perhaps even for her last act of folly, she sighed and closed her eyes.

Then the fuel caught and raging flames exploded from inside the van, scorching the earth, searing the air, and devouring everything within reach. Instincitvely, Ben rolled away, then climbed onto all fours, shielding his face from the heat of the blaze that erupted from the van and reached to the heavens.

And Freya, the woman he had loathed and loved, who, with her spite and charm, had broken and mended his heart, was lost to the inferno.

CHAPTER FIFTY-FOUR

Strong arms dragged him to safety. Yet he kicked and fought at his saviours. The van was ablaze. Thick, black smoke smothered the ground. Bright flames soared from inside as the vapours that had collected ignited.

And a limp, dark form fell to the ground.

"Freya," he yelled, but the hands held him tight. He tore at them, digging his heels into the earth until he broke free and scrambled across the dirt to her.

The heat was immense, and thick smoke stung his eyes.

"Guv, leave her," one of the uniformed officers shouted over the blaze.

Ben turned on him. He wanted to grab the man and hold him in the flames until he felt what Ben was feeling. Until he felt the hurt like he did.

Instead, he just snarled at him, "Give me your jacket."

"Guv, don't–" the officer protested, but Ben had already begun clawing at him, tugging at the man's bright coat until he relented. Using the jacket to cover his head, Ben crawled towards Freya. She was still and flames burned in places he never thought possible. So intense had the heat been that flames danced across her skin. He lay flat on the ground, the heat tearing from the open van door above him, flames licking at his hand as he reached for her, groping for her clothes. Twice he had to withdraw, clutching at his burned skin. But he couldn't let her stay there. He couldn't just leave her to burn.

A body dropped beside him, though he couldn't see who it was.

"I'm with you, guv," the officer called, and he felt a reassuring hand on his shoulder.

"On three," Ben called. "One." He prepared himself, flexing his hand to ready the already seared skin. "Two." He dug his heels into the soil to give him purchase. And then he took a final breath. It was going to hurt. But it would hurt a lot more if he just left her there. "Three."

Together, they reached out, groping for purchase. His fingers found material, enough to pull on, and so he did, and she moved. Together, they dragged her from beneath the flames until the air was cool enough to breathe. He ripped the jacket from his head and tossed it away, then stared at her in disbelief.

And just like the first time he had seen her, mid-winter, on that icy, remote beach, it was an image he would never forget.

"Help me," the officer said, as he climbed to his feet, then bent to grab hold of her limbs. Ben followed suit and together they heaved her away from danger, toward the cars, and let her rest on the ground. Without the overbearing rush of flames and crinkle of steel, a sound from the sky caught his ear. A distant thumping like the cavalry's heavy boots.

"Help's coming," he told her. "Just wait, Freya. Just hang on." But once he'd started speaking to her, he found he couldn't stop. "I'm sorry," he said, falling to his knees and resting his head on her chest. "I'm so sorry. I told you to keep away. Why couldn't you just do as I said for once? Why, Freya? Why do you have to be so bloody pigheaded?"

"Guv?" the officer said, resting a hand on Ben's shoulder, which he shrugged off, turning his attention to Freya again.

"It doesn't matter about the wedding, okay? None of it matters. We don't have to do any of it. Just...just don't go, Freya. Just be strong, will you? Bloody listen to me. Open your eyes, Freya."

He touched her blackened skin and felt the heat from within. Those few places on her face that were not black were fiery red, as was his hand. But his hand was insignificant. His hand would heal. Her eyebrows had gone, as had her fringe and much of the hair on the left side of her head. Her ear had the look of melted wax, dotted with ebony ash and filth from the field.

But it was her face at which he couldn't stop gazing. Not the crust of charred skin that ran down the left side. Not the angry and inflamed flesh surrounding her left eye.

But her lips. They appeared to be unscathed.

Yet they were motionless. As was her chest, which no longer gently rose and fell like a turning tide, but was as still as a millpond. He lay his head against her chest as the yellow helicopter prepared to land in the field. The heavy rotors washed the thick, black smoke from the scene, kicking up dust in giant plumes.

"Freya? Don't go, sweetheart. Stay with me. Please, just stay with me."

"Guv?"

"I can't hear her heart," he snapped at the officer. "She's gone."

It seemed to take an eternity for the helicopter to land, but when the huge bird finally settled in the soil, and the engines wound down to a whining idle, the team inside were out and running towards them in a heartbeat.

"Freya, help's here, okay? You're going to be okay, Freya," he said. "Okay? They're going to help you."

"Get this man away," a man with a doctor's badge on his chest called as he dropped beside Freya. The officer who had helped Ben grabbed him beneath his arms and helped him to his feet.

"Come on, guv. Let them do their thing," he said, as the doctor checked her vitals. Another man ran to his side, opening a collapsable stretcher as he ran, which he dropped beside her. "What do we know about her?" the doctor asked and looked up at Ben and the officer. "Come on. What happened here? Who is she?"

"Guv?" the officer said, shaking Ben from the horrors in which his mind was indulging.

"I need a name," the doctor said.

"Freya," Ben said finally. "Detective Chief Inspector Freya Bloom."

"Was she in there?" he asked, gesturing at what was left of the van.

"Outside," Ben said. "But close enough to be caught in the blast."

"Are there any more?" Ben stared at her motionless body. "I said, are there any more? Is she the only casualty?"

"There's one in the van," Ben told him. "But he won't have survived."

The doctor had little time for gratitude or opinions. He signalled to the pilot that they were ready, and then together, he and the other paramedic executed a lift, placing her gently onto the stretcher, then prepared to carry her to the waiting helicopter.

"Is she..." Ben began, then felt every muscle surrounding his heart contract. "I work with her. She's my...she's my boss."

The doctor must have seen something in Ben's face as he paused for a fraction of a second to look him in the eye.

"Get your hand seen to," he told Ben. "We need to get her to Lincoln and we need to do it now."

"But she's alive?" Ben asked, as they carried her towards the chopper. "She'll make it, right?"

He made to follow them, but again, the officer restrained him. "Let them do their jobs, guv," he said. "Just give them space."

But Ben tore his arm free and ran after them, catching up just as they placed the stretcher on the deck. Oblivious to Ben, the paramedics climbed in beside her, reached out, and slammed the door closed.

The motors whined into action, and the rotors, which had been slowly idling, gained momentum. Undeterred, Ben pressed his face against the glass in time to the doctor leaning over Freya, performing CPR while the paramedic held an oxygen mask to her mouth.

"Freya," Ben called out, slamming his hand against the window. "Freya, can you hear me? I'm here, Freya."

Strong arms wrestled Ben from the side of the helicopter, but he held fast in time to see the doctor drop back into a seated position and shake his head at his colleague.

"*No*," Ben said, banging on the door again. "No, keep trying. Keep trying. Don't stop. She's alive. I know she is."

With a concerted effort, the officers dragged him from danger and across the dirt, kicking and fighting. The rotors gained speed. The high-pitched whine drowned every other sound out, even the grunts of the officers who knelt on Ben's chest to keep him down.

"Freya," Ben screamed as the rotors kicked the dust into the air once more. "Freya, I'm here. Freya? Don't leave me." The ascent was faster than the descent had been. The skilled pilot turned as they climbed and all Ben could think of was the doctor sitting back and shaking his head.

In seconds, Freya was nothing more than a distant thumping on the horizon. A yellow dot that faded to nothing.

Like her heart.

The officers relaxed their grip on Ben and he lay there in the dirt, watching the chopper's journey for as long as he could. "Don't leave me," he said. "Please. Don't leave me."

A hand squeezed his shoulder. Aside from a few pops and crackles coming from the burning van, the air was silent.

"You had to let her go, guv," a voice said. "They did what they could."

But Ben was in no mood for empty consolation. In the space of a few minutes, his world had turned as black as the skin on Freya's face.

"Where is she?"

"Who?"

"Kerry Finch," Ben said, and he dragged himself to his feet, stumbling once but regaining his balance. "Where is she?"

The two officers stared at each other, then back at him.

"She did a runner, guv," one said, and Ben's head snapped to attention. He stared across the field to where he had last seen her. "But she can't get far."

"Wait here."

Both of them climbed to their feet, clearly distressed.

"Guv, I'm not sure if you should go–"

"I said wait here," Ben snapped at him.

"We've got units on every road," he replied. "They'll pick her up. She won't get away with it."

"No, she won't," Ben told him, as he wiped his eyes with his sleeve and started off across the field. "Not if I have anything to do with it."

CHAPTER FIFTY-FIVE

Mud clung to his shoes and clothes so heavily that he felt he was wading through water. The smoke had smarted his watering eyes and his hand felt as if it was on fire.

Yet he trudged onward, unrelenting, unwilling to sit and wait, unable to let somebody else bring Kerry Finch down, shove her face into the dirt, and snap the cuffs onto her wrists. It had to be him.

But with every step he took, he seemed to leave a piece of his reason behind. The solitude, as he scoured the land for movement, and the silence, allowed his mind to work overtime, until he was nothing but an embittered man stumbling through farmland, fuelled only by a hateful vengeance.

He could see her face. Kerry Finch. He could see her consoling Rachel MacMillan on the very first day of the investigation. If only she had come clean then. If only she hadn't mowed Holly Carson down. If only Holly Carson hadn't been walking along the lane in Haverholme Park. If only Liam Finch had stayed faithful to his wife. If only Reggie Jarvis had been a kinder man to his daughter.

If only.

But he hadn't been a kind man. She had wanted to leave. And for that, she needed money.

And Liam Finch hadn't been faithful to his wife.

And Holly Carson had been walking along the lane.

And Kerry had knocked her down.

"Kerry Finch," he said aloud to himself. He could see her in his mind's eye. He pictured her face, her makeup, her hair, her eyes.

And he imagined it burning.

He could see her now, her ear melting like candle wax, her hair singed, her scalp scorched. Flames licked at her eyes, angering her skin, and she screamed. She screamed, loud and hard, so hard that her flaming lips peeled away from her teeth and her face blackened and crinkled like paper under a flame.

And Ben's hand, swollen and scarred, held her against that flame.

He stumbled and regained his balance, but it was enough of a disruption for his daydream to fade and for Freya's face to return to the forefront of his imagination. She was lying on the helicopter deck and the doctor sat back. But in Ben's mind, he didn't share his opinion with the paramedic. Instead, he turned to Ben, who peered through the window as a lost little boy.

And then shook his head.

"She's gone," he said, his gravelly voice somehow overcoming the thundering rotors and the closed door.

Ben stopped and bent over to catch his breath, cradling his swollen hand in his good arm as he straightened. He scanned the horizon, taking in the smoking ruins behind him, the distant road where a fire engine hurtled along, and the far side of the field, towards North Kyme where they had set up the roadblock.

The roadblock was gone now, but there was no other way out. Dykes crisscrossed the farmland, closing off any other means of escape. He considered running alongside them to see if she had jumped down into the water to hide. But something caught his eye—a kite circling high in the sky. Riding the breeze as a boat skips across the lapping shore.

And directly beneath it, crawling through the dirt on her hands and knees, was Kerry Finch.

Ben gave chase. It was like a dream; his legs felt as if they were working against him. He knew he could run faster, but his body denied the claim. Twice he stumbled to his knees and twice he clambered back to his feet before he lost momentum. He was three hundred yards from her by the time she thought to look back, and even from that distance, he recognised the fear in her eyes. No longer did she crawl through the mud in search of safety. Now she was on her feet with any hopes of escaping unnoticed gone.

"Stop, Kerry," he barked, to no avail. "There's no way out."

To his side, a liveried police car with its spinning blues closed in. They must have been watching Ben from afar and were vying to close off her escape.

But there was no way he would let them get to her before he did.

He doubled his efforts, searching deep inside for some source of energy other than his depleting adrenaline. He had the advantage. She would be running on fear alone. Fear that would obscure her judgement. Fear that caused her to look back, stumble, and fall, allowing him to close in.

She reached the far edge of the field and dropped out of sight, and moments later, Ben hurled himself into the ditch behind her. He landed and rolled into the cold water, just as she was scrambling up the far bank to the road. He reached and caught her boot, but she tore herself free.

"Stop, Kerry. It's over," he yelled.

But his words went unheard. She pulled herself out of the dyke and froze at the roadside.

Inch by inch, Ben forced himself on, dragging himself from

the water, grabbing hold of thick grass tufts to yank his sodden weight up the bank behind her.

Eventually, he reached forward. His hand touched flat grass, his fingers dug into the soil, and he heaved himself to the road-side, where he was met with the sight of her two leather boots and the wheels of passing traffic motoring past.

"It's over, Kerry," he said, his mouth dry, his lungs heaving, and his broken heart hanging by a thread. "No more."

His initial reaction was to push himself to his feet before she could run again. But she stayed where she was. He had hoped to find her crying, or angry, or showing some kind of emotion. Freya deserved that much, at least.

But she wasn't. Her face was calm, as if she had found peace in her attempt to escape. As if she had come to terms with her bleak future and accepted her fate.

"I told you no more blood, Kerry," he growled at her. "Do you know what you've done? Do you know who you've just murdered?"

Her face paled and Ben took a sodden step forward.

"I could have helped you, you know? I could have pushed for manslaughter. I could have pushed for mental instability. But you had to, didn't you? You had to push it. There's no help now, Kerry." He took another step forward. "By the time I'm done with you–"

The hate-filled speech he had prepared during the chase, while images of Freya's melted flesh had hijacked his mind, faded to nothing but meaningless words.

Brakes squealed on the tarmac, car horns rang out, and then the sound of broken glass brought the ensemble to a close.

Those two leather boots that had belonged to Kerry MacMillan lay on the ground a few metres from where she had been standing as if somebody had tossed them from a car, discarded, like the lives of two young girls...

And Freya.

CHAPTER FIFTY-SIX

He hadn't moved an inch, save for dropping to his knees at the roadside. He stared at the streak of blood that led from the tarmac before him to some dark place beneath the bus that hit her.

Uniformed officers had spoken to him. But what they had said was anybody's guess. It was just noise. All of it was just noise. Unnecessary noise.

A hand squeezed his shoulder, and for a moment, he thought it might be the officer who had helped him.

Until the gruff Glaswegian spoke.

"You alright there, fella?" Gillespie said. "Jeez, look at this place."

Ben remained facing forward, staring at the spot where she had been standing with tears streaming down his face.

"I could have stopped her, Jim," he said eventually. "I could have reached out and stopped her."

"Ah, come on. Even the bus driver saw it happen. He said there was no chance of stopping her."

"But if I could have, Jim, if I could have gotten to her..." He looked up at his old friend. "I don't think I would have."

Gillespie sighed heavily, then dropped down to the ground beside Ben, hugging his knees into a more relaxed position.

"Listen, mate. She knew her time was up. Whether she did it here, at the station, or in prison, she was going to do it. She had to. You had her bang to rights. Though, if I'm honest, I still don't understand how we got to this point. I was all up for nicking Nick MacMillan."

"We're long past that," Ben told him. But before he could explain about the fire and how even MacMillan's DNA would have been burned to a cinder by now, and how Freya had...

"Listen, I've spoken to the team, and, well, in light of what happened today, we've decided that we'll write the reports up. You know? One less thing for you to worry about."

"Ah, the reports. Where would we be without the bloody reports, eh?"

"They need doing, Ben."

"People died today, Jim. Lives were torn apart. But the force still needs reports."

"We just want to help, mate. Look, I just need the facts, then you can go and...do whatever you need to do to get past this. You can leave it all to me. But the longer you leave it, the harder it'll be. And God knows you won't want to relive today, will you?"

Ben glanced his way and offered a weak smile of thanks.

"You're right. Cheers mate."

"Ah, it's the least we can do, fella," Gillespie replied. "So let me get this right? Holly Carson was Liam Finch's bit on the side. Holly Carson was walking home when Kerry Finch knocked her down? Is that right?"

"It was the photo," Ben said. "The last photo in the pile. It's in Freya's file."

The mention of her name stung like a knife to his heart and turned away to wipe his eyes.

"The last photo in the pile?"

Ben closed his eyes. Did they have to do this now? No, but it was probably Gillespie's way of distracting him from reality. Besides, with the images his mind was conjuring, who knew what that reality might look like in a few days?

"The wardrobe," Ben explained. "It was Freya who found it in the MacMillan house. The clothes she had worn were tucked in a little space beneath the floor of the wardrobe."

"Aye, I see," Gillespie said.

"Kerry Finch then asked Nick MacMillan to help her get rid of the body. Hence the burning van with the man himself inside. She must have realised we were closing in and decided that too many people knew."

"But how did Deborah Jarvis know?" Gillespie asked. "What, did she see it happen or something?"

"That's what she did," Ben replied. "She wanted to get away from her abusive dad so much that she would break into people's houses searching for something to have on them. An affair, an accident, cheating in exams–"

"A dirty fetish?" Gillespie said, to which Ben nodded. "So it was Kerry Finch who nabbed Deborah that night?"

"It had to have been," Ben said. "Liam said they were packing the house up. None of us even questioned if *she* was home all night. We were too busy looking at Liam and Kevin. All she had to do was pop down the road to the forest, wait for her moment, and then drag her to the priory. There's blood on the wall in the priory. My guess is that she hit her with something, thought she was dead, and left her there wrapped in plastic until the house was empty."

"Kerry Finch?" Gillespie said. "You think she did all that alone, do you? She's a wee lass. She couldn't have dragged Deborah up to the priory and she certainly couldn't have carried her back wrapped in plastic." Ben stared at him thoughtfully. "She had to have someone help her, Ben."

"Someone like?"

"Her husband?" Gillespie suggested. "Or maybe her son? They

both had something to lose. I mean, we've got them both in custody. We could go back and question them."

"No," Ben said, his tone a little too sharp. "No, you're right. She did have help. But it wasn't either of those two."

"Who then? Not MacMillan?"

"Who would you ask to help you?" Ben asked. "Your son? Your husband?"

"The man who had helped her before," Gillespie said. "The man who couldn't say no."

"He had as much to lose as she did. If Deborah reported what she knew about Holly Carson, they'd both go down for it."

"But he lived with her beneath his floor for five years, Ben. Five bloody years knowing that a wee lass is lying there."

"Compared to serving life sentences, it doesn't seem like much. All he had to do was wait for the right time to renovate his house."

"Aye, but his wife beat him to it, eh?" Gillespie said, shaking his head, and Ben stiffened at the sight. "You okay, mate?"

Ben shook his head.

"No, not really," he said.

"Why don't you take some time off, eh? Granger wouldn't mind, would he? I mean, you've been through it."

"As it happens, I was thinking of taking some time off," Ben said.

"Good for you, mate. A month or two would do you the world of good. Go somewhere new. Breathe fresh air and all that."

"I was thinking longer than that," Ben said. "Much longer."

"Well, a few months is plenty of time. You wouldn't want to come back and find me in your spot, would you?"

"Wouldn't I?" Ben asked. "The truth is, mate, that right now, nothing would give me greater pleasure than seeing you and Anna leading the team."

"Eh?"

"I'm not coming back, Jim," Ben said. "I'm done."

"Ah come on," he said. "You're just messed up because of all this. You're not thinking straight."

"I'm serious," Ben said. "Besides, you deserve it. You work hard enough. Anna too. You could both run the team with your hands behind your back."

"Aye, I mean, we could run the team," Gillespie said, never one to let modesty impede a compliment. "But we couldn't manage the boss like you can. I mean, when she gets going, the rest of us just back off, if you know what I mean."

Ben squeezed his eyes closed and let his head fall back while Gillespie rambled on.

"And as for her mood swings," he said. "Jeez, I don't know how you do it–"

"She's dead, Jim," Ben said, cutting Gillespie short. He swallowed and took a deep breath.

"You what?"

They were words he couldn't bear to repeat and prayed that Gillespie had heard.

"I watched the air ambulance take her away, mate," Ben mumbled. "I dragged her from the..."

"Easy now," Gillespie said, and he rolled onto his knees to sit before Ben. "Just take it easy."

"I watched them try to save her. I watched them give up, Jim. She's gone." He leaned forward into Gillespie's arms. The tears he'd been fighting for the past hour flowed freely and he sobbed into his friend's chest like a child; despite his efforts to hold back, the tears and sobs just kept coming.

Gillespie held him and rubbed his back as if coaxing the tears to come.

"That's a bit of a blow," he said after a short while. "I just sent Cruz to buy flowers and grapes."

His words waited at the peripheral of Ben's fertile mind until they saw a break in the flow. His sobbing stopped as he pieced the statement together.

"You what?" he mumbled into Gillespie's chest.

"I thought you'd heard, mate," Gillespie said. "Freya's alive."

"She's not, Jim. I saw them trying to save her. I saw them stop. I saw him shake his head."

"You didn't see them giving up, Ben," he said, pulling Ben's head away so he could look him in the eye. "You saw them save her."

CHAPTER FIFTY-SEVEN

Peering through the little window into the hospital ward reminded Ben of how he and Freya used to watch the team through the incident room door. With both of them gone, Gillespie would toss balled paper across the room, usually aimed at Cruz. Or he would be on his feet, inciting a heated debate about the perfect chocolate bar, the best TV show, or preferred takeaways, usually based on time to deliver and portion size as opposed to the quality of food.

Ben would have given anything to be watching a paper ball fight or a debate. Instead, a doctor added notes to a clipboard, nurses fussed over machines, and Freya lay there with her face and arms wrapped in bandages and an oxygen mask covering her mouth and nose.

Her chest rose and fell, but from where he stood, it was hard to see if the machines were producing the effect, or if her own efforts were stable.

It was a nurse who first saw him, like a schoolboy peering through a window at something he shouldn't, and in turn, she alerted the doctor. He was of Asian descent and carried himself with a confident authority when he approached the door.

"May I help?" he asked, his accent more akin to Freya's than to his ancestors.

"I..." he began. "How is she?"

"Alive," he replied. "Are you family?"

Ben considered lying but found himself shaking his head before the words could form.

"I'm afraid you can't be here."

"I'm all she's got," Ben said hurriedly. "Her parents are dead and she has no siblings. I'm all she has."

The doctor seemed reluctant at first but then submitted. He egded from the room, closed the door behind him, and with a firm but gentle hand coaxed Ben along the corridor.

"You care for her," he began. "I can see that. But I'm afraid you must prepare yourself, Mr..."

"Savage," Ben replied. "Ben Savage."

The doctor accepted Ben's introduction with casual indifference. With his arms behind his back, he strode thoughtfully, perhaps seeking the most suitable means of phrasing Freya's condition.

"Just tell me," Ben said. "How bad is it?"

"Miss Bloom has suffered severe trauma," the doctor replied. "Without knowing the details of the accident—"

"It was no accident," Ben told him. "I was standing beside a van filled with petrol. A burning jerry can was thrown at me."

"And if it hadn't been for Miss Bloom?" the doctor said, finding the words that would have brought Ben to his knees. It was all he could do to nod in response and swallow the emotion that had taken root in his throat. "She was caught in the blast, I presume?" the doctor said, and again Ben nodded. "Well, that explains a few things. I consider her to be very fortunate."

"Fortunate?"

"It could have been a lot worse," the doctor replied. "She was in a state of deep shock, which given the circumstances, is understandable. Had the fire been anywhere else, then I'm quite sure you wouldn't have been able to pull her out." He glanced down at the angry skin on Ben's hand. "As it happens, the fact that she fell to the ground probably saved her life, with the fire being a foot or two above her, her burns are...shall we say, less severe than they could have been."

"So she'll make a full recovery?" Ben asked.

"She'll recover sufficiently enough to walk the earth," the doctor replied. "Her burns can be treated and I would imagine some plastic surgery would be required. Her ear, for example, is particularly injured, as is the skin on the left side of her face and arm. But these are superficial wounds. She'll need to come to terms with her physical scarring, but the large part of her rehabilitation will be in her mind, Mr Savage." The doctor stopped walking and turned to face Ben. "She'll need help. She'll need... good friends. Someone to stand by her."

"Then she shall have it," Ben replied without hesitation, to which the doctor nodded once and eyed Ben as if to reinstate his analysis. "It'll be several hours before you can see her. Why not take the time to collect some of her belongings?"

"Clothes and stuff, you mean?"

"Among other things," the doctor replied, then turned on his heels and began walking back to Freya's room, calling out over his shoulder. "Perhaps something to remind her that she is alive, Mr Savage. Give her a purpose." He stopped at the doorway and looked back at Ben. "Your friend has a long journey ahead of her, and believe me, she will be questioning her existence with every step."

CHAPTER FIFTY-EIGHT

His knees shook and his feet felt as if they were not his own. He rested against the corridor wall, letting his head fall back. He could have just slumped to the floor and slept. His mind was a whirlwind of thoughts, reenactments, and regret. Mostly the latter. Footsteps passed by, of nurses and visitors all going about their business.

But Ben's world had come to a grinding halt. He was living a dream in which he faced parallel lives. One showed him and Freya in the field with the van, but their positions were swapped, and it was Ben who had slowly crept around the vehicle while Freya had tried to stop Kerry Finch. And it had been Freya who had stood before the open van door, and Ben who had shoved her away. It had been Freya too, who had watched the air ambulance arrive, who had witnessed Ben's body being carted off.

But when the doctor sat back in the helicopter and shook his head, Freya wasn't there to see it. She was already on Finch's heels. She hadn't wasted those precious moments. She had brought Kerry down before she had reached the road.

He opened his eyes, dabbed them with his sleeve, and glanced along the corridor, only to find a man peering in through

Freya's window. Ben shoved off the wall, curious as to the man's identity. He was too short to be Gillespie and too tall to be Cruz. He took a few slow steps towards the room, studying the man. A bunch of petrol station flowers hung by his side, and when caught sight of Ben approaching, he stepped away from the window.

"You?" Ben said.

"I heard about it," Godfrey replied. "I just came to..." He glanced down at the flowers. "Well, you know?"

"You?" Ben said again, his pace quickening. He reached the man in seconds, grabbed hold of his lapels, and shoved him against the wall. "How dare you come here?"

"I didn't mean to—" he began, but Ben pulled him away from the wall, only to slam him back into place.

"Do you have any idea of what you've put her through?" Ben snarled at him. "Do you have any idea at all? She has spent the past six months going out of her mind, wondering if she was going mad or if somebody had it in for her."

"It wasn't supposed to be like that—"

"Well, it was," Ben shouted, his face inches from Godfrey's. "You planted a piece of false evidence, Godfrey. Do you have any idea of the repercussions? What if that had been used in court? What if a murderer had walked because we couldn't say where that evidence came from?"

"It was just meant to slow her down, that's all."

"Why? Because she had a go at you at a crime scene? Because she showed you up in front of other officers? Man the hell up, Godfrey. If she showed you up, it was because you deserved it and she was the only one ballsy enough to pull you up."

"It wasn't just that," Godfrey said.

"Oh, no. Of course not. You're not alone, are you? Someone put you up to it, didn't they? Someone orchestrated the whole thing. The complaints against her and the rest of it. And what about the arrest? What about when two of your officers came to her door and arrested her for leaving the scene of an accident? How do you think that would have affected her career?"

"I wasn't thinking," Godfrey said, and Ben held him even tighter. "I...we just wanted to–"

"To what?" Ben said, and he forced him back hard enough for the man's head to collide with the wall. "To what, Godfrey?"

"We just wanted...to put her back in her place," he said.

"She's a DCI. Pulling officers up on scrappy police work is her job. Making sure procedures are followed is her job." Ben pulled him from the wall, turned him around, and dragged him sideways to the door, where he pressed Godfrey's face against the glass. "Look at her. Look at her, Godfrey. Do you see that? Do you see what she is now? Is she back in her place, is she? Is that what you wanted?"

"No–"

"She deserves this, does she?"

"No–"

"No, she doesn't," Ben said. "But she wouldn't be here if it wasn't for you and your petty mates bullying her. If you weren't so bloody sensitive and could take a few harsh words. Do you know how hard she was trying to get things right? Knowing that if we couldn't finish the investigation, if we couldn't get to the bottom of it, then it would all fall on her shoulders? And why? Because people like you are out there actively trying to bring her down. Now you tell me she deserves that?" Godfrey said nothing. His breath fogged the glass and Ben pressed even harder. "Tell me she deserves it, Godfrey. Tell me."

"She doesn't," he said. "I'm sorry, alright? I'm sorry. It went too far."

Ben pulled him away from the glass and then shoved him along the corridor. He collected the flowers from where Godfrey had dropped them and threw them after him. "You know what you can do with those."

Godfrey stood there for a moment while Ben straightened his jacket.

"Well? Go on then. Piss off. You're not welcome. And you can tell your mates too," Ben said. "All of them. If any of them come near her, they'll have me to deal with. Do you understand me, Godfrey?"

But Godfrey was still as if defying Ben to come at him again.

And Ben prepared to do just that. He marched up to the man, balled his fist, and was about to knock him into the middle of next week when Godfrey reached into his pocket and pulled something out.

"What's that?" Ben asked as he lowered his fist, and Godfrey looked at the floor, ashamed.

"I found it under the floor in the MacMillan house."

Ben held out his hand, and Godfrey dropped a scrap of old, yellowed newspaper into it. He recognised it immediately from the MacMillan kitchen walls.

"You know, it wasn't my idea to bring her down, don't you?" Godfrey said.

Ben nodded slowly. "Say his name," he growled and grabbed onto Godfrey's shirt. "I said, tell me who put you up to it." He waited a few seconds and was happy to force the name from Godfrey's lips when he spoke.

"Steve Standing," Godfrey whispered.

"Standing? You're sure about that?"

"He's had it in for her since day one. She's upset a lot of officers. People who are loyal to him. People who think it an injustice to see him behind bars."

"Yourself included?" Ben asked.

"Like I said, she made a lot of enemies by putting him away."

"He abused his position," Ben said quietly. "He killed a man. A family is out there grieving. Should Standing be walking the streets? Is that what you call justice?"

"He's a good man," Godfrey said. "And he was a good officer. Is your conscience clear? Mine certainly isn't."

"We've established that."

"And hers?" Godfrey said, and his eyes narrowed as if he knew the answer to his question.

A fire burned in Ben's heart. "You don't get to talk about her," he said. "You don't even get to think about her. Now get out of my sight." He turned his back on Godfrey and strode over to the window. One nurse remained, tending to the machines and Freya's drip. "And Godfrey," he called, catching the sergeant as he walked away. "Remember what I said. No more sabotages, no more complaints, and no more attempts to bring her down. This ends now."

Godfrey stared back at him, nodded once, then resumed his exit, straightening his shirt as he walked.

Ben stared through the window. He wondered if Freya could hear him, or if she even knew he was there. He wondered if she had heard their altercation.

He hoped not. Some things were best left unspoken.

It wasn't until a few moments later that Ben felt a presence beside him. A man as tall as Ben but older. He peered through the window in the other door.

"Did you..." Ben began.

"Hear it?" Granger said, and he nodded slightly. "I heard enough."

Ben remained facing forward. Freya's chest rose and fell, and the nurse went about her business.

"She's going to make it," Ben said, to which Granger said nothing. But what could he say? What value could he add to the statement?

"For what it's worth, Ben, I thought you handled the situation very well."

Ben squeezed the scrap of newspaper in his sweaty palm and then pocketed it.

"It could have gone another way," Ben admitted. "Part of me wishes it had."

"I hear you're thinking of taking leave," Granger said, and he rolled back and forth on his heels and toes with his hands in his pockets.

Once a bobby, always a bobby.

"You've been talking to Gillespie," Ben replied quietly. "Has he put his name forward already? He didn't waste any time, did he?"

"Actually it was I who sought him out," Granger replied, and his eyes rolled sideways to meet Ben's. "Let's just say that I was required to diffuse a certain situation with one of the locals in Haverholme. It appears that his past came back to haunt him."

"And did you?" Ben asked. "Diffuse the situation, I mean? Did he walk away with a reprimand?"

"My dear, Ben. We all have chapters we would prefer to remain unpublished," Granger replied. "So, will you be seeking some time in warmer climes to recover? Should I pull in some resources from another team?"

"No, I'm not going anywhere, guv," Ben said, staring at Freya, and wondering what lay beneath those bandages. He turned to find Granger's sympathetic eyes drilling into him, and he looked away again, finding comfort in the rise and fall of Freya's chest. "At least not for the time being."

"You know, Gillespie would make a good number two, Ben."

He searched Granger's eyes to read the true meaning behind the statement.

"So would Anna Nillson," he replied, to which Granger nodded his agreement.

"What I'm saying is, Ben, that if you're staying," Granger began, "I need you to step up."

"I figured as much."

He stared through the window at Freya, and a pang of betrayal tugged at his heart.

"A few days ago, I gave the pair of you a choice,' Granger said. "Now it's you who has a decision to make."

"And when she's back on her feet?" Ben asked. "Am I to step down?"

Granger took a final glance at Freya, then took a step back, preparing to leave.

"I suppose that all depends," he said flatly.

"On what?"

"Circumstances, Ben," he replied. "Who knows when that will be? And who knows what will happen between now and then?" He nodded a goodbye, turned, and strolled along the corridor. "It's your team, Ben," he called out. "It's always been your team."

"Guv," Ben called out before Granger disappeared around the corner. He turned back, eyebrows raised in anticipation. "Standing," he said. "If you heard my conversation with Godfrey, then–"

"I shouldn't worry too much about Standing," Granger said. "I doubt he'll be influencing any officers in this neck of the woods for much longer."

And with a friendly wink, Granger turned and left Ben alone.

The nurse opened the door and smiled politely up at Ben as she went about her day. But as the door closed, a familiar scent emerged into the corridor. He knew he must have imagined it. After all she had been through during the past day, it had to be a figment of his imagination, his senses yearning or his memory toying with his heart.

But he relished the fragrance nonetheless.

"You hang in there, Freya," he whispered. "And that's an order."

CHAPTER FIFTY-NINE

The first thing Ben noticed when he pushed open his front door was the smell—fresh linen, or at least an air freshener that smelled like fresh linen. The second was something that caught his eye. A key on the doormat. It stopped him in his tracks for a moment, but then he bent to pick it up and dropped it into his pocket.

He moved through to the living room where he dumped his bag down, kicked off his shoes, and padded through to the kitchen. The fridge was fuller than he remembered. Not with food, but with wine. Wine that he hadn't bought but did recognise. He reached for a bottle and held it up to the light to read the label. It was the Sauvignon Blanc they had enjoyed in Woodhall a few weeks ago. He remembered the lunch, and how he had commented on the wine. But she hadn't replied. He thought she was just ignoring him, as she so often did.

The Chablis, too. They had been out for dinner in Horncastle and shared a bottle.

He dropped to a crouch to study them all and could name the places of all six bottles.

And all the time, he had thought she had been ignoring his comments on the wine.

And then he saw it. The note on the kitchen work surface.

"Hello?" a voice called from the front door, female with a faint Edinburgh accent.

"In here," he called back, folding the note and slipping it into his pocket just as Jackie appeared in the doorway.

"How are you holding up?" she asked.

"I could ask the same."

She stepped into the kitchen, dumping her bag on the counter, and then wrapped her arms around him. "Don't deflect," she mumbled. "It's okay to be upset, you know?"

"I'm fine," he replied, holding her close to prevent her from seeing the lie in his eyes. "At least I don't have tubes coming out of my nose. I'm not wrapped in bandages. And as far as I'm aware, I'm not being kept alive by machines."

"Is she that bad, Ben?" Jackie said, pulling back.

But he just shrugged and turned away. "Who told you anyway?"

"Granger," she said. "He suggested we have a little chat. You know? I talk about what I saw, and you talk about..."

"What I saw?"

"It helps, you know?" she said.

"So I've heard. But I'm not really the talkative type, am I?" He stared through the window into his garden. But it wasn't his window; it wasn't his garden. Freya was there, hijacking his mind as she had done since the moment he had met her. "The truth is, Jackie. I'm at a loss for words. It all happened so fast. One minute we were about to put the cuffs on Kerry Finch, and the next minute... The next minute, we weren't." He shook his head. "I keep replaying it over and over, Jackie. Different versions. Things I could have done. Things she could have done. Should have done."

"Such as?"

"Listen," he told her. "I told her, Jackie. I told her to stay put. To stay where she was. But you know wat she's like. She–"

"Ben, Ben, Ben," Jackie began, cutting him off. "You can't change the past. You just can't. Things happened and now we must face the consequences."

He closed his eyes to the world and exhaled, long and slow.

"You know I asked her to marry me, don't you?"

"What? No. Ben, you should have said–"

"She hadn't given me an answer. Not properly, anyway. I mean, she would have married me, but there were conditions." He turned to her and lost himself in those big, beautiful eyes. "Compromises."

"Granger?" Jackie asked, to which Ben nodded.

"I couldn't see it before, but there's no escaping it, is there? He didn't want a married couple on the team. He said it was too risky in case one of us gets hurt."

"Ben, you couldn't have known."

"I suppose none of it matters now, does it? He was right. One of us got hurt and the other one needs to carry on somehow. Pick up the pieces, write the reports, and carry on as if nothing happened. Because that's what we do. I've got to get through the very situation he was trying to avoid." He laughed, but it faded as fast as it came. "And I have to do it while the woman I love is in hospital having her face rebuilt, and that's before we even talk about her mind. She might come through all of this and decide to just bugger off again."

"No, she wouldn't do that."

"Wouldn't she? She did it before."

"Oh, Ben," Jackie said in that way only mothers can. "What can I do? How can I help?"

"You can't," he told her. "I need to get to her place. I need to pack her some things." He reached for her hands and held them tight. "Can you imagine if she wakes up wearing a hospital gown that dozens of women before her have worn?"

Jackie laughed quietly.

"Heads would roll," she said.

"It would be an affront to her sense of style and decency," Ben told her.

"Then let me do it," Jackie said. "Let me help. I can pack her some things. She wouldn't mind. In fact, she'd probably prefer it, me being a girl and that."

"You'd do that for me?"

"Of course," she said, as if the answer was obvious. "Do you have a key?"

He grinned inwardly.

"As it happens, I do," he replied and fished the single key from his pocket. She reached for it, but Ben held it tight for a moment.

"I didn't tell you, but we had an argument the other day."

"You didn't need to tell me, Ben. It was written all over your face."

"Was it?" She grinned up at him, as a sister might. "Well, it was bad enough that I posted the key she gave me through her letterbox. As far as I knew, it was over between us."

"So how did you get this one?" she asked.

He shook his head.

"I suppose, she must have known what I would do," he said. "And she must have been clinging onto whatever it is we have."

He stared up at Jackie, one of his oldest friends, trying to read whatever it was in her eyes.

"What, Ben? What is it?"

"I don't know," he replied, thinking of the key on the mat. He let the key go and brushed an eerie sensation away from the forefront of his mind. "It's nothing."

"No, come on," she pressed. "Talk to me, Ben. It's me. You can tell me anything."

"It's just..." he said, then paused as a plan began to fruit. "Do you mind if I come with you?"

"To Freya's? Of course not."

"Stay here," he said, pushing past her to get to the stairs.

"Ben, you're acting weird. Do you think you should have a lie down. It could be shock setting in."

"No, it's not shock," he told her from half way up the stairs. "I just need to fetch something. Something for her to cling to."

CHAPTER SIXTY

The key opened the door with ease, just as Ben knew it would. But the house was different somehow. Even though he had been the last person there, it felt altered, as if something was missing.

"She's furnished the place well. I'll give her that," Jackie said, and he recalled the trips into town to order her dining table, chairs, and the rest of it.

"She was never going to make do, was she?" Ben replied. "Only the finest. That's her to a tee, is it not? I still have the table my dad gave me, and as for my bed, I think it was the one I was conceived in."

"Oh, well, thanks for that image," she said, then rubbed her hands together as if warming them. "Right then. Upstairs, is it?"

Ben presented the stairway with a sweep of his arm then followed her up, and that pang of betrayal returned with a vengeance. Following Jackie up to Freya's bedroom felt more than a little uncomfortable. So much so that he steered her into the spare bedroom, which Freya used as a dressing room.

"Wow, an entire room dedicated to clothes and makeup," Jackie said. "Every girl's dream." Her wandering eye landed on the table and chair Freya had set up, and then the pieces of paper that were laid out and pinned to the wall. "What's all that?"

She stepped closer, reading some of the names Freya had written.

"Sergeant Godfrey?" she said, glancing inquisitively at Ben. "Isn't he the one who–"

"Led the internal search team at the MacMillan house," Ben finished for her. "He also led the search in Boothby Graffoe last month." Jackie seemed perplexed. "And he planted a piece of rogue evidence, hoping to catch Freya out or trip her up or something."

"What about these names?" Jackie asked. "Sanderson?"

"It turns out that Freya has managed to upset a few people since she arrived in Lincolnshire."

"A few?"

"Well, more than a few. But it just so happens that the loyalty of some of those individuals lies elsewhere."

Jackie traced the lines Freya had drawn from each of the names to a single name at the top of the table.

"Steve Standing?" she said. "But he's–"

"In prison," he finished for her again.

"Bloody hell. Isn't there something we can do? Surely we can report it? If he's had visits or calls from police officers, then–"

"It's been dealt with," Ben assured her. He reached past her, pulled all of Freya's research into a pile, and then screwed the entire bundle into a ball, which he then unceremoniously dumped into the waste bin. "It might be best we keep this to ourselves," he told her. "Nobody needs to know, and with any luck, when she comes around, it will be a figment of her imagination." Jackie smiled at his loyalty. "Anyway, I'll leave you to it. You'll find her bags and whatnot in the wardrobe."

"I'll find it," Jackie said and watched as Ben edged from the room and into Freya's bedroom, where he found himself staring out of the window at the church. He recalled their conversation only a few days before when some other happy couple had emerged from those two wooden doors, ready to embark on a new chapter of their lives.

Then the image blurred, his throat tightened, and he wiped the tears from his eyes.

But still, they fell.

He stepped back and perched on the edge of the bed, holding his head in his hands.

Did he have what it would take to help Freya back to her feet while managing the team?

It would be a new chapter in their lives. A chapter that had yet to be written. A story that could unfold in any number of ways. Nothing was in his control. He was lost at sea at the mercy of the tide.

But he did have an oar. A single oar which he could dig into the waves to plot a new course.

He checked behind him to make sure Jackie wasn't looking, and then reached into his jacket pocket. He positioned the photo frame exactly how Freya had, mirroring the frame on her side of the bed.

"I'm done," Jackie said, coming to the door holding Freya's holdall. "Are you ready? You don't want her to wake up alone, do you?"

"No, of course not," he replied, wiping his eyes before standing to face her. He glanced around the room, taking a mental image that he might recall in the coming days and weeks. "In fact, that's the last thing I want."

The End.

BURDEN OF TRUTH - PROLOGUE

The Wild Fens Murder Mysteries - Book 14

The world passed by in a blur. The horizon was in the dying throes of azure, clinging on as darkness claimed its space. The field he ran through was a sea of honey stems, crunching underfoot, tripping him and cutting into his bare skin.

And the air he breathed was lacking, as if his body needed more.

He stumbled and fell, and lay in the crops, listening for footsteps above his thumping heart as the darkening sky above him swirled like vultures.

Something scurried nearby, a mouse or a vole.

Or maybe it was *him* growing close. His captor. Maybe he had found his path through the broken stems and was on the hunt.

Lee Constantine sat up. But still the world span. His eyes, unable to focus on a single stem, found only shadow, and that distant strip of light to the west.

Again, he ran.

Even the ground was a blur, and each mistimed step was like miscalculating the final stair. Sometimes his feet hit the ground earlier than he had anticipated, while other times, the soil seemed to have disappeared altogether.

Ahead of him, a line of trees marked the edge of the field. In the light of day, when the world did not turn, and his eyes could focus, he might have named his position.

But in the meagre, mid-evening light, he could have been anywhere; Scotland, Yorkshire, Cornwall. Any number of places. A part of him, that part that he recalled from an hour or so ago, knew the field was a Lincolnshire field. But the mind has a way of giving in to the doubt that delusion propagates.

"Lee?"

A whisper. A hiss in his right ear.

He stopped, turned, but found nobody.

"Lee?"

The same whisper. The same voice, but this time to his left.

And still nobody was there.

"Leave me alone," he screamed, first to his left, and then to his right. "Just let me be."

He edged backwards.

"There's nowhere to run," the whispered voice taunted. "I know what you saw."

"I didn't see anything," Lee replied. Even his repeated blinking would clear the blur, and the tears that rolled from his eyes only served to make focusing harder.

He reached behind him, feeling the bushes of sharp thorns digging into his skin. But he pushed through. It was his only escape. With one hand reaching through the thicket and the other covering his genitals, he forced himself into the bush to the tune of his captor's laughter.

"Where are you going, Lee? You can't get away. I'm in your head."

"Just leave me alone. I won't say owt."

He stayed there, with sharp thorns pressing into his backside and his sides. He couldn't get him here.

Could he?

But then he appeared. A face. A sneer.

Anger.

"No," Lee said, and forced himself through the hedge as a hand groped for him. He fell through the second half and landed in a heap on the ground. He scrambled clear, backing away on his hands and feet.

But nobody came after him.

No voices called out.

No laughter taunted him.

He was alone.

Slowly, he climbed to his feet, blinking to regain some clarity but finding only the inescapable blur.

He took a step back, searching for movement where detail lacked. Listening for footsteps, for a breath, for anything.

"I know you're there," the whisper came, and Lee froze as the face emerged from the hedge and grinned at him. "Found you."

Lee backed away, one step, two steps.

But the third step was different. There was no hard ground to take his weight. It was that gut-wrenching sensation of descending the stairs again. Imagining that his foot would find the step.

But no such step existed, and he felt his weight shift. He groped the air for a hold on something. Anything.

But nothing was in reach, and as he fell backwards, his captor grinned at him.

The image of that grin filled Lee's mind until his broken body hit the rocks below, where the sneering face faded into the swirling sky above.

And the darkness gave way to a light so bright that Lee had to squint.

But there was clarity. The world around him was as vivid and detailed as he could ever remember. So clear was the dying world, so detailed, that he saw his captor peer down at him from above. And that grin was gone from his face.

He let his head rest on the rocks. He let a smile form on his cracked lips. And he let peace take him, along with a deadly secret.

VIP READER CLUB

Your FREE ebook is waiting for you now.

Get your FREE copy of the prequel story to the Wild Fens Murder Mystery series, and learn how Freya came to give up everything she had to start a new life in Lincolnshire.

Visit www.jackcartwrightbooks.com to join the VIP Reader Club.

I'll see you there.

Jack Cartwright

ALSO BY JACK CARTWRIGHT

The DCI Cook Murder Mysteries

A Winter of Blood

A Secret to Die For

The Wild Fens Murder Mysteries

Secrets In Blood

One For Sorrow

In Cold Blood

Suffer In Silence

Dying To Tell

Never To Return

Lie Beside Me

Dance With Death

In Dead Water

One Deadly Night

Her Dying Mind

Into Death's Arms

No More Blood

Burden of Truth

Join my VIP reader group to be among the first to hear about new release dates, discounts, and get a free Wild Fens novella.

Visit www.jackcartwrightbooks.com for details.

A NOTE FROM THE AUTHOR

Locations are as important to the story as the characters are; sometimes even more so.

I have heard it said on many occasions that Lincolnshire is as much of a character in The Wild Fens series, as Freya is, or Ben. That is mainly due to the fact that I visit the places used within my stories to see with my own eyes, breathe in the air, and to listen to the sounds.

However, there are times when I am compelled to create a fictional place within a real environment. For example, in the story you have just read, Haverholme Park, the Priory, and the towns are all real places, whereas the houses that are described are not. The reason I create fictional places is so that I can be sure not to cast any real location, setting, business, street, or feature in a negative light; nobody wants to see their beloved home town described as a scene for a murder, or any business portrayed as anything but excellent.

If any names of bonafide locations appear in my books, I ensure they bask in a positive light because I truly believe that Lincolnshire has so much to offer and that these locations should be celebrated with vehemence.

I hope you agree.

Jack Cartwright

AUTHOR

AFTERWORD

Because reviews are critical to an author's career, if you have enjoyed this novel, you could do me a huge favour by leaving a review on Amazon.

Reviews allow other readers to find my books. Your help in leaving one would make a big difference to this author.

Thank you for taking the time to read *No More Blood*.

Best wishes,

Jack Cartwright.

COPYRIGHT

Milton Keynes UK
Ingram Content Group UK Ltd.
UKHW041452121024
449426UK00001B/42